Peter Driscoll was born in London in 1942, and went with his parents to South Africa after the war. At seventeen he joined the Rand Daily Mail as a cub reporter. He has worked as a scriptwriter in London television, a stoker, labourer and film extra. He now lives in Ireland.

Peter Driscoll

The Barboza Credentials

Futura Publications Limited
A Macdonald/Futura Book

A Macdonald/Futura Book

First published in Great Britain by
Macdonald & Jane's Publishers in 1976

This edition published by Macdonald &
Jane's Publishers in association with
Futura Publications in 1977

ISBN 0 8600 7553 2
Printed in Great Britain by
Hazell Watson & Viney Ltd
Aylesbury, Bucks

Futura Publications Limited
110 Warner Road
Camberwell, London SE5

Author's Note

Soon after the coup which overthrew the Caetano regime in Portugal in April 1974, it became clear that the country had lost the will to hold on to its empire in Africa. In the case of one of the three African colonies, Mozambique, the guerrilla war which had been waged for ten years by black nationalists against the Portuguese was effectively over within two months. By September a transitional government had been formed under African control, and in June 1975 the People's Republic of Mozambique achieved full independence.

The capital, Lourenço Marques, has been renamed Maputo. Since it is still better known by the earlier name this is the one I have used, even though most of this story is set in the period after independence.

To the best of my knowledge there has never been a village called Goronga. No United Nations committee has been into Mozambique to investigate war crimes, but evidence of Portuguese atrocities against civilians was collected from refugees in Tanzania and published by the UN in December 1974.

Operation Zebra, the rounding up of former Portuguese secret police officers, is fact. It took place in mid-1974. Operation Terno Branco is my own invention.

PETER DRISCOLL

Glossary

Frelimo: Frente de Libertação de Moçambique (Mozambique Liberation Front). Commenced guerrilla operations against the Portuguese in 1964 and formed the first government of Mozambique at independence in 1975.

PIDE: Polícia Internacional e de Defesa do Estado (best translated as Frontier and State Security Police). Formerly the main instrument of internal security both in metropolitan Portugal and the overseas territories, it was officially disbanded in 1970.

DGS: Direcção-Geral de Segurança (Directorate-General of Security). Successor to the PIDE, it performed the same functions and was disbanded in turn after the Portuguese coup in 1974.

PSP: Polícia de Segurança Pública (Public Security Police). The national gendarmerie.

Flechas: (arrows), a refinement of the Grupos Especiais or special airborne commando units of the Portuguese Army. Flechas were trained in field intelligence work as well as for search-and-destroy operations against Frelimo guerrillas and were usually commanded by DGS officers. The rank and file were almost exclusively black.

Prologue

The armed men came like phantoms from the bush. The first the boy knew about it was when a woman suddenly screamed, a single cry of alarm that was cut off in the middle by a shallow explosive *plop*.

He had been dozing in his father's hut. As he sat up sleepily on his mat he heard other sounds, intrusive and harsh, the voices of men barking commands across the village, shouting, bullying. Within a few moments there was a crunch of boots at the doorway and a man stood there, blinking into the gloom inside. Then he stooped and entered the hut, his ungainly shadow bulking against the ceiling. There was a rifle slung from his shoulder. He bent over the boy, seized his arm and dragged him off the mat.

"Fora! Ande!"

Not understanding, the boy knelt and stared up at the dark outline of the man's face until he felt the shock of a kick in the ribs and went sprawling across the dung floor. The intruder took his arm again and dragged him through the door, cursing incomprehensibly as he struggled to get himself, the rifle and the equipment strapped to his body out by the narrow opening. The boy wore only a ragged pair of shorts; although the air was warm he shivered as he got to his feet, his sleepy bewilderment hardening into fear.

Across the village a hut had been set alight. Flames tore through the grass walls and the bamboo frame and a second later were leaping high above the roof. People were being driven in ones and twos towards the centre of the village. The woman who had tried to scream a warning lay in an awkward posture at the door of her hut. Taking in the obscene mess of blood and pale matter, the boy realized, incredulously, that the back of her head was blown away.

"*Ande!*"

The rifle butt thumped him between the shoulder-blades and he stumbled forward, still dazed, joining the drift of people towards the quadrangle of baked mud. Most of the villagers were already assembled there, squatting or sitting in a tight huddle. There was terror in their bearing, the women clutching their children tightly to them, the men still and watchful. He saw his father, the village *regulo*, squatting at the edge of the crowd and went and sat beside him.

"What do they want?" he asked softly, taking some slight courage from the presence of the headman.

"Be still," the old man murmured. He watched the intruders with the wary attention of a dog expecting a beating. Eight or ten of them had closed in to surround the villagers while others still moved among the huts, the alien quality of their walk and their stance setting them apart as much as their appearance did. They looked clumsy and overdressed, weighed down by weapons and packs. One, evidently their commander, a tall, spare man, gave an order in the language which the boy did not understand. Several more huts were set alight and soon the village was a sea of flame. Then the air was shaken by terrified bellowing and the stink of scorched hide filled everyone's nostrils. The cattle were being roasted alive in their kraal.

"What do they want with us?" the boy whispered urgently. "What will they do?"

The old headman did not reply. His son had overheard the talk of trouble. Since that morning, when the white man and his soldiers had come down in their helicopter and spoken to his father, there had been arguments—and the *regulo* was in the thick of them. The boy himself had been torn between apprehension and curiosity; he did not often see either a white man or a helicopter.

The commander was on the other side of the square. The guards, who had grown restless, began to exchange sniggering comments about the people who cringed in front of them. One of the men suddenly stepped in among the villagers, seized a young girl by the wrist and jerked her to her feet. He shoved her out in front of the group, where she stood bewildered, shaking with fright. He put a hand to the top of her long *khenga* and ripped it off. She wore nothing beneath. Helpless and ashamed, the men of the village averted their eyes. The guards' laughter was swift and ribald, but its tone changed as they took stock of the firm, sleek body.

The girl tried ineffectually to cover her breasts and pubis with her hands, staring at the guards with a face made ugly by fear. But her terror only stimulated them. Two men took her arms and twisted them behind her back. The one who had stripped her thrust the muzzle of his rifle between her clamped thighs and pushed it upwards, forcing the tip of the long front sight into her vulva. The girl whimpered and squirmed. Then the headman was on his feet.

"Leave her!" he called hoarsely.

The men turned to him in surprise.

"Leave her. Kill me, if you want. But don't touch the women."

The man who had been tormenting the girl jerked the rifle free and walked up to the *regulo*. His eyes shone with lust and spite. He reversed the weapon, raising it to shoulder height so that the butt was poised a few inches in front of the old man's face.

"*Que é que tem, avô?*"

"Leave the women alone."

The guard grinned and smashed the rifle butt into the headman's face. The old man gasped and fell to his knees, his cheek split open to the bone. Blood welled from the pale tissue and began to drip rapidly on the ground. The boy stared, wild-eyed but no longer petrified, beginning with a growing sense of panic to understand what was about to happen. Did no one else recognize it, or were they telling themselves that it couldn't, that even in a vicious war there were some things that men would not do? All he knew was that his father's gesture had been futile. He had offered his life, but that had already been judged worthless.

The guard turned away. But now the men's superior was coming back across the square. He saw the naked girl and exchanged some sharp words with the two who were holding her. Then he looked down at the headman, who still knelt bleeding on the ground, and spoke one sentence in their own language.

"You know the price of treachery, grandfather."

The *regulo* stared into the alien, frightening face and said nothing. The commander snapped his fingers; reluctantly the men let go of the girl and pushed her back among the villagers. The guards stationed behind the captives were moving away, leaving only an arc of men in the front. An order was called; with a series of sharp metallic clicks they cocked their weapons.

Everyone was already silent but a more intense hush seemed to fall, muting even the crackle of the flames and the dying moans of the cattle. Collectively the villagers cringed. The boy leaped to his feet and ran.

His panic erupted, sending him in a blind rush through the gap between the two nearest guards and across the quadrangle. Someone shouted. The man at the end of the arc swung round, bringing the rifle to his shoulder, letting the sights follow the running figure briefly before he fired. The boy heard the smack of the bullet through his flesh and felt as though he'd been kicked violently behind the knee. He stumbled and fell in the dust but got up again and went on. His right leg was wobbly and cumbersome but he could still run on it, and now the mango grove at the edge of the village was only a few yards away.

There was another shout and two more shots as he plunged in among the trees, tripping and staggering, bruising and grazing himself but moving deeper into the cover of the mango grove until he found the thinly marked footpath that led north into the bush. Thorns tore at his arms and his shorts. His bare feet pounded along the track till they were numb.

He ran until his legs collapsed under him and he fell, exhausted, on the prickly grass beside the path, his breath coming in hoarse, choking sobs. A minute later he vomited. Then he sat up, aware for the first time of the pain in his leg. The bullet had gone through the muscle behind and just below his right knee-joint; the entry and exit wounds oozed dark, glutinous blood and the surrounding flesh was swollen and bruised.

From what seemed a long way behind him there came a ragged volley of automatic fire mingled with screaming. Then a few residual cries were choked off by single shots.

He took off his shorts, tore them into strips and made a crude bandage which he wrapped tightly round his knee.

But now when he tried to stand the pain was agonizing and the leg gave under him. He crawled along the path until he found a fallen acacia branch which was straight and strong enough to support his weight. Hoisting himself up onto his left foot, with the right one stuck out behind, he clung to the branch with both hands and used it to hop and hobble for as long as he could until he fell again. This time he knew he was too weak to get up. He dragged himself and the stick off the path, as deep into the bush as he could go, then crawled behind an anthill and lay there, naked and suddenly cold. His mind seemed paralyzed with shock.

Soon he heard the men searching for him, calling to each other and tramping heavily along the footpath. They had followed the trail of blood, but it ended at the point where he had put on the bandage. The men did not look much further. They made a few desultory attempts to break through the bush but soon, after some discussion, turned round and went back to the village.

Somehow, the boy fell asleep. When he woke up he was astonished to find it was dawn. He was bruised and stiff and chilled and his leg hurt dreadfully, but he was most conscious of a raging thirst. He took the stick, crawled out onto the path and hauled himself upright, considering. Back at the village he could drink at the stream. But what if the men were still there, waiting for him?

To the north there was sanctuary of a sort. It was a long way, but there was no choice. He turned and began to hobble along the path.

PART ONE
Saturday, November 15

1

Moamba, two thirds of the way from Lourenço Marques to the South African border, was a village I had often driven through without really noticing, a dozen or two clay-coloured buildings scattered along the roadside like pieces of earthenware set out tò dry in the sun. There was a railway station, a small garage with a single hand-operated petrol pump, a Catholic church and a fly-ridden cantina with old political slogans daubed on its walls and a sort of permanent encampment of Africans lounging and dozing on the veranda. Unexpectedly, twenty yards down a dusty track that led off towards some peasant plots, there were also the premises of an undertaker.

The building had a pair of shopfront windows curtained off in dusty purple velvet. I held the screen door open for Inspector Akimo, the black police officer, who stepped through without acknowledging the gesture, and followed him inside. It took my eyes a few seconds to adjust from the glare to the half-light of the funeral parlour. Gilt frames for photographs of the dead and plastic flowers encased in transparent crucifixes were displayed on the walls, relics of the Portuguese taste in funerary ornament. A Goan in a black satin waistcoat was standing up and bowing to us from behind a desk.

Akimo introduced himself curtly.

"Concerning the late Ricardo Gomes?"

"Correct. Senhor Joseph Hickey for identification."

"Deepest sympathy, deepest sympathy," the Goan murmured mechanically in my direction. "If you'll step this way?"

He was used to seeing bereaved relatives hauled in for the ritual. It irritated me vaguely to be taken for one, but I couldn't be bothered explaining. I was hot and tired. The undertaker ushered us through a small showroom full of coffins into an enclosed loading bay at the rear which was shared by an ancient Dodge hearse and a pair of deep-bodied refrigeration cabinets. He opened one of these to expose three drawers, the bottom one of which he slid out on rollers. He pulled back the shroud and Akimo beckoned me over.

Once I had been a policeman myself, so I'd seen the bodies of enough road-accident victims to know what to expect. The effects of being thrown forward through a windscreen as the result of sudden deceleration from about eighty kilometres an hour to zero, without the benefit of a safety belt, are much the same on everyone. Ricardo Gomes, until that morning my business representative in Lourenço Marques, was unsightly but still recognizable. There had been laceration, though not so much as there might have been at a lower speed. There had been concussion, massive internal bleeding and compression of the brain, all instantaneous. Gomes had been lucky, if that was the word; he probably died within a second of hitting the ground forty yards beyond the concrete-filled barrels of the roadblock he'd tried to crash.

Akimo waited for a barely decent interval. "Well?" he demanded.

"It's him," I said. "Of course it's him."

"Sign."

The inspector thrust the identification form at me, with personal details scrawled into the blank spaces in an over-neat, ill-educated hand. He was a gruff, balding man with heavy jowls and coarse, pitted skin like worm-eaten mahogany who had met me off the DETA flight from Johannesburg an hour earlier. After examining my passport he had tucked it with an absent-minded air into the breast pocket of his shirt and had so far neglected to return it.

I rested the form on the roof of the hearse, scribbled my signature and handed it back.

"Is that all?"

"For now."

"I don't mind you wasting your own time. Mine happens to be valuable."

"Waste, hm?" Akimo scowled at me suspiciously. "You say you were police yourself. In . . . where? Kenya?"

"A long time ago, before I knew there were better ways of making a living."

"Positive identification, first step in investigating a death. You should know."

"Why pick on me? There must be plenty of people down here who knew him."

"Suddenly not many are keen to admit. He had no relatives in Mozambique."

"He had an ex-wife."

"Know her?"

"I've met her," I said neutrally.

"I'll be speaking to her. But yes—one reason for bringing

you out here was to talk. You knew him as well as anyone."

"I wouldn't say that. Obviously I didn't know him well enough."

"So you keep telling me," Akimo said with another scowl. Although by no means stupid, he was a little slow on the uptake and distinctly single-minded, qualities that had been typical of the Polícia de Segurança Pública under the Portuguese and which a few months of independence had done little to improve. He seemed still to be convinced that I must have had something to do with Gomes's desperate behaviour. The reason he'd tried to break through the roadblock had emerged when the police searched through the wreckage of his undistinguished, meticulously kept Opel Kadett: Packed into a tartan duffel bag under the driver's seat were just over thirty thousand United States dollars in used bills of various denominations and a one-way ticket for that evening's South African Airways flight from Johannesburg to Rio de Janeiro. And at his apartment in the Alto Maé district of Lourenço Marques he had left signs of a hasty departure.

A fan in the wall of the loading bay stirred the sluggish air, cooling the sweat that had stuck my shirt to my back like an adhesive bandage. The Goan had slid the refrigerator drawer back into place and now hovered restlessly behind us.

"Still say you know nothing about that money, Hickey?"

"Don't let's go over that again," I said. "I didn't need Gomes to smuggle money out of the country for me."

"The fact remains, he was on his way to the border with thirty thousand dollars—"

"Which I have never seen in my life," I interrupted firmly.

"—and was doing what every white man left in Mozambique would like to do: getting out and taking money with him. Hard currency too, hm? Dollars—scarcer than gold bars these days. You admit you were closing down your office here. Gomes never made money like that in his life. If it wasn't yours then where he get it?"

"How many times must I say it? I don't know."

"Guess. I want you to guess."

I gave a helpless shrug. "He had a sideline of some kind. Presumably an illegal one. That would be a very good reason for not telling me about it. I didn't know much about him personally. I'm in a legitimate business—"

"Sanctions-busting? You call that legitimate?"

For a moment I stared at him blankly. The Goan was holding the door open for us. Akimo remained planted where he was, cap off, wiping his bald patch with a grubby handkerchief. I said, "You've been listening to gossip."

"LM is a small town, hm? Word gets around. You're a fat cat in the import business. The word goes that you opened your office specifically to shift machinery through here to Rhodesia. That you were turning over two million escudos a month, maybe even three million."

A more subtle man might have been playing dumb, leading me on, but I had guessed by now that he had no proof. Gossip couldn't hurt. I said, "So what? I haven't done a cent's worth of business here since independence. I haven't broken the laws of the People's Republic."

"I've got no quarrel. I'm a policeman. All that stuff is politics." Akimo made a dismissive gesture which was not entirely convincing. "What interests me is where Gomes came into it."

"Off the record?" When he nodded I said, "All right, I import specialized mining machinery for the whole of southern Africa. Some of it goes to Rhodesia. Quite a lot of it, in the past, was shipped through Lourenço Marques. Ever since independence the new government has been threatening to close the route. It could happen at a moment's notice, which is why I'm pulling out. The Portuguese winked at sanctions-busting for ten years, and if I hadn't taken advantage someone else would have. I employed Gomes to smooth the way down here, nothing more. He ran a small office—you've seen it—a one-man operation that handled no big money, nothing like thirty thousand dollars. You've seen the books too; you know there's no way to disguise an amount like that. We kept a small escudo account for out-of-pocket expenses—"

"Small? It's got a hundred and twenty thousand escudos in it right now."

"Call that two thousand sterling or five thousand dollars and it sounds less impressive. Frankly, the less of your Monopoly money I have to handle the better."

"It is an offence to slander the currency," said Akimo, straight-faced.

"Look, could we get going? And talk on the way back?"

Akimo thanked the Goan perfunctorily and led me out through the funeral parlour. I still wasn't sure whether he mistrusted me on principle, because I was white, or out of a kind of envy, because I was an ex-policeman who had succeeded at something else. Akimo had the stamp of a career copper, although I gathered that before joining the PSP back in the bad old colonial days he had, like many black Mozambicans, done a stint on the South African gold mines. That was where he had learned his English, which was still pretty sound, certainly better than my rudimentary Portuguese. The epaulets on his shoulders were stiff and new against the worn khaki shirt. Like other African policemen—*cipais*, the Portuguese had called them, and the name still stuck—Akimo had done well out of independence, though the earlier years of marking time as a sergeant while white men were promoted over his head had made him surly, inclined to heavy sarcasm. To my mind he still had the qualities of a natural sergeant: He was solid, methodical and a trifle unimaginative.

Outside, the heat was colossal. A couple of hobbled goats had taken refuge on the undertaker's front porch. As we crossed the road to where the police car was parked in the shade of a fever tree I glanced at my watch: ten past four on a searing November afternoon. When the rains were late, as they were this season, this was the worst time of year to be in Mozambique. The heat made people lethargic, irritable, depressed, and though the weather had nothing to do with my own state of mind it didn't help either. I was obscurely angry—with myself and with the lump of battered flesh in there that had called itself Gomes. I had lost nothing material through his death—indeed, to be cynical, I had been spared paying him another two months' salary in return for too little work—but I had confirmed an uneasy feeling I'd had ever since I first met Gomes, a feeling that in some way he was living a lie.

I climbed into Akimo's battered and incredibly dusty Peugeot, recalling how the news had reached me through the fog of a hangover at nine fifteen that morning. I'd been out until three, entertaining some hard-drinking clients from Salisbury, so that when the phone at my bedside rang it awoke me simultaneously to awareness of a headache and to the fact relayed by my secretary that Gomes was dead. He had slowed down at a militia roadblock near Moamba, then panicked and tried to crash through. I asked her to book me on the first available flight to Lourenço Marques and check that my three-month multiple-visit visa was in order. While I showered and dressed and packed there was one thought I couldn't put out of my mind: that it was quite unlike Gomes to behave in this way. He'd had his moments of oddness, yes, but whatever else he might be he was not a precipitate man. Even when a report came through of the finding of the dollars in his car (it was illegal to possess foreign currency, let alone take it out of the country), there did not seem to have been sufficient reason for a suicidal escape attempt. I decided that Gomes had been afraid.

There would be a lot for me to do in LM. Winding up the business of the branch and clearing out and closing the office—work that Gomes would otherwise have done— would take four or five days that I could scarcely afford to spend away from Johannesburg. So I was not inclined to be helpful when Inspector Akimo waylaid me at the airport and drove me to Moamba, particularly since his most insistent question was the one that I couldn't answer: Where had Gomes got the money? Akimo had already opened and thoroughly searched his apartment and the office, and turned up details of his private bank account and few small investments, without finding any clues.

I was curious, of course, and in a different frame of mind I might have found the mystery challenging. Thirty thousand dollars was the official equivalent of three years' salary for Gomes. Even if he had somehow managed to save every penny he had earned from me, though, he would never have been able to convert it all to hard currency—not legally anyway—and on the black market the same quantity of dollars would have cost him three or four times as much. He'd obviously been squirreling money away from some profitable and illicit sideline.

Akimo pulled away from beneath the fever tree and swung onto the Lourenço Marques road. In the dry air a layer of red-brown dust hung permanently over the bush and the village, and the sun burned angrily through it from a steely, cloudless sky. Heat and the residue of the hangover had brought back my headache. My throat was parched.

"I want to know about your business down here," Akimo said. "And your relationship with Gomes."

"Let's have a drink," I suggested.

"Hard-boozing *bwana,* hm?"

"When I need it, yes. And I need it now. A couple of beers will do us both good."

He gave me a look and then stopped the car outside the cantina. I pulled a hundred-escudo note from my pocket and held it out to him but he shook his head, got out and went up the steps, watched by the listless crowd on the veranda. A boy wearing only a filthy vest, with his skin covered by the obscene raspberry growths of yaws, approached my side of the car diffidently to beg. On impulse I thrust the hundred escudos into his hand. He stared at it incredulously for a second and then, fearing I would change my mind, bolted into the bush behind the cantina. I guessed there wasn't much chance of its going on penicillin.

Frelimo vencerá, democracia triunfará, said the largest of the slogans on the wall, outdated in spite of the future tense. Frelimo, the Mozambique Liberation Front, had already won. Whether democracy had triumphed was a matter of opinion, I supposed, depending mainly on whether you were rich or poor, white or black; the alternatives were more or less interchangeable. When I had first visited this vast, backward slab of south-east Africa (you were supposed to call it "developing"), it had been part of the world's last real colonial empire. The war between the Portuguese and Frelimo's black guerrillas had then been rumbling away for several years, remotely and indecisively, in the far north. With the nearest war zones eight hundred miles from Lourenço Marques, this prosperous colonial capital in the south remained untouched and you were likely to see more tourists than soldiers on the streets. In the last eighteen months all that had changed—and in a way few people could have foreseen.

The coup in Lisbon had brought to power a group of radical young army officers, many of them frustrated by the futility of colonial wars in Africa which they knew they could not win in the long run. Once installed, their first act had been to dismantle the DGS, the notorious secret police organization that had bolstered the old regime. Their next had been to disengage from the African territories.

In Mozambique the fighting had dragged on for a few more months, with the guerrillas pressing home their advantage against demoralized Portuguese troops. Who, after all, wanted to die for a cause that already seemed lost? As it became increasingly clear that Frelimo would settle for nothing less than full independence, the white *colonos* reacted in panic. It had been an ugly conflict, fought with all the weapons of modern guerrilla war: not just napalm and landmines, defoliants and booby traps, but the brutal methods used by both sides to win the allegiance of black civilians. The result at the end was deep mutual distrust. There were race riots, killings, burning, looting. When Frelimo finally emerged from the bush to take firm control, the country was in a mess. Half the Portuguese civil servants, including most of those on whom Gomes and I had relied for special favours, had fled.

Frelimo's rule was absolute, socialist and austere. This would not have worried me if it were not for another factor. After all, I had seen Kenya overcome its teething troubles under a black government and prosper in spite of the White Highlanders sneering into their Pimm's. Frelimo, however, was committed to applying the United Nations' mandatory sanctions order on trade with the neighbouring rebel colony of Rhodesia, an order which the Portuguese had been quietly ignoring for ten years. And that was bad news for me.

Akimo returned clutching some cold bottles of Laurentina lager. We drank as we drove and I began to tell him—with a certain amount of circumspection—about myself and Gomes.

2

We had met four years ago over lunch at Spaghi's restaurant in Johannesburg. Gomes had had word that I was looking for someone to represent me in Lourenço Marques and had flown up at my expense for a meeting. He sounded like the kind of man I wanted: local, with good contacts, business experience and, above all, discretion. By then I was well established in my second career and had few regrets about my forced retirement five years before, at the age of thirty and with the rank of chief inspector, from the Kenya police. I had been one of the early victims of "Africanization"; the Kikuyu whom I'd once hand-picked from among the annual crop of police-college graduates to become my personal assistant had stepped into my job as deputy head of operations in Nairobi.

With hindsight, I knew that he'd done me a favour by forcing a decision that might have taken me years to make for myself. Even at the time, I hadn't been bitter. I had immensely enjoyed my twelve years in uniform but knew that much of what had made them enjoyable couldn't be recaptured: youth, excitement, the edge of danger, the hedonistic life of Kenya in the fifties. But there was a new order in Africa, and even if there had been a future for me in an independent black nation, middle age and seniority would have meant a headquarters job, commuter hours, pontification at staff meetings, pressure from politicians, responsibilities which I would prefer to take on my own behalf.

Several of my British colleagues found themselves redundant at the same time as I, but while they accepted the inevitability of going "home," I was determined to stay in Africa. This was home to me. I had been born on a farm in Devon but had come to Kenya at the age of ten, with parents bent on making a new and freer life for themselves, and had grown up on a cattle ranch east of Nakuru. On the couple of return visits I had made to England I had found it a damp, cheerless and overcrowded place. Weeks of overcast weather depressed me, the London tube trains gave me claustrophobia and the pursuits of the average Englishman, both at work and at leisure, seemed tame to the point of being pathetic. It wasn't just that I missed the sun, the clean air, the outdoor life and the dusty taste and smell of Africa. I could not feel at home in England because it was over-civilized; it lacked that curious sense of excitement—adventure, if you like—that I was used to feeling in the fabric of the society around me.

After the Mau Mau emergency in the fifties, and then the series of droughts that had ruined their ranch and their dreams, my parents returned to England. I chose to stay on. My addiction to Africa would prove expensive, but like any addict I considered the expense justified. Police work there was like nothing else on earth. It had nearly killed me once or twice, the first time at eighteen, within months of my joining up, when my patrol was ambushed in the Aberdare forest by the remnants of a Mau Mau gang we were hunting, and I'd taken a .303 bullet from an ancient Lee-Metford through the shoulder and almost bled to death. Later I'd fought running gun-battles with poachers and commanded a para-military General Service Unit against Shifta rebels on the Somali frontier. The job had kept me fitter than a marine and sharpened my instincts for aggressive self-preservation to their utmost. Nothing improves your reflexes better than the knowledge that a man is lying in the bush with a gun and waiting for you. After that first time, nobody ever got the chance to shoot before I did.

My addiction had cost me my marriage, however. Miriam was a stockbroker's daughter from Surrey, one of a number of English girls I had slept with during their two-week visits to Kenya on what the travel firms like to call camera safaris. Once she came back to marry me she grew gradually to dislike the climate, to hate the demands and dangers of my job and to fear the blacks. After three years of increasingly desperate exhortations to take her back to England she finally went on her own. With the preliminary divorce papers I got a letter accusing me of being wilful, obstinate and aggressive. I suppose I was all those things to some degree. I suppose, too, that they helped me make a success of my new career.

The transition was an odd one, but it worked. I had seen too many others like me, unqualified to be anything but policemen, go innocently into civilian life expecting the authority and competence they had carried in the pips on their shoulders to go with them. It didn't work that way. They ended up as security guards and hotel detectives, living on their memories and drinking away their boredom. Three days after my summary retirement I caught a plane from Nairobi to Johannesburg; like so many other East African whites in those early days of *uhuru* I had decided, reluctantly, to move south. At least it was still Africa. I put my savings and severance pay carefully away in a two-year fixed-deposit account, I took a job at a meagre salary with a trading firm that specialized in importing machinery from Europe and North America for the booming South African mining industry, and I set about learning the business from bottom to top.

The dynamics of it were easy enough to master, and by studying textbooks and manuals I managed to catch up on the technical knowledge I needed. I cultivated contacts in the buying and planning departments of the big mining conglomerates and soon earned some trips to Canada, the United States, Sweden and Germany, where I met manufacturers who would later be useful to know. It also did not take me long to find out that some of what we were importing was destined not for South Africa but, very unofficially, for Rhodesia.

The breakaway British colony was then in the second year of its unilaterally declared independence. With the connivance of the South African and Portuguese governments, the Rhodesians had so far succeeded in evading most of the trade sanctions that the United Nations had imposed. Middlemen like ourselves had found markets for their tobacco, chromium and asbestos exports and had procured material necessary to the survival of their economy—in our case computerized winding systems and sophisticated drilling machinery for the copper, chrome and coal mines.

The procedure was fairly simple. Orders would be placed overseas in the name of one or another of half a dozen South African "mining companies" which existed only on paper and were actually subsidiaries of our own. The goods would be shipped to Cape Town or Durban, where we arranged for customs clearance and forwarding to the fictitious companies. In fact they went into storage for a few weeks before being re-sold as "second-hand" to the Rhodesians. This meant that through a legal loophole their origins could be declared on the consignment notes as South African, which did not offend the sensibilities of the Pretoria government about allowing their country to serve as a pipeline to Rhodesia. Everyone concerned knew exactly what was going on. It was a seller's market, the mark-ups were high, the profits were excellent and competition among the firms that went in for these clandestine deals was fierce. When the two years that I had allowed myself were over and I formed my own company and went freelance, I decided to specialize in doing business with Rhodesia.

I did not do so out of political conviction, and even less with any sentimental notion of propping up the white regime in the face of threatening black hordes. International business, as I had learned early on, is apolitical and unsentimental. The Rhodesians themselves understood this; they couldn't do without people like me and they often complained that we were bleeding them to death. In answer I pointed to the risks I was taking. At the British Embassy in Pretoria a hive of men who called themselves political counsellors buzzed away over South African import and export statistics and kept in touch with agents in Salisbury and Bulawayo as well as in countries whose laissez-faire attitudes had encouraged sanctions-breaking. Once they had traced a supply route and fingered the middlemen, the British would do whatever they could to embarrass them—and to cost them money. A word in the right ear could lead to the seizure of a shipment in an unfriendly black-African port of call en route to Cape Town, for instance. More seriously, as a British subject myself I ran a high risk of having my passport invalidated if I should come to the notice of those busy little men in Pretoria. Without a passport I'd be ruined; it was that simple. Prevented from travelling, I would quickly lose the essential benefit of personal contact with both suppliers and purchasers. My competitors would be eager to fill the gap, and I would soon be out of business. And so I was very careful to keep my personal involvement in all Rhodesian transactions down to the minimum.

It wasn't long before my small initial slice of the market was growing and I secured a couple of exclusive franchises from manufacturers in Germany and Canada. By the time I met Gomes I had ten employees in my main office in Johannesburg and two more running small branches in the ports of Durban and Cape Town. I lived alone in a cottage on the countrified fringes of Johannesburg's northern suburbs, drove a Jaguar XJ-12, worked hard and was moderately rich, not short of women and reasonably content with life. As my business acumen had developed I had adjusted to some ways of doing things over which my conscience a few years earlier might have been uneasy. I was not more dishonest than I had been, simply less fastidious.

The regrets were few, but they were there. Policemen often see people at their most violent, deceitful and degraded levels, and they learn that their own authority rests finally on an unspoken threat of violence. The bad ones become cynics; the good ones know that the last thing they can afford is self-satisfaction—something I caught myself feeling once in a while. On these occasions I would wonder whether my cushioned existence really suited me, whether I really needed the money I had always managed without before. And I would regret that those finely honed instincts of survival had fallen into disuse, instincts which had sometimes made all the difference between life and death.

I could not honestly tell Akimo much more about Gomes than I had learned at that first meeting in Spaghi's. That was one of his curious abilities, to let you know just so much about himself and no more: that he too was divorced, an accountant by training whose small travel agency in Lourenço Marques had collapsed through no fault of his; that he'd had some job in the Portuguese civil service (I could never establish exactly what) and had been posted to Mozambique many years before, liked it, and stayed. He was a lean man with a bony face and yellowish colouring caused by a severe dose of hepatitis; on account of this he was forbidden by his doctor to drink alcohol and compensated after a fashion by consuming vast quantities of a bottled mineral water called Pedra de Agua. This was one of a number of eccentricities which I gradually came to notice and which, lacking any real insight into a personality which seemed otherwise very ordinary, I always found surprising.

He favoured citified European clothes—turtle-neck jersey shirts and slacks instead of the ubiquitous safari suit—and in most other ways was unlike the typically extrovert and slightly puerile *colonos* around him: an introspective man with an orderly mind in spite of its odd quirks, an impersonal manner and a preoccupied air. Mostly we talked shop; sometimes he would tell me about a big bass he had caught across the bay or make oblique references to some recent sexual conquest. These latter, I was suddenly to discover, were pathetically imaginary, but it was a chink in his armour which I did not care to probe. I had only once seen him ill at ease, and that was when the two of us bumped into his ex-wife and he was forced to introduce us. Joana Gomes was, surprisingly, much younger than he was, self-centred, beautiful, and with a vaguely discontented air about her. The marriage had been brief and disastrous.

Being inscrutable, Gomes was also unpredictable. I discovered quite by chance that his political views were on the lunatic fringe of the far right.

I had no strong opinions of my own in this area, but

since the success of my business depended on the continuance of an existing political situation, I took a keen interest in all developments concerning Rhodesia. I happened to be in Lourenço Marques just after the British General Election of 1974, and I wondered aloud to Gomes whether the new Labour Government would bring more pressure to bear on Salisbury than the Conservatives had been doing. He replied that it wouldn't make much difference, since both Wilson and Heath were paid agents of the Communist Party in any case.

Like all serious fanatics, he presented this statement as one of fact, not opinion. Encouraged by my silence he launched into a tirade: Liberal decadence had permitted the Russians to infiltrate every government in the West; any day now Europe would be delivered into Moscow's hands; the rot had begun with the colonial powers meekly surrendering their empires to savages barely out of the trees, et cetera. It was the usual formula of the right-wing *colono*—reds and blacks ganging up to destroy Christianity and civilization—and there was no point in arguing with him. After that he would expound other strange theories to me from time to time. With a conspiratorial air he dropped dark hints about having inside knowledge of various political developments. Finally there had been his public outburst over the massacre at Goronga.

"What happened?" Akimo asked.

"You remember Goronga, of course?"

"Hard to forget."

It had been a village in the bush south of the Pungwe River. In June of the previous year, in the dying days of the war, it had been destroyed and its inhabitants, about fifty of them, shot to death. As I remembered the story a troop of Flechas—black soldiers recruited in Mozambique and trained by the Portuguese in aggressive counter-terrorist tactics—had been hunting a Frelimo band in the area. The villagers had misled them as to the whereabouts of the guerrillas, and the troops had returned and murdered them. There were no survivors. It was one of the ugliest outrages of the war, and it had much the same effect on world opinion as the My Lai massacre in Vietnam had had a couple of years earlier. It demoralized the Portuguese, most of whom had no heart left for the fight anyway, swung further support behind Frelimo, and hastened the inevitable cease-fire and the promise of independence. Since a white officer of the DGS had been in command of the Flechas, it also helped precipitate the mass arrests of Portuguese secret policemen that followed soon afterwards.

After independence the Frelimo government had invited the United Nations to send a committee to investigate the atrocity. It was just after their report had been published, two or three months ago, that Gomes had put on his weird performance.

"I was down here to get some formalities out of the way so that this end of the business could be wound up," I told Akimo. "Gomes and I were walking back from a visit to our local lawyer when he offered to buy me a beer. I think what he really wanted was a mineral water for himself. We went into one of those noisy little bars across from the market; these days they're always full of Frelimo soldiers and party cadres, and we'd hardly been there a minute when one of them started haranguing us. He'd had too much to drink. The UN report had just come out, and this fellow was breathing beer and wagging his finger in Gomes's face and lecturing him on the brutal mentality of the Portuguese.

"Gomes worked himself up into a fury. I'd never seen him like that before. Suddenly he was shouting at the top of his voice. He said one day the world would know the full story of Goronga and then that UN document would be worthless. He had inside knowledge of what had happened. . . .

"Well, the mood was getting ugly. The Frelimo man took a swing at Gomes. I knocked him out of the way and grabbed Gomes's arm and we ran. We got away through the market. Make of that whatever you will; he never mentioned Goronga again."

"I make nothing of it," Akimo said. "Where the hell would he get inside information about Goronga? He sounds crazy."

I had refrained from telling Akimo that Gomes had contributed to the black soldier's anger by addressing him as *macaco,* monkey—a term he had used habitually in the old days but had largely and wisely dropped since independence. On the whole I hadn't disliked Gomes, but I had not been able to take too much of him at a time.

Akimo swallowed some lager with a gargling noise and said, "Well, you gave him a job, back in whenever. Then what?"

"I gave him a month's trial. He proved himself more than adequate, and I took him on. I didn't need to be mad for his company; I would only be spending two or three days a month down here. And in business I couldn't fault him."

The car sped us along the fast, narrow road back towards the coast. I stared out of the window as I talked. There was nothing between Moamba and Lourenço Marques with any right to be called a town, but African villages could be glimpsed through the thin bush, scatterings of thatched bamboo and mud huts, lean-tos made of beaten tin, just occasionally a rectangular brick building with a dark doorway opening into some fetid cantina. Villages like this were what Mozambique was really all about. The Portuguese had been here nearly five hundred years, but for much of that time their rule over the greater part of the country had been purely nominal. Slave traders and a few lethargic officials had worked in the relative safety of the coastal settlements, while in the hinterland warlike blacks had kept the Portuguese garrisons penned up, sweltering and dying of malaria, in their tiny stone forts. Even in recent times their grip on parts of the interior had remained tenuous. Development had been sketchy. Today there were only three cities and a dozen towns, most of them still on the coast; for the rest it remained a thinly populated country of vast distances, poor communications and scattered administrative outposts. Even the big European-owned cotton and sugar plantations, many of them now being nationalized by Frelimo, were separated by great tracts of virgin bush. Pioneering hadn't been encouraged by the climate; for nine months of the year the country lay under a blanket of heat, alternately damp and dry, which sapped the energies of all but the hardiest white people.

Four years ago, the only thing in Mozambique that had interested me was a five-hundred-kilometre stretch of narrow-gauge railway line that linked Lourenço Marques with the Rhodesian border at Malvérnia. The Portuguese had always been more blatant in their disregard of sanctions than the South Africans. Oil had been flowing openly through Malvérnia, and there seemed no reason why I should not use the same direct route in addition to my South African ones. If goods could be consigned to Johannesburg via Lourenço Marques and then re-routed from the quayside, I would cut out some of the time-wasting and expensive business of storing them and transferring ownership. I would gain an edge over the competition in improved delivery times as well as profits. Once again my name would have to be kept clear of all transactions;

there was, after all, an overstaffed British consulate-general in Lourenço Marques as well. What I needed down there was a good organization man who could pull strings discreetly on my behalf. Gomes fitted the bill.

"What did you pay him?" Akimo demanded suddenly.

"Fifteen thousand escudos a month. Later I raised it to twenty."

"More than I make in twice the time," the black man said sourly. "What made him worth it?"

"He was good. I couldn't have managed without him. He . . ."

"Go on."

"He could fix things," I said, knowing I was on slightly dangerous ground. "He had influence with people who counted. Some of his work involved—well, unofficial approaches."

"What you mean," said Akimo, pausing to raise the Laurentina bottle to his lips and suck at it noisily, "is bribery." He took his eyes off the road momentarily to glance at me. "Am I right? The *consideração* system, hm? With the right contact and the right *consideração* you could get almost anything. He'd need people who could falsify consignment notes, duplicate bills of lading, that sort of stuff. More important, he'd need clearance with the Interior Department to do business with Rhodesia in the first place. That was liable to cost him too. Hence the size of your petty-cash float, hm? Frelimo has been stamping the system out. Another reason you're leaving?"

I nodded slowly. "Everyone was in it to some extent. You had to be to survive."

"You're a hell of an ex-policeman," Akimo muttered.

"I've learned not to think like a cop, that's all. And now I've told you everything."

It hadn't taken long either. I had even tried to convey

to Akimo that other impression, indefinable but indelible, that I had always had about Gomes. He hadn't seemed very interested. What Akimo understood was evidence, and I hadn't the slightest scrap of that. Things I had noticed while visiting the office—phone calls from men who refused to leave their names, packets that clearly had nothing to do with business, delivered by hand and marked *personal*—these added up to exactly nothing, but they confirmed my feeling that Gomes had somehow been more than he seemed.

We were on the outskirts of Lourenço Marques now, the bush giving way to market gardens and peasant smallholdings, and soon across the estuary of the Espírito Santo the city came into view, fashionable apartment blocks arrayed on the cliffs above Delagoa Bay and thrown into bold relief by the rays of the late afternoon sun. The evening stink of the *bairros populares*—"popular districts" was the euphemism for the black shantytowns sprawling around the western edge of the city—wafted through the car. The smell was always the same, a compound of woodsmoke, excrement, rotting fruit, and who could say what else fermenting among the tin shacks and grass hovels.

Akimo came doggedly back to his subject.

"Who were his friends? What were his interests, pastimes?"

"He seemed to have a lot of acquaintances, no real friends. We never met socially, so I could be wrong. Pastimes? The only one I ever heard about was fishing."

"There was no fishing tackle in his apartment."

"Maybe he kept it somewhere else. I know he used to fish across the bay."

"Sex?"

"He talked about it occasionally." I paused. "The fact is he wasn't much good at it. He was virtually impotent."

"He told you that?" Akimo asked swiftly.

"No. His ex-wife did."

"Were you that close to her?"

"On one occasion."

I counted five seconds while Akimo thought about the phrasing of the next question. In the end he said bluntly, "You screwed her?"

"Once. There was nothing illicit about it," I added quickly. "They'd been divorced two years. We were unattached adults."

"So Gomes knew about it?"

"No," I admitted. "Look, it left me feeling like a bastard, if you really want to know. He had no claim on her, but I still felt as though I'd been disloyal to him. Besides, that kind of thing isn't good for business. That's why it was just the once. It wasn't an affair, it was just . . . what you called it: a screw."

We drove up the Avenida Pinheiro Chagas, one of the two long boulevards that bisect Lourenço Marques from west to east. Along sidewalks that had once been the preserve of Portuguese troops and strolling bourgeois couples the Frelimo soldiers, lean, loose-limbed black men in the shabby green camouflage they had worn as bush fighters, sat at the tables of pavement cafés or gazed into the windows of poorly stocked shops. I'd been half expecting Akimo to take me down to police headquarters in Central, but instead he carried on to the end of the boulevard and turned left towards the Polana Hotel, where I'd told him I would be staying.

"No more questions?" I asked.

"You'll be around. I'll come back to you if I have any new ones."

"I'll be here for a few days shutting up shop."

He swung into the hotel driveway and stopped under

the awning outside the front door. At last it was a little cooler, and the leaves of the scarlet-flowered flame trees in the hotel gardens quivered in a slight sea breeze. A smart little African in white ducks opened my door. Akimo waited for me to get out.

"I think you're forgetting something," I said.

He grinned sarcastically and tapped the passport in his shirt pocket. "You've got a note of the number?"

"Yes."

"That's all you'll need when you check in. I want to be sure you *are* around if I need you, Hickey. That you don't decide on a sudden trip back to Jo'burg."

"You can't do that. My consul—"

"Don't threaten me with the British consulate, Hickey. You are sanctions-breaker, hm? That's the last building in LM you are likely to walk into asking for help. You can have this back when my inquiries are complete—and that should be within the few days you say you will be here. That's assuming, of course, that I find no charge for you to answer. When you want to leave you'll give me notice, a clear twenty-four hours' notice. Understood?"

I knew when I was beaten. I shrugged and climbed out of the car. I opened the back door and let the boy take my grip and attaché-case off the seat.

"You've got my phone number," Akimo said. "In case you have any second thoughts, hm?"

I watched him drive the dust-smothered Peugeot away. He was an annoying man. He was also a plodder. I couldn't have guessed at that moment quite how far he would plod.

PART TWO
Wednesday, November 19

1

It was four days after Gomes's death that I discovered I was being watched.

I had spent most of the time doing what he had been meant to do, settling the affairs of my Lourenço Marques office, paying bills, going through the files and records and throwing most of them out preparatory to vacating the premises, the lease on which would expire at the end of December anyway. By Wednesday morning I knew I had only a few hours' work left. If it wasn't for Akimo's tiresome insistence on twenty-four hours' notice before my departure I could have caught a plane out the same afternoon. As it was, I decided I might as well finish the work I had to do that morning and spend the afternoon lounging by the Polana swimming pool. I could then take the first flight out the next morning and go straight to my office from the airport.

The Polana had given me the top-floor suite that I liked; since the South African tourists had been scared away and half the other hotels in Lourenço Marques had closed, my regular custom had been doubly welcome. I breakfasted early on coffee and hot rolls and then made a few phone calls—to my secretary to find out what was happening in Johannesburg, to a couple of clients in Salisbury whose business demanded my personal attention, and finally to Akimo. I'd heard nothing from him since he had vanished with my passport in his pocket on Saturday, and that was all to the good; it meant he had found better things to bother about than trumping up charges of currency-smuggling against me. I informed him of my plans; he listened in a preoccupied way and told me I could have the passport back; he'd return it himself sometime later in the day. At eight thirty I took a taxi downtown, to the quiet old office block on the Avenida da República where my company had shared the first floor with a firm of insurance brokers. They too had moved out, either to Portugal or Brazil, since independence.

The part-time secretary Gomes had employed, together with the African errand boy, had been dismissed months before, so the office was now unoccupied. When I was not there I left the door locked with a note pinned to it advising callers to leave messages with the newsagent on the ground floor. So far there had been no messages; the only thing in the mail that morning was a telephone bill, receipted. Gomes had been nothing if not efficient.

He had also managed the office extremely well. He'd been tidy to the point of obsessiveness; correspondence, invoices, bills of lading, customs declarations, accounts, bank statements, were all scrupulously filed and readily accessible. Just a glance through them last Saturday had told Akimo he would have to look elsewhere for clues to the origin of the thirty thousand dollars. Tidiness, however, reinforced an impression of impersonality. Gomes had never let his own name be typed at the foot of a letter; his illegible signature was followed simply by the title of the company, and there was not a single stamp of individuality in any of the other documents.

I resumed working as I had been since Sunday, reading through everything, discarding a lot of stuff, dropping it in a big dustbin for the cleaning woman to throw out, and keeping back only what was necessary for my own records in Johannesburg and what the local civil administration people would want to see when I applied to have the branch wound up. I had already made arrangements for the removal and sale of the furniture, apart from a single filing cabinet full of essential records which would be sent by rail to Johannesburg in due course.

By eleven o'clock I was finished and glad of it. This was the hottest day since I had been here. The electricity had been cut off some weeks before so I could not run the air-conditioning unit, and although I had left the outer door and all the windows open to catch any breeze that was going, the office was stifling. I went into the small adjoining washroom, stripped off my shirt and sluiced myself in cold water. As I dried myself on the remains of the roller towel I studied my reflection critically in the mirror above the washbasin. The couple of pounds I had put on since my Kenya days had been absorbed into a slight, almost imperceptible thickening at the waist. At six feet two I did not look tall because I was proportionately broad; the muscles were heavy but not well defined, providing strength without grace—a wrestler's build rather than a boxer's. In the hollow between the right shoulder joint and the collarbone and pectoral muscle was the small crater of pale dead flesh that marked the entry wound of the Mau Mau man's .303.

As for my face, twenty-odd years in tropical climates had not been kind to it. There were more wrinkles than I deserved at thirty-nine and the skin had coarsened and acquired a permanent tan, the kind of deep tawny colouring that comes to fair people after long exposure to harsh sunlight. The light brown hair was streaked with yellow, the blue eyes looked out from under thick thatches of brow that were bleached nearly white. There is a look common to policemen everywhere that allows me to recognize them almost without fail, but I had never found it in my own face. Miriam had said it was there, in the eyes: a curiosity that was both intense and calculating, distant yet disquieting. Miriam had said it made her uncomfortable, but then so did a lot of things.

As I turned away to put on my shirt I thought I heard a creak on the wooden landing outside the office door, as though someone had been standing there and was moving away. A visitor? It seemed hardly likely. By the time I'd buttoned up my shirt and walked across to the door there was no one in sight on the landing or down the stairs, so perhaps I'd been mistaken. I decided I could do with a beer.

I took a final look round the office, locked up and went down to the newsagent's shop. I bought that morning's *Notícias*, yesterday evening's *Star* from Johannesburg and a copy of the *Southern Africa Financial Mail* which I'd asked them to reserve for me. Outside in the fierce glare of the midday sun, I walked to the big café on the corner of the Avenida da República. A heat haze had built up over the bay and even the hardy blossoms on the flame trees looked ready to wilt. There had still been no rain. I brushed off the swarm of lottery-ticket sellers and beggars who descended on me as I approached the café, sat at a table in deep shade under the awning and ordered a Laurentina. For a minute or so I picked my way through a story in the Portuguese paper and then looked up. Suddenly I was certain that I was being followed.

The man had been lingering outside the street door to the office when I went in before nine o'clock, and when I'd come out I had seen him in a corner of the newsagent's, paging with elaborate concentration through a copy of *Newsweek*. Now he stood watching me uncertainly from beyond the furthest row of tables, a small, pale, plump Portuguese with the look of a minor government *funcionário*: grey safari suit, polished black toecaps, dark glasses, cheap briefcase tucked importantly under one arm. I remembered the step on the landing and suddenly it clicked: He'd been wondering whether to approach me, perhaps lost the courage.

I could do one of two things: ignore him or make it obvious he was found out. Like other foreigners visiting Lourenço Marques I had grown used to furtive approaches of one kind and another. I fixed my gaze on the two dark lenses and stared at him hard. For a full minute we watched each other, and then he stepped hesitantly forward and made his way between the tables towards me.

"*Desculpe.*"

The little man stopped and hovered in front of the table, the briefcase clutched protectively across his chest. He bounced up and down once or twice on the balls of his feet, as though there were springs in his heels.

"*Desculpe, senhor.*" And then in English, "It is Senhor Hickey, yes?"

"You've been following me," I said. "Yes?"

"Forgive me." He gave another bounce and uttered a nervous laugh which made his pale cheeks wobble. "Following, no. I wished only an opportunity to talk to you. In confidence, that is."

"If you're trying to buy foreign currency you're wasting your time."

"Senhor!" The man made a shocked face. "The black

45

market! No, certainly not. If I might just take five minutes of your time . . . ?"

He was bound to be in some kind of racket, I thought. At one time only black pimps and beggars were likely to pester you. These days it was the whites, trying to off-load their escudos, pleading with you to smuggle things out for them. I said, "You've been hanging around in my vicinity for the last three hours. You sneaked up the stairs to my office, didn't you? Why couldn't you speak to me then?"

"Ah. I had to be sure you were the right person. The principal of the late Senhor Gomes, yes? I waited until I could ask in the newsagent's."

He bounced again and gave a quick, shifty smile that sent his soft features into folds like raw pastry. I said slowly, "It's about Gomes?"

"It is, senhor. A tragic occurrence," he added with a sudden show of solemnity.

"And who the hell are you?"

"It would be simplest to call me Filipe."

The studied furtiveness, the air of anxiety, were faintly comical, yet I detected beneath them a kind of dangerous, barely suppressed hysteria. Seizing the opportunity of a pause in the conversation, Filipe sat down quickly on the chair opposite me. He placed the briefcase flat on the table, crossing his small, plump hands on top of it as he leaned forward to speak in an urgent whisper.

"I was not, myself, acquainted with Senhor Gomes. Like him, I must answer to a principal. Let me take you into my confidence, senhor; we Europeans should trust one another in these difficult times, not so? I need hardly tell you that Gomes was well connected with certain people in the civil administration before independence, particularly in the Department of the Interior. He used these contacts, unofficially, to your advantage." Filipe raised one hand as if to still any possible protest on my part. "It is known. Why pretend? It is natural that he should use them to his own benefit also. Some time ago he agreed to help in solving a small bureaucratic problem on behalf of a group of people with whom my principal and I are connected."

"What kind of group are you?"

"Oh, we are very informal," Filipe said carelessly. "We don't go by any particular name. We are engaged in—well, charitable work, broadly speaking. For a time Gomes was associated with us. This service he agreed to perform, however, had to be paid for. A sum of money changed hands."

"How much?"

"I do not know. That is the concern of my principal. The point is that Gomes was killed before the transaction was complete. He had taken the money but had not handed over what was due in return."

"You don't expect me to be responsible for his debts, I hope."

"Not exactly."

"Not at all," I said with an edge of anger. "If some crowd of amateur do-gooders have been buying favours through Gomes and burnt their fingers, it just isn't my problem."

Filipe, agitated, managed a couple of bounces on his backside. "The money is of no great consequence. What is important is that certain documents were in Gomes's possession." He lowered his voice. "It is a delicate matter. I wonder whether you have come across them in the course of going through his papers? And whether you would let me have them? There would be a consideration."

"What papers are they?"

"Personal documents. A passport, an identity card, a birth certificate and a few more. They are in the name of a man called Barboza." I thought Filipe had hesitated for a fraction before pronouncing the name. "Luis Pinto Barboza, architect, resident in Vilanculos. You wouldn't know him."

"Is he the man you call your principal?"

"No."

"Then who is? And where does he come in? All this anonymity bothers me."

"It would hardly be appropriate to name him, senhor. Otherwise why would he use me as intermediary?" Filipe gave his pastry-fold smile. "But I will be candid with you. He is a wealthy man, a philanthropist. He is concerned with the welfare of the white people of Mozambique, especially those who have lost their livelihood and faced other hardships since the blacks took over. Our small group does what it can to help such people and he provides much of the financial support. We feel it wise at present not to attract attention to what we do. The organization is, as I said, informal, and so are some of our methods. I am being quite frank. About eighteen months ago this Senhor Barboza approached us in difficulty over his personal papers. He had been born in Goa and was living there at the time of the Indian invasion in nineteen sixty-one. He opted to remain and become a national of India, which meant that he lost his right to claim Portuguese citizenship.

"Subsequently he came to Mozambique and set up an architectural practice in Vilanculos. At the end of the war the building industry came to a virtual halt and he realized he would no longer be able to make a living here. His only recourse was to go to Portugal, but with his irregular status he would not be admitted.

"My principal took the problem to Gomes. Through his contacts in the ministry a plan was devised to adjust the records. Barboza would be shown to have been born in the *metrópole,* not in Goa. Frankly, it was illegal. It would mean the issue of a new birth certificate, followed by a new identity card, passports and other papers—in other words, a complete set of new credentials. All this was done just before independence, but for the sake of security Gomes was to keep the papers until Barboza could wind up his affairs and leave. He is ready to leave now. But Gomes is dead. The documents are missing. You will appreciate that if the police find them Barboza will be in trouble."

"So will your group," I said. "And the man you call your principal."

"You can hardly disapprove of the motives, senhor. It was an act of charity."

Filipe gave me a pious look. I said, "It was also, as you say, illegal."

"Laws are not immutable, Senhor Hickey. They change to reflect the attitudes of those who make them." He lowered his voice again. "Consider. People who only last year were considered terrorists and murderers are now the lawful government of this country. When society's values change so rapidly, surely we are entitled to adhere to some of our own?"

For a few seconds I looked into Filipe's fat, pale, anxious face. I didn't like the way he had taken my connivance at this queer little conspiracy for granted. Nor was I convinced, in spite of his protestations of frankness, that he was telling the whole truth. Two questions arose from his story. If the luckless architect Barboza had forfeited his Portuguese citizenship in nineteen sixty-one, how had he subsequently been allowed to live in Mozambique, where the same rules of residence had applied as in metropolitan Portugal? And why had it taken him as long as eighteen months to wind up a defunct business? But I didn't ask the questions. I shrugged.

"Well, I haven't found the papers."

"But it's possible that you may."

"I doubt it. I've just been through every scrap of paper in that office. And on the day he died both the office and his apartment were searched by the police. I'd have heard if they had found anything like that."

From nowhere a face appeared grotesquely between us at the level of the table-top, a finger pointing into its gaping mouth: a *mutiladore,* one of the Africans who had had their legs blown off by the landmines planted by one side or the other during the war and had drifted south to beg. Filipe dismissed him with a wave and he shuffled off resignedly on his rubber stump-pads.

"The documents exist, so they must be somewhere. Why don't you try to find them for me, senhor? As his former employer, you see, you are in a far better position than I am to search, to make inquiries if necessary. You have a legitimate excuse; I do not. And as I say, there is a consideration involved."

"Does your principal have access to hard currency?" I asked casually. "Dollars, for instance?"

"He has ample means, that is all I can say."

"Thirty thousand dollars? Is that what he paid Gomes? Would he pay the same to me?"

"It would not do to try to take advantage of his generosity," Filipe said evenly.

"Oh, we're only talking theoretically. If I should find these Barboza papers, you see—which I admit is unlikely— it would be my duty to hand them to the police. I should also, to safeguard myself, report this conversation to them."

I'd said this lightly, hoping to startle him, so his reply was quite unexpected.

"That would be regrettable." He gave one of his quick, neurotic smiles but I knew suddenly that there was no laughter behind the dark glasses. "It would also be foolish.

You misapprehend me. No money is being offered. But I think this will interest you."

One fat hand had been surreptitiously at work on the zip of the plastic briefcase. The other delved into it and came out holding a sheaf of greyish foolscap papers. Filipe slid them across the table to me. They were photostats, perhaps a dozen of them, stapled together at one corner. The top sheet was blank but for a small pale rectangle in the centre containing a few lines of typing. There was a long serial number and some meaningless headings and sub-headings in Portuguese. Standing out among them like a bewildered foreigner was my own name, in capitals: JOSEPH HICKEY.

"What's this, for Christ's sake?" I demanded.

"A copy of a file. The original is in the hands of my principal. The subject of it is you, Senhor Hickey, or rather your business activities in Mozambique. More precisely, your involvement in Rhodesian sanctions-breaking. Please look through it; you'll find it quite comprehensive. The bookwork of the DGS was always impeccable."

I suppose that the look I gave him was incredulous. The Direcção-Geral de Segurança had been the Portuguese secret police, disbanded after the coup. I said blankly, "Why should the DGS have kept a file on me? No—I don't believe it."

"There is the proof, senhor. Like all political police they made work for themselves; they needed to justify their existence. You were a foreign businessman operating on Portuguese soil; they were bound to take a certain passing interest in you. Of course they did not object to what you were doing—far from it—but they kept files on people out of habit, friends as well as enemies. To the friends, of course, some of what they learned may now be embarrassing."

Disbelief had given way to hostility and then suddenly

to apprehension. I removed my gaze from the unyielding dark lenses and for a minute paged through the file. The text, although in Portuguese, was easy enough to follow; it consisted of a series of entries of a few lines each, set out in chronological order. Some of the dates were familiar; so were many of the invoice and consignment note numbers, and of course I recognized the names of the foreign suppliers and the consignees in Salisbury and Bulawayo. What it amounted to was a pretty detailed record of all the business I had conducted through Lourenço Marques with Rhodesia, including lists of the "strategic goods" embargoed by the UN, from the beginning four years ago until the DGS themselves had gone out of business last year. What it meant was that for all that time someone had been informing on me to them.

"Where did you get this?" I asked coldly.

"I am not the principal; I do not have such information. But you are satisfied that it is authentic, surely? Let us just say that it fell into our hands—and that we thought you would not care for us to send it to the British consulate. At least, not if you valued your passport."

The threat was offered obliquely, almost hesitantly, a winning poker hand presented by a novice not quite sure of the rules. But in the end there were three aces on the table and Filipe knew it. In the hands of the British authorities that file contained enough information to lose me my passport a dozen times over. And more, much more: the British were quite capable of making evidence as solid as this public, embarrassing the foreign firms who had supplied me and putting pressure on the governments that had condoned what they were doing. Even though it hadn't been my fault, the leak would have happened at my end. Nobody in my line of business would ever trust me again.

"All right," I said grimly. "I've never been blackmailed

before but I recognize the symptoms. What's your price?"

"What else but the Barboza papers, senhor?"

"I haven't got the bloody things. I—"

"They should not prove too difficult to find."

"I wouldn't even know where to start looking."

"Then you must think. And quickly."

"There isn't time. I'm leaving first thing tomorrow."

"No." Filipe took the photostats from my hand and slipped them into the briefcase. "This is business, Senhor Hickey, and business makes unusual demands on one's time. Of course we cannot prevent your leaving—but if you go, the original of this will be in the hands of the British consulate by tomorrow evening. That is the consideration I was talking about. You cannot run away from your past. If you notify the police the same thing will happen." He stood up and tucked the briefcase under his arm. "As I have said, you are in a better position than anyone else to locate the documents. And I think you are a resourceful man. You have twenty-four hours. You stay at the Polana, I believe? Please be there to receive a phone call at mid-day tomorrow. If you have the papers we will arrange a further meeting."

"And if not?"

He smiled again and patted the briefcase. Like many small and insecure men he enjoyed the chance to bully. "That," he said, "would be unfortunate."

I'd been doing some swift thinking. Maybe this was the prelude to an orthodox blackmail demand after all, an attempt to soften me up and raise the stakes. I said, "I'll offer you an alternative. I'll phone Jo'burg right this minute and have ten thousand rands in good hard South African currency deposited in a bank account under any name you give me—"

"You cannot buy your way out," Filipe said. "My principal has no need of money. It is the papers that he wants."

"It's ludicrous! If they can't be found then nothing you threaten me with is going to make me find them!"

"On the contrary, you have an excellent incentive."

He made a slight formal bow, as if we had just concluded some mutually beneficial piece of business.

"Twenty thousand," I said desperately.

"*Até amanhã.*"

He gave a final bounce and turned away. I stared incredulously after him as he disappeared among the crowds hurrying home for lunch and the midday siesta.

2

Bewilderment had turned to worry when I got back to the hotel an hour later. I kept telling myself that the whole situation was ridiculous, but this did nothing to diminish the fact that it was also full of menace. I had spent the time back in the office, searching with increasing desperation for some nook which might have served Gomes as a hiding place for the absurd set of papers. The task had been hopeless from the start; Akimo had been over the place once, and while he wasn't the most imaginative of men he was an experienced and methodical police officer. I started by going to the obvious places: the backs and undersides of the furniture, the lavatory cistern, the cavity in one outer wall where a ventilator grille had been blocked off when the air-conditioning had been installed (new scratches in the slots of the screws that held down the metal plate told me that Akimo had thought of that too), and the air-conditioning unit itself. Nothing. There was no point in digging through the remaining office papers again; the Barboza documents would certainly not have escaped my notice even if Akimo had chanced to miss them. I examined the walls—all solid brick, no stud partitioning—and checked the plaster of the ceiling; the place hadn't been painted or re-plastered since we had taken it over, so any signs of tampering would have been noticeable. The floor was solid concrete overlaid with strips of linoleum; no room there for concealment.

By now I'd had a bit of time to think, and I was more certain than ever that I was wasting my time. I had to remind myself that if things had happened as Gomes had intended, he would now be alive and well and living in Brazil. He had planned with that in mind, and he would not have left the Barboza papers here because once his disappearance was noticed this and his apartment would have been searched automatically. Would that have mattered to him? Yes, I thought it would. Although the Mozambicans couldn't have touched him, the discovery of falsified Portuguese papers would have been reported to the authorities in Lisbon, and they might well have requested his extradition from Brazil, a country friendly to Portugal's military rulers. The most sensible thing, then, would have been to destroy the stuff. Unless—yes, a possibility that Filipe and his mysterious principal did not seem to have considered—unless Gomes had intended to keep his part of the bargain once he was out of the country. That would mean leaving the documents in some safe place to which he could subsequently direct his clients.

Two enormous questions remained. Why had Gomes been running? And what was so damned important about those papers that it was worth turning down twenty thousand rands to get hold of them? Come to think of it, twenty thousand rands, give or take a bit, was almost as much as the thirty thousand dollars that Gomes had been carrying with him when he died. Was that really the price he'd been paid for arranging the falsification of a few papers? If so, what made the welfare of one small architect from Vilanculos worth that much?

I had no answers. I knew only that I was suddenly the victim of a vicious, unreasoning form of blackmail. Unless from somewhere I managed to conjure up the Barboza papers, I was pretty certain Filipe would pass that file on to the British consulate; those busy bees would soon be swarming all over me. And if I took the plane tomorrow the escape would be illusory; the result would be just the same. The whole comfortable world I had made for myself was threatened, the world that I sometimes caught myself, with regret, feeling complacent about. I was anything but that now. I *had* to find those papers. The threat might seem ridiculous, but it was also very real.

To go through Gomes's apartment, even assuming I could get into it, would be highly risky and would probably prove as pointless as my search of the office had been. If he had not destroyed the documents I felt sure he had left them in some private place, a place where no one would think of looking after he vanished. Which left me right back at the start: with nowhere to look either.

Back at the Polana, having nothing better to do, I decided on a swim. It would freshen me up after my second session in the baking office, and perhaps help me to think more clearly. I changed into my bathing suit, went down the back stairs of the hotel, crossed the terraced lawn and dived into the pool. There were only a few people out here, a couple of children splashing about in the shallow end and some local Portuguese having drinks under the coloured umbrellas on the grass. I swam half a dozen lengths and scrambled out, and as I was walking back across the lawn I saw Joana Gomes.

She sat alone at a table in the shade of an umbrella a few yards ahead, watching me with a wry, rather private smile. She was wearing dark glasses and a lime-green cotton trouser-suit. There was a huge rawhide handbag on the grass beside her and a tall glass full of melting ice on the table. Bacardi on the rocks, that would be; she liked her drinks and most other pleasures strong and undiluted.

"Hello," she said.

I stopped in front of her. "What brings you here?"

"I sometimes call in for a drink. My apartment is just along the road. Remember?"

"I'm sorry. I suppose I should have looked you up, offered my condolences. I wasn't even sure you were still in the country."

She shrugged. "I'm not exactly a widow. What do you call the divorced wife of a dead man anyway?"

"Wasn't it a shock?"

"I felt sorry for him, I suppose. It was like hearing about the death of—not a stranger, exactly, but someone I'd known slightly. One doesn't expect it."

I might have found this cool detachment a bit distasteful if I hadn't recognized it as part of her manner, languidly sardonic in her view of everyone, including herself. Not for the first time I wondered what she had seen in Gomes, but then the same question is asked just as often of successful marriages as of the failed ones. She looked as I remembered her: slim, athletic figure, dark, oval Latin face framed by short, tightly curled black hair like Persian lamb's-wool. Silly hair, but with an odd appeal. The moment we'd first met I had wanted to run my fingers through it.

Suddenly I wondered whether she might be able to help me. "Are you in a hurry?" I asked. "Or can I buy you a drink?"

"What if I said neither?"

"I'd have to take the hint, I suppose."

She removed the dark glasses and smiled, relenting the slight sarcasm. "All right, I'm not in a hurry. I'm bored, if you must know. I'm on a week's holiday from the newspaper. I'd planned to go up to Jo'burg and do some shopping; you can't buy a thing down here any more. Unfortunately our black socialist government doesn't approve of such frivolous expeditions. I wasn't able to buy any foreign currency."

"There's still Bacardi around. Still your drink?"

"Yes."

I signalled to a waiter hovering nearby, who brought me a chair from another table. I sat down and gave him the order: Bacardi and ice for her, Laurentina for me. There was that slight awkwardness between us of intimacy reduced to politeness, the participants in a sexual encounter recalling the circumstances better than they remembered each other.

The setting, at the start, had been an odd one: a tourist launch manoeuvring within camera range of hippos and basking crocodiles on a sightseeing trip up the Incomati River north of Lourenço Marques. In those days there had still been tourists. I had unwisely chosen to drive rather than fly down from Johannesburg for that particular monthly visit. The first torrential summer rains had then arrived and washed away part of the road back to the border, so that I found myself stuck with my Jaguar in LM over a week-end. Gomes, whom I rarely saw outside working hours, felt moved to entertain me, and on the Sunday we drove to Vīla Luisa at the mouth of the Incomati and took one of the launches upstream. He seemed disconcerted to find Joana among the other passengers; after mumbling an introduction he disappeared, clutching a mineral water, to another part of the boat, leaving me to talk to her at the small cocktail bar in the stern.

She showed no interest in the crocs or hippos and spent the whole trip drinking Bacardi at the bar. She was on her own, killing time. She was a newspaper librarian, though quite unlike any other librarian I had met, with *Notícias*, the local morning paper, which meant she worked most Sundays and, she said, hated the ones she had off. I was struck by her looks—the brooding, discontented expression, the fullness of the lips and the slight flare of the nostrils that suggested a deeply sensual nature—and by a matching, almost primitive taste for vividly coloured clothes and enormous handbags. She was about twenty-eight at the time; although she was wholly European there was something indefinably African about her, as though the continent had left its stamp there, so I was not surprised to learn that she'd been born into a colonial military family in Mozambique and had spent all her life here.

She told me her mother had died when she was young and she'd been brought up by her father, a Portuguese infantry officer, on a succession of army bases around the country. There'd been great affection between them, to judge by the amount she talked about him, and his death in the first few weeks of the war against Frelimo had been a terrible shock. Nine years later she still spoke of it with remarkably obsessive bitterness.

"He was blown to pieces by a landmine. No man should die that way. They had to pick bits of him out of the thorn trees so that there'd be enough of him to bury. The funeral was held in secret, so that civilian morale wouldn't be affected. Who would have cared? Down here in the south they didn't know there was a war on. They still don't. They sit in their cafés reading about politics in Lisbon and fashions in Paris. Is that what he died for, to let them live like that? I wish every one of them had been forced to see my father before he was buried—a plastic bag full of bloody pieces of flesh!"

At the time she had been in the first year of a degree course in English at Lourenço Marques University. She gave it up and went to stay with her godfather, an old friend of the family who commiserated and doted and also, I suspected, allowed her to indulge in a deep well of bitterness on which she still drew, encouraging her not to forget her father's death or forgive those who had killed him. In time she did resume her studies, and later came her calamitous marriage to Gomes.

She told me matter-of-factly why it had failed; there was a hint of defiance when she mentioned the affairs she had resorted to. Our conversation at that bar counter had become very frank. What was left unsaid, though, was really more important—the current of mutual physical interest that drew us along as the hot afternoon progressed and the drinking continued. The signals were unmistakable: Joana was available if I wanted her, and I did. We arranged to meet back in Lourenço Marques for dinner, and later in her apartment we made love with greedy abandon.

That was how it began and ended, as a swift physical release, compensating me for a wasted week-end, relieving her of her Sunday bout of boredom. When I left her to drive back to Johannesburg the next morning I was vaguely depressed by the feeling that we had merely used each other and by that sense of disloyalty to Gomes. She was no longer his wife but he was the common denominator between us, and even as she had writhed and clawed at me in bed I had been reminded of the occasions when Gomes had been unable to perform. Joana suffered from no such remorse. I supposed there was no reason why she should—she seemed to have known him no better than I did—but I wished somehow that she'd been able to keep the derisive tone out of her voice when she spoke about him. We had not seen each other since.

"Still with *Noticias?*" I asked conversationally.

"Sure. The same old drudgery, duller if anything. These days I file reports on cashew-nut collectives instead of the Governor-General's receptions."

"I'd have thought you might join the exodus back to Portugal."

"What for?" She dug into the vast handbag for a packet of Camels. Apparently remembering my habits, she didn't offer me one. "I belong here."

"Even with a black government in power? You don't sound contented, exactly."

Lighting a cigarette, she shrugged the suggestion aside. "What about you? I gather you're not in too good an odour."

"Predictable. My Rhodesian connections—I need hardly explain. I've been questioned by a black police inspector—"

"Akimo," she said. "So was I. I couldn't tell him anything."

"He's not entirely convinced that I didn't put Gomes up to smuggling that money out to South Africa."

"He was on his way to Brazil, wasn't he?"

"Via Johannesburg. It's the quickest way there."

"Why there? And why now?"

The drinks arrived and I signed for them. "It's very big and very far away. And it's Portuguese-speaking. It's the best place in the world for anyone Portuguese to drop out of sight. Why now? Well, he was running from something. Any ideas?"

Joana shook her woolly head. "I didn't know the man. Akimo wouldn't believe that either. I tried to explain that even though we were married officially for two years, in practice it was all over within a few weeks. You know why."

It was a thing that Gomes had apparently refused to explain or even discuss after his few limp and fumbling attempts to make love to her.

"I couldn't get through to him intellectually and I couldn't excite him physically," she said, with an edge of the old bitterness. "What else was left? The most exciting thing we ever did together was go fishing from his shack across at Catembe." She sipped her Bacardi and gave a rueful smile, managing now to see the thing as a joke against herself. "Actually, I quite enjoyed the fishing."

A question was in my mind. I paused before asking it but decided I had nothing to lose. "Did he ever have anything to do with a man named Filipe?"

"Filipe who?"

"I don't know. A little man, pale, fat, neurotic—like a pot threatening to boil over. Claims to belong to some charitable group," I added casually. "He was round asking about some papers of theirs that Gomes seems to have mislaid."

"It rings no bells," Joana said indifferently.

"You don't recall his having any connection with an organization like that? An informal charity, Filipe called it, concerned with the welfare of displaced white people."

"Gomes wasn't much of a joiner, and he certainly wasn't into charity work. There was Ficamos, but that hardly fits."

"Ficamos?"

"Never heard of it?"

"No. Can you explain?"

She shrugged again. "The word means *we stay*. It was one of the settler movements that used to spring up from time to time before independence. Far-right, ultra-white. It was rumoured that they had the backing of the DGS. . . ."

"Them," I said. The memory of that file recurred to me

at once, together with the first question I had asked about it: How had it reached the hands of Filipe and his organization?

"Gomes was a member," Joana said. "They were all anticommunists, dedicated to fighting for the white man's right to stay in Africa. A pressure group, really; they wanted to make sure Lisbon wouldn't sell them out to the blacks, which in the end was exactly what happened. It was all quite legal. They were more cranky than sinister, but they had influential friends in the white community: bankers, farmers, businessmen. And, as I say, the secret police."

"Are you sure about all this?" I demanded.

"I spend my days reading and filing newspaper reports. I have an excellent memory for facts. Besides, Gomes was involved."

"Any idea where they got their funds?"

"That's something that was never reported. Unofficially, yes, I do have some idea." The look in her eyes was guarded. "What's all this to you, Joe Hickey?"

If I wanted to learn more I was going to have to trust her. And I thought I could. In spite of the question, she was really too self-centred to sustain more than a mild curiosity in other people's activities. I hesitated only a second before saying, "Between us?"

"Okay."

"This man Filipe. He represents some group that he refuses to name. There's someone behind him, a wealthy man whom he calls his principal. They want these missing papers, and they're pressuring me into finding them."

"Is that a euphemism for blackmail?"

"Call it what you like. They're in a position to hamstring me, ruin my business, unless I give them the documents. And with the best will in the world I don't know where to find them."

"The threat is meaningless, then."

"It means a lot to me, I can tell you. It occurs to me that if I knew who this principal was I might be able to bypass Filipe and approach him direct. Maybe I could talk sense to him. If Ficamos and this organization are one and the same—"

"As far as anyone knows, Ficamos died a natural death three years ago—which isn't to say that it might still not be operating in a clandestine way. I wouldn't know. What I can tell you is this, and it must go no further: There was a rich German sugar farmer mixed up with them, a man called Emmerich." She watched me carefully for a few seconds. "Know the name?"

"Yes. He's about the biggest producer in the country, isn't he?"

"He's very powerful. An old-time *colono*, very right-wing. During the war he raised a sort of a private army up on his estate near Beira—mostly paratroopers with dishonourable discharges from the army—to help him keep Frelimo at bay, and they're still there, still waiting for the siege. He swears he'll go down fighting rather than let them nationalize his property. He used to make secret contributions to Ficamos. Large ones. The only reason I know is because they were paid through Gomes. The money was filtered through the books of his previous business, the travel agency."

"Gomes let you in on this?" I asked.

"No, I found out by accident. A couple of weeks after we were married I opened a packet addressed to him and pulled out a hundred thousand escudos, in cash. I got an explanation out of him: It was Emmerich's monthly subscription."

"Jesus," I said softly. "Did you tell Akimo any of this?"

She shook her head and put her dark glasses on again. "It's not wise to become involved in the inquiries of the black police. Besides, what I know was not relevant to Gomes's death."

"It might be very relevant," I said. "He was carrying thirty thousand American dollars. Emmerich is a big exporter, right? The kind who can always get his hands on foreign currency somehow or other."

"Why should I incriminate Emmerich? Or anyone else?"

A tall South African in shorts walked across the lawn, sat down at a table near us, called a waiter and ordered whisky in a loud voice. Joana drank some more Bacardi, watching me over the rim of the glass.

"I always suspected Gomes was a man with secrets," I said, "but I never came close to finding any of them out. You seem to have had more success."

"Not really. What made you suspect?"

"Nothing I could put my finger on. His manner, mostly. Then there were those odd phone calls from people who would never leave a name, and mysterious packets that kept arriving for him. They added up to a feeling that he was living—well, in two worlds, for want of a better phrase. I'd get hints: his queer political ideas, and the bits of misinformation he would come up with—he must have picked those up somewhere, and he would blurt them out at the most unexpected moments. That stupid business over the Goronga incident. . . ."

I repeated to Joana the story I had told Akimo, about how Gomes and I had been lucky to escape a beating in the bar opposite the market. She listened thoughtfully and nodded.

"Yes, I've seen him do that sort of thing. Never quite so publicly. On the other hand that UN report on the massacre *was* just a public-relations exercise."

"I never read it."

"The UN were invited in simply so that Frelimo could

wring the last possible drop of publicity out of it. They went through the motions of holding an inquiry and their finding was the one that Frelimo wanted: that fifty people had been murdered by a troop of Portuguese Flechas under a DGS officer named Antonio Gil."

"You mean they should have reached a different conclusion?"

"I don't say they could have. It's just that the conclusion was so obvious beforehand that they took no trouble to back it up. After all, by the time they started their investigation the name of Goronga was already a legend, like My Lai, Sharpeville—name any other atrocity you like. They are symbols of everything that seems bad about one set of people and good about another set. The truth may just lie somewhere in between. That's *poder de opinião* for you. You know the phrase? The power of public opinion?"

"You can't seriously think that Gomes had access to any hidden information, can you? Or that it had something to do with his trying to skip the country?"

"I suppose not," Joana said. "How did he react to the original news of the massacre?"

"Should he have reacted at all? I don't know that he did. In fact," I said, searching my memory, "I believe he was away from the office just after it happened. Yes, I remember because I had to come down here myself and fill in for him over a week-end. There was an urgent shipment to be seen through to Salisbury, and on the Friday morning he phoned to say a cousin had been killed in a race riot up in Nampula, that he had to fly up there and help the family. The papers were full of Goronga at the time."

"He had no cousin in Nampula," Joana said coolly. "He had no relatives in Mozambique."

Suddenly I remembered Akimo telling me the same thing. "It was a lie, then," I said. "Why?"

"A coincidence, perhaps. Goronga happened on a

Wednesday, the twelfth of June. That means he must have called you on Friday the fourteenth." She was more interested now, the dates tallying with some fact in her librarian's memory index. "Do you recall what was going on around that time? The army coup had been in April. In Lisbon the military began breaking up the secret police apparatus almost at once, rounding up officers and agents of the DGS. Here in Mozambique the position of the DGS was ambiguous. They were disliked, yes, but they were still fighting side by side with Portuguese troops against Frelimo. There was confusion and delay. The thing that finally pushed the army into taking action was the massacre at Goronga.

"On the fifteenth, Saturday, they began picking up DGS men. The operation was code-named Zebra. Some escaped —including Gil, the man who was supposed to have been in charge at Goronga. But that's by the way. Notice the dates?"

"You're suggesting that Gomes went into hiding? That he was afraid of something?"

"He was afraid of something when he tried to run away the other day."

"But he came back, after three or four days in Nampula or wherever it was. And he's worked for me ever since, for nearly eighteen months."

"Maybe something happened to make him afraid again. I don't know." She finished her drink and rose from the chair, smoothing down the creases in her trouser-legs. When she straightened up her untethered breasts strained perhaps a fraction more than they needed to against the thin cotton, outlining uptilted nipples.

"I have to go. I enjoyed the drink."

"Thanks. It was interesting, but it's not going to help me find those papers."

From behind the dark glasses her eyes lingered on me,

as though she was reluctant to leave. I'd been too preoccupied with the Barboza documents to sense something that must have been obvious to her from the start—a feeling that, with Gomes now dead, the way in which we stood to each other was different, subtly redefined. I said, "Did you know I was in town?"

"I might have guessed you would be. Don't flatter yourself, Joe, I didn't come looking."

In spite of the sharpness of her tone I understood the signals again. She had nothing better to do. I had a lot on my mind—too much, I would have thought, to be stirred by any interest in Joana. But I was stirred, perhaps subconciously seeing in her a promise of escape. I said, "Can you stay for lunch?"

"Sorry. I have to spend an hour in the office."

"Dinner, then?"

The South African at the adjacent table called the waiter and ordered more whisky. He had a booming voice that could be heard everywhere in the vicinity of the pool. He'd been watching the two of us openly, probably trying to work out our relationship, and I'd have bet he had it wrong. Joana gave me a long cool look and then smiled knowingly. It was a smile that managed to suggest she saw through me, even if she didn't.

"All right, dinner. As long as we don't spend the evening talking about Gomes."

"Promise. Eight o'clock in the Polana bar? And then we'll choose a good restaurant, if there are any left in this town."

"I like to eat prawns," Joana said firmly. "Giant prawns, freshly caught, grilled, served with butter and lemon. Delagoa Bay still has the best prawns in the world; that's one thing Frelimo hasn't been able to change."

"Prawns, then. There was a place called the Peninsula

that used to—" My memory was jolted. "You said something about a shack. A fishing shack."

"Across the bay. It's where Gomes used to keep his tackle."

"Think it might still be there? Still in use?"

"I've not the slightest idea."

"It's just occurred to me. Those papers: He might just possibly have hidden them there. Where exactly is the place?"

"On the beach east of Catembe. It's one of a row of Goan fishermen's huts. You have to cross the estuary and then walk down the beach, probably for the best part of a kilometre. If I'm not mistaken his was the end one in the row. The fishermen could tell you."

"I don't want to advertise my interest. You didn't mention it to Akimo?"

"There was no reason. Gomes liked to keep the place to himself; I'd practically forgotten its existence."

It didn't sound like the kind of place where anyone would hide confidential documents, but there seemed no harm in trying. Anything would be better than complete inaction. Joana hitched the big handbag onto her shoulder and stood ready to go. I was grateful for her lack of curiosity. I said, "By the way, have you ever met this Emmerich man?"

"Yes."

"What's he like?"

Her hand went out in an eloquently meaningless gesture. "He runs an empire, and behaves a bit like an emperor."

"Perhaps you'd tell me what you know about him this evening."

"I'll do better than that. I'm going into the office; I'll copy some of our files on him." She paused as she was about to turn away and said, "A coincidence strikes me, perhaps a silly coincidence. The village of Goronga is—was —just a few kilometres from his sugar estate. He was asked to give evidence to the United Nations inquiry. He refused."

"I see." The information was meaningless and yet somehow disturbing. The slaughtered village seemed to hover like a ghost in the background to Gomes's death. I said, "Well, till tonight."

I watched her walk away, swivelling her hips as she passed between tables and chairs. Then I discovered that the loud South African was watching too. He turned to give me a chummy, approving nod which I didn't acknowledge. My mind was in a turmoil.

3

It was all very easy. A little too damned easy, as I might have realized if only my thinking hadn't been dominated by anxiety, if the need to find the Barboza papers and put myself in the clear with Filipe hadn't driven most other things out of my head. Gomes, Emmerich, Ficamos, Goronga, the DGS: They were names and titles with little meaning, locked together in some confused relationship that might or might not have some bearing on the reason for blackmailing me. What mattered to me was the blackmail, and the very faint hope I had now been given of fulfilling its demands.

I didn't allow myself any optimism when I set off for Catembe to visit the fishing shack. It sounded a pretty insecure hiding place, after all. Once I had changed from my bathing suit into slacks and a loose shirt, I had another beer and a quick steak sandwich in the bar downstairs and caught a taxi down to the Baixa, the old part of the city.

From my first day I'd been aware of the slight possibility that Akimo had put a tail on me. Till now it hadn't mattered; today I had to be sure. There was also a faint risk that Filipe or someone connected with him might attempt to watch my movements. I paid off the taxi outside the old Portuguese fort, the last relic of the days when Lourenço Marques had been a tiny trading post exporting ivory and slaves, and followed a roundabout route towards the docks through narrow cobbled streets, past crumbling colonial buildings whose yellowed plaster hurled the glare of the sun into my eyes. The heat was stunning. The Portuguese had all fled to their air-conditioned apartments up the hill; some beggars and shoeshine boys dozed in doorways but by now the streets were practically deserted. The PSP were an unsophisticated police force and I reckoned I could count on their being clumsy at surveillance work; no one could have followed me at that time of day in any case without marking himself out, as I presumably did, as eccentric or foreign. By the time I reached the ferry landing I was certain that there had been nobody. I had just a couple of minutes to wait before the half-hourly boat left for Catembe at one thirty. There were only a few other passengers, most of them African women taking trussed chickens and boxes of vegetables home from the market. Behind us the skyline of Lourenço Marques was thrown into vivid relief above the ships lining the wharves.

Unless you were interested in beach fishing, the only point in making the crossing was to see the view. Catembe was a dull, dusty little village well sunk into the torpor of the siesta. The community of Goan fishermen lived further along the shore, towards where the muddy river widened out into the bay, in wooden shacks built on stilts above the beach. I'd heard that their numbers had been dwindling over the years; presumably Gomes had secured one of the shacks when it was left vacant. It was an ideal base for fishing. There were mullet and shad to be caught close in-shore, and with a boat you could go after kingfish, bonito and even sharks out in the bay. The spot was isolated and the Goans were a closed community; it was the kind of place that would have appealed to the secretive side of Gomes.

Approaching the huts, I took to the cover of the scrub that grew above the beach and circled behind the row. Probably I need not have bothered, for this village was in the grip of the siesta as well. Upturned boats lay between the stilts under the shacks and nets were spread out to dry on the baking sand. No one stirred. Most of the huts, which were set well apart from each other, had open doorways curtained with strips of plastic that hung limp in the still air, but as I drew near the one at the end I saw that it had a fitted door and a pair of crudely made shutters over the single window. I felt sure that Joana had remembered correctly. That would be Gomes's place.

When I was level with it I walked cautiously down the beach, round to the front of the hut and up a creaking stepladder onto a narrow platform that served as a kind of porch. There was a rusty bolt secured with a padlock on the door, but the wood which held it looked damp and soft. Experimentally I placed my shoulder against it and brought pressure to bear on the staple. The screws that held it gave slightly, with a protesting squeak. Suddenly I was aware of a movement under the nearest hut, perhaps thirty yards away. A grey-muzzled mongrel that had been lying in the shade stood up, gave two perfunctory barks and flopped down on the sand again, its tongue lolling, watching me with indolent curiosity. I had tensed and turned my back to the door. I waited two full minutes, mentally rehearsing the story I had prepared, before I was sure no one was coming to investigate. By now the old dog had got used to me and was scratching itself. I turned back to the bolt.

As I had thought, the door and its frame were of raw timber, and the soft woods of southern Africa do not last in seashore humidity. With two quick shoves I had wrenched the staple out of the wood and drawn back the bolt. The door swung open. I glanced around; the dog hadn't barked again and there was still no one in sight. I entered the hut quickly and closed the door behind me.

I stood blinking in the dim light that seeped through the gaps in the planking. The hut consisted of a single room, perhaps fifteen feet square, with a screen door connecting it to another platform at the rear. And Gomes had used it recently, that was certain; I recognized the neatness and impersonality. The only furniture was a camp bed, with a sleeping-bag rolled up at its foot, and a folding chair. A shelf had been built along one wall to hold a camping gas-cooker, some plates, a saucepan or two and a regimented row of cans and jars containing basic provisions. Against the opposite wall, three fibreglass fishing rods rested horizontally on racks: a long surf-casting model fitted with an expensive Abu multiplier reel, a stout little boat rod and one of medium length for spinning. There was another low shelf on which stood a wide wooden tray divided into compartments to hold lead weights and hooks of every size, spinners, spoons, made-up tackles and wire tracers. An old rucksack lay on the floor and I searched it; it contained two more reels, several hundred metres of spare line, knives for scaling and gutting fish, and a dozen other accessories that Gomes had accumulated over the years. I rather envied him this private enthusiasm; he could have spent weeks out here without anyone's knowing. Could this, I wondered, be where he had come last June when he was supposed to be in Nampula?

I stood in the centre of the shack, looking round me and feeling vaguely cheated. There were no cupboards or drawers; the walls, the floor and the roof were all made from single layers of planking supported by crossbeams, so there were no cavities in which anything might be hidden. I checked through the cooking utensils and provisions on the shelf, opening the jars and shaking the cans; then I took one of the scaling knives, slit the lining out of the sleeping-bag and shook its filling out on the floor. Nothing had been concealed inside. Disappointment began to swell to dismay.

An ingrained thoroughness, certainly not the hope of finding something, prompted me to open the screen door and check the wooden platform at the rear of the hut. It had a broken handrail and, like the walls and the floor, consisted of a single row of planks. There had once been an opening through which, presumably, a second stepladder had led down to the beach, but it was now boarded up. It wasn't till I was turning to close the door that my eye caught a tiny glint of new steel in the sunlight. I went out on the platform and knelt down to examine the planks that had been used to cover the opening. They were as old and discoloured as the original wood and had probably been cannibalized from some other hut, but the nails that secured them were new and shiny. They were not the galvanized kind that resisted rust; given the rate of corrosion in this climate they could hardly have been there more than a couple of weeks. Without quite knowing what I expected to learn, I lay down on the platform and peered cautiously over the edge. The opening had been boarded up from below as well. What on earth for?

Then suddenly I understood. Between the upper and lower layers of planking there must now be a kind of well about eighteen inches square and corresponding in depth to the thickness of the original wood, which was two or two and a half inches. Excited by the discovery, I went back inside and took the largest of the scaling knives from Gomes's rucksack. I returned to the platform and got to work on the wood. Here at the rear of the shack I could not be seen from anywhere else in the village, and the job took only a couple of minutes. The planks were as rotten as the door had been. When I twisted the first one off I saw what I had already come to expect, a thin bundle tightly wrapped in a plastic bag. No, not just one bundle. Hastily I tore out the rest of the planking and then stared in puzzlement at what the cavity contained: three separate sets of paper, all carefully wrapped in plastic. I chose one, tearing off the adhesive tape that sealed the mouth, unfolding the bag and letting the contents tumble out. The three basic documents were there: a Portuguese passport, a birth certificate and the *bilhete de identidade* of a Portuguese citizen. Along with a couple of moisture-absorbent tablets to prevent condensation and mould, there were also a record of baptism, a yellowed school-leaving certificate from a *liceu* in Lisbon, an international health card, a driving licence and half a dozen other documents. It was a testimonial to a life—a complete set of credentials, as Filipe had called them. The trouble was that they were not the credentials of Barboza, but of someone named Casimiro Nunes.

The next bag I opened held a similar set of papers in the name of Francisco Gouveia Machado, his life fully documented from birth. The third revealed a package within a package—a thick blue plastic wallet with AMERICAN EXPRESS embossed on it, one of those things that travel agents give their customers to keep tickets and documents in. This, in turn, contained the Barboza papers.

Again, apart from the three basic items there were about

twelve other documents which between them provided a fairly comprehensive record of the man's existence.

I squatted on the narrow platform looking over the array of papers and asking myself what the hell they could mean. That two other white men with the same kind of citizenship problems as Barboza's had come to Gomes for help? Perhaps he hadn't simply been providing a one-off service to Filipe's "principal" but with the help of his civil service contacts had been running a sort of wholesale business in the straightening out of inconvenient documents. It wasn't such an improbable idea. Back in South Africa, where a black man's place of birth or length of residence in a particular town could make all the difference to where he was allowed to live or work, falsifying personal papers was quite a cottage industry. The change in Mozambique's status must have brought similar problems to many Portuguese.

Or did it go deeper than that? Filipe's story about Barboza hadn't rung true, particularly after he'd refused my offer of twenty thousand rands as an alternative to producing this stuff for him. Even then, though, I might have given him the benefit of the doubt if it wasn't for finding these other sets of papers. Clearly they'd all been brought out here pretty recently, and in some haste. I'd been right about the shack: it wasn't a secure hiding place, which probably meant that Gomes had intended it as a temporary one. Perhaps he'd meant to notify Filipe's "principal" of the whereabouts of the documetns once he reached Brazil—all of which led me back to the conviction that Gomes had been running because he was afraid.

Searching for a clue, a common denominator of some kind, I read more carefully through the details on the passports and identity cards. Barboza might indeed have been born in Goa, but his place and date of birth were here firmly recorded as Lisbon, 1933. His profession was given as consulting architect. Nunes, salesman, had been born at Sintra in the Estremadura in 1928, and Machado, dental technician, at Luanda, Angola, in 1937. They were now resident respectively in Vilanculos, Lourenço Marques and Beira. Nothing there, nothing to suggest even that these three average-sounding men might have known each other. But there were two significant things about the passports: they had all been issued by the Portuguese Interior Ministry office in Lourenço Marques around the same time—May and early June last year—and none of them appeared to have been used since. There were no entry or exit stamps.

May and the first part of June: that had been the very uncertain period Joana and I had talked about, between the coup and the Goronga massacre. But in the absence of any obvious connection I could not pursue the thought. I studied Barboza's passport photograph in the hope that it might reveal something. It showed a man of forty-plus with a very fat face; features which had probably once been strong and aquiline were blurred by puffy fat. He had heavily ringed eyes framed by rimless glasses, black hair brushed back and forming a widow's peak where it had thinned, a pencil moustache. He was described as one metre eighty-five in height—about six feet one, which was tall for a Portuguese. I compared his picture to those of Machado and Nunes. They showed three very different men, with differing expressions ranging from deadpan to self-conscious smirk, but there was an underlying sameness about the photographs, a similarity of tone and texture that I didn't understand at first. And then suddenly I had it. They had all been taken in the same artificial light, at the same camera setting, with the same hazy background —in other words, by the same photographer and in the same studio—three men who were supposed to live in different parts of Mozambique three or four hundred miles apart.

My sceptical instincts had warned me from the start that Filipe had been lying, but it was only now that the possibility occurred to me that the man called Barboza did not actually exist—at least, that neither he nor Machado nor Nunes existed under those names; that the identities themselves, not just the specific facts about them, were elaborate fakes; and that the implications of this were far more serious than Filipe had wanted me to believe.

I did not wish to pursue the thought to an uncomfortable conclusion. Against all my expectations I had found what Filipe wanted. Good. I'd wait for his call at midday tomorrow, hand the stuff over, retrieve the DGS file and be off, no questions asked. But inevitably questions were crowding into my mind. Had Filipe told me that silly story about the architect because the real story would have scared me, even more than the threat of losing my passport? And since he had been discredited by my discovery of the other two sets of papers, was it possible that he hadn't known about them?

Now I faced a stark set of alternatives. Whom did I fear more, Filipe and his anonymous organization or Akimo and the police? The presence of three lots of false personal papers suggested that they were meant to provide cover for some criminal or subversive activity. Not to report this to the police would make me a party to it. If I were caught, the question of having my passport confiscated would be the least of my worries. On the other hand, if I did go to Akimo with these documents, I could be quite certain that Filipe would send that file to the British.

It was a question of weighing a probability against a certainty, of comparing the short-term chances of self-preservation offered by either choice. And Filipe won.

Once again I glanced briefly through the papers, finding their ordinariness and banality reassuring: the laboured official handwriting and the coffee stain on Nunes's birth certificate, transposed figures on the issue date of Barboza's driving licence. If these were fakes they were extremely good ones; a small mistake like that could lend more authenticity than perfect accuracy would have. Maybe they were genuine. Maybe I was letting my imagination run away with me. All I knew was that the misgivings I'd had about this business had strengthened, in the few hours since I'd met Filipe, into a very deep disquiet.

Recollecting myself, I knew I should not be lingering. I wrapped up the bundles of paper, replaced Machado's and Nunes's in the cavity and laid the planks loosely over the opening. Carrying the American Express wallet I went to the front door of the shack, opened it a fraction and looked out. The fishermen's village was still asleep. I stepped out and closed the door behind me, making sure the bolt—at least from the distance at which anyone was likely to look at it—did not appear disturbed. Then I went down the ladder, walked up the beach into the scrub and headed back to the ferry landing. Only the dog had witnessed my visit.

Back in my suite at the Polana I thought for several minutes about where to keep the wallet until tomorrow. It was two inches thick and too bulky to carry on my person. Theoretically the best place would be the hotel safe, but I did not trust the reception-desk staff. Under the Portuguese all hotel desk clerks had had a reputation, whether deserved or not, of being DGS informers, and I wouldn't have been surprised if some of them were now giving the same service to the black police. I considered hiding it in the lavatory cistern or the air-conditioning unit, but in the end I simply left it in the most obvious place, the drawer of the bedside table. If a thief should break in while I was out he wouldn't spare it a second glance, and no determined searcher would miss it wherever it was hidden. But nobody, I thought, was likely to come looking.

4

"Under the Portuguese he was virtually a law unto himself," Joana said. "A big landowner, a major export earner; he couldn't do a thing wrong and he had the whole administration in his pocket. Açúcar Emmerich Limitada is the name of his firm; it still supplies something like sixty per cent of the country's total production. What he's doing up there can't be called farming, it's 'agribusiness': growing sugar, milling it himself, refining, packing, exporting. Most of it goes up the Persian Gulf to the Arabs. They have a sweet tooth, I'm told."

"And they pay in dollars out of their oil revenue surpluses, presumably."

"Frelimo would like to do without him, but it seems they still can't. In a country that's supposed to practise revolutionary socialism, you would think he'd be first on the list for a state takeover. Others have been bought out, but not Emmerich. Perhaps he still manages to have someone in his pocket. Still, pressure is building against him. Someone in the government referred to him the other day as the last *prazeiro* in Mozambique."

"What does that mean?"

Our second cup of coffee arrived, and I ordered two more glasses of vanilla-flavoured brandy. The service was prompt; the waiters had too little to do these days. The only other customers in the Peninsula were four Frelimo soldiers at a corner table who were drinking dark beer and having an argument in Portuguese. It was odd to hear the language spoken among black men; they were from different tribes and it was the official lingua franca of the movement. Joana was doing her best to pretend they weren't there.

"*Prazeiros* were the first white settlers here. In the seventeenth and eighteenth centuries they were given a free hand to take whatever land they could and enslave the blacks living on it. They made their own laws and recognized no higher authority. Eventually the system was abolished, but the *prazeiros* went down fighting. One of them beat off four attacks and wiped out a column of infantry before he surrendered his territory. It's not too fanciful to imagine Emmerich doing the same."

Accustomed to marshalling facts, she gave this explanation concisely and clearly, but I was not too sure that there wasn't some sneaking admiration in her tone. Most people admire a stayer. I had asked her for the information on Emmerich because I had two grounds for suspecting that he might be the "principal" behind Filipe: One was his association with Gomes through the Ficamos movement; the other was the presence of the thirty thousand dollars in Gomes's car. But I did not really want to know about Emmerich any longer. Additional knowledge only increased my uneasiness, my feeling of involvement in something beyond my understanding. I had found what Filipe wanted; I would pay him his price and get out. However, Joana had brought with her to the Polana bar photocopies of newspaper reports on Emmerich over the past three years and I had to appear interested. She had not asked me about my visit to the fishing shack.

Over Bacardis before dinner she had helped me translate some of the clippings. The papers—at least before independence—were always repeating his life story, the rags-to-riches tale of a successful planter. Like other Germans in Africa, denied the backing of a colonial empire such as the British, French and Portuguese had had, he'd set about making one of his own. The "sugar king," as the newspapers had called him, was in fact a baron—the Freiherr Heinrich von Metzradt-Emmerich, scion of a family of minor Saxon aristocrats, who had lost what money he'd had as a young man in the Depression, worked his passage on a freighter to Africa and landed penniless in Beira, the second city of Mozambique. With a loan scrounged from one of the chartered companies that were then administering large tracts of the country, he bought ten hectares of rich, silt-laden land adjacent to the Pungwe River and put them under sugar-cane.

In that part of Africa the crop had never been tried on a year-round basis under intensive irrigation. It proved phenomenally successful and the enterprise grew without check. Açúcar Emmerich now owned six thousand hectares of productive land—in my terms about fifteen thousand acres, or nearly twenty-four square miles of sugar-cane—and I could understand his reluctance to give it up.

Long ago there had been a wife, a German woman for whom the loneliness of life on the estate had eventually become too much. Emmerich was a man's man; it showed in the newspaper interviews. His friends had been bachelor farmers and soldiers stationed in the area; his idea of a good time was an all-night poker game or a drinking session in the officers' mess in Beira. The wife had gone back to Hamburg. There had been no children.

The Portuguese soldiery was no longer there, nor were many of the neighbours. In his sixties now, Emmerich lived alone in a house at the centre of his dominions.

There were a few pictures which had come out reasonably well on the photocopies. One showed him clutching an automatic rifle and scowling aggressively out from behind a pile of sandbags stacked around his front veranda. It had been taken a year before the war ended. Around this time he had begun recruiting Portuguese ex-paratroopers as security guards and had publicly invited the Frelimo guerrillas who were infiltrating the area to attempt an attack on his property. Apparently they had never responded to the challenge, but the private army was still in his pay, still carrying weapons. For Emmerich, it seemed, the war was not yet over.

Stubbornness was evident in the heavy set of his features, the bullet head with its cropped grey hair, the slope of his powerful shoulders. The country had been wide open when he'd first arrived, and few legal restraints had been placed on any European who was prepared to pioneer in that wild hinterland. So for a long time Emmerich had been accustomed to doing pretty much what he pleased. Still running his business on old-fashioned lines, he was firmly paternalistic towards his African workers and an enemy of reform—in other words, a *colono* of the old school, refusing to adapt to the changes around him. He was what I might have been myself, had I been older, richer, and a bit less cynically realistic. Ficamos was only one of a number of right-wing settler movements to which he had belonged at various times.

Joana had arrived at the Polana carrying a handbag the size of a hatbox and wearing a yellow cotton caftan which showed off her figure to the fullest advantage. From there she'd driven us in her Volkswagen to the Peninsula, where we had duly ordered the prawns that she wanted. She'd eaten with sensuous, unself-conscious gusto, letting butter run down her chin and gulping down glasses of chilled *vinho verde*.

Now we had finished our second glass of brandy. A waiter approached to offer more coffee and I raised my eyebrows at Joana. She glanced at the Frelimo men in the corner. With the flow of beer their talk had become progressively noisier.

"I could do with some less discordant sounds. There's a *boîte* over in the Baixa where they still have real *fado* music. Feel like moving on?"

The Baixa had been hot and somnolent when I had walked through it on my way to the ferry this afternoon. At night one of its streets came to life: the Rua Major Araujo, where a dozen seedy saloons, a few discreet nightclubs and the one-room apartments of countless black prostitutes catered to a need for liquor, entertainment and sex which the puritan zeal of Frelimo had not yet succeeded in stamping out. Up a narrow stairway between two bars, the *fado* house was a tiny smoke-filled room where we found ourselves crammed together behind a low table, drinking more raw brandy and listening to the soulful singing of the Lisbon tavernas.

"Why did he refuse to help the UN inquiry?" I asked in a break between songs.

"He said the whole thing was a waste of time, a way of rubber-stamping the obvious; besides which, he knew nothing about the incident. They said all they wanted from him was background information; he'd known the village well, since it was so close to his property. He still said no. Short of asking the government to go in and bring him out forcibly, there was nothing the committee could do."

"The real reason, of course, could be that he had something to hide."

"Perhaps."

"And that might just tie in with Gomes sounding off

about what had really happened at Goronga. Exactly what did happen, anyway?"

"That's just it. No one can say with absolute certainty, so everyone feels free to speculate." She took out a Camel and lit it. "No survivors were ever found, and the men who did it weren't caught. It was right near the end of the war. It seems there was a Frelimo band operating in the area; the previous night they had ambushed a military convoy and killed some soldiers. The Flechas came to the village and questioned the people about the whereabouts of the guerrillas. The story goes that they were deliberately misled. Apparently they came back later that day, lined up the whole village and shot them. The bodies were found next morning. A priest from a mission station nearby notified the military. There was some bungling and delay. By the time anyone got round to asking the right questions the Flecha unit had disbanded and destroyed their muster-rolls. And the white DGS man in charge, Gil, had disappeared too. Plenty of speculation about him as well, naturally; like all the best Nazi war criminals, he's rumoured to be in South America. People even claim to have spotted him in Caracas. And in Salisbury, Durban, Macao, Melbourne. A lot of that type did get away, of course, in spite of Operation Zebra a few days later."

The melancholy music began again. We ordered more brandy, and soon Joana's head was resting on my shoulder. I ran my hand through the tight black curls and she twisted her face round and kissed me hard. A shudder ran through us both. The longing was sharp and urgent, and this time there was no need for me to feel guilty towards Gomes.

Her apartment was up the hill in the Cronistas district, not far from the Polana. In the bedroom the caftan fell off her at the pull of a string. Like her face, her body had something African about it, with a long-waisted suppleness, slender legs, and breasts that were both high and full.

In the moment of her orgasm she gasped and tore at me. Yet even at her most furiously abandoned there was some quality of inwardness about her pleasure, as though I were its cause but not a participant. Later, running a hand over me, she discovered the small indentation in the right shoulder and asked what it was.

"Bullet scar. Mau Mau."

"Black bastards," she murmured.

She squirmed closer and the hand groped downwards, eager to arouse me again. If the onrush of renewed desire hadn't driven everything else from my mind, I might have had reason to think about that comment.

5

When we had made love again I fell asleep with Joana curled in beside me. I woke with a start, groping for the light switch and my watch, and discovered it was only ten to twelve.

I had had some hopelessly confused dream in which the Barboza papers and all those disconnected names had figured—Gomes, Emmerich, Ficamos, Filipe—and through which a single vision had leaped out at me, a vision of myself opening the drawer of the bedside table in the Polana and finding the wallet gone. The image had been terrifying enough to waken me in a sweat. It was stupid, of course—no one knew anything, no one could have gone looking—but for my own peace of mind I should have put the papers somewhere less accessible. I tried to put them out of my thoughts, but they wouldn't go. After lying there for a couple of minutes I knew I would have to go back to the hotel and check. Irrationally but decidedly, I wouldn't feel easy until I knew the documents were safe.

I tried to leave the bed without waking Joana, but she stirred beside me and muttered, "What is it?"

"I have to go back to the hotel for a minute."

She felt for my hand and pressed it between her thighs, warm and still moist from our last coupling. "You can't do that, Joe. I want more of you."

"Later. There's something I must do."

"What?"

"I have to take an important call from Salisbury. I've just remembered."

"Get it transferred here."

"I have to consult some notes. They're in my suite."

I took the hand back and rolled out of bed. There was no use trying to explain the real reason, not even to myself, and I was too aware of urgency to feel foolish at interrupting our lovemaking. Joana watched resentfully as I pulled on my clothes. I went round the bed and kissed her on the shoulder but she turned away, sulking.

"I'll be fifteen minutes, no more."

"That's what you say. You've had what you wanted and you're leaving. Have you got another woman?"

The sudden scent of jealousy in her was so odd that I laughed. "Don't be ridiculous! I'll be back."

"Go then, if you must. Take my car."

"It'll be as quick to walk."

I went downstairs and out into a soft warm night heavy with the scent of jasmine. As I strode along the deserted road overlooking the bay, my mind was filled again with that meaningless sequence of names and designations. Only now they had started to make a little more sense when they were paired and grouped together. Filipe and Emmerich, yes. Gomes, Emmerich and Ficamos, yes. The DGS and Ficamos, the DGS and the butchered village of Goronga. Somewhere there had to be another name, another entity which, like a particular and vital loop in a tangled fishing line, would unravel the whole thing once it was found.

It took me five minutes to reach the Polana. I turned in at the gates, walked up the driveway, entered the wide Edwardian lobby and collected my key at the desk. There were only two or three guests still sitting in the cocktail lounge; one was the loud-voiced South African who'd been at the pool that morning, and he nodded a greeting to me. I took the lift up to the top floor.

Opening the main door of my suite I caught the reek of coarse tobacco, the cheap shag favoured by Africans for their foul, hand-rolled cigarettes, and thought the roomboy must have been in to turn back the bed. Before I'd had a chance to wonder why he should come so late I had shut the door behind me and stepped forward. Then I was aware of a movement in the bathroom doorway, to the right and slightly behind me. Before I could react my right arm was seized and twisted behind my back. I opened my mouth to shout for help. A sweaty hand was jammed over it and I bit down hard, sinking my teeth deeply into the palm, hearing a hiss of pain as it was withdrawn. My arm was released, but only for an instant before a vicious kick in the base of the spine sent me staggering against the wall. Two men had come through the door from the sitting room, Africans in kepis and khaki drill outfits. One of them was calling an urgent word of command to the man behind me, whose hand I had bitten.

The order came too late. Something hit me square across the back of the head, slamming me several feet forward into the arms of one of the khaki-uniformed figures before I slid to the floor. In a moment of numb detachment as unconsciousness closed in on me I recognized Inspector Akimo; I also recognized the American Express wallet that he clutched in one hand.

PART THREE
Thursday, November 20

1

When I was marched up from my cell to the office for the second time I wasn't sure what to expect. The first session, during which I'd stood swaying and stupefied by the pain in my head, unable to comprehend the questions or formulate the answers properly, had been a grim little business quite as unreal as everything that had preceded it: the police half dragging me down the back stairs of the Polana to dump me in a car; the man I had bitten and who had hit me with his truncheon sitting beside me on the drive downtown, alternately cursing, sucking his palm and giving me vicious little pinches by way of further retaliation.

At the end of the interview I had asked Akimo to notify the British consul of my arrest. Instead of replying he had punched me, a single hard jab in the stomach that had doubled me over on the floor in front of the desk, an inarticulate venting of anger, tiredness, exasperation. After that, back in the cell, I'd lain awake for a long time on the thin, urine-stained palliasse.

It smelt like all the police cells I had ever known, the carbolic never quite overpowering the odour of bodies and the special rankness that sweat seems to have when it is induced by fear. The walls were painted a shiny green that bounced the hard overhead light into my eyes, inhibiting sleep and bringing a sense of timelessness. The fierce pain gradually subsided to a throb. Apart from the guard stationed along the corridor, who'd given me water to drink from a jam tin, the only person I saw was the bitten policeman, who would appear at intervals outside the barred door to wave a bandaged hand at me and jabber threateningly in pidgin Portuguese. Eventually he was chased away.

At some point I must have fallen asleep, for I was startled awake by the shriek of unoiled door hinges. The guard motioned me out, and I stood up and shuffled awkwardly into the corridor. My shoelaces had been taken away, together with my belt, money and wristwatch.

"*Que se passe?*" I asked.

"*Não sei, camarada. Para lá—ande!*"

"*Tem horas?*"

"*Seis e trinta.*"

Six thirty. So I'd been here more than six hours. There'd been plenty of time to reflect that I was in the worst trouble of my life and that it was mostly of my own making, but I had one immediate concern: the British consulate. Sanctions-buster or not, I was in desperate need of their help.

The guard stayed a yard behind me. We tramped past more cells, then went through a steel door that was unlocked for us by another policeman and up a flight of concrete stairs to the ground floor of the headquarters building. Outside one of a row of doors in a long, bleak corridor, my escort told me to stop. The nameplate of some Portuguese former occupant had been replaced by a roughly stencilled card that read JORGE AKIMO, INSPECTOR. The guard knocked, gestured me inside and closed the door behind me.

I screwed up my eyes at the sudden flood of daylight from the uncurtained window. It looked out on a residential street. Akimo's office was as stark and functional as my cell, with bare linoleum on the floor and what little furniture there was all crowded into one corner: three hard chairs, an empty bookcase supporting a rack with pigeonholes for official forms, and the battered desk on which the papers lay spread out, not just the Barboza documents, this time, but all the others from Gomes's shack. Passports, identity cards and the rest were set out in rows like cards in a game of patience. It was a pretty damning array of evidence.

This time, too, there was another African in the room, a lanky man leaning back against the window-sill with his arms crossed tightly over his chest and long hands thrust round under the armpits so that he appeared to be hugging himself. He wore a Chinese-style cotton drill suit, the outfit fashionable among Third World politicians anxious to maintain their proletarian images, though this one fitted his athletic frame well enough to suggest personal tailoring. His face was long and narrow, handsome in a rather forbidding way, but most readily distinguished by the tribal scars that covered his cheeks and forehead. I recognized them as the scars of the Makonde tribe from the far north, people who'd been prominent in the fight against the Portuguese, a complex pattern of zigzags and chevrons stained dark blue against the shiny black of his skin. The dark eyes as he returned my gaze held a peculiar intensity. They were not a policeman's eyes. I put him down as a party member, one of the new breed of zealous young men who had stepped into the senior civil-service jobs vacated by the Portuguese.

Akimo, seated behind the desk, watched me sourly. In contrast to the other man's crispness he looked rumpled and weary, with a greyness under his pitted skin and big sweat-marks on his shirt, though the morning was still cool and the overhead fan not yet running.

"I have more questions," he said. "This time you will co-operate."

"I have requested to see my consul," I said.

"The request is noted."

"What the hell does that mean? Have you informed the consulate or not?"

"Suddenly you are anxious for protection from the British, hm? After four years of working against their interests, what help do you expect?"

"I have the right to insist on—"

"Don't speak about rights," Akimo snapped. "In this building you have none. You were police yourself, you should know. If indictment is made the consul will be notified."

"You mean you're going to charge me?"

"It depends." He glanced significantly towards the man by the window. "Whether or not, the legal process is slow. It can take some months to decide."

"I see," I said grimly.

"Sit."

Akimo pointed at the chair facing the desk and I sat down, not at all reassured by the small courtesy. In the presence of the Makonde he was trying to sound correct —not an easy thing for him—but he'd already made it clear that he didn't believe a word of my story. He did not even believe that Filipe existed, and his mind, once made up, was hard to change.

He'd made me look pretty stupid all the same. He had gone to the Polana to return my passport late the night before. When he learned that I hadn't been in all evening he'd become suspicious and decided to make sure that I hadn't for some reason chosen to do a bunk after all. So he'd obtained a pass key to my suite and searched it. It had been that simple.

Akimo indicated the documents spread out before him. "You don't deny possessing?"

"The ones in the name of Barboza, obviously not. The others were in Gomes's shack, where I told you you'd find them."

"A technicality. You knew where they were."

"Since yesterday only."

"And you know the real identity of the man named Barboza."

"Only since you told me."

Akimo made a sceptical face at the man by the window. The scarred face remained immobile.

"This is not a good start, Hickey. Your only chance is to co-operate in full. You want to stick to this story about a man who approached you in the street?"

"It happens to be true."

"And within a couple of hours you just happened to find the place where the papers were hidden, hm?"

"Yes, it was by chance. I didn't know the shack existed until Senhora Gomes mentioned it. Ask her."

"An attempt to make an alibi," Akimo said dismissively. "Anyway, if you found the papers and thought they were suspicious, why didn't you bring to me?"

"I've told you. Because I was afraid of what Filipe would do."

"More afraid of him than me?"

"At the time."

Akimo watched me malevolently through tired, angry eyes. The temptation to hit me again must have been strong.

"Filipe lives only in your imagination, Hickey. What can you tell us about him? Nothing."

"Because he wanted me to know nothing."

"Not his surname, not where he comes from. . . ."

"I can produce him for you, if you'll give me the chance."

"Like hell."

I'd already made the suggestion once but Akimo, set on his course, had dismissed it as a diversionary tactic.

"Filipe is due to phone me at the Polana at midday," I said wearily. "Let me go up there and take the call, arrange a meeting with him, and you can have him."

"You're supposed to be scared of him."

"He can lose me my passport and a whole lot besides. I'd rather that than rot in a Mozambique jail. Filipe can lead you to Barboza. That's what you really want, after all."

Akimo shifted his gaze to the man at the window, uncertain of himself, seeking guidance. The Makonde merely sighed as if growing bored; the thin, cicatrized face and the hunched body remained as still as one of the grotesquely handsome blackwood figures carved by his fellow tribesmen. Encouraged, Akimo said, "It is you from whom we expect information, Hickey. You will tell everything, starting with what you left out the first time we talked about Gomes. You still deny that you knew?"

"Yes."

"He worked four years for you. In all that time you never guessed?"

"Never. With hindsight it makes sense, of course."

"You lie," said the policeman evenly.

There was no point in arguing. Suddenly the Makonde spoke.

"Perhaps not."

They were the first words he had uttered. Both of us turned to him. He was still propped against the window-sill, still hugging himself; his brown eyes with their curious bright stare were fixed on me but he addressed no one in particular and spoke of me in the third person.

"Perhaps he is telling the truth—at least on this point. Gomes would have had deep cover. There would seem to be no advantage in having his employer know anything."

His tone was matter-of-fact; it did not invite contradiction. Seizing the chance to argue my case I said, "If you believe that you can believe the rest of my story. Why should I have known about the Barboza business? Let me prove it. Let me finger Filipe for you."

"That is one possibility," the Makonde said.

"Do you believe he exists?"

"So far my mind is open."

"I'm glad somebody's is," I said with a sidelong glance at Akimo. He was being upstaged—or simply outranked— and was visibly resentful. It was the old antipathy between professional policeman and politician, and there seemed no harm in rubbing it in a little. "It's nice to hear some sense spoken," I said. "May I know who I'm talking to?"

"Raoul Sousa. District Governor, Beira district. I flew down when I was notified of your arrest."

"I'm flattered."

"Don't be. The interests of the country concern me, not yours."

Raoul Sousa pushed himself off the window-sill and came round behind me. His walk had a finely balanced tension to it like that of a prowling cat. I recognized the name. He was a soldier turned administrator, something of a revolutionary folk-hero, too. During the war he'd built up a reputation as a daring and elusive guerrilla leader, and when independence came he was appointed to replace the Portuguese governor of one of the ten districts into which Mozambique was divided. Outside the central government in Lourenço Marques, these were the most important political jobs in the country. In speeches I had read, Sousa had stressed his tribal and peasant origins in the remote Makonde homeland, but I knew that like most of the leading Frelimo officials he had entered the movement at its intellectual end. The story had been repeated a thousand times all over colonial Africa: a mission-school education had led to a white *liceu*, a couple of eye-opening years on a college scholarship in Lisbon or Coimbra, and perhaps a couple more somewhere like the Lumumba Friendship University in Moscow. Along the way he'd become a Marxist and a devotee of the nationalist cause, and eventually he'd returned to join the "armed struggle."

From his speeches, too, he sounded vain, humourless and puritanical, dedicated not only to collectivizing the country and abolishing private property but to stamping out such remaining traces of colonial decadence as drunkenness, prostitution and bullfighting.

His English was fluent but a little over-precise and colourless in tone. The accent, for some reason, was faintly American.

"Do not mislead yourself, Hickey. I am not taking your side. You belong to a class that is opposed almost by definition to our revolution."

"In other words I'm a white capitalist hyena. That doesn't mean I haven't more sense than to intrigue against you."

"We in Frelimo are not racialists. But we must face facts. Until recently almost everything in Mozambique was owned by three per cent of the population, and almost every member of that three per cent was white. Many have left since independence. Those who remain must adjust to a society that distributes wealth more fairly. They must learn. There are others, however—former officers and agents of the DGS, still at large—who can only be dealt with by means of revolutionary justice. There are still those who secretly sympathize with them. That is why a white man in your situation is automatically suspect. Akimo, tell him what you have learned about his late employee."

The policeman gave a sullen shrug; clearly he considered it a waste of time.

"Gomes had a friend in the Ministry of the Interior. A good friend and former colleague. A Portuguese named Andrade, an old *colono*, near retirement, who stayed on after independence to safeguard his pension. On Friday night he phoned Gomes with a warning. The Ministry had just found, in their basement, a batch of DGS files that had been missing since the time of the coup, files that the DGS had not had time to burn. They were secret personnel dossiers. And Gomes's own file was among them."

Akimo paused, scowling at me.

"So now we know why he was running, hm? Your employee was also a full-time agent of the Portuguese secret police."

"Funny," I said. "I used to think I could recognize a policeman anywhere."

2

The room had grown warmer in the short time I had been there and I could feel new patches of damp forming under the arms of my shirt, already stale with dried sweat. Akimo was feeling the heat too; he wiped the balding crown of his head with a handkerchief and then stood up, went to a switch on the wall and turned on the ceiling fan. It ground noisily into life. He returned to slump into his chair and go on with the story.

News of the existence of the file had not filtered through to him until late last Monday, but once it did the reason for Gomes's attempted flight became clear. The old civil servant Andrade was soon singled out as the probable source of the tip-off, and once he was arrested he admitted to this and a lot more besides.

Gomes had told me he was originally sent out from Lisbon as a civil servant too. Strictly speaking, this was true. He'd had a desk job with the documentation section of the PIDE, the secret police organization that had preceded the DGS. By 1970 the PIDE had become so unpopular and powerful that it was officially disbanded, though most of its employees were simply absorbed into the new apparatus. Gomes was given a new job, one that was designed to avoid the scrutiny of squeamish politicians in Lisbon. In effect, he was to do undercover what he had done routinely before: provide credentials and make travel arrangements for DGS officers and agents operating out of Mozambique into neighbouring territories. It was an unglamorous role but an important one; hostile black countries like Zambia and Tanzania provided bases for Frelimo guerrillas which the DGS was constantly trying to penetrate. Using the travel agency that was set up for him as a cut-out address and message centre, Gomes worked closely with Andrade and officials in other departments to provide false documents for the agents—usually Africans posing as refugees—who would cross the borders and attempt to infiltrate Frelimo.

'By the time I met him he had been doing this job successfully for over a year. But the DGS suspected that one of their men who had penetrated the Frelimo headquarters in Dar es Salaam had since gone over to them. The travel agency cover was in danger. It was decided to send it into liquidation and transfer Gomes to a less conspicuous position—with me. With the help of his powerful employers it was easy enough for him to win all the business favours he needed to keep me happy, and to run the office efficiently on my behalf as well as theirs. It was he who had supplied the information which had allowed the DGS to build up their dossier on me.

Then had come the coup in Portugal, turning the DGS from a feared elite into hunted men. Late in April Andrade received an urgent request from Gomes for a dozen sets of credentials. This was not routine DGS work: he was to be paid a private bonus of fifteen thousand dollars for them. They were to be issued to white men and would be more sophisticated than anything he had supplied before—documents that could stand up to scrutiny not just across the borders but anywhere in the world.

"They worked out a system between them," Raoul Sousa said, taking over the explanation. "When a man died his *bilhete de identidade,* passport and birth certificate had to be returned to the Ministry for filing, together with the record of death. Dozens of such papers passed through Andrade's hands each day, and within a week he had found suitable identities for all twelve men. He kept the documents back from the files and gave them to Gomes.

Gomes would then use the birth certificate as identification and apply for a new identity card in the name of the dead man, claiming to have lost the original. The records, of course, showed that the men were alive, and so the cards were issued. After a few days Gomes would apply for a passport in each name, this time sending in the *bilhete* as identification. From then on it became easier; the original documents were destroyed and copies of driver's licences, health certificates and so on could all be obtained on the strength of the *bilhete*. Some could even be back-dated with the help of Gomes's other contacts."

Sousa was pacing tensely up and down behind my chair. "Within a few weeks Gomes had built up a full dossier of documents for these twelve identities. The original holders were safely dead but officially still alive. None had close ties in Mozambique, so the chance of inquiries from relatives leading to discovery of the falsification was remote. Barboza, for instance—an architect, a bachelor in early middle age, both parents dead; he was drowned while spear-fishing off Vilanculos on the twenty-ninth of April last year."

The black man paused and looked at me. "When the time came for these twelve men to leave the country they had simply to step into their new identities and go. Andrade, of course, had no idea who they really were. But he has given the twelve names to Akimo, here. Immigration records show that nine of them left Mozambique during June last year. That left three sets of credentials unaccounted for—until just a few hours ago. You will recall what happened last June?"

"Operation Zebra," I said numbly.

"The roundup of DGS men. We know that some crossed into Rhodesia and found sanctuary there. Others, like Gomes, stayed free because their connection was not discovered—though he did take the precaution of going to ground for a few days, it seems. But of the twelve most wanted men, it soon emerged that nine had vanished without trace. Two of the other three were caught because by chance they had not received the timely warning of Operation Zebra they had been expecting—again, from Andrade. These two were handed over to us by the Portuguese· They are awaiting trial on charges of crimes committed during the war—murdering Frelimo sympathizers and torturing suspects. And these are the two."

Sousa stepped over to the desk, selected two of the three identity cards from the ends of the rows and tossed them into my lap. "Casimiro Nunes and Francisco Gouveia Machado. Their real names are Camacho and Strauss, both inspectors of the DGS. The photographs show them as they were meant to look on departure: contact lenses, changed hair-styles, and so on. But they did not have time to assume these new identities.

"Naturally they were questioned about the whereabouts of the other nine: the murderers, the interrogation experts, the commanders of the Flecha groups. It appeared that those who had most to fear from a change of government in Portugal, and from African rule here, had made careful plans. This group of twelve gave a code name to their operation. They called it Terno Branco."

For a moment both black men watched me for a sign of recognition. "What does it mean?" I asked.

"It is Brazilian Portuguese. It means *white suit.* There is a sort of jocular myth in Portugal that all men in Brazil wear white tropical suits. It was an esoteric title, one that Africans were not meant to understand." Sousa didn't laugh. "Their object was to acquire new identities that would allow them to travel to Brazil and begin new lives there. Under their own names they could not consider themselves safe anywhere.

"Each man knew only his own new identity, and neither

Camacho nor Strauss had any contact with the source that supplied the documents. In other words, they knew nothing of Gomes. All they were told was that a coded warning would reach them, that they would be instructed when and where to collect their papers. Until it was safe to leave they would remain in hiding with white civilian sympathizers who could be trusted. These civilians were all former members of the Ficamos movement."

I said nothing. Sousa resumed his pacing.

"Remnants of the Ficamos reactionaries were involved in supporting and financing the operation. They undertook to provide two safe refuges to each DGS man—they called them first and second billets—as a precaution in case one was discovered, and to help them out of the country one by one. Apparently the plan succeeded. Of the original twelve, none of the missing ten was ever found and it was assumed all had escaped—ten men using false identities of which we had no trace, ten out of the thousands of Portuguese flooding out of the country at that time."

He reached for the two identity cards I was holding, replaced them where they belonged and picked another card out of the third row.

"Among those ten men is one we have always wanted more badly than the rest. You recall Goronga?"

I nodded slowly. The Makonde was staring intently at the card.

"I have a personal interest in what happened there. Goronga was a village in the district I now govern. And at the time I was commanding a guerrilla unit engaged in that area in operations against the Portuguese. The entire village, around fifty people, all unarmed civilians, were massacred by a troop of Flechas. They were shot down in cold blood as a reprisal for giving help to my band. The man who carried out that massacre was one of the ten who vanished. We have always assumed that Operation Terno Branco got him to Brazil with the rest. Now it seems that he is still in Mozambique."

Sousa thrust the card in front of me. The hand holding it shook slightly, and I looked up in surprise at the black man's face. Within the grooves of the livid scars there were beads of sweat, and his eyes were dilated by the pressure of strong emotion.

"Luis Pinto Barboza," he said. "Otherwise Antonio Carlos de Nobrega Gil, superintendent in the DGS, wanted for fifty murders. It appears that he was about to leave the country—and that you, Hickey, were about to help him."

Gil had been the missing entity, the vital loop in the tangle. I jerked my head at Akimo. "He's already told me."

"You knew all along," the policeman growled.

"Whether you did or not," Sousa said with a remote look in his eye, "you are going to help us find him."

"How?" I said blankly.

"Through this man Filipe—assuming he exists. Let us say for the moment that he does. We shall not arrest him; we shall give him what he wants. You will be released for long enough to meet him and hand over the Barboza documents—under observation by the police, naturally. You will then be returned to custody until Gil makes his attempt to leave. Either we get him or we keep you. I take it you value your own freedom more highly than his, Hickey."

3

At eleven o'clock I was released under the close escort of two black detectives. They were both dressed in floral shirts and pale linen suits, and while they did not exactly handcuff me between them they could hardly have made their presence more conspicuous.

Akimo, as if still reluctant to let me go, accompanied me to the door of the headquarters building, and I stood on the steps with my eyes screwed up against the brightness of the day. I felt dirty and tainted, the stench of the cell still clinging to me, the dull pain in my head already burgeoning in the oppressive heat. I had returned the laces to my shoes, but the other things that had been taken from me on arrival were now in an envelope that I clutched under my arm. So was the wallet containing the Barboza documents.

One of the *cipais* had got into the driving seat of a dented Chevrolet parked at the kerbside. The other was holding the door open for me. I turned to Akimo.

"This isn't going to work. Not with those two treading on my heels."

"You expect us to let you out of sight? With that stuff you're carrying?"

"Look, Filipe is a nervous type. He's also not stupid. If I turn up to meet him with that pair in tow he'll crawl right back under his stone again. Let me do this on my own; it's the only way."

"The only way for you to do a flit, hm?"

"Without a passport I won't be running anywhere."

"Nothing doing. If I had my way you'd still be in that cell. I hope this little exercise will prove to Sousa what I still believe: that your friend Filipe is imaginary; that it's you, not he, who's involved in the Gil business. You'll go down for a long time, Hickey, ten years, maybe fifteen. And I'm not taking the risk of losing you, with or without a passport; there's a lot of bush to hide in out there. Now go. In four hours' time you'll be brought back, Filipe or no Filipe."

Further argument would be pointless. I had spent an hour trying to convince Sousa of the importance of letting me meet Filipe on my own, but he wasn't the kind of man to concern himself with details and in matters of police procedure he had been guided by Akimo, who was pig-headed enough to ruin the whole thing. I said, "Well, I'm not driving up to the Polana with those comedians. I might as well arrive in a riot truck. I'll walk; they can follow."

Akimo saw my point even if he wouldn't admit it. Blear-ily setting course for the hotel, I realized that the British Consulate-General was just round the corner from here, an old colonial mansion with a reassuring air of solidity and discretion. I could, I supposed, make a bolt for it, go in there, come clean with them, take any protection they could offer—but no, Akimo had been right on one point. I couldn't expect much sympathy from that direction. There was no one I could rely on but myself.

Four hours. I had until three o'clock to take Filipe's call—and I could only pray that he would phone on time —make contact with him and hand over the Barboza wallet as if nothing had happened, all under the gaze of two men whose idea of a discreet tailing operation was to kerb-crawl their Chevrolet in low gear ten yards behind me as I trudged up the road. It was insane.

Nobody in the Polana had witnessed my arrest, so there were no raised eyebrows when I entered the lobby after an absence of eleven hours. As I approached the lift with the two *cipais* close behind me, however, the hall porter came up with a sheaf of telephone message slips. All were from Joana. She had called at four, seven and ten o'clock that morning. I smiled to myself; curiosity had got the better of her after all.

I tried to ignore the black detectives—not an easy thing to do, since they crowded into the lift behind me and then followed me doggedly down the third-floor corridor. One had a straggling beard, the other was clean-shaven; that was about all that differentiated them. I opened the door to the suite. Once we were inside the bearded man held out his hand for the key, locked the door and slipped the key into his pocket. Then they sat down in opposite corners of the sitting-room, watching me in uneasy expectation.

The time was twenty past eleven. We had forty minutes, possibly longer, to wait before Filipe phoned. I could do with a drink. I went to the phone, picked up the receiver and was aware of a swift movement behind me. The bearded man pulled the handset from my grasp and crashed it back on the cradle.

"No telephone," he said.

"I only wanted room service."

"No telephone," he repeated.

I shrugged. "Okay. You don't mind my taking a shower, I hope?"

He did not reply. From the questioning look he exchanged with the other man I realized suddenly and rather ludicrously that neither of them understood English—at least, no more than a bare minimum. I left them there and got undressed and showered, letting the tingling needles of cool water soak away the smell of jail and some of my aching tiredness while I tried to put the events of the last twenty-four hours into perspective. I had started out being blackmailed by a little fat man named Filipe and now I was preparing to betray him—that is, if a ploy designed to bring a mass murderer to justice could be called betrayal. I had a role to play and if I played it—or was allowed to play it—right, the process leading to the capture of the man named Antonio Gil, alias Barboza, would have begun. I would also retrieve the DGS file and eliminate the threat that it offered. If I went wrong, the file could hardly matter against the likelihood of ten or fifteen years in a Mozambique jail. Raoul Sousa had explained the alternatives clearly enough: We get Gil or we keep you.

The balance was a delicate one and would be easily upset. It rested on Filipe's willingness to trust me, and that in itself depended on more than just doing what he wanted, more than Sousa and Akimo understood.

"You are a European," Sousa had said. "And so he relies on you not to oppose his interests."

"Like hell," I'd replied. "Why does he need to blackmail me?"

"As a safeguard. Fundamentally he *wants* to trust you. You are his lead to the Barboza papers, just as he is our only lead to Gil. You will wait for his call, arrange a meeting, hand over the papers without comment or discussion. The moment Gil attempts to leave the country we will have him."

"Filipe isn't a fool. And he knows I'm not one either. He'll guess that I haven't swallowed that story of his about Barboza, especially now that I've seen the documents for myself. If I make things too easy for him he's going to be suspicious. It's my neck that's at risk; let me handle this my way."

But they wouldn't. There was a lot at stake for Sousa as well, I thought, as I stood soaking in the shower. It was a question of what sort of man Filipe thought he was dealing with, of how he expected me to behave—with the self-preserving instincts of a comfortable businessman or the aggressive, suspicious ones of an ex-policeman. A bit of each, perhaps. Left to manage without those two clowns following me. . . . Suddenly I knew that I would have to get rid of them.

How? I had no idea. All I knew was that if this plan was to succeed they had to go. If the police were too incompetent to handle the job properly I would have to do it myself.

I had mentioned to Sousa my suspicion that the sugar farmer Emmerich might be the "principal" behind Filipe. I had done so when Akimo was out of the room for a minute, because it wouldn't be beyond him to send some ham-fisted policeman in asking questions. Sousa had watched me intently.

"What makes you think it may be Emmerich?"

"Two things: his connection with Ficamos and the dollars in Gomes's car. Given his extremist views it's in character, too, that he should sympathize with a war criminal like Gil. And it squares with his refusal to testify to the UN committee on Goronga."

"We would have to be very sure of his involvement before we acted."

"Against a capitalist jackal like him?"

"His business is a mainstay of the economy. One of these days it will function without him, for the benefit of the people as a whole, but in the meantime he remains a power in the land. He cannot be lightly accused. If we had sound evidence of a crime, of course, that would be different. That would give us reason to remove him."

Sousa had sounded as though he would enjoy that. Then he'd changed the subject abruptly and shown me a photograph, the only one on record, of Gil without the Barboza disguise. The difference was startling, even though no un-natural-looking artificial aids such as wigs and make-up seemed to have been used. The thick, curly, prematurely grey hair of the earlier photograph had been dyed black and trained backwards in the Barboza pictures; the widow's peak had been created by shaving either side of the front scalp to present a receding hairline. The blue eyes were darkened by tinted contact lenses, and the rimless glasses and the moustache had helped to blur the features further. But the most striking change was in the outline of the face itself. The lean, aquiline Gil had become puffy and almost moon-faced. Only after a close comparison of the two pictures was it possible to believe they were of the same man.

"How did he do it?" I asked.

"I can't be sure, but I have an idea. Certain drugs can upset the metabolism and the level of fluid retention in the body. Cortisone, for instance—it is used to treat rheumatic diseases, and one of the commonest side-effects is an accumulation of fat, especially in the face. It can distort the appearance quite severely. Assume that this picture was taken sometime between the coup in April and Gil's disappearance in June. He was preparing for the possibility of having to go underground; he wanted to look quite different to the way he would be remembered by anyone who mattered. If he was taking really big doses of cortisone, four or five hundred milligrams a day, for instance, he could easily have achieved an effect like this in that time. And he would have to keep taking it until he left the country, of course."

"Sounds pretty risky."

"Only if the level of fluid retention becomes dangerous. Or if there should be other serious side-effects. The drug itself cannot kill."

"You seem to know a lot about it."

"I was a medical student once."

There was a puzzle here. "His disguise is pretty effective," I said, "and his papers would have got him out of the country any time in the last eighteen months. Why has he stayed?"

"I trust we will find that out," Sousa said remotely.

He'd read me extracts from a file on Gil. He was now forty-four years old. He had enlisted in the PSP in Portugal at the age of twenty. Like many of their more promising young officers, he was subsequently recruited into PIDE and sent to Africa. When war broke out in Mozambique in 1964 he was one of the first men to assigned to the *contra-terror* department, which was responsible for preventing the spread of subversion among the black civilian population.

"In effect," Raoul Sousa had explained, "it meant making people more afraid of the Portuguese than of Frelimo. It is the philosophy of winning the minds by threatening the flesh."

"You mean people were actually afraid of Frelimo?" I'd asked, mock-innocently. "I thought you were an army of liberation, welcomed in every village."

"There were always reactionary elements." The gleam in his eye had gone a fraction colder. "There were chiefs and headmen in the pay of the Portuguese, and others who were simply stubborn. They refused to learn. It was sometimes necessary to practice exemplary discipline . . ."

"And revolutionary justice?"

"Yes," said Sousa, either missing or choosing to ignore the sarcasm.

Joking aside, there were several deaths or disappearances for which Gil could be held directly responsible. It was part of the way this war had been fought. Africans taken in as suspected Frelimo supporters had been killed "while trying to escape" or had simply never come home.

By 1970 Gil was a chief inspector in the DGS, as PIDE

had now become. From the town of Tete, in north-western Mozambique, he was seconded temporarily on to the staff of Zamco, the international consortium engaged in building the big Cabora Bassa hydro-electric dam on the Zambezi River, as chief security adviser. With the site threatened from outside by the guerrillas, his job was to weed out Frelimo sympathizers and potential saboteurs among the thousands of African labourers in the work force. Apparently he was successful, for the dam had not suffered a single instance of sabotage during its construction. When his job there was over he was promoted to district superintendent for Beira.

This area, too, was extremely sensitive at the time. The guerrillas, who already controlled large parts of the country further north, were infiltrating the bush settlements and the rich farming hinterland west of the city and threatening its road and rail communications. Tension was high among both whites and blacks. It was in this atmosphere that the massacre at Goronga had occurred.

I turned off the shower, towelled myself down, went to the bedroom and dressed in lightweight clothes. It was ten to twelve and I was walking through to the sitting room when the telephone rang.

It stood on a table by the window. The two detectives started out of their chairs, glancing at each other and then staring intently at me. The bearded one signalled me to answer, and as I walked across the room and lifted the receiver they crowded in beside me. I said hello and heard Joana's voice.

"Bastard," she said evenly.

"I'm sorry about last night," I said. "I got your messages, but I haven't been able to call back."

"You didn't intend coming back to me after all, did you?"

"Of course I did. Something cropped up. That call I

113

told you about . . . there was a sudden crisis. It happens in my business."

"What kind of business takes you out from midnight till ten in the morning?"

I sensed that she was play-acting to some extent. She wasn't really angry, and even the hint of jealousy was meant to cover something else, something equally unaccountable: curiosity. Why else all those calls? Aware of the tense, uncomprehending faces of the *cipais* at my side, I said defensively, "I'll explain, but not now. I can't really talk at the moment."

She gave an exaggerated sigh. "See you around, Joe."

"Wait." Suddenly a wild idea had occurred to me. While I'd been talking I had been looking out of the window, across the hotel pool and terrace to where the ground dropped away in a steep, bushy slope to the shore of the bay. There was a road that traversed this hillside and met up with the marine drive at the bottom.

"What?" Joana asked. I gave the black men a nervous glance. I would be taking a hell of a chance on their lack of English, and perhaps an even bigger one on Filipe's punctuality.

"Are you at home now?" I asked.

"Yes. Why?"

"I want you to do me a favour. No, please listen. It's important. Can you drive down to the bottom of the hill in front of the Polana? And meet me at the intersection in exactly ten minutes' time? I'll explain when I see you."

I had kept my tone casual but the urgency must have got through to her. She said, "I'll be there," and rang off.

I faced the detectives. They hadn't understood. There was puzzlement but also hostility in their looks, as though they sensed I had taken advantage of them.

"Who?" demanded the bearded man.

"Not him. Someone else. A woman."

He studied me suspiciously for several seconds, then shrugged his shoulders and turned away. They both resumed their seats, the bearded man picking his teeth with a matchstick as he watched me moving restlessly about the room. I could not think of anything now but Filipe's call and whether it would be on time. More than ever it seemed like my only lifeline, and it was vital that nothing should go wrong with our meeting.

The call came at exactly twelve o'clock. It lasted thirty seconds. When I put down the receiver my heart was pounding.

"Him?" said the bearded man, standing beside me again.

"Yes." I went to the chair on which the plastic wallet lay, picked it up and tucked it in the waistband of my trousers. My hands were clammy. "The rendezvous is in thirty minutes."

Now the bearded man went to the phone. He asked for a number and spoke a few urgent words. Then he went to the door. He unlocked it, stepped outside and waited for me and the other *cipai* to join him before closing and re-locking the door. I started off down the corridor and the two of them fell into step behind me.

We had to wait half a minute for the lift, which was set in the centre of the building's main stairwell. Once on the ground floor there would be too many people around; it would be too late to act. Up here the three of us were alone. My mouth had gone dry.

"You take taxi," the bearded man said. "We follow. What place we go?"

I didn't answer. The lift arrived then, empty, and the man with the beard stepped into it and held the door open for me. I'd managed to position myself so that his companion was just behind my right shoulder.

"What place?" the bearded man demanded.

Again I said nothing. I raised my right leg and with the flat of my foot kicked the door shut as hard as I could, sending him staggering back against the rear wall of the lift car. Before the other man knew what was happening I'd made a half turn, seized him with both hands by the lapels of his linen jacket and flung him head first against the door. Then I hurled myself down the stairs.

Confused shouting came from behind me as I bounded down the first flight six steps at a time. On the second floor I turned right and raced along the corridor to the end of the wing, depending on knowing more about the building than they did. There was a back stairway here which people in bathing costumes were supposed to use to get to and from the pool. I turned down it, crashing almost at once between a pair of girls in bikinis whose outraged hisses followed me on my headlong descent. In twenty seconds I was out of the ground-floor exit and running across the lawn bordering the pool. Waiters and sunbathers stared bemusedly. I reached the balustrade at the end of the terrace, sat on it and swung my legs over. I saw the *cipai* with the beard coming across the grass in the instant before I dropped into the shoulder-high scrub beyond the wall. And he had seen me.

I went slithering down the slope, breaking through low branches that jabbed and scratched at me. When I'd gone thirty yards I glanced back to see the bearded African vaulting the balustrade behind me. I could only hope that the other one was, as I'd intended, too stunned to have gone for their car.

The slope was steep. I concentrated on getting down it as fast as possible without going into a headlong fall. The grass underfoot was thick and tangled, and the scrub tougher to break through than I had imagined. I tried to ignore the sounds of crashing pursuit, but before I was halfway down I knew he was catching up on me. He must have been running more recklessly than I; besides, he had only to follow the path I was breaking through the bush.

I tried to move faster, but in less than half a minute I could hear the black man's footfalls and harsh breathing just behind me. He reached out and grabbed the back of my shirt collar. I shook him off but he lost his balance and fell forward, knocking me over, and we rolled several yards through the scrub together, flailing at each other with our fists.

When we stopped he was a couple of yards below me. He came scrambling up the slope, reaching out to seize my arm. I punched him on the forehead and he fell down. He got up again, his linen suit smothered in red dust, and this time he ducked skilfully below my punch and dived at my feet. Too late, I realized he wasn't trying to trip me. The wallet containing the Barboza papers had slipped from my waistband and he had grabbed it and was scuttling away like a crab, on his knuckles and toecaps. I ran after him desperately. He was getting to his feet when I aimed a wild kick that just missed his head. He flinched, however, and caught between crouching and standing he slithered several yards down the slope, his feet scrabbling for a hold. Without warning his left ankle caught in the fork of an exposed root; off balance, he reared over backwards and the joint broke with an audible snap.

I retrieved the plastic wallet and stood panting over him for a few seconds. He lay whimpering and gasping in turns, trying feebly to reach the ankle that was still trapped and twisted in the root. He'd be found soon enough, I guessed; I scrambled and slid the remaining couple of hundred yards down the hill and found Joana parked under the eucalyptus trees beside the marine drive. She could not have seen anything of what happened from here, but she was staring at me incredulously. I realized I was patched with sweat and red dust.

"What *is* going on with you, Joe?"

"Drive along the north shore. I'm going to take up your offer to lend me the car, just briefly. I'll have to ask you to wait."

We were out of the city in a few minutes and speeding between the beaches and apartment blocks of a bayside resort called the Costa do Sol. It was obvious that I couldn't tell Joana the truth about what was happening—not just because to talk to anyone would have been a security risk, but because I wasn't quite sure I would have her sympathy. If she knew I was being forced to help Frelimo would she be willing to help me? Right now I depended on her help. I told her a story that I made up as I went along: That call at midnight had been from a worried customer in Salisbury. I'd ordered a shipment of diamond drill bits from Holland for him, and the Dutch customs authorities were demanding proof that they were destined for South Africa, not Rhodesia. The proof had had to be cobbled up in a hurry. I'd had to wake up the South African trade commissioner and had spent most of the night sitting in his office while he made phone calls on my behalf. I was now on my way to a hurried meeting with someone else who could pull strings for me.

Joana looked thoughtful but seemed convinced. At least she asked no more questions.

Most of the beach bars had closed down for lack of business since independence, but I found one that was open and asked Joana to stop and wait for me over a Bacardi. She was back now to being her old incurious self. I drove on alone.

A couple of miles on, the road suddenly crumbled into a potholed track between the conical huts of an ill-defined

African *bairro*. Goats tugged at the hard grass, chickens scratched a living from the sand and black women in their gaily coloured *khengas* sat in the shade of the malala palms selling cockles plucked from beds along the seashore. Anyone turning left here onto a road that ran past a tidal salt pan would find himself within a couple of minutes inexplicably driving on the runways of an airport. At least, the runways were there but the rest of the Costa do Sol airport had somehow never been built. No one knew why; the reason was lost in the chaos of Portuguese bureaucracy. A grid of metalled runways stood deserted and shimmering in the heat, with a few goats nibbling at the weeds that had sprung from the cracks. It was a monument to inefficiency, but it was also a very good place to meet someone if you wanted to be sure he was alone. You could see everything that moved within a radius of a mile, and in case you had to leave in a hurry there were tracks going off into the bush in a dozen directions. Filipe had chosen his spot well. I was now quite certain that I'd been right to ditch the two detectives—no matter how much trouble I had made for myself from Akimo.

I nosed Joana's VW towards the car standing where two arms of the runway grid intersected. It was a white Fiat 127, its outline from a distance quivering slightly in the heat thrown up from the tarmac. Making a mental note of the Lourenço Marques registration number, I pulled up alongside. The driver's door was open and the cheap briefcase lay on the seat. Filipe leaned against the side of the car just to the rear of the doorway, pale and tense behind the dark glasses as he watched me get out and approach him. For a couple of seconds we stood sizing each other up.

"You brought the file?" I said.

"I think I am entitled to the first question, senhor. May I see the documents?"

"Certainly." I took the wallet from my waistband and

held it up. "It's just that there are a few things I want to know first."

"Know?" His stare was blank and pasty.

"I don't enjoy being blackmailed, Filipe, but I like being lied to even less. You lied to me about these, didn't you?"

He had started bouncing on his heels. "This was not in our agreement. You were to find the papers and hand them over, nothing more."

"Since you haven't kept your part of the bargain, I don't see that I'm bound to keep mine."

"Betrayal!" he shouted suddenly. "Banditry! You're in no position to make threats, Hickey, do you understand?" His cheeks quivered and his voice rose to a pitch close to hysteria. "It is not too late to give that file to the British. We'll do it, I tell you!"

He was bouncing furiously and at the same time edging into the car doorway. He made a grab for the briefcase. I dropped the wallet, stepped forward and hit him in the mouth. The blow spun him in a half turn against the side of the Fiat and he stood huddled there, cowering, staring at me with a froth of blood and saliva forming in the corner of his mouth.

"Don't talk to me about betrayal, Filipe. There's no such person as Barboza, is there? That story about his being born in Goa and losing his citizenship was all crap. There are no men called Nunes or Machado either. I found their papers in the same hiding place, you see, and I didn't need to be a genius to work out that all of them were fakes. What was Gomes doing with three sets of false identity papers, Filipe?"

He was too frightened to speak. I jabbed him in the stomach and he made a retching noise and fell forward on his hands and knees.

"Barboza is a fugitive, a criminal of some kind. And you were trying to trick me into helping him out of the country, risking not just my passport but my neck. Am I right?"

Filipe still said nothing. He crouched like a baby on all fours, panting and dripping blood on the tarmac.

"All right," I said, "don't tell me, I don't really want to know. You know as well as I do that I can't take this stuff to the police. But then I don't have to give it to you either. I'll start by taking what I came for—that file."

Filipe was beyond reason. He got up on one foot and made another clumsy lunge for the briefcase. I stepped swiftly in to block him, grabbing the front of his safari jacket and jerking him back so that he sat down hard on the ground. His dark glasses had fallen off to réveal small blue eyes frantic with rage and fear. I reached into the car for the briefcase. Its zip was undone. I upended it and let the contents spill out on the seat: a packet of Kleenex, a capsule of Librium sedative pills, a DETA airline ticket and a Browning .25 automatic. There was no file. I picked up the gun and jerked the magazine out of the butt. It was fully loaded and there was a cartridge in the breech.

"Were you afraid I wouldn't deliver?" I asked. "Or did you intend to kill me anyway? I can see the advantage in that. It would keep me quiet about your friend Barboza. Yesterday you were very strong on all us Europeans sticking together; I can't say you're setting much of an example. Now where's that file?"

Filipe, blood drying on his chin, sat still and watched me as if hypnotized. I shoved the magazine back into the small pistol, flipped the safety catch and pointed the gun between his eyes.

"Where is the file?" I repeated.

He made a helpless gesture and croaked, "Not here."

"*What?*"

"With my principal."

I felt as though I'd been kicked in the stomach. My whole strategy had depended on securing the file, retaining the initiative. But I kept the gun pointing at the little man's forehead.

"What do you mean? You were supposed to bring it with you."

"I never said that." Filipe spoke indistinctly through swelling lips. "You are to come to Beira for it."

"Like hell!"

"Believe me, there is no alternative. It is arranged. That ticket."

Keeping the gun trained on him with my right hand, I groped with the left on the car seat and picked up the airline ticket. I held it at half an arm's length and flipped it open. I read HICKEY in the segment marked off for the passenger's name. Below that, the reservation section had been filled in for the next afternoon's flight to Beira. The return date was left open. The ticket had been issued the day before by the DETA office in Lourenço Marques.

"You were pretty confident that I'd find what you wanted, weren't you? But my business instincts tell me this is a seller's market, Filipe. You need the Barboza papers more than I need that file. Why should I—?"

"I would not count on that."

Perhaps sensing uncertainty beneath my tone, he was caught between fear and a sort of hesitant defiance. He still sat absurdly in the middle of the runway with the sun beating down on him. "Personally I do not care what you do; I have no taste for this business. My principal wants you to bring the documents to Beira, that is all I know. The file will be waiting. . . ."

"And another loaded gun? You're not talking to a beginner, Filipe."

"It is the only way. Unless you take that plane he will send the file to your consulate."

"Who is this goddamned principal, anyway?"

"It is worth more than anything you can do to me to tell you that."

I hesitated for several seconds. The one thing I hadn't been prepared for was an ultimatum like this, and in responding to it I had to balance bluff against counter-bluff. I knew I was right—that the Barboza documents were vitally important to Filipe and his principal and Gil—but since I wasn't supposed to know quite how important, I could not appear too sure of my ground. I couldn't afford to push. And if I rejected the idea outright I risked not only being exposed to the British but losing contact with Filipe and the people who were hiding Gil.

"I'll think about it," I said.

I lowered the Browning, pumped the single cartridge out of the breech and tossed it away. Then I sent the gun and the loaded magazine, in turn, skimming for fifty yards in opposite directions along the runway. I picked up the American Express wallet, got into the Volkswagen and slammed the door.

"The afternoon flight," Filipe said. "You will be met."

"I'll decide in the morning. Don't lose any sleep over it. Take some Librium."

He sat watching me drive away. I thought about the expression on his face and decided that he didn't have the look of a man who would ever be much good as a criminal. On the other hand, he did have the look of a man who would like to kill me.

4

I reckoned that no matter what sort of mood he was in by now, Akimo would stop short of hitting me in public. And so I chose a public place to give myself up: the Aquario Bar, one of the dives on the Rua Major Araujo, where there were bound to be a few whores, pimps and seamen hanging about even during the siesta.

I'd collected Joana on the way back to LM, asked her to drop me in the Baixa and told her I would be in touch later on. Perhaps we could meet for a late lunch. In the cool of the Aquario Bar I ordered a beer and phoned Akimo, and I was sitting in a cubicle at the rear when he arrived eight minutes later. He had Raoul Sousa and a couple of plainclothes *cipais* in tow. Anger made the veins in his temples stand out, throbbing, against the sweaty dark skin. He stood beside my table and thrust his face close to mine.

"You've had your last chance," he hissed. "The very last, hm? What the hell you think you were doing?"

"Only what had to be done," I said. "I met Filipe. And I made sure he wasn't frightened off by those two idiots."

"You broke a man's ankle, you—"

"He broke his own ankle."

"So still nobody but you has set eyes on this Filipe. Very convenient, hm? We still have no evidence that he exists."

"There's that car number," I said. "You could try checking it out."

Sousa, who as before was allowing the policeman to let off steam, said, "Sit down, Akimo." They sat, Akimo opposite me where he could glare, the Governor on my right. The *cipais* hung about at the door. Almost at once a black bar-girl in a sequinned miniskirt sidled up to the table. Akimo dismissed her with an irritable gesture but she went

124

to Sousa and rubbed her belly provocatively against his shoulder. With his bright, obsessive gaze fixed on me, he did not appear to notice. The Aquario was one of those saloons where white men and black sharing a common interest in sex and liquor had always mixed without remark.

"Why couldn't you hand over the stuff?" Akimo demanded. "Why not do what you were told?"

"That would have made it too easy for him. He thinks I'm a bastard, but he understands bastards. The furthest thing from his mind is the thought that I might be doing this for you."

"Why the trip to Beira?"

"I don't know."

"I can think of an explanation," Akimo said. He snatched at the bowl of cashew nuts that had come with my beer and crammed a handful of them into his mouth. "Could be you planned the delay between you. Could be you don't want Gil to have those papers and come into the open. Could be you're just being true to the colour of your skin."

"Sounds like you've actually started to believe in him," I said.

"You expect us to let you go free now, to catch planes around the country?"

"It's the only way you'll get Gil. Oh, and I'll need my passport back, of course. Because of those security checks you have on internal flights."

The girl, still standing behind Sousa, began kneading his shoulder muscles through the cotton tunic. Coming out of his strange reverie, the scar-faced man seemed suddenly to become aware of her. He seized her wrist and flung her arm violently away. She spat a word at him in the vernacular and flounced off. Wagging a long finger at her retreating back, he called in Portuguese, "You must learn some self-respect, dignity! Your sort will soon be a thing of the past here!"

The dozen or so other customers exchanged glances.

Sousa turned back to me. For a moment I had caught a glint of fanaticism in his eyes; he was always trying to teach people. He said, "We have learned something, at least. Filipe's principal is in the Beira district."

"Which increases the odds on its being Emmerich," I said.

"Throw a raid into his property," Akimo suggested, scooping up another handful of nuts. He'd been told by now of my suspicions. Sousa regarded him coldly.

"Do you want Gil frightened even deeper underground? We do not know what resources these people may have. Besides, it is not so easily done; there is the threat of armed resistance. I would need a better excuse—just one excuse, but the right one." He turned to me. "As chief administrator of the area I assume overall responsibility in the search for Gil. I am returning there tonight. You will go back to your hotel now and stay there. If Filipe wishes to communicate with you again it will not do for you to be absent. Tomorrow you will take that flight. It seems that Filipe intends to make contact with you upon arrival. Give him the documents, retrieve your file and return to Lourenço Marques. You cannot, of course, expect your movements to go completely unobserved."

"Just as long as I'm not shadowed by any lunatics like those two today."

"No," said Akimo, with a significant look at Sousa. He chewed with his mouth open, expelling tiny fragments of nut as he spoke. "This time I do it myself."

"Jesus," I muttered.

I went back to the Polana, phoned Joana, and asked her to join me for lunch. I had it sent up to the suite, and afterwards we locked the door and made love through the rest of the siesta. I told her I had to go to Beira for a day or two and she made a face.

"There's nothing to do in Beira."

"There's business."

"I thought you were due to fly home."

"I was, until everything went haywire last night."

Later, after we had parted reluctantly, Akimo called round with my passport. His usual sarcastic belligerence was subdued. He had checked the registration of the Fiat and found it belonged to a rental firm which had hired it out the day before. The driver's licence they had been shown was in the name of one Filipe Jaime Pereira, of the Hotel Braga, Beira.

"I got our people up there to do some checking for us. Pereira was a member of Ficamos several years ago. He is also the owner of the Braga. Two years ago he found himself in debt and had to mortgage the hotel for six hundred thousand escudos. The mortgagee is Emmerich."

PART FOUR
Friday, November 21

1

Like every other business DETA, the Mozambique airline, had suffered since independence from an exodus of skilled Portuguese staff and a loss of custom. The Boeing 737 that left Lourenço Marques on Friday afternoon for Beira, Quelimane and Tete was only one third full, so the passengers—Frelimo soldiers going home on leave, a party of nuns on their way to mission schools in the north, and a sprinkling of white businessmen and civil servants—were told to sit wherever they pleased. I chose a window seat halfway down the cabin. Akimo, who'd arrived at the airport in an ancient and ill-fitting civilian suit, placed himself three rows behind me. We had given no sign of recognizing each other.

The last passenger to board was the loud-voiced South African who'd been hanging around the Polana. He was a tall, tanned man in his forties. As he came down the aisle he gave an exaggerated show of surprise at finding me and promptly sat down next to me, uninvited.

"Good to see a familiar face," he said, struggling with his seat-belt.

"We haven't met, I believe."

"Are you for Tete?"

"Beira."

"Me too. Stopping over. On my way to the Cabora Bassa dam—if I can get through the red-tape barrier, that is."

For much of the way north the plane flew a course parallel to the coast, with the Indian Ocean on the right, the marshlands and bush of the coastal plain to the left. A few villages and footpaths could be picked out, and here and there a meandering river debouched its muddy water into the sea. Far inland, almost obscured by the heat-haze, stood the mountains marking the edge of the interior plateau. From thirty thousand feet it was easier to appreciate just how wild some of this country was. What had Akimo told me? "There's a lot of bush to hide in out there." For ten years it had sheltered Frelimo guerrillas from the Portuguese, and suddenly I was struck by the conjecture that it might be protecting Antonio Gil from Frelimo. Why not? Hiding out in someone else's house made sense in an urban environment, but not in a country like this. As a counter-insurgency expert Gil would know just how secure a well-chosen campsite in the bush could be, even for as long as eighteen months. With the right equipment and a regular supply of provisions brought to him by his Ficamos sympathizers, it should be possible to stay out there almost indefinitely, and as long as he kept clear of tribal villages there wasn't a chance in a million of someone's stumbling upon him accidentally.

But this was just a passing thought, snatched during a pause in the flow of talk that came from the South African beside me. His name, it seemed, was Aubrey Slater, and he had only one real topic of conversation: himself. In the first half of the ninety-minute flight I learned a great deal about Aubrey Slater; so did everyone else who understood English and sat within earshot of his stentorian voice. He had a wife and four children and lived in Houghton—the wealthiest suburb in Johannesburg, he pointed out, in case I should be unaware of the fact—in a house which was now worth three times what he had paid for it. He owned a champion Labrador and a vintage Bentley, played scratch golf, and ordered his shirts made to measure from Hong Kong. He was a hydraulic engineer with his own consultancy firm and had been commissioned at a staggering fee by Zamco, the consortium which had built and now helped to run Cabora Bassa, to advise on possible improvements to the flow-rate controls of the water turbines. He reported with a deprecating laugh the remark of the Zamco contracting engineer that he, Slater, was the only man in Africa qualified to solve the problem.

Altogether he was remarkably pleased with himself. He was also a monumental and aggressive bore.

"Not that you'd think they wanted me up there," he said. "This is my first visit, and Jesus, the crap that I have to carry round with me! To do with security, they say. Want to see?" He needed no encouragement to produce from his jacket pocket a small bundle of papers. "I had to be issued with a special identity card. I said what's wrong with my passport? If it's good enough to get me into the country it ought to be good enough to get me onto the crappy site. Nothing doing. I had to have this card. There's not even a photograph on it. What's the good of an identity card without a photograph, I ask you? Plus a pass to allow me from one part of the site to another. Plus a special air ticket with a clearance stamp. It cost me two days in LM to put this bunch of crap together. It must be easier to get into Fort Knox. Why, for Christ's sake?"

"Partly it's a relic of the war," I said. "Frelimo swore to destroy the dam while it was building. And partly it's because the Portuguese and Zamco are still in charge of things up there."

But the question had really been rhetorical. "The war's over," Slater said. "Frelimo's running the crappy country."

Weary of his talk, I said, "Bureaucracy is self-perpetuating. If they stopped issuing all those permits there'd be a dozen people out of work."

It was true, though, that the situation at Cabora Bassa was anomalous. Before independence Frelimo had opposed the building of the dam on the grounds that most of the hydro-electric power it produced would be going to South Africa and would be of little benefit to Mozambique. Once it was built it was built, however; since the new government refused to accept the debts incurred in its construction it was still run by the Portuguese and the South African-dominated Zamco company. With both these groups nervously guarding their massive investment, it remained an enclave of colonial economic dominance in the wilds of the Zambezi Valley.

"There was one man who instituted all those controls," I said. "A DGS officer named Gil."

I had weighed the remark carefully but Slater didn't seem interested.

"Well, I've planned things now so that I don't arrive till Sunday afternoon. I'm giving myself a day or two in Beira."

"There's nothing to do in Beira," I said, echoing Joana.

"No?" He gave me a sly smile. "Think I haven't done my research? All the South Africans make a point of stopping over. Local colour, you know? Forbidden fruit where we come from."

"Black girls? There are plenty of those in LM."

"Those saloons in the Baixa? No thanks, too public and

too close to home. You're liable to find your local church-warden getting his end away in the room next door. Beira has nice discreet spots, I hear, and people who'll make private arrangements for you without your ever having to go near a knockshop. And what those coon-girls won't do for a few rands is nobody's business, they tell me. Look, if you're not doing anything tonight why don't we—?"

"Thanks, but I'll be busy."

"Well, we can share a taxi from the airport, anyway. Are there any decent hotels? Where are you staying?"

"I'm being met." The last thing I wanted was to get landed with Slater. "Hotels—well, some have closed but I believe the Ambassador's still going. That's fairly central."

I was grateful at this point for the arrival of the drinks trolley. While Slater ordered a Scotch I took from my grip the copy of the United Nations report on the Goronga massacre which Joana had procured for me from the *Noticias* library the afternoon before. We had glanced through it together in my hotel suite, but now I made a point of looking busy by reading it in full.

My reasons for wanting to see it in the first place were mixed. Some of it had to do with the fact that I was un-willingly involved—with Sousa and Gil and perhaps Emmerich—and felt that the more I knew about the back-ground the better. And some of it arose from the doubts that had been cast on that background, and on the validity of the report itself, first by Gomes, then by Joana. Perhaps I was employing all those dormant instincts of mine; I be-lieved in that old saying that time spent on reconnaissance is never wasted. Gil himself might not be waiting in the bush for me with a gun, but the people protecting him were likely to be just as dangerous as if they were.

The UN committee, although the outcome of their inquiry had been a foregone conclusion, did at least seem to have collected and examined as much information about the Goronga incident as had been offered to them. The evidence they had gathered, together with their conclusions, occupied thirty printed foolscap pages.

There were of course no known survivors, but a dozen other witnesses had come forward to tell the committee what they knew. There was the woman from the neighbouring village who had discovered the massacre on the morning of Thursday, June 13, the day after it had happened. There was the Portuguese priest whom she had called from the nearest mission station and who had notified the authorities. Then there was Raoul Sousa, something of a star turn, I imagined, the bush fighter with his dramatically scarred face and his revolutionary jargon.

He had been invited firstly to tell what he knew of the methods of the Flechas, the black shock troops selected for their aggressive qualities, trained and commanded by the DGS for combined intelligence and attack operations. They would saturate an area the moment they knew of the presence of a guerrilla band. They would question the chiefs and headmen, try to find the whereabouts of the guerrillas by any means they could, then go in after them. Any tribesman who refused to co-operate was likely to be taken for a Frelimo sympathizer. He might have his hut burned, his cattle confiscated, perhaps worse.

Sousa had gone on to describe events surrounding the incident. The report of his evidence reflected his colourless, declamatory style of speech, beneath which there lurked a certain boastfulness.

In the first week of June my unit came from our base area near Inhaminga to the country south-west of Beira. My comrades and I travelled as we always did, by night, on foot. We were given guidance, food and shelter by people in the villages along the way, as well as information regarding the disposition of enemy forces. Our objective was to attack military transport on the road leading south to Nova Lusitania and make it unsafe for the colonialists.

A forward base was already established south of Goronga. Our plan was to make a series of attacks at different points along the road—to hit and run, hit and run, using the tactics we had employed successfully for ten years to wear down the morale of the imperialist troops. On June the tenth we passed by the Emmerich sugar estate, and on the eleventh we carried out our first ambush, destroying a jeep and a truck with landmines. The surviving occupants tried to resist but were quickly finished off by fire from our Kalashnikovs.

We withdrew to the east, passing through Goronga before returning to our camp. There we spent most of the next day. In the afternoon we fired on a Frelon helicopter that came over. It was damaged but landed safely and eighteen or twenty Flechas, black puppet soldiers, deplaned. Adhering to sound principles of guerrilla warfare we naturally refused to engage a superior force and withdrew eastwards, soon leaving the colonialists behind.

The next day we heard that the leader of this criminal band had taken his Flechas back to Goronga. In his frustration at our escape, in a fury at the villagers for their heroic refusal to inform on us, he burned their huts, killed their cattle, and shot. . . .

At this point, the report noted in respectful parentheses, Sousa was overcome with emotion. I'd noticed myself how tense he became when discussing the incident; to know that fifty people had died in retaliation for his actions must have been hard even on his messianic conscience. I thought I understood his eagerness—his need, almost—to see Gil captured and punished.

There was evidence from people who had witnessed the progress of the Flechas from one village to the next in pursuit of the guerrillas. Goronga had been the first stop; the people there had given accounts of the visit to others who had passed through during the day. The huge Super Frelon troop-transport helicopter had landed in a clearing north of the village, and Gil had questioned the headman and the elders. Some had known him by reputation and been apprehensive. He had called them lying *macacos* and warned them that if they had not told the truth they would take the consequences. Then the helicopter had taken off again.

Sometime later, after stopping at several more villages and unsuccessfully engaging Sousa's band, it seemed the Flechas had returned to Goronga. Exactly how things had happened there would never be known. The priest who went there the next day testified that the Flechas seemed to have followed their usual retaliatory practice of burning the huts and had then burned down the cattle pen with the beasts inside. It seemed as though the villagers had been made to watch all this from the central square before being shot where they sat. The bodies were left where they had fallen. By the time the priest found them, jackals and vultures had already been at work.

The Boeing drifted down across the Pungwe estuary, the muddy river bisecting a featureless landscape of brown blotched with green, and began circling for the landing at Beira. Slater, lacking someone to talk at, was reading a newspaper.

News of the Goronga incident had reached the outside world quickly. Nevertheless, the Portuguese administration was in such confusion at the time that it took several days before any high-level inquiries had begun. By then Gil seemed to have received his tip-off that Operation Zebra was about to begin, and had vanished. The Flechas, too, had had contingency plans; as black men who had fought for the Portuguese they had everything to fear from a Frelimo takeover. Within three days of the massacre they had disbanded and scattered, and their muster-rolls and other unit records were destroyed. Most of them would have gone back to their villages, a couple of dozen spread out in the bush among a population of eight million. Even the flight logs of the first Super Frelon—which had been damaged by gunfire—and the one which had been sent to replace it were found to be missing from the air base at Manga airport; the crews of both had gone back to Portugal.

A full reading of the report had disappointed me, even more than my cursory look through it the day before had done. I wasn't sure why; it was no direct concern of mine. But I had seen Joana's point.

"It's difficult to get to the bottom of anything like this," I had said. "But I can't give the UN committee much credit for trying. All right, they reached the only possible conclusion: that the massacre was carried out by the Flechas under the command of one Antonio Gil. Perhaps I'm nitpicking, but I'm used to following the rules of evidence, to strict investigation procedures. Half of what they heard was hearsay; the rest was circumstantial. There were no autopsies carried out, no forensic or ballistics reports—"

"You're asking too much of the local police. They were incompetent even before the blacks took over."

"At least the committee might have visited the site for themselves. They didn't bother. Instead of facts they dealt with suppositions."

Joana had shaken her head. "You're a legal absolutist, Joe. It comes of your police training. This wasn't a legal process, it was a piece of political showmanship. Frelimo invited that committee in here to help publicize the horrors of life under the Portuguese and imply that everything was much better now. They have *poder de opinião* on their side, remember—world opinion. Facts don't matter so much as the disposition to believe. Why do you think the My Lai massacre caused such a commotion? Americans who've been in Vietnam can tell you that the Viet Cong did things just as bad, sometimes worse. But what the world wanted to hear about at that time was American atrocities, not Viet Cong ones." She gave a cynical smile. "The Portuguese in Africa became like the Americans in Vietnam—no better or worse than they had ever been, simply unfashionable."

Thin, clinging, sticky rain was falling as we touched down at Beira but it seemed that the wet season had still not begun, for the preliminary shower was over by the time we had walked across the apron into the airport building. It was five thirty and still stifling hot. We were six degrees nearer the equator now and well into the tropics.

Just inside the terminal I paused near a group of hotel touts and porters, looking for Filipe or whoever else might have come to meet me. Slater, who'd accompanied me from the aircraft, glanced uneasily at the Frelimo guards leaning on their Kalashnikovs. I saw Akimo cross from the door to the baggage conveyor and wait there, although I knew that, like me, he had brought only a small overnight bag which he'd kept with him in the cabin.

"Senhor Hickey?"

An African stepped forward from among the group of porters. He had a cigarette dangling from his mouth and wore a faded green uniform with threadbare braid on the epaulets and a peaked cap with a name embroidered on its band: HOTEL BRAGA.

"Senhor Hickey? You have a reservation with us."

It was a statement, not a question. It seemed I was intended to spend the night under Filipe's roof. He couldn't, of course, have known that I was aware of his connection with the hotel.

"I am sent to drive you."

"To the Braga?" Slater spoke from beside me. "Is it any good?"

"I've no idea."

"I may as well try it too."

"If you have no reservation . . ." the driver said.

"Reservation? Don't be funny, Sambo. Half the hotels in this country have gone bust and the rest are almost paying people to stay at them. What makes the Braga so special that I need a reservation?"

"I was told to pick up one. Senhor Hickey."

"Well, now you'll get a bonus for finding an extra customer. A good one, too. I always take the best room and I tip well. Remember that. If the management want to quibble over a ride from the airport they can quibble with me."

The driver shrugged, guessing as I had that it was impossible to argue with Slater. He took both our bags and led us out to the forecourt, where more Frelimo men were hanging about and sitting in battered jeeps and Berliet trucks, vehicles abandoned by the Portuguese Army and made precariously roadworthy again. Among them the Hotel Braga's small bus was parked, an old petrol-driven Leyland with about twenty seats. In a minute we were bumping along the potholed road that led into the city. Glancing casually behind I saw Akimo riding in the passenger seat of a Ford Taunus that had picked him up at the front of the terminal. Everything was as we had planned it, apart from the presence of Slater. Slater had begun to worry me. What made him so eager to stay at a hotel he had never heard of? Was he really more interested in keeping close to me? I had told him my name and volunteered the information that I was on a business trip; he hadn't wanted to hear any details, and I distrusted people who asked too few questions as much as those who asked too many.

Beira hadn't changed much in the year or so since I had last seen it. Africans sat sleeping in doorways and whites were clustered in immobile groups round the café tables in the central square, as if mesmerized by heat and lassitude. This had been a boom town at the end of the nineteenth century, full of foreign adventurers lured by the promise of gold in the interior. The gold had never materialized; the real wealth of the area lay in the rich farming soil that was subsequently exploited by latter-day *prazeiros* like Heinrich Emmerich, and though Beira had never become a ghost town it had a kind of incompleteness to it, an air of having missed its chance in life. The official map optimistically showed many streets on the outskirts which had never come into existence, and even in the city centre, right beside some smart new hotel or office block, a patch of unkempt bush would suddenly appear as if to emphasize that Africa was still on the doorstep.

The Hotel Braga was neither smart nor new. It dated from the boom days, a long, single-storeyed building in the barrack-like style characteristic of colonial Africa, with a wooden-railed veranda along its front. The roof and outer walls were made of galvanized iron on which the red paint had been scorched rusty-brown by years of sun. It looked out across the Chiveve, the narrow, fetid stream which bisected the city. Dusk was beginning to fall as we arrived. The driver led us into a narrow lobby, dropped our bags, banged the handbell on the counter of the deserted reception desk, and then vanished. We waited a minute; no one approached. Beneath a carpet colourless with age the floorboards creaked as we shifted our weight. The rack of room keys behind the desk was almost full.

"Weird sort of place," Slater murmured. "What brought you here, for Christ's sake?"

"Someone made a booking for me. Are you sure you want to stay?"

"Now that I'm here. . . ."

From somewhere deep inside the building came the faint sound of a woman's voice upbraiding someone in Portuguese. Leaving Slater in the lobby I followed the sound around a corner at the end of the hall, through a deserted lounge and into a dining-room with about twenty tables, half a dozen of them set for dinner. The scolding voice came from behind a swing door that led into the kitchen. I pushed it open. The woman turned sharply.

"*Sim?*"

"There's no one at the reception desk. Are you . . . ?"

"Senhora Pereira, wife of the proprietor. You must be Senhor Hickey? One moment."

The other person in the kitchen was an African chef, languidly stirring the contents of a stewpot. The woman turned back to chide him again, in a stream of Portuguese too rapid and idiomatic for me to follow. The chef ignored her, raising a spoon to his lips to try out his stew. Senhora Pereira stalked out, drawing me in her wake, a stocky little woman in a blue overall, with the build and brusqueness of a Madeiran peasant. I had never thought of Filipe as having a wife, and I wondered immediately what he had told her about the purpose of my visit—if anything.

"These blacks nowadays," she confided as she led me back through the dining-room. "Impossible! Sullen, cheeky, late to work. Give them independence and they think the country owes them a living. They don't understand, senhor, that we have had to work hard for what we've got—and that is little enough these days."

We had reached the lobby. When Senhora Pereira saw Slater waiting she stopped and looked at me. "I understood you were alone. My husband said—"

"Mr. Slater happened to come in on the same plane. He'd like a room for a couple of nights."

"You have no booking?" she asked him.

"Lady, is there something about me?" Slater's voice resounded through the vestibule. He pointed at the key-rack. "You've got thirty-five rooms, of which as far as I can see thirty-three are empty, and suddenly everybody wants to know if I've got a booking. Just let me have your best suite."

"There are no suites. You should try the Ambassador. . . ."

"A room with a private bath, then. Tell me you've got none of those either."

"A few," she admitted. She looked at us both uncertainly and then sighed, went behind the desk and passed over two registration *fichas*. We filled them in and took the keys that she gave us.

"Is your husband around?" I asked casually.

"He will be here later." She looked about in exasperation. "Now where is that black devil of a porter?"

We carried our own bags to our rooms. They were at opposite ends of the building. Once I had unpacked the few clothes I had brought, I showered and changed into a clean shirt, slacks, and a lightweight cotton jacket.

Just after seven o'clock I left my room and went down the corridor to the small lounge. Taking no chances with the Barboza papers this time, I carried them in spite of their bulk in the inside pocket of my jacket, where they made an awkward lump. I had hoped to avoid Slater, but I found him installed at a table drinking whisky. Having nothing better to do, and no better company to do it in, I had a couple of drinks with him and listened with one ear to accounts of recent coups he had pulled off: in seducing women, in dealings on the Johannesburg Stock Exchange, in playing golf. At eight o'clock we went in to dinner, an indifferent meal of canned soup, a ragout made of fatty beef and a dessert that was far too sweet for my taste. It was served by the bus driver, transformed to a waiter by virtue of a white drill jacket, and supervised by Senhora Pereira, who at intervals could be heard through the kitchen door scolding the cook. The other two guests had appeared, a pair of Portuguese commercial travellers who sat together and ate in stolid silence.

Slater complained loudly at the quality of the food and, when he was finished, tried once more to persuade me to accompany him on a tour of the *boîtes*. I refused and he went out, abruptly and somewhat to my surprise, on his own.

Senhora Pereira served me a second cup of coffee herself. She said, "Your friend did not enjoy his meal?"

"He's hardly a friend, just someone I met on the plane."

"I cannot say I blame him," she said candidly, ignoring my disownment of Slater. "This cook is an impudent *macaco*. Useless, too, but I cannot find another who would be any better. We have known more prosperous times, senhor. We would have left before independence if not for . . ."

"What?" I prompted. I had already guessed that she was given to imparting confidences.

"My husband is a good man," she said, lowering her voice, although by now there was no one else in the dining-room. "But he has a weakness. Before we married he was a gambler, a bad gambler—one who lost. His nerves are bad; he has not the temperament for it. Under my influence he stopped. For fifteen years he bet not a single centavo. Things changed for us. He was assistant manager of the best hotel in Beira and well on the way to a directorship. And then the hotel was forced to close. With our savings we bought this." She shrugged eloquently. "It made us a living but was not of the class to which we were accustomed. One day business took him to Swaziland. The casino there. . . . The germ never leaves a gambler, senhor. He had a few wins on the first spins of the roulette wheel and began to think he was on his way to big things. In one night he lost almost everything we had. The hotel had to be mortgaged. And now we cannot even pay our way. He talks of some venture that will allow him to pay off the mortgage and get us out of here, back to Portugal. It is a gambler's dream. He dreams of a tourist hotel on the Estoril. . . ."

I finished my coffee and walked out through the lobby to the front veranda. The two commercial travellers sat at a table playing chess by the light of a hurricane lamp. They paid me no attention. So I had learned one more thing about Filipe. I'd known that Emmerich had underwritten his debt of six hundred thousand escudos; now Filipe was hoping to cancel that debt—for services rendered, no doubt. It seemed almost certain that Emmerich, the financial backer of Ficamos, must be Filipe's "principal" and the protector of Gil. Clearly, and wisely, Filipe had kept his wife in ignorance of the venture by which he hoped to write off his mortgage.

I was more concerned with the problem of Slater. Who or what could he possibly be? Not even a theory sprang to my mind. I went down the veranda steps and stood looking casually around, across the malodorous Chiveve and up and down the dark embankment. Under some jac-arandas fifty yards to the right a few cars were parked, and I recognized among them the pale Taunus that had picked Akimo up from the airport. The policeman still distrusted me; this had a lot to do with his determination to keep track of my movements. The setup made me uneasy, but since Akimo was so close I wondered if I dared risk making contact. I stood at the foot of the steps for a couple of minutes and then, affecting to decide on an after-dinner stroll, I walked slowly to the right along the deserted pavement. The Taunus was on the opposite side of the road. I went well past it before pausing in a patch of shadow to be sure I had not been followed from the hotel. Then I crossed to the embankment side and doubled back.

As I walked past the other parked cars I checked to be sure they were all empty. A burly silhouette scrambled out of the Taunus as I approached.

"What in hell you want?" Akimo whispered fiercely.

"Information."

I glanced around. The street lamp above was conveniently out and we were well hidden in the shadow of the jacarandas. There was another African in the driving seat of the Taunus.

"I'm worried about this Slater man," I said.

"What you find out about him?"

"That's what I came to ask you. Engineer on his way to Cabora Bassa—at least according to a fistful of security documents—but he just doesn't seem real."

"I know." Akimo waved a dismissive hand, glad to score a point off me. "I heard on the plane. You can't help hearing a man with such a voice. I checked with LM. His credentials seem OK. There's an Aubrey Slater due up at the dam site on Sunday. Description fits."

"Then at least I know he's not one of yours."

"Where would we get a white man to front for us?"

"The same place you got me, perhaps. What about Gil's people? It's at least possible that they might have put someone in to watch me." I paused. "Filipe isn't at the hotel. What if he arranges a rendezvous somewhere else?"

"Then we follow. I have men round the back too. You will be seen leaving."

"Tailing at night is bloody risky, Akimo. One bad move and it's all over. Why can't you just leave it to me?"

"Because I have to be sure, Hickey. Sure of you."

I left the car, walked past the hotel and on for another hundred yards or so along the embankment, then crossed the road and returned to the Braga. Filipe was waiting for me in the lobby.

2

He was dressed, incongruously in these shabby surroundings, in a dinner jacket with a velvet bow tie. Against his pale complexion the bruised, swollen lips were plum-coloured, and in place of the dark glasses he wore a rimless pair with non-reflecting lenses, through which the blue eyes watched me with hostile wariness. I supposed the dinner jacket was a way of keeping up appearances for a man who had known better times, and I could recognize in his bearing now some of the ingrained deference of the hotelier. Though he wasted none of this on me, his manner was as anxious as usual. He bounced on his heels once or twice.

"Where have you been?"

"Out for a stroll. You weren't exactly quick to appear."

"We must not be seen talking." He glanced round the deserted lobby. "Come in here."

He led me past the reception desk into a tiny room behind it which contained a couple of filing cabinets and a telephone switchboard, at present unmanned. When he had closed the door he pressed his back to it and said, "Who is this Slater?"

"I've no idea. He attached himself to me on the plane."

"And you let him accompany you here?"

"He invited himself. He's not easy to get rid of. Ask your wife: she's the one who let him into the hotel."

"She knows nothing," Filipe said impatiently. "What is he doing in Beira?"

"He's supposed to be en route to Cabora Bassa." If neither side could account for Slater, he was either harmless or more dangerous than any of us knew. "He claims to be stopping over to screw a few black girls. He ought to be out for the next few hours; why don't you search his room?"

Perhaps I had underestimated Filipe's cunning. "I already have," he said. "There's nothing unusual. He has passes and security papers for Cabora Bassa; they look genuine enough."

"But then so do the Barboza documents."

He gave a convulsive bounce, as though the very thought of them was enough to upset him. "You have them on you? May I see them now?"

I took the American Express wallet from my pocket and handed it over. He went through the papers quickly, glancing over the tops of his spectacles at each one in turn before putting it aside. When he looked up at me there was relief on his face. He nodded several times.

"Good. Very good." He shuffled them into a stack, returned them to the wallet and passed it pointedly back to me. "Yours—until the transaction is complete. And now if you please we shall go."

"Go? Where?"

"To effect the exchange, the file for the documents. It is a drive of some distance. The sooner we leave the better."

"Now just a minute," I said, dismayed. "I agreed to come as far as Beira, that's all. I expected you to have the file here."

"My principal will not release it until he has seen these for himself. And I think that is reasonable, don't you? He cannot come here. We must go to him."

"What do you call a drive of some distance?"

Filipe shrugged carelessly. "Ninety minutes?"

"Each way?"

"I am afraid it is unavoidable."

"It isn't good enough, Filipe. When I brought you those papers yesterday you told me I'd have to come to Beira with them. Now you expect me to go off on a three-hour jaunt into the bush with no way of knowing what's at the other end. And still with no guarantee that I'll get that file."

"The file is of no value to my principal except as an inducement to you. There would be no advantage in his cheating you out of it, if that's what you are afraid of. Is it?"

Once again he'd put me in a quandary. Certainly I was afraid, but I couldn't tell him why and I couldn't afford to let on just how apprehensive this new development made me. I knew things that I was not supposed to know. I said, "You keep changing the rules to suit yourselves. That doesn't inspire much confidence."

"The more powerful side always makes the rules, Senhor Hickey." He enjoyed telling me that. "The file is waiting. We can be back here by midnight."

I shrugged and said reluctantly, "All right, let's go."

"I am glad you see the sense of co-operating. We must

not leave the hotel together. Go out by the front door, turn left and walk towards the fishing dock. Wait on the first corner while I bring the bus around. Unless you want anything from your room first?"

"No."

"I will be five minutes."

We emerged from the tiny office and Filipe hurried away to the rear of the building. As I rounded the reception desk I noticed the day's collection of completed *fichas* lying on a shelf beneath the counter, presumably for delivery to the police the next morning. The lobby was as deserted as usual, and I had some time in hand. I took the registration forms off the shelf and examined them. Slater's was the one that interested me; it was on top of the pile. He'd given his first names as Aubrey Harold, his nationality as South African, his occupation as engineer and the purpose of his visit as business. The home address was in Houghton, Johannesburg. There were no inconsistencies there. I glanced idly at the other *fichas*: the two commercial travellers were named Garcia and Sorgentini and both had given addresses in Lourenço Marques. That accounted for three of the four guests in the Braga. The form I had filled in was not there.

I replaced the three slips of paper carefully on the shelf and went to the door. Outside on the veranda the two travellers were still hunched over the chessboard. I stood for a minute beside them under the hurricane lamp, pretending to be interested in the game and making sure that Akimo would see me leaving, before I went down the steps and began walking towards the fishing dock. It might not be such a bad idea to have the black inspector around after all.

It was nearer ten minutes than five before Filipe drove up to where I stood on the corner. He was at the wheel of the Leyland bus. It must have been parked at the back of the hotel, for it came from the direction of a narrow street that ran behind the Chiveve embankment. The articulated doors slid open for me and I climbed up three metalled steps. Filipe, still in his dinner jacket, sat erect and tubby with his arms extended across the steering wheel on its upright column. He worked a lever on his right and the folding door clattered shut. The interior of the bus was in darkness, so it was only as I was about to slide into the seat behind the driver's that I saw the other man. He was slouched in the far corner with his legs stretched out on the long back seat. I could see him only in silhouette; he was wearing what looked like the soft-peaked forage cap of a Portuguese soldier. He sat very still and he was watching me.

"Who's that?" I demanded.

"His name is Henrique,' said Filipe. "He is here for our protection."

"Why do we need protecting?"

"On country roads, late at night, one can never be sure."

I sat down. Filipe swung round the corner and drove past the hotel and the shadowy spot where Akimo waited in the car. From where I sat I could look into the driving mirror and get almost the same view as Filipe. We had driven a couple of hundred yards along the embankment before I saw the tail-lights of the Taunus come on and the beam of its headlights rake across the street as it turned to follow.

Filipe crossed the Chiveve by a bridge some way east of the hotel and headed out of the city. The centre of Beira was quickly left behind, and the road travelled flat and straight across a landscape dotted at intervals with bleak new apartment blocks where the poorer whites lived —those that were left. Beyond these were the usual sprawl of huts made of mud and tin and planks. Glancing into the mirror from time to time I saw Akimo's car following steadily. I was grateful to note that his driver was properly trained; he took the precautions necessary in light traffic, keeping the bus as far in front as possible without the risk of losing sight of it, never coming up close behind, and getting other vehicles ahead of him whenever he could. The outer fringes of Beira ended quite suddenly and then we were out in the bush, enveloped in the deep, soft darkness of the African night. The traffic thinned to about one car every five minutes, with an occasional dangerously wobbling bicycle in between. Akimo's car dropped back. It had been safe enough since the war ended to venture out on the roads at night, but after living for years with the threat of ambushes and landmines people had got out of the habit.

The security guard called Henrique did not speak but stared idly out through the rear window. Insects swirled and eddied in the headlight beams and were flattened in a steady stream against the windscreen. Filipe worked the water spray and gave the wipers a couple of sweeps. I said, "Who is it we're going to see? No harm in telling me now."

"He would prefer to introduce himself."

"Rich, you say?"

"Yes."

"And you owe him money."

He gave me a swift glance across his shoulder but said nothing.

"I know you're not in this business for the love of it, Filipe. This is the big spin, isn't it? The one that's going to pay back the debt you owe. Haven't you heard about the theory of probability? You can't win at roulette."

"You've been talking to my wife," he said huffily.

"She's been talking to me."

"She talks too much for anybody's good."

We drove steadily inland. The road was level and fast and for much of the way was raised on an embankment ten or twelve feet above the surrounding bush. These were the Pungwe Flats, wet and fertile from the rich silt that was spread across them regularly by the flooding river. Here and there the headlights caught the outline of a village in their glare—a few huddled huts, a cattle kraal, a small grove of mango trees—but for the rest there was only the low dark bush, relieved occasionally by lofty acacias, malala palms, and the fever trees that were vividly marked out by the sickly yellow-green of their bark. We'd been driving for more than an hour and had covered, I estimated, a little over a hundred kilometres. I kept an eye on the mirror. Along the flat road the Taunus could afford to stay as much as a couple of miles behind. Sometimes it vanished for a minute or two; sometimes it was discernible by a pale glow thrown up from behind some slight rise. Sooner or later the headlights would reappear, but never soon enough or predictably enough to suggest that there was just one car back there, to create any impression of steady pursuit. Akimo's driver was doing well.

And then Filipe missed a turning.

We were approaching another sleeping village when he braked and swung the bus into a sudden U-turn. "I always overshoot in the dark," he muttered. He drove back the best part of a mile and with alarm I saw Akimo's car approaching, its headlights on full beam. The driver dipped them just as Filipe began slowing down and signalling right. We got a split-second view of the Taunus as it passed before Filipe took the almost invisible turning, onto an unsurfaced road to the south with a bent signpost pointing down it that said NOVA LUSITANIA, *80 quilómetros.* I recognized the road by name; somewhere along here the ambush of the military convoy by Raoul Sousa's band had taken place in June of last year, the incident that had led to the massacre at Goronga.

The road was tricky, little more than a track, with bone-jarring corrugations on its surface and sharp, unexpected twists. In a couple of places where it crossed dry stream-beds there were alarming little bridges consisting of narrow rows of planks supported by precarious-looking uprights. When we had driven a couple of miles I caught the faint glow in the mirror again, the reflection of lights bouncing over a rise behind us. It lasted only a second. Then the voice of the man named Henrique hit me like a physical blow.

"Car behind us."

Filipe bounced once in his seat. "Well?"

"Not more than a dozen cars a day use this road. We'll stop and take a look at the fucker."

Filipe slowed down. Henrique stared intently to the rear while I sat in a mesmerized silence, my gaze riveted on the mirror. The glow did not appear again, but I was horribly aware of the truth of what I had told Akimo. It needed only one wrong move. The tail car had only to be spotted once.

In half a mile or so Filipe had found a spot where the roots of a big fever tree, clinging tenaciously to the soil, had survived surrounding flood erosion to form a steep-sided sandy mound twelve or fifteen feet high. He stopped and reversed behind the mound, turned off the lights and cut the engine. We were in shadow, invisible from the road. The sudden quiet magnified the shrill song of crickets.

Henrique came forward down the aisle. By the starlight that filtered into the bus I made him out as a stocky man dressed in army fatigues and clutching something in his right hand that looked like a length of metal piping about eighteen inches long. Ignoring me, he squatted beside Filipe. I strained to follow their Portuguese.

"It's probably someone going to Nova Lusitania. On the other hand, there was a car behind us just before the turn-off. If it's the same one. . . ."

"Two people missing the turn-off within a couple of minutes," Filipe said thoughtfully. "Yes, that could be more than coincidence."

I recognized a dangerous combination of qualities in these two: Henrique's alertness and Filipe's cunning. Yet they weren't very sure of themselves. Perhaps I could talk them out of this. I said, "You think someone might be following? That's ridiculous. Nobody knows—"

"It could be your friend Slater," Filipe said grimly.

"Impossible. He didn't even see me leave the hotel."

"All I want is a look at the fucker," said Henrique.

A couple of minutes dragged by. The crickets' chirping seemed to have slowed down, like the beat of a metronome set at half speed. There was no further sign of the headlights; I wondered whether Akimo and his driver might have heard the changed note of our engine as we reversed, and stopped to reconnoitre on foot. Henrique, whose manner seemed to alternate between restlessness and a sort of studied boredom, said, "Could be they've gone back."

"I'm sure they have," I said. "We're wasting time."

"Have you some interest," said Filipe, agitated, "in convincing us of that?"

"You're imagining things. You're—"

"Shut up!" snapped Henrique. "Listen!"

I heard it in a rising panic, the hiss of tyres on sand and the whine of a motor in low gear. In a few seconds the pale shape of the Taunus came dimly into view from our left. The headlamps had been doused, presumably when

Akimo and his man had lost sight of our own lights, and the car crawled cautiously forward with its parking lights on, searching for some sign of the bus. None of us breathed. The Taunus entered the gap in front of us and then stopped, its engine idling.

Henrique snapped something into a slot about halfway along the metal pipe, something that stuck out from it at right angles. I recognized an FN machine carbine with its magazine in place.

"It's the same one," Henrique muttered. "Let's get a better look."

With a quick movement Filipe switched the headlights on at high beam. The car, broadside on to us and fifteen yards away, was thrown starkly into view. The astonished faces of the two black men were turned blinking into the glare.

Violence, once begun, acquires an insane momentum of its own. The Africans stared at us for several seconds before Henrique said, "See if they scare."

Filipe started the engine, crashed into gear and drove the heavy bus straight at the Taunus.

"Stop!" I yelled, half rising from my seat as we bore down on the car. Akimo's driver recovered his wits just in time to hit the accelerator. The rear wheels spun in the sand; the bumper of the bus clipped the car's back mudguard but it surged forward. Filipe swung out on to the road behind it.

"What are you doing?" I shouted. "You're both mad!"

"They were following!" Henrique yelled back. "Why the fuck you think they run?"

I tried to make a grab for the handbrake but the sharp turn to the right swung me off balance, onto the seat across the aisle from mine. I knelt there and clung to the handrail. Akimo's driver, still confused, was moving blindly on his parking lights and Filipe, bucking in his seat, was gaining fast. For a moment I thought he would ram the Taunus from behind, but instead he swung out to the right and began to edge alongside, trying to force the car off the rutted road.

Once again the black driver's reflexes saved him at the last moment. He turned on his headlights and accelerated. Filipe lost a few yards but the bus had plenty of momentum by now and he put his foot flat as well. He was screaming unintelligibly over the roar of the motor and the awful jarring and shaking. And he went on picking up speed. Too appalled to move, I crouched on the seat. We must have got up to sixty miles an hour, on a road that would have been dangerous at half the speed, but the car was moving a fraction faster, stretching a lead of five yards to ten and then fifteen.

Henrique spat out a word and reached across Filipe to shove back the lever that opened the folding doors. Dust billowed blindingly in. The guard dropped into the stairwell across from the driving seat, clinging to the sloped handrail with one hand as he crouched on the bottom step, with the other steadying the machine carbine against the rubber lining of the doors as he took aim.

I watched what followed in numb disbelief. Akimo and his driver were about twenty yards ahead when Henrique emptied the whole magazine at them in a single brief burp. Bullet holes pocked the rear window and the boot lid and the car started to slither out of control. Then, inexplicably, Filipe stood on the brake.

My head slammed against the handrail of the seat in front of me. The rear of the bus slewed violently to the right. Spinning the wheel to turn into the skid, Filipe over-corrected and we teetered on the edge of a roll before performing three clockwise circles on locked wheels. My brain whirled. I was vaguely conscious of a series of explosive metallic crashes and the sounds of breaking glass. Then I realized that the bus had stopped and that we were still upright. It wasn't we who had crashed.

I had fallen off the seat onto the studded steel deck, and I lay for several seconds watching the ceiling of the bus reel. When I managed to sit up, dizziness and nausea rushed on me. Filipe was scrambling out through the driver's door. I got up and lurched down the steps. Henrique had fallen off the stairwell, but not when we'd been moving fast enough for him to get hurt. He came running towards us, covered in dust, still clutching the carbine. Filipe was shining a torch into the dark gully that lay like a gash across the road. I looked down and saw the Taunus lying on its roof in the stream-bed twenty feet below. Its doors had burst open.

Dazedly I began to realize what had happened. Akimo's driver, hoping to shake us off, had been going at full speed for the narrow wooden bridge that spanned the gully. Filipe, knowing the heavy bus could not possibly take the bridge at the same speed, had braked just in time. The bus had come to a halt with its rear two feet from the edge.

Now he stood shaking and reeking of nervous sweat and staring down at the wreck. I seized the torch from him, flashed its beam along the rim of the gully, and found a place where the side was less steep. I clambered down, discovering that I was shaking myself, and Filipe and Henrique followed. At the bottom I almost tripped over Akimo.

He lay slumped back against the bank of the dry stream several yards from the car. His eyes were closed; his breathing was regular but there was a deep gash in his forehead which had sent blood running down his face and over his chest; it gleamed darkly in the torchlight. At a guess, he had banged his head violently against the dashboard as the car went into the gully, then fallen from one of the open doors. I stepped over to the car. One glance at the driver was enough. A bullet had taken him in the base of the skull and blown out his right eye to leave a messy jelly hanging on his cheek. I turned away quickly. When I shone the torch on Akimo again, Filipe started to go through the policeman's pockets.

"That can wait, can't it?"

"We must find out who they are."

"You *are* bloody mad, the pair of you."

Henrique had calmly stripped down his carbine and was squinting up the short barrel to see whether any dirt had got in when he'd fallen. Filipe continued to dig in Akimo's pockets. He found only a soiled handkerchief and a ballpoint pen, nothing that would identify him. When he stood up I handed him the torch, knelt beside the black man and felt his pulse. It was steady but slow. Between thumbs and forefingers I forced his eyes open. One pupil was distinctly dilated, a sure sign of a serious internal head injury.

I stood up and looked at what I could see of Filipe's face, a pale moon in the darkness behind the torchlight.

"Congratulations," I said. "You've really screwed it up."

"Have we?" he asked. He was extremely nervy, but there was a diffident menace in his tone. "For whom?"

"What do you mean?"

The torch was still shining directly in my face, but an edge of the beam was caught by that small hotel manager's gun that was now in his other hand. It wasn't exactly pointing at me, but neither was it pointing at anything else in particular.

"Why were they following, Hickey? What did they know?"

"Why the hell ask me?"

"Because it could just be that you led them here."

My scalp crawled. I said quietly, "It could be, but it isn't."

"Then why else did they follow?"

"You don't know that they were following, Filipe. They could have been innocent travellers on their way to Nova Lusitania, who missed the turning just like you, and who just happened to be driving with their headlights off. Ridiculous? Ridiculous things happen. Like having a bus suddenly charge at you out of the bush. If that had happened to me I'd have done just what they did—run like hell. Admit it, Filipe: you over-reacted. You don't know who they are and you can't speculate. All you can be sure about is that one of them is dead and that between you you murdered him."

I wanted to scare him and I thought I'd succeeded. The torch beam quivered in time with his trembling hands, though the gun did not waver noticeably. "If we are responsible, so are you," he said.

I was already more grimly aware of this than Filipe could guess. I didn't know how I would ever explain to Raoul Sousa. Akimo had suspected me from the start of being implicated in protecting Gil, and in the last minute before his senses had been slammed out of him he must have had the suspicion confirmed in his own mind.

"I didn't drive the bus. And I didn't shoot anyone."

"Perhaps not. This changes things, all the same." Filipe watched my face closely in the torchlight. "Have you ever seen either of these *macacos* before, Hickey?"

"No." The lie came with surprising ease. "But I have seen a lot of head-injury cases. Without treatment this man can only get worse. He needs to go to hospital."

"That would mean exposing ourselves," Filipe said. "And that is one thing we cannot afford."

"And if he dies?"

"Then he is one more dead *macaco*. On the other hand, he may regain consciousness. We cannot leave him here. He will come with us."

"Moving him will just make it worse."

But Akimo's condition was not uppermost in Filipe's mind. "Have you spoken to anyone about Barboza, Hickey? Let anything slip?"

"Of course not."

"Not to Slater, for instance?"

I had an inspiration. Whoever and whatever Slater might be, Filipe's paranoiac attitude to the man made him a useful scapegoat.

"I've said nothing to him. But I must say I don't trust him. He managed to be on the same flight as I was and to end up in the same hotel. It could be he's keeping a check on my movements. I can't imagine why."

Filipe was uncertain of himself, unable to pursue the thing further. But the pistol remained in his hand.

"I hope you are telling the truth, Hickey. Slater worries me. I intend to learn more about him. Meanwhile we have wasted enough time. Help with him." He gestured at Akimo.

"Help to kill him by moving him? No, thank you. I'm not going to be an accessory to—"

"You are involved, whether you like it or not. And you had better remember, Hickey, that your only value to us lies in those papers in your pocket. You, yourself, are expendable. And so you will help."

The facts were unarguable. And the direction in which the gun pointed was now a little more specific.

"What about all this?" I said, looking at the wrecked car with the body in it. "You think you can just leave it here, to be found by the next passing motorist?"

"There will be no motorists till morning. And by then it will all be gone. Where we are going such things can be arranged."

"That will only delay the problem. You can't make two men and a car disappear without expecting questions to be asked."

"But not questions that we will have to answer," Filipe said. "If these men followed us from Beira they have been driving for over an hour, just as we have. For all that time they were out of touch with whoever sent them. They could be anywhere; they cannot possibly be traced to our destination."

For the moment I almost wished this were true. I bent down and gripped Akimo's ankles. Henrique took him under the armpits and then, with an exclamation, let him go again to pick up something that had been lying on the ground beneath the policeman's bulk. It was a Mauser pistol; it must have fallen from a pocket or a hand as he rolled out of the car.

"What do you say about that?" Filipe asked excitedly.

"On country roads, at night, you need protection," I said. "You told me that yourself."

3

With a lot of strain and a stream of cursing from Henrique, the three of us managed to drag the dead weight of Akimo up the steep side of the gully. We hauled him clumsily up the steps of the bus and laid him down on the steel deck between the rows of seats. What the shaky ride would do to him I didn't like to imagine. The wound was no longer bleeding, but I knew that wasn't where the real damage was anyway. Anyone who stays unconscious more than a few minutes is likely to be suffering from cerebral compression which will kill him unless it can be relieved by medical means—usually a lumbar puncture to draw off cerebro-spinal fluid. In the torchlight there was now a greyish hue to the dark pitted skin of his face.

I was appalled, but as we took our seats in the bus I had time to realize that I ought to be worrying about myself as well. Whether Akimo lived or died I was in trouble —about twice as much trouble as before. The possibility that the black man had been following us—and luckily I had managed to convince Filipe that it was no more than a possibility—inevitably caused suspicions about me that would not otherwise have been there. And that meant more danger. The sooner I could get tonight's business over and head back to Beira the better. Explaining to Sousa would not be easy, but he would have to accept that what had happened had not been my fault. If the fools had trusted me in the first place . . . but it was no use going over all that again.

Filipe took the bus gingerly across the bridge, a squat figure looking more ridiculous than ever in his dinner jacket; beneath it the starched shirt was soaked in sweat and stained with Akimo's blood. Henrique had returned to his post on the back seat.

Dust boiled in our wake. Except for deep and sudden gullies the country remained flat, and there were no longer any signs of human habitation; whatever villages there were must have been well away from the road. We had left the site of the shooting at ten o'clock, and it was about ten minutes later that I saw lights ahead and to the left. At first there was just a faint glow against the sky and then, as we drew nearer, the points of illumination became defined. There was a pattern, roughly rectangular, formed by hundreds of powerful lamps positioned over what must have been a very large area. They were still a long way off, but readily visible across the flat terrain in the clear, dry air. Then I realized that there was a barbed-wire fence running parallel to the road on our left, and that what stood behind it was not the usual straggling bush but a dense growth of uniform height, a man-made forest of slender stems with the light foliage at the top swaying and rustling in the air-flow as we passed. For a couple of miles it went on as the lights drew closer, one edge of what was obviously a vast plantation, until we came to an intersection with an illuminated signboard pointing left. I read the name on the board without surprise, but with an edge of apprehension.

The new road had a better surface and ran straight, flanked by the swaying masses of sugar-cane, for perhaps two miles into the heart of the estate. The pattern of lights came closer. Now I could see that the lamps stood on tall poles, floodlighting an inner perimeter fence which surrounded an area that might have been twenty or thirty acres; in the dark it was hard to tell. The nearest of the lights stood above a pair of steel-framed mesh gates with strands of barbed wire along the top and a small gatehouse just inside. A Land Rover with a radio aerial on its roof was parked alongside. There was another notice with the name of the company and a warning: PROPRIEDADE PRIVADA! PROIBIDO ENTRAR SEM PERMISSÃO! To make the point, two guards in jungle fatigues and with automatic rifles slung from their shoulders stood behind the gates.

Filipe pulled up a few yards short, climbed out of the bus and approached them. He spoke for a few moments through the mesh and one of them let him in and re-locked the gates behind him. He followed the guard into the gatehouse; I heard the clicking of a manual telephone being cranked. Another pair of guards appeared from the left, paused beneath the light and then continued a patrol of the fence.

Filipe was on the phone a couple of minutes. When he returned he was tense and subdued. He climbed back into the bus, drove forward and halted for long enough to let both guards flash torches in my face, record it in their memories and nod. They exchanged greetings with Henrique as we went through, crunching along a gravelled road that led straight across the large floodlit rectangle.

No sugar-cane grew here. This was where it was brought to be milled, where the extracted juice was refined and the crystallized product prepared and packed. For a factory site it had been made as pleasant as possible; the buildings were set among wide, well-watered lawns dotted with malala palms and fringed by flowerbeds. After the miles of parched bush it was an oasis. Past a long brick bungalow housing a row of offices, the bus bumped over a series of narrow-gauge railway tracks that crossed the road to converge on a loading platform beside the huge, silent mill. Small diesel locomotives and high-sided tipper trucks that brought the cane in from the fields were drawn up in rows. The whole factory area was illuminated like a football field.

At intervals we passed more of the uniformed guards, some stationary, some patrolling in pairs. They were all white men; they had walkie-talkies strapped to their web belts and they carried their weapons with familiar assurance. These would be the ex-paratroopers, men who'd stayed on after the war to become mercenaries because they liked Africa and had a taste for fighting and were now paid three times their army wages for the training and experience that had given them the willingness to kill—a willingness which Henrique had demonstrated tonight.

In one corner of the rectangle were the lights of what I guessed was a workmen's compound. Opposite, the road made a turn towards the south-eastern perimeter and travelled up a palm-covered slope to a rocky ridge which must have been one of the few elevated sites in this flat terrain. Backing onto the ridge, partitioned from the factory area by a low split-pole fence and a row of casuarina trees, was a large house.

It was a bungalow, built rather in the style of an old Saxon farmhouse around three sides of a small courtyard, in which Filipe pulled up. It looked out across the dark canefields, and the two east-facing wings were raised on concrete stilts to give the house an aggressively imposing air. The spaces between the stilts served as carports; there was a white Mercedes in one, a Mini-Moke in the other. The garden was an orderly jungle of tropical vines and creepers, oleanders, malala palms and pawpaw trees.

Akimo still lay unconscious in the aisle of the bus. Leaving him in Henrique's charge, Filipe and I got out and climbed onto a wide, balustraded veranda. Apart from some elaborate wrought-iron burglar guards on the windows, there was no sign of the Portuguese weakness for ornamentation. Filipe rang the doorbell. Chimes and savage barking sounded from deep inside the house. In a minute a young African houseboy in tennis shoes and a white drill suit let us in and led us silently through the entrance hall and into a living-room the size of a barn. Filipe looked nervously at a door at the far end, from behind which came scratching and whimpering.

"Dogs," he said. "He keeps vicious dogs. *Traze o senhor,*" he ordered the houseboy sharply. "*Ande!*"

The boy looked startled for a second. Then he hurried away, moving with a stiff-kneed limp in his right leg. I looked around the room.

A vast picture window formed one side of it, giving a view across the lighted courtyard to the canefields. One wall was made of rough stone, another was panelled with pine. The furniture was extremely simple: a massive oaken chest, a heavy blackwood settle and matching chairs, a low central table, lamps of Portuguese marble, three or four Persian rugs scattered about on the highly polished stone floor. At the other end was a dining alcove. It was all essentially masculine—the home of a man with plenty of money, some taste, and little use for luxury.

From somewhere behind us came a snarl. Filipe gave a yelp. I turned to see a big Doberman pinscher in the far doorway, teeth bared as it strained towards us on a short leash held by a man whose face remained hidden in the shadow of the hall. Then he stepped forward and I got my first look at the Freiherr Heinrich von Metzradt-Emmerich, owner of the Açúcar Emmerich sugar estate, financial backer of the Ficamos movement . . . and Gil's protector.

He was a squat man, short and very powerfully built. His cotton shirt was stretched as tightly over his chest as over his stomach. He wore the combination of lederhosen, dark ankle-socks and sandals that invariably identifies a German in a warm climate. He let the dog haul him across the room and reined in the choker leash at the right distance to let it sniff at us suspiciously. Another growl bubbled in its throat as Filipe cringed. Emmerich gave an amused grunt.

"He won't harm you. Not unless I tell him to. Perhaps I should, after the mess you made of things tonight."

"I don't like dogs," Filipe muttered. "I can't pretend to."

"They know it, too." Emmerich spoke in English, presumably for my benefit. His tone was peremptory. "A dog will assess your attitude in a moment. Never show fear; never run. Arouses his hunting instinct. Nino!"

The houseboy re-entered the room, carrying a tray with a tall stone bottle of Schimmelhagen and a tiny shot-glass. When he had lowered this to the table he took the leash from Emmerich and led the Doberman away.

"Nino, now—he was terrified of them at first, and they slavered to get at his throat. Once he built up the courage to handle them they started to like him. Choose their own friends, you see. Pity we can't all do the same. Eh, Filipe? When I go to bed at night they're let out to run free. They'll attack any stranger and they're trained to kill. They did, once. So this is Hickey."

He did not offer his hand. The heavy, aggressive face swung towards me as purposefully as a revolving gun-turret. The eyebrows, the bristly moustache and the hair, thin on top but cropped to half an inch all round like a Prussian officer's, were of a uniform iron grey. The eyes were deep blue and hard in spite of a slight rheuminess.

"Know who I am, Hickey?"

"I've heard the name."

"I'm on this land forty years and I don't intend leaving now. You saw the security outside? It was set up during the war. Frelimo didn't frighten me when they were terrorists and they don't scare me now that they call themselves a government. One of these days they will attempt to subject me to what they call their Revolutionary Agriculture Programme. Know what that means? Dividing my land among a thousand *macaco* farmers who wouldn't get ten per cent of my productivity out of it. Paying me some laughable compensation in blocked escudos. No, thank you. I will stay, and if necessary I will fight to stay. But we have business to discuss. A drink first. Schnapps?"

"Scotch," I said, wondering what the purpose of this little diatribe had been. What did Emmerich need to prove to me? He roared for the houseboy again and then turned his attention to Filipe, who was bouncing in agitation beside me.

"Please, that car . . . the *macaco* in the bus."

"All in hand," the German said brusquely. "The breakdown truck is on its way. In an hour's time no trace of the accident will remain. The car will be brought here and hidden safely enough never to be found. Six thousand hectares is a lot of land. But that does not excuse your bungling, Filipe."

"It just . . . happened," the little man said awkwardly. "It seemed the right thing to do at the time."

"It was the wrong thing. You should either have lost them or lured them into a corner where they would have had no chance of escape. Anything would have been better than to chase them along a public road. If Henrique's shooting had not been accurate they would have got away."

The brief reproof also contained a threat; it was the tone of a father whose authority is absolute. Emmerich had the gruff certainty of a man whose assertions are never challenged, the unmistakable self-confidence that only money or power or a combination of both can bring, and Filipe seemed genuinely in awe of it. He said meekly, "You are right."

"From now on no more bungling, Filipe. We cannot afford it. Go and help Henrique bring in the injured one. Nino will show you where to put him."

The houseboy approached, was given some instructions in the vernacular—he was from one of the local Shona tribes, I guessed—and went limping away with Filipe following. When they had gone Emmerich looked at me.

"You say you have never seen either of those who were in the car?"

"Never."

He nodded in a preoccupied way, leading me towards the table where the Schimmelhagen stood. The casualness of his attitude, after Filipe's near-hysteria, surprised me; it was as if he regarded the incident as an inconvenience rather than a threat. I thought the time was right to have my say about Akimo.

"That injured man," I said, "is badly hurt—more badly than you realize, perhaps. Unless a doctor sees him he'll die."

"What qualifies you to say that?"

"I know a little about head injuries, that's all."

Emmerich seemed to consider for a few moments, then shook his head decisively. "It's out of the question. There is no doctor between here and Beira; even if we got one to come out, the circumstances of the accident would have to be explained. And he would be bound to report them to the authorities. There was a doctor in Dondo once—my tame doctor, I used to call him—who was ready to overlook such formalities, but he is back in Portugal now."

"So you'll let him die? Just like that?"

"What is he to you? A stranger—or so you say."

"He's a man who doesn't need to die."

"He is also a man who was carrying a gun and may have been trying to follow you here. What colour are these susceptibilities of yours, Hickey? Pink humanist? White parlour liberal? I'd have thought you had lived in Africa long enough to know better. There's no one to whom his own life is cheaper than a *macaco*."

"Maybe so, but the law puts its value a little higher—and the law is being made by *macacos* these days. What I do know about Africa is that it's changed. I've learned to recognize the fact and to adapt. What have you learned in the last forty years?"

Emmerich glowered at me for a second or two but then

his eyes slid away as if he sensed a fault in his own argument. If there was no compassion in him, there was perhaps the residue of a sense of honour. "It is not your concern," he muttered. "If he dies that is my responsibility. You don't understand how high the stakes are; I cannot take unnecessary risks." He pointed to a chair and sat himself down on the edge of the settle. "Show me those papers."

I took the plastic wallet from my pocket and placed it on the table. He poured a tiny glass of schnapps and drank it at a swallow. It was, I realized, by no means his first of the evening. A slightly unsteady hand confirmed what the watery eyes and the volubility had only suggested. He went through the documents, holding them close to his face in the manner of someone short-sighted who refuses to wear glasses. Again I was surprised at his carelessness; he gave each paper only a cursory glance. Finally he replaced them in the wallet and grunted.

"Help yourself." He waved at a tray which Nino, returning, had put at my elbow. It held a full bottle of Johnnie Walker Black Label, a silver bucket of ice, a soda syphon, a jug of water and a crystal tumbler. I poured myself a stiff one, aware of Emmerich's gaze; for the moment, at least, he seemed more interested in me than in what I had brought him.

The wallet was back on the table. "What do you make of all this, Hickey?"

"I prefer not to make anything of it."

"Meaning you'd rather not know. That's sensible. But you're not a fool, you must have had thoughts. Tell me your thoughts."

I was reluctant, but it would have been dangerous to sound naïve. I said, "Barboza isn't Barboza. That is to say, he's not some little architect who came to you for help. He's more than that. It's important to you to get him out of the country safely. Important to the tune of paying Gomes thirty thousand dollars. And of refusing twenty thousand rands from me to buy my way out of this arrangement."

Emmerich nodded. "More important to me than that file could possibly be to you, Hickey."

"So it *was* a seller's market after all. Speaking of the file—"

"It's here, in the safe in my study. It is best left there until you go."

Something in his tone prompted me to look at my watch. It was eleven o'clock.

"I don't intend lingering."

"I thought that since it was so late you had better stay the night. I might even enjoy your company, Hickey. I don't have many guests these days."

"Flattering—but no, thanks."

"Unfortunately it is already arranged."

As his gaze shifted to some point beyond my left shoulder I realized that Filipe was back. I stood up quickly, turning to face the little man, and with a start he dropped something he had been holding on to the stone floor. It was my overnight bag, fully packed. Emmerich spoke from behind me.

"I told you I could not take unnecessary risks. And it would be a risk to let you go tonight."

"Why? I don't understand."

Filipe was enjoying my bewilderment. He sent his left cheek into a pastry-fold. "You have checked out of the Braga. In fact, officially you never stayed there."

I remembered the missing *ficha* and the ten-minute wait for Filipe to pick me up on the corner and silently cursed my stupidity. He'd spent the time in my room, removing the traces of my occupancy. I said, "I'm not staying."

"But you must. It is a safeguard."

"It's no deal."

I spun towards the table and made a grab for the wallet. But the old German was on his feet now and he stepped in to block me, seizing my forearm and holding on to it with surprising strength. I swung my left fist at his head, missed, got hold of his shirt collar instead and twisted it into his throat. For several seconds we stood grappling in the middle of the room until Filipe shrieked, "Let him go!"

The Browning was in his hand again. It was pointing at me, but Filipe was bouncing on his heels and shaking with nerves, and Emmerich released my arm just as quickly as I let go of his collar. We were both afraid of being shot by accident. We stood a couple of feet apart, glaring angrily at each other.

"Is this your way of doing business, Emmerich?"

"It is a matter of necessity. Those papers are to be used sooner than you probably imagined: in point of fact, at two thirty tomorrow afternoon. Barboza is to take the weekly direct flight from Beira to Lisbon. From there he will transfer to a flight for Rio de Janeiro. Until he has arrived there safely—that is, late on Sunday evening, our time—you will remain here. You shall be my guest for the week-end, Hickey."

I continued to watch him closely, hoping the defiant stare would mask the panic that had suddenly filled me and threatened to overflow. "Guest?" I said sarcastically. "You mean hostage."

"I want you here as a guarantee of your own good faith. If I released you now there would be very little to stop your going to the police."

"Very little? You could keep the file until Barboza was safe. You'd still have the power to lose me my passport."

"A trifle compared with what I have to lose, Hickey. Of

course there is something else to consider," he added in a dangerously negligent tone. "How do I know that you have not already been to the police?"

"Why should I have done that?"

"I don't know. The matter of those two *macacos* is still unexplained. Two black men, one of them armed, driving just a short way behind you on a lonely road like that . . . it makes me wonder, that's all."

I'd have been surprised if he wasn't doing more than just wonder. But I said, "I don't believe they were following. Even if they were, why blame me for it? How good is your own security? How do you know who else might not be interested in Barboza?"

"Slater, for instance," muttered Filipe from his corner. We'd been forgetting about Filipe. He was still pointing the pistol at me and blinking anxiously through his rimless lenses. And he was on about Slater again; the man was proving useful.

"Put that away," Emmerich ordered Filipe, then turned back to me. "You've had your thoughts about Barboza, Hickey—uncomfortable thoughts, perhaps. Some of them may be right; others are certainly wrong. I do not choose to discuss them. There is more involved in this than you could possibly know. One day you may hear the whole story. Meanwhile just be aware of this: I have a vital interest in seeing that Barboza gets out tomorrow. Vital. The papers are perfect. Provided he reaches Brazil you will be released at once, with your precious file. If he fails be under no illusion: Only one person can have betrayed him."

Emmerich turned to the table and poured himself more Schimmelhagen.

"If you know something, Hickey, if you are hiding something, it will be better to admit it now. Things will go easier for you. If Barboza is arrested you will take the consequences—and you will have only yourself to blame. Understood?"

I nodded grimly. "I'd go the same way as that car and its driver tonight, I suppose—to a quiet spot in the canefields. I've heard you called the last *prazeiro*, Emmerich. How long do you think you can go on acting like one?"

"I'm too old to change now," he said imperturbably. "And I have not achieved what I have by being squeamish. I repeat: You are my guest until Sunday. You have the freedom of the property, but resist the temptation to leave. You have seen some of the security arrangements. They kept Frelimo out and they will keep you in."

I understood my situation better than Emmerich knew. Tomorrow when Antonio Gil tried to leave Mozambique under the Barboza identity he would be arrested. It was just what Sousa wanted—but the one thing neither he nor I had considered was the possibility that at the time of the arrest I would be helpless in the hands of Gil's protectors. And I had little doubt that Emmerich would have me killed.

Escape, on the other hand, seemed impossible, and to attempt it in any case would alert Emmerich to the deception. He would cancel the Barboza travel plans, Gil would still be free, and Sousa might well believe I was deceiving *him*. We get Gil or we keep you, he had said. Jesus! How had a plan that had looked reasonably logical until an hour ago turned into such a bloody mess? But even as I asked myself this I knew I must stem the flood of panic, wait until I had the chance to think. And that in the meantime I must learn everything I could, everything that could possibly help me survive.

My drink still stood on the table, untouched. I picked it up and swallowed half of it.

"So once again you're rewriting the contract to suit yourselves," I said. "I'm to be stuck here doing nothing for two days. What guarantee have I got that you'll give me the file at the end of it? How do I know you've even got the bloody thing?"

"You will take my word for it," the German growled. He drank off his glass of schnapps. "I don't go back on my word, Hickey. Everyone I have ever done business with knows that."

"But I've never done business with you," I pointed out. "Show me that file. Just show it to me, as a sign of *your* good faith."

He stood and glowered at me, his features slightly blurred by alcohol, and I had the curious impression that I had offended that old-fashioned sense of honour. He picked up the blue wallet and looked at Filipe.

"You have things to do in Beira. Preparations to make."

"Yes."

"Then go. Hickey, come with me."

4

Emmerich led me down a corridor into the north wing of the house. About halfway along it was a closed door with one of the armed guards leaning against the wall beside it. Obviously that was where they had put Akimo, and they weren't taking any chances on his making a sudden recovery during the night. Emmerich walked past the room without giving it a glance and showed me into his study at the end of the wing. It had a partridgewood desk marked in several places by circular stains from bottles and glasses. On the wall behind it was a framed, hand-drawn surveyor's map of the Açúcar Emmerich estate, and on a table by the window stood a short-wave receiver-transmitter and a master control unit for the Pye walkie-talkie system used by the guards. Unlike the living-room the place had a cluttered, lived-in air, and I guessed that this was where he spent his evenings, working, brooding, drinking. This was his nerve-centre, the throne-room of his empire. He gestured me into a swivel chair and I noticed two pictures standing at one end of the desk. One was a framed print of the newspaper photograph I had seen, Emmerich with his rifle behind the sandbags. The other was a faded group photograph taken on the lawn in front of the house, on the occasion of some party. Emmerich, slightly slimmer and a good deal younger, stood at the centre of a row of a dozen men laughing or smirking into the camera, several of them in Portuguese Army uniform, all of them clutching glasses: his cronies from the old days. Between Emmerich and one of the officers, each of them with an arm around her shoulders, stood a pretty pony-tailed girl of eleven or twelve in one of the full skirts that had been fashionable in the mid-fifties. One of the friends' daughters, I supposed. I searched the faces quickly for Gil's; it wasn't there.

Filipe had left to return to Beira. The houseboy had followed us to the study with the bottles of whisky and schnapps. Emmerich went behind his desk to push aside the map and reveal a small safe set in the wall at chest height. He twisted the combination knob back and forth. To judge by the squinting and grunting that went on he was having trouble seeing the figures, but finally the door swung open. He dragged out a foolscap-sized file cover; three bundles of money and a couple of papers slipped to the floor. The money was American, thick wads of used twenty-dollar bills. He tossed the file onto the desk in front of me. On the cover was a gummed label—the pale patch on the photostatic copy—with my name and the unintelligible Portuguese headings. A glance at the entries inside told me it was authentic. Emmerich was holding out his hand. I surrendered the file reluctantly, though knowing it could now make little difference whether I had it or not.

"Satisfied?" Emmerich said. "It's yours as soon as I am sure you have fulfilled your part of the contract." He scooped up the money and shoved it back in the safe, cramming the file and the American Express wallet in after it. "Meanwhile it stays here, along with my pile of emergency dollars. Why should I give it to the blacks at the exchange control and take their worthless escudos in return? That's why it is useful to have friendly buyers overseas."

He closed the door and twisted the knob to lock it. Then he poured the last drops of schnapps into his glass and shoved the Johnnie Walker bottle at me.

"Do you intend giving me a bed?" I asked.

"Better, Hickey, better; you're becoming reconciled. Adaptable, as you say. You are a guest. The guest suite is in the other wing; Nino will show you. Drink with me first. I don't get much company."

I considered for a moment. I wanted to be alone to do some hard thinking. On the other hand it might be more valuable to stay here for a while with the old man, especially if the drink was making him garrulous. I poured some more Scotch. Emmerich slumped into the chair behind the desk, watching me blearily.

"You married, Hickey?"

"I was."

"Difficult bastard to live with, are you? I suspected. Like me. I was married once. She couldn't take the climate, the loneliness. Those things are tolerable if there's companionship, but I didn't give her enough of that. I was thirty-five before I married, and working eighteen hours a day, seven days a week, to build up this place. Set in selfish bachelor ways too, I suppose. It turned out she couldn't have children; otherwise things might have been different. That's the only thing I envy other men for—their children, the sense of continuity they bring. I used to look at my friends' children and think. . . ." He gestured vaguely at the group picture on the desk. "Too late now. The friends are gone as well."

Sensing that he was growing maudlin, he stopped and drank the schnapps in his glass. Then he grabbed the bottle, shook it and bellowed, "Nino!"

The houseboy, silent as ever, appeared from down the hall, placed a new stone bottle in front of his master and removed the empty one. The drill was so practised that I realized this was how the evenings must pass here, with Nino hovering and the old man yelling occasionally for more drink. He was lonely even if he wouldn't admit it, a solitary planter clinging to the only way of life he knew. I might have managed to feel sorry for him if his mawkishness hadn't stood in contrast to his disregard for the man dying in the next room, if the barbed wire and the armed guards outside hadn't underlined the fact that even as an anachronism he was still a dangerous one.

Perhaps he guessed something of what I was thinking; he looked at me with a foggy knowingness.

"Nino—all the family I have now. Follows me about like a puppy. I'm all that he has too, you see. He addresses me as *father;* in a matriarchal society the title is transferable. You'd know that, of course. He's fifteen. He lost his parents during the war. Lucky to be alive himself. That limp: bullet wound."

This didn't seem to be leading us anywhere. Emmerich broke the seal on the new bottle of Schimmelhagen and poured himself some. By now he was pretty far gone, but his appetite for the stuff was unabated. Though his speech was slurred he chose his words with the care of a practised drinker.

"His mother and father were shot. So was everyone else in their village. It was a place very close to here. Name of Goronga. Heard of it?"

I stared in astonishment. What was he trying to do? Did he think that I might have guessed at Barboza's real identity? If not, why raise such a dangerous topic at all?

"Heard of the place?" he repeated.

"Yes, of course."

"Then why look so flabbergasted?"

"Because no one was supposed to have survived the massacre."

"No survivors were traced. That's not saying the same thing. Nino survived. He was the son of the headman. After they'd set fire to the huts and lined the people up to be shot, Nino panicked and ran. They got him in the leg but he managed to keep running and reach cover. He spent the night in the bush—they didn't find him in the dark—and then set off northwards. It was the following afternoon when I found him. Here." Emmerich reached out and stabbed at a point on the map. It looked about halfway from the factory area at the centre to the south-eastern perimeter of the estate. "I was out inspecting the cane and found him lying unconscious in a field of stubble. He'd drunk water from the irrigation sprays; that was all that had kept him going until he collapsed. I brought him back here and called in my tame doctor. Told him the boy worked on the estate and had been wounded in a shooting accident. The story went no further. He was given transfusions, injections. There wasn't much that could be done about the knee; the cartilage had been damaged and the joint stiffened up. Somehow he just stayed on. There was nowhere else he could go. He became a house-servant and learned a little Portuguese."

Still shaking my head in amazement, I said, "That's what you had to hide, then. But why?"

"Hide?" His look was wary.

"You refused to give evidence at the United Nations inquiry. If you had you'd have been forced to reveal Nino's existence; he would have had to testify too."

"Pah!" The old man made a sound of disgust. "United Nations—united in greed and dishonesty and empty rhetoric, nothing more. You'll hear better sense spoken at a *macaco* fish market."

"Maybe so, but you must have realized the importance of what Nino could have told them. He's the only one who knows exactly what happened at Goronga, the only witness."

"Apart from those who did the killing." Emmerich's tone was level.

"Were you afraid of something he might tell them?"

"Listen," Emmerich said, impatience edging into his voice. "We're talking about a boy of fifteen—fourteen when it happened. He can't read or write, he's never been more than twenty kilometres from his own village, he's not even heard of the United Nations. He didn't even know enough to think of recourse to the law, do you realize that? I really do wonder how long you've been in Africa, man. These tribal people are fatalists. What happened that night was like an act of God; nothing Nino could say to anybody would change it. Nothing would bring his family back. Besides, I refused on principle to talk to that UN committee. You should have seen them: They came to Beira and sat hearing evidence in an air-conditioned hotel lounge, three complacent little men: a Mexican, a Liberian and a Pole. What did they know about life in the Mozambique bush? They wouldn't have listened to Nino anyway; they came here with their minds made up."

"Poder de opinião," I murmured, remembering Joana's phrase.

"What?"

"World opinion was on their side."

He glared at me. "It's over now. Gone, forgotten. Goronga is a bare patch of earth in the bush. Soon the bush will have taken over."

He sounded as though the thought satisfied him. We had talked all around the subject of Gil without mentioning his name—Emmerich didn't know how much if anything I had guessed, and I could not afford to seem too interested —but the disclosures about Nino were something quite different. They added a puzzling new dimension to Emmerich, and in spite of my caution I wanted to know more.

"If the committee had made up their minds beforehand," I said, "then surely nothing Nino said would have changed them? Or was there just a chance that it might have?"

"I couldn't care either way. I tell you I would have nothing to do with that committee."

"Do you believe they reached the right conclusion?"

Emmerich reddened and banged his glass down on top of the desk, slopping schnapps over the blotter. "Why shouldn't it have been right? Who's been putting ideas into your head?"

The anger seemed unwarranted. "Nobody," I said. "It's just that I've read their report. I was a policeman; I know what evidence is all about. And I know that it wouldn't have been hard to hide evidence from that committee. Particularly since they didn't even trouble to visit Goronga for themselves."

"A waste of time. There's nothing to see."

"What makes you so sure?"

"God damn it!" he roared. "What gives you any right to cross-examine me? Policeman, eh? Well, go and see the damned place for yourself. See what you make of it. See if it changes any of your smart-arsed progressive views."

The suggestion startled me. I said, "Are you serious?"

"Of course. Go and look tomorrow morning. It'll use up some of your time here. It may also stop you asking ridiculous questions. The place is five kilometres from my boundary fence. I knew it well; we used to recruit extra labour there, if there were any specially big crops to be cut. Yes, go and look, Hickey." A drunken gleam came into his eye, as if he were challenging me to a contest which he didn't believe he could lose. "You'll find a scar in the bush and a mass grave, nothing more. The place is as ordinary in death as it was in life—simple, open, communal. It's difficult to hide anything in a community like that, even the circumstances of its own destruction. Life in a bush village is a matter of survival; a village like that thinks in terms of getting by from one crop of maize to the next, never beyond that. When Frelimo came to such a village they would offer a choice: Support us or the Portuguese; you cannot do both. In Goronga they opted for the side that gave them the best hope of survival in the short term. They made their choice and it happened to be wrong, and the price of the mistake was annihilation. Evidence? There's your evidence, Hickey, a village that no longer exists. Yes, go and see. And come back and tell me what you have learned that could have made the slightest difference to the findings of the UN committee."

"Very well," I said blankly. The proposal had been made on a drunken impulse, but I sensed there was more to it than that. My company was a novelty of a sort, and he was playing a game with me. Was there really something out there that he was daring me to discover for myself?

"Good," he said, pleased now with his idea. "I am to drive to that corner of the estate in the morning. I will drop you off at the fence and you can walk—not alone, naturally. A couple of guards will accompany you. The *macacos* around here won't go near the place, but I don't imagine you are superstitious."

Emmerich refilled his glass while I sat staring at the map behind him. Nothing I might learn out there would help me out of my predicament, and there would be no chance of escape, so I was letting myself in for a ten-kilometre walk in the heat for nothing. On the other hand, there would be the opportunity to improve my knowledge of the estate and the surrounding country. And anything would be better than waiting here.

"I'll send Henrique with you," Emmerich said. The idea was now crystallized into a project. "Henrique, yes— he knows the way. One of my best men, one of the first to join me. I started recruiting around the time that was taken, when Frelimo had come south of the Pungwe for the first time."

He made another clumsy gesture and I realized he was talking about the other photograph on the desk, of himself on guard behind the sandbags.

"We installed steel window shutters and barricaded the buildings against rocket attacks. The Portuguese offered me a couple of platoons to guard the estate. I said no, thanks, I'm recruiting my own. Ex-paratroopers, seasoned fighters—all I wanted was the weapons to arm them. The local military governor was a friend of mine; he gave me six light machine-guns, forty G-threes and a hundred thousand rounds of ammo, and when the Portuguese pulled out they quietly forgot to reclaim the stuff. I wasn't going to be left helpless. I challenged Frelimo to attack me."

"But they never took up the challenge."

"Oh, but they did. Of course they never talk about it. It happened just once, two nights before the Goronga business. A band of them, the same band that went on to Goronga afterwards, crept up through the ripe cane and cut the inner fence. My paras shot two and the Dobermans killed another one. The rest ran in a panic. Nothing scares a man more than a dog trained to attack. You can't frighten it off, you can only kill it—if you get the chance. They never came back."

"I see." This debacle had been absent from Raoul Sousa's account to the UN committee of the events that had led up to Goronga. Understandable, perhaps; he was a vain man who would resent such a failure deeply. But it was one more piece of evasiveness in the background to the incident, a background that had begun to look distinctly murky.

"The *macaco* who led that raid," Emmerich said, as if he'd been reading my thoughts again, "was a man named Sousa. He is now the governor of Beira district. It was the only time he ever picked on someone who could hit back, and he has not forgotten it. He would avenge himself if he had the chance. He would like to expropriate my property; he'd use any excuse he found to move in here and take over. *Any* excuse." The old man watched me through watery eyes, then muttered, "We shall see who wins in the end. If it comes to a fight then I will fight. We're ready for a siege here, and my paratroopers will stand by me. They all have their own reasons for hating Frelimo. Well." He finished his drink and stood up. "I'm an early riser. You won't see me at breakfast. Be ready to move at eight. Nino will wake you in good time."

Emmerich stamped out of the room. Nino appeared silently in the doorway, carrying my bag, and led me past the guarded room where Akimo lay, all the way down the long U-shaped passage to a door near the end of the south wing. He opened it and stood by as I entered. I said softly in Portuguese, "You come from Goronga, I hear."

He did not reply.

I said, "The senhor told me how you came to be here. You must have seen the man who commanded the Flechas. The one who gave the order to kill."

Nino said nothing but stood watching me with still brown eyes and a face empty of expression. It was a look I had often seen, the impenetrable gaze of Africa. Whether he understood or not was impossible to say, and no amount of questioning would help. I dismissed him with a nod; he shut the door and I listened to the soft uneven squeak of his tennis shoes as he limped away along the stone floor. It was still difficult for me to grasp the paradox of Emmerich's having given refuge to both Nino and Gil, one a victim of the Goronga incident, the other the perpetrator of it. Stranger things had happened, I supposed. Could there be secret guilt as well as prejudice there?

I'd been perplexed to learn of the hostility between Emmerich and Sousa. It made me wonder about Sousa's motives, and whether it was entirely coincidental that the trail I had been forced to follow had led here. Sousa could not, surely, have suspected Emmerich of harbouring the killer, at least, not until two days ago, because until then it had been assumed that Gil had escaped with the rest of the missing DGS men to Brazil. On the other hand, it would be highly convenient for Sousa if he could implicate the old man in the Terno Branco conspiracy. It would give him that one excuse he needed to arrest him—which, in effect, would probably mean entering the Açúcar Emmerich estate by force and taking it over on behalf of the People's Republic.

The guest suite was comfortably anonymous, a bedroom

and sitting-room, pine-panelled, with a bathroom between them, air-conditioning units and windows that looked out through the ornamental burglar-proofing towards the black sea of sugar-cane. As I unpacked my bag and undressed I considered my position carefully.

When Gil tried to leave on that two-thirty plane tomorrow he would be picked up, because once he came into the open under the Barboza identity he was finished. And so was I. I could of course still come clean with Emmerich and tell him why I was really here, but in Sousa's eyes that would look like defection, with the injury to Akimo and the death of his driver to explain on top of it. No. The only way I could save myself was to escape—and, what was more, to time the escape so that it would not be too late to prevent Gil's being captured. Just how the hell was I to accomplish that?

I wondered whether Gil might have been living here, in this house, but dismissed the idea at once. There'd be far too much risk of curiosity and gossip from servants. Somewhere in the factory area, then? The same problem arose with workmen and guards. The more I thought about the twenty-four square miles of cane that surrounded us, the more I was convinced that the ideal hiding place would be somewhere out there or in the adjacent bush. Assuming Gil was out there now, he would presumably be given the papers tomorrow morning and then driven directly to the airport or to somewhere in Beira to prepare for his departure.

I had a shower, and when I came out of the bathroom the house seemed very quiet. I pulled on my bathrobe, went to the sitting-room door and tried the knob. It wouldn't turn. I crouched and examined it; it was one of the kind that can normally be locked from the inside by a button set in the centre. Instead of a button, a keyhole faced me—a keyhole for which I had no key. The lock had been reversed; Nino had twisted the button after closing the door on me. This was the only exit from the suite.

Emmerich obviously wasn't relying only on the deterrent value of dogs and armed guards. I had the freedom of the property, he'd said, but that didn't include the freedom to snoop about the house. I went across to the open window and tested the strength of the wrought-iron burglar bars. Ornamental, perhaps, but they wouldn't budge. As I closed the window a lean dark shape came hurtling across the lighted courtyard and flung itself at the wall just beneath me, barking and snapping furiously. I turned on the air-conditioning to drown the noise and went to bed.

I slept patchily, full of nameless misgivings about what the next day would bring. Sometime during the night, while I was lying awake, I heard a disturbance in the corridor. Nino's squeaky footsteps were followed by the tramp of boots. I got out of bed and went quietly to the door and listened. Emmerich had been wakened; there was a murmured conversation between him and one of the guards. I picked up enough of what was said to know that Akimo had died.

Emmerich had let him die, coldly, deliberately. The stakes were too high, he'd said. If there'd been any slight doubt left in my mind that he was prepared to kill me as well, it was gone. If ever I needed those instincts which had kept me alive more than once in the bush in Kenya, it was now.

PART FIVE
Saturday, November 22

1

Nino knocked on the outer door to call me for breakfast at seven o'clock. Presumably he released the locking button at the same time, for the door opened when I tried the knob. Trusting that Emmerich in the sober light of day hadn't changed his mind about the Goronga trip, I chose from among my few clothes those most suitable for walking: lightweight denim trousers that fitted well enough not to chafe, a short-sleeved voile shirt, a cotton T-shirt to absorb sweat, rough suede ankle-boots with crepe soles. When I'd left the suite and walked into the central section of the house I glanced down the corridor that led into the north wing. There was still a guard outside Akimo's door, which meant they hadn't yet got rid of the body. It was tough about Akimo; there hadn't been much liking between us but it was a miserable way to die.

The table in the dining alcove was set for one, and a maid in a starched white apron was in attendance. Breakfast on an African farm is the most important meal of the day, and this one came with German variations: half a pawpaw, bratwurst, rump steak, fried eggs, pumpernickel, hot rolls and strong coffee. I hadn't much appetite but I forced myself to eat, uncertain of when I would get my next meal, and stared out between the casuarina trees towards the mill and the refinery that formed the nucleus of the estate. The African labourers had been at work since dawn. Sugar-cane under irrigation was a year-round crop, planted, watered, and then cut at the moment when it would yield the optimum quantity of liquid sucrose. The trick was to stagger the crops so as to ensure a constant supply to the mill. Workers not employed to cut or process cane were mostly busy quenching its enormous thirst, maintaining the machinery that ran the irrigation system and the generators that ran the machinery. The estate by daylight was an impressive sight: As far as I could see across the canefields, brilliant green in the morning sun, great arcs of water drawn from the Pungwe River ten or fifteen miles away were being flung from whirling sprinklers that stood at intervals of a couple of hundred feet.

At two minutes to eight there was an impatient hooting outside the front door. I finished my coffee and went out. At the foot of the steps Emmerich sat behind the wheel of the white Mini-Moke, a kind of imitation jeep with open sides and a canopy that was now folded back. Henrique and another uniformed guard sat in the back, and there was a bulging army kitbag and a plastic jerrycan full of water on the floor behind the front seat. I went down the steps and hopped in beside Emmerich, who thrust a bush hat with a floppy brim into my hands.

"You'll need that," he said.

Without another word he slammed into gear and accelerated across the gravel.

The factory area hummed with quiet efficiency as we

drove through it. The loudest noise came from the huge corrugated-iron building where slow-moving milling machinery cut up and crushed the cane. Where the railway lines crossed the road we had to stop and let one of the toy trains rumble across to the front of the mill, its high trucks piled with freshly cut cane. When we moved on and got a view towards the other end of the building, I noticed how close it stood to the western perimeter fence. Five or six Mercedes diesel trucks formed a queue alongside the fence facing the rear of the mill. Worth remembering.

"What are they doing?" I asked Emmerich.

"Collecting trash. That's what is left of the cane when it is crushed. An efficient mill extracts ninety-nine per cent of the sucrose. What's left is dry enough to burn as fuel. I sell it by the truckload to a brickworks near Beira."

A sickly sweet smell wafted across from the refinery. Two Indian clerks who'd been gossiping on the veranda of the office building withdrew hastily, like mice into their holes, to separate doorways at the approach of the Moke. The man on the gates hastily swung them open and saluted as we passed through. Emmerich enjoyed his power, and I understood his reluctance to give it up.

We raced on towards the junction with the Nova Lusitania road. Half a mile short of it there was a gap in the fence where Emmerich turned left onto a bumpy track that ran straight across a canefield. It was like a corridor between the massed stalks that towered six feet above the small car, one of a grid of driveways intersecting at intervals of about two hundred yards. When these fields were ready for harvesting, the driveways would make them accessible to tractors and cutters; now, deserted but for us, they were simply confusing.

We made innumerable turns, and my sense of direction went completely. Occasionally we would cross more railway tracks. At other intervals we passed small boards staked into the ground with numbers stencilled on them, which Emmerich used to find his way about. No landmarks were visible above the cane. Presumably the numbers corresponded to grid references on a map of the estate that he carried in his head. Once in a while he stopped, groped under his seat for an eighteen-inch panga that was kept there, got out of the car and examined a few stalks of cane carefully. He would hack a stalk off a foot or two from the ground and suck the cut end to test the concentration of sucrose. Then he would grunt, whether with satisfaction or not I could not tell, and climb back behind the wheel. He was not in the least talkative this morning, but showed no after-effects from the vast quantity of schnapps he had drunk. Nor did he so much as mention Akimo.

Every minute or so as we drove we would be hit by a spray of water from one of the tall sprinklers. Even when we pulled up the canopy it got to us through the open sides of the Moke and we were soon soaking wet. The day was growing hotter, though, and the dousings weren't really unwelcome.

I'd been wondering about the kitbag and the can full of water, and suddenly they made very simple sense. Emmerich was on his way to Gil's billet. Somebody had to keep the fugitive supplied with provisions, and the least obvious and safest way was for Emmerich to stop in while conducting his regular inspection tours of the estate. That way only he needed to know the whereabouts of the place. This morning he would call in as usual after dropping me at the fence, I thought, and would then move Gil to some other rendezvous, probably with Filipe. The Nova Lusitania road was only a few miles west of here. Gil would be installed in some safe place in Beira—perhaps the "second billet" that had been set aside for him—until the time came for him to go to the airport. Sometime between one thirty and two o'clock I would have to make my move and hope that all this guesswork was right.

It took about an hour of zigzagging through the cane before we broke out into open country again. To judge by the position of the sun we were roughly south of the house and the factory areas; I couldn't have hazarded a guess as to how far, and Emmerich offered no information. The track on which we emerged twisted for about half a mile over uncultivated land until a barbed-wire fence appeared. This was the boundary of the property. Emmerich kept to the track, which turned to run parallel to the fence, for a couple of hundred yards before stopping. In front of us was a footpath that approached from the north, went under the fence and meandered off into the bush on the other side.

"The way to Goronga," Emmerich said, and glanced at his watch. "It's ten kilometres there and back, a comfortable three-hour walk. The guards go with you."

I glanced round at Henrique, who gave me a grin. He picked up his machine carbine from the floor, and he and the other man climbed out after me.

"I will collect you at twelve thirty," Emmerich said. "Be sure you are back in time."

He drove off in a froth of pale brown dust, and the guards and I climbed the fence. It was only head high, designed to keep cattle and game out of the canefields, and we got over it without difficulty. In a minute we were picking our way through the bush along the thinly marked path, avoiding huge thorns that could rip clothing and draw blood at a touch. Henrique kept a few yards ahead of me, whistling tunelessly and slapping at the thorn bushes with a stick. The other guard walked behind. Even if there had been any point in escaping at this stage, I knew that

I couldn't possibly get away with it. Besides, I had too little idea of the geography of the surrounding country and too much respect for the capacity of the bush to confuse. My only point of reference was Goronga, and all I knew about the site was that it was several miles east of the Nova Lusitania road. In that much bush you could walk in circles till you fell from exhaustion; you could die of thirst fifty yards from water without knowing it was there.

Heat was building up. The sparse foliage of the thorn trees offered little protection from the sun and I was soon sweating, though the going wasn't difficult. The land was perfectly flat, with just here and there a little knoll, rock-strewn and thickly overgrown, rising above the tree-tops. The exercise had begun to seem a little pointless. I'd established what I wanted to know, which was the layout of the factory area and the canefields in its vicinity, and I'd worked out that there was only one place where there was any possibility of getting over the inner perimeter fence in a hurry. I would be better off conserving my energy. The challenge implied in Emmerich's offer to send me here now appeared unreal, a product of my own imagination. But I had agreed to come, so I would have to trudge on.

After three kilometres or so we stopped for a rest and I said to Henrique, "You've been here before? To Goronga?"

"Sure. There's fuck-all to see, chief."

"When the village was there, I mean. When the people were alive."

"Yes." He grinned. I waited and he expanded reluctantly. "When there are big cane crops to be cut we go out recruiting extra *macacos* from the villages around here. Recruiting—well, they take some persuading sometimes, know what I mean?" He laughed and slapped the stock of the carbine. "Lazy fuckers don't want to work even when they're starving; that's a *macaco* for you. Goronga wasn't bad, though. We'd usually get some who would come willingly from there."

"They'd work for Emmerich, even though they supported Frelimo?"

"Them? They didn't give a fuck for Frelimo. Let's keep moving, chief."

I continued along the path, talking to his back. "They were supposed to have helped the guerrillas. The band that attacked the convoy that night before the massacre, the same band that tried to attack Emmerich's place."

"Maybe so," Henrique said indifferently.

"But you don't think so?" I persisted.

"Listen, in a village like that the *regulo*, the headman, makes all the big decisions. Well, this village had an old-fashioned *regulo*, the kind who respected white men. I don't see what way he'd have helped Frelimo."

"The United Nations report said they were Frelimo supporters."

"What the fuck would the United Nations know?" Henrique hawked and spat. "By the time they came out here Frelimo was on top. Find me a *macaco* today who won't tell you he's been a Frelimo supporter all his life."

"If they weren't for Frelimo, why were they killed?"

"Who knows? Could have been a mistake."

"A mistake that cost fifty lives?"

"It happens."

He wouldn't be drawn further. We made good time and reached the site an hour and a quarter after setting off from the fence. The path went round the foot of another overgrown mound, slightly larger than the rest, through a cluster of malala palms, their dead fronds rattling in the breeze, and a grove of mango trees. Then the clearing opened in front of us, a patch of brown earth sloping slightly away from the hillock, towards where the cattle kraal and the few acres of flat arable land that had kept the village alive had lain. In a gully running across the centre of the clearing was a stream, reduced at this time of year to a trickle. The footpath entered on the north side, passed across the site and left on the south. Although the ground was baked and cracked, hardy savanna grass was already well established and it was easy to see that after a few more rainy seasons the thorn forest would be well on the way to covering the site. Goronga had never appeared on any map, not even the ordnance survey, and soon even its physical presence would be erased.

"Is this all?" I asked.

Henrique gave me a told-you-so look. "Across the stream is where the huts were."

We went up the slope and stepped over the stream. On the ground here were circular black blotches ten or twelve feet across, reminding me of patches of scorched earth where campfires have been. A few charred pieces of wood lay scattered about, but the huts had been mostly of bamboo and thatch and had burned like paper.

Henrique had brought an army water-bottle which he unslung from his web belt. He gave me a sip and took some himself, and then the two guards went and sat in the shade of a wild fig tree at the edge of the clearing, watching me idly. Across the stream, among the stalks of a few dry reeds hung with intricately woven nests, brightly plumed weaver birds squabbled excitedly.

"Where are the bodies buried?" I asked.

"Down beyond the kraal."

A metal bowl, rusted and holed, lay in what had been the open space at the centre of the village. It was here that the shooting had taken place. When I walked down the slope to the large black rectangle where the cattle pen had stood I discovered a cowhorn and several pieces of bleached bone scattered among the tufts of new grass. The cattle had not been buried but left for the undertakers of the bush to dispose of—vultures, jackals, perhaps hyenas.

The mass grave looked remarkably small, a rectangle perhaps twenty feet by ten, distinguished from the surrounding earth only by the darker brown of the subsoil that had been thrown on top; it rose in the centre to form a low mound on which savanna grass had already gained a foothold. I remembered the evidence of the priest at the inquiry: there had been no time for finesse. When the bodies were discovered they were already decomposing. Little attempt was made at individual identification. A hole was dug and when it was just big enough they were thrown into it. Probably it was the priest who had subsequently erected the cross; it stood about three feet high and was made of two lengths of blackwood dovetailed and nailed together. One side of the upright had been planed flat and bore a crudely cut inscription: GORONGA and the date of the atrocity. There were no names.

I walked back to the clearing past the shamba, the communal vegetable garden of the village. Pumpkins and squash had run wild, and my eye was caught by a dull brassy glint among the anarchic growth of stalks and leaves. I bent down and picked up a cartridge case.

It was a rifle shell which had once held a bullet of military calibre. The opening was choked with soil. I parted the leaves to look for more but saw none. Then I realized how unnaturally discoloured the metal was, as if it had been immersed in a gentle corrosive. I got down on my knees and scrabbled in the soil around the pumpkin roots, and almost at once found two more cases. A little deeper there were another three. They had been buried; a new growth of stalks had pushed the first one to the surface.

Acidity in the soil would account for the bluish discoloration. I went to work systematically, uprooting one whole plant and digging out the soft soil all around it to a depth of about a foot. In five minutes I had discovered between sixty and seventy cartridge cases. I had no doubt now that they had been deliberately buried here. By the priest too? Hardly likely. He hadn't mentioned finding any shells. The killers must have picked up every single one and buried them in the shamba. Why? Was it a clumsy attempt at a cover-up?

I studied the cartridge cases more closely. They were all rimless centre-fire high-velocity shells from automatic rifles. The calibre would probably be 7.62 mm, a bore common to several types of military weapon, although the breeches varied in size and shape from one type to another. To an untrained eye, the indentations of the firing pins in the centre of the primer caps all looked identical; a good ballistics man would have been able to list the number and type of weapons used and the number of shots that each had fired. Once again I was irritated at the negligent way inquiries into the massacre had been conducted. Nobody had even stopped to ask what had become of the spent shells. Could this be what Emmerich had known about and had been teasing me to find? It seemed barely possible; it was by sheer chance that I had come upon the things, and reasoning didn't enter into it. . . .

A short burst of shots boomed across the clearing and I jumped to my feet with a start. The bush came alive with alarmed birdcalls. Henrique still sat with the other guard under the fig tree; he was lowering his carbine and grinning at me. Across by the stream a shower of yellow feathers floated to the ground from the shattered nest of a weaver bird among the reeds. Henrique was getting bored.

I slipped two of the cartridge cases into my trouser

pocket. With my foot I shoved the rest back into the hole I had dug and kicked some soil over them. Then I walked up to Henrique.

"Next time give me some warning."

"Scare you? Sorry, chief." He grinned unrepentantly. "Noisy little bastards were getting on my nerves."

I gauged the distance from the fig tree to the reeds. A weaver bird's nest is about the size of a tennis ball; to hit one swaying on a reed thirty yards away with an inaccurate weapon like a 9-mm carbine is an impressive, not to say frightening, achievement

"We may as well go," I said.

"There's time in hand, chief. If we leave now we can stroll."

2

We crossed the stream and set off back along the footpath. The heat was intense. There was still no sign of rain, and each day the air became drier, its arid heat catching at the back of your throat as you inhaled. The bush was scorched yellow-brown. Henrique was behind me now, the other guard in front. We set a slower pace than we had on the way in.

When we'd been going a few minutes I said, "What weapons did the Flechas carry?"

"G-threes, chief. Standard rifle for all Portuguese forces."

"What calibre?"

"Seven-six-two."

"Standard NATO cartridge?"

"That's right. They're German guns, made under licence in Portugal."

"The same as the ones you use to guard Emmerich's property? The ones he got from the army?"

"Sure." Henrique's sluggish curiosity was aroused. "Why do you ask?"

"I just wondered."

"Find something interesting among the pumpkins, chief?"

"Just a cowhorn," I lied. "Dragged there by the jackals, probably."

In a nervous moment I had started walking faster. I slowed down deliberately. Henrique ambled behind, swiping with his stick at the undergrowth. When we were about halfway back to the fence we stopped for another sip of water.

Henrique's long but watchful silences disturbed me. I said, "What made you leave the army?"

"The army did." He corked the water-bottle. "Dishonourable discharge. I was court-martialled for shooting a *macaco* private."

"I see."

"Fucker wouldn't go into an attack. I was a platoon sergeant in a front-line unit up in Cabo Delgado province. We had a Frelimo band surrounded on a hillside; we were ready to move in on them. That's the only way to fight guerrillas: on the ground, on their own terms. Well, this bastard wouldn't go in after them. He broke and ran. I got him behind the ear—not bad for a moving target at forty metres. And then they court-martialled me for it. They'd turned soft; at one time they'd have congratulated me." Henrique spat on the ground, his spittle rolling past me in a little dust-ball along the path. "No wonder they'd started to lose ground to Frelimo. Their morale had gone. A white man with the right training and the right spirit is still a match for three *macacos*. Look at that mob that tried to attack Emmerich's place. They didn't know what had hit them. They ran—out through the cane, into the bush—and they didn't stop running till the next evening."

"How would you know that?"

"I knew it as well as they did. We were chasing them."

I wasn't sure that I had heard right. "You? The guards from Emmerich's place? You went into the bush after Sousa's band?"

"Sure." He gave me a grin and then watched me for a few seconds, wondering how much he should say. In the end the temptation to boast was too strong. "It can't matter who knows now. It was like this. They attacked on the Monday night and we chased their black arses right off the property. Emmerich should have called in the military right away and left the rest to them—that was the rule—but we asked him to let us have a go at them. To flex our muscles, huh? We were soldiers too; we'd had a little action and we wanted more. We wanted those *macacos* all to ourselves. He said OK and we went, about fifteen of us. We followed them for the rest of that night and the whole of the following day, and they just went on running. They didn't even have the guts to set an ambush for us."

"You followed . . . how? With the dogs?"

"Those dogs aren't trained for tracking. No, we did it like the Flechas did, only we had no helicopters. The only way to travel through this bush is on the footpaths, and all the footpaths lead to villages. It was a matter of following them from one village to the next, asking questions after they'd passed through: Which way had they gone, how long ago? And making sure, of course, that the *macacos* told us the truth."

Henrique paused. I said nothing.

"Well, they kept just far enough ahead to avoid contact with us, and at nightfall on the Tuesday we had to give up and go home. We weren't equipped or rationed for a long march. That night the military convoy was ambushed and everything became official. The Flechas were brought in. We did what we could to help them. We set out again on the Wednesday morning and called at a few more villages—"

A question loomed in my mind and I had blurted it out before I could stop myself. "Not Goronga?"

Henrique grinned again and shook his head. "Not Goronga. Definitely not. Let's go, chief."

I led the way along the path, puzzled and alarmed. Here was more evidence that had never come to light. On the day of the massacre there had been not one but two armed groups out hunting the guerrillas: the Flechas and Emmerich's mercenaries, all men of the same ruthless and determined calibre, and all equipped with the same kind of weapon. It proved nothing, but the implications were frightening. Emmerich must have had a good reason for keeping quiet about the involvement of his men. Had they been to Goronga, in spite of Henrique's denial? Put bluntly, could they have been implicated in the atrocity?

By asking more questions I might be stepping on dangerous ground, but I was driven by a compulsion to know. I called across my shoulder, "You helped the Flechas, you say. Did they want your help? Or need it?"

"Unofficial co-operation. It went on all the time. First thing in the morning they called in at the estate. Dumped that big chopper right down on Emmerich's driveway. They needed directions, local advice on where to start looking. We told them they'd be best heading due south while we covered as much of the country as we could on foot south-east of the estate. We met up again towards dusk, when they looked in on their way back to base."

So Emmerich must actually have seen Gil that day,

both before and after the killings had happened: another good reason for his reluctance to appear at the UN inquiry. But something seemed out of place in Henrique's chronology.

"You say the Flechas were returning to their base before dark?"

"Right."

"But the shootings happened at night, didn't they?"

"Who says so?"

"I'm not sure, come to think of it. It was just an impression."

"Couldn't be. It was nearly midwinter. It gets dark around six or just a little after, and it must have been all of ten to six before they landed on the estate. I saw them arrive; we were just in ourselves. They spent a few minutes there and left just as night was falling."

"They could have gone back to Goronga at that stage, couldn't they?"

"Listen," said Henrique indulgently, "they were in a Super Frelon helicopter, one of those big bastards with twin rotors, carries anything up to twenty men at a time. You try putting one of those big fuckers down in bush like this in the dark, with no ground lighting; it's impossible. That's why they had to cut short the search in the first place. I saw them leave, anyway; they were heading north-north-east, back towards Beira. They'd been at Goronga sometime in the afternoon, that's for sure."

We plodded on along the narrow path. Why did there seem to be two versions of every story about the massacre? Someone said the villagers of Goronga had been supporters of Frelimo; someone else said they hadn't been. Henrique said Gil and the Flechas were out of the area before nightfall, while I'd had the notion that the killings had taken place after dark. Typically enough, the UN committee had not attempted to establish the exact time of the incident.

Then I remembered where that impression had come from: Emmerich. He had told me that after the houseboy, Nino, had run from the scene, the killers had been unable to find him in the dark. Which meant that even if the shooting itself had happened in daylight, the men had stayed in the area of the village until after nightfall.

Emmerich might have good reasons for trying to mislead me. So might Henrique. I shouldn't be letting these discrepancies bother me—I had enough problems of my own—but I couldn't help it. I also couldn't help wondering why anyone who showed the callous disregard of opinion that it took to slaughter fifty people should go to the trouble of picking up and hiding every one of the cartridge cases.

There were two people who knew for certain the answers to this and other questions about Goronga: Gil and Nino. Both of them, by some curious coincidence, were now virtual dependants of Emmerich.

We reached the boundary fence and climbed it with twenty minutes to spare before the German drove up in the Mini-Moke. He came from the direction in which he'd gone when he dropped us, to the west and parallel to the fence. We rose from where we'd been sitting in the shade of an acacia. Once again I climbed into the front passenger seat, and as the two guards got in at the back I noticed that the kitbag was gone and the jerrycan was empty. With a slightly panicky sense of triumph I knew I'd been right. Gil was—had been until this morning—in a hideout in this vicinity. By now he must be well on his way into Beira. The time was twelve thirty. The next hour would be crucial, for me as well as for him. Things would have to be arranged so that at just about the time Gil was checking in for the Lisbon flight—one thirty, say—I could cross the wire on the west side of the sugar mill and run for it. Emmerich was bound to have someone at the airport making sure Gil departed safely, so news of the arrest would get back to him pretty quickly. Of one thing I had to be sure: that I wasn't around when that happened.

"Did you learn anything?" Emmerich inquired, as we set off towards the canefields.

I had thought some more about the cartridge cases and decided not to mention them. I said, "Only by talking to Henrique."

The German twisted his head to give us both a swift look. "Talking about what?"

"About the day of the massacre. About how the Flechas made two calls at your place. That was bringing it close to home, wasn't it? It could have been an embarrassing piece of evidence if it had come up at the UN inquiry."

He bumped the Moke with controlled savagery into one of the cross-cuts that led through the canefields. "There was nothing embarrassing about it. I knew the local military well. Farmers co-operated with them against the common enemy."

"But not usually to the extent of sending their own hired gunmen out after guerrillas. Henrique told me that as well. If it had got around after the massacre it could have been more than embarrassing, couldn't it? It might have been damned dangerous. Someone might have had the fanciful idea that your men could have had a hand in the killing. Or even have done it themselves."

"That is nonsense," Emmerich said with a studied calm, starting straight ahead.

"Fanciful, as I say. But you still can't afford to have it known. To quote Henrique, every *macaco* is a Frelimo supporter these days."

"I have done nothing of which I need be ashamed. Nothing," he repeated, giving me an emphatic sidelong glance. "I am not a racialist, Hickey. I give a man his due. I fought Frelimo not because they were black, but because they threatened my life and property. And I oppose them now because sooner or later they will threaten my livelihood."

The route by which he drove back was no less confusing but much quicker. At a few minutes to one he stopped at the foot of the steps leading to the front door of the house. I got out of the Moke expecting him to accompany me, but he and the two guards remained in their seats.

"Nino will give you a drink if you want one," Emmerich said. "I have to meet a visitor. I will be back shortly."

He drove back down towards the factory area. I ascended the steps and entered the breath-catching cool of air-conditioning. From some distant quarter came the clattering of dishes and the voices of servants preparing lunch, but this part of the house seemed deserted. This was a piece of unexpected luck. Thirty minutes now before Gil would be picked up at the airport; it was too early for me to make my move, but I could put the occasion to good use. I walked to the right, into the north wing. The guard was still on duty outside Akimo's door. Why the hell hadn't they dumped the body yet? I nodded to the man familiarly, taking a chance that he had no idea who I was, and carried straight on to Emmerich's study door. It was open. I entered quickly and went straight behind the desk to examine the map of the estate.

The scale was large, perhaps as much as six inches to the mile, so each of the hundreds of small square canefields was individually marked. The grid numbers that Emmerich had used to find his way around them were absent, but they would have been no great help to me anyway. The property was roughly trapezium-shaped, with the shorter of the two parallel boundaries on the western side. The Nova

Lusitania road ran beside the boundary fence for some way, as I had seen last night, but then made a wide loop off the map to the west, reappearing within a couple of miles of the south-western perimeter. Now I could put this morning's trip into perspective. The factory area and the house were in the centre of the trapezium. I couldn't be sure at which point we had crossed the southern boundary fence to reach Goronga—which was not shown—but wherever it was we could not have travelled more than four miles in a straight line to get there.

The scale of the map was also big enough to show the factory area in some detail. As I had guessed, the mill was the building closest to any of the inner perimeter fences, no more than forty yards at its western end. The fence was about ten feet high; the road along which the high Mercedes trucks queued to reach the loading bay ran right beside it. Within the next half hour I would have to find a way of getting down there. Luckily, it seemed that the truck-drivers did not take a siesta; they had still been lining up beside the fence as we had driven past the mill on our way to the house.

I had learned all that I usefully could have about the layout of the estate. I was about to leave when I saw a couple of sheets of paper, stapled together, lying on the desk blotter. I remembered seeing them fall from Emmerich's safe the night before when he had taken out the file to show me. With his wits fogged by schnapps he had obviously forgotten to replace them, and the servant who'd tidied the room this morning must have put them on the desk.

I don't know what it was that made me pick up the papers, but when I saw the printed letterhead on the top sheet, GOVERNADOR DISTRITAL DE BEIRA, I had to read on. There were three sheets in all, the punch-holes in their left-hand margins suggesting that they'd been removed from a file in the company office and brought here for safe-keeping. They were letters, three separate letters, an exchange of correspondence between Raoul Sousa, in his official capacity as District Governor of Beira, and Emmerich. My knowledge of Portuguese was just good enough to permit me to follow.

Two of the letters were from Sousa. They were carelessly typed and their tone was cool and impersonal. The usual cordial greeting, *Amigo e Senhor,* was absent. Instead there was simply a heading: *Programa Agrícola Revolucionária.* The first letter gave notice that the district revolutionary council under the chairmanship of the Governor had decided to expropriate Açúcar Emmerich. Emmerich was required to acknowledge the letter and accept the instruments of expropriation within a month. Compensation would be paid in due course at the value assessed by a specially appointed valuation board.

Apparently Emmerich had not replied. The next letter from Sousa, dated August 15 of that year, noted this and gave what it described as a final warning. Unless the estate was surrendered peacefully within seven days, it would be taken by force.

This time there had been a reply, a single typed paragraph dated August 18, the carbon copy of which was stapled behind Sousa's two letters. Emmerich had not referred directly to the threat of expropriation. He'd merely stated that he would be visiting Beira on Wednesday the twentieth and would call at the Governor's office to discuss matters of mutual concern.

There the correspondence ended, as abruptly as it had begun. A final warning, three months old? Raoul Sousa, in spite of his revolutionary jargonizing, was a man who meant exactly what he said, and yet here was Emmerich still firmly in control of his land. What could have happened at that meeting on August 20 to change Sousa's mind? What influence could Emmerich have exerted—a man who was not only a sworn opponent of Frelimo's policies but who had attracted Sousa's personal hostility as well? And could the answers to these questions have any bearing on the events of that day nearly eighteen months ago, when three separate groups of armed men had been at large in the bush near Goronga?

The letters gave no clue. And there was no time to think about them now anyway. I glanced at my watch. Ten past one, twenty minutes to go. I replaced the papers on the desk and turned to leave the study, my mind seething with questions, and found Nino standing just inside the doorway.

He watched me with the same opaque stare I had seen the night before. I had no idea how long he had been there.

"Come here," I said in Portuguese. Once again he did not reply, but this time I was determined to get one question answered.

"Come here. I think you understand. There's something I need to know."

He turned suddenly to leave the room. I'd been ready for that and I sprang after him, seized his arm and spun him round to face me.

"This time you're going to answer," I said. "You're going to tell me one thing: What time did the shooting at Goronga happen?"

He stared back at me. There was no fear in the look but perhaps just an edge of anxiety. Outside the house a car door slammed and there came the sound of several voices. I had only a few more seconds alone with Nino.

"What time?" I demanded. "Five, six, seven?"

The voices approached the front door. One was a woman's. Emmerich's visitor? It was startlingly, unbelievably familiar. I felt a leap of panic. Nino still said nothing. I seized him by the front of his drill jacket and pushed him against the wall. The back of his head banged into it hard. I watched his expression change to shock.

"I do not know what time," he said. "I had no watch."

"Before dark or after? Just tell me that."

He stared at me numbly. "I do not know."

I shoved my hand into his face and slammed his head against the wall once more. "What do you mean, you don't know? You know the difference between day and night! Tell me!"

"Please. . . ." He cringed as I raised my hand again. "I cannot say. It is the senhor. He told me I must speak to no one about Goronga. No one, ever. If I disobey, the punishment will be very hard."

The front door opened and a group of people, four or five of them, came down the corridor towards us. I didn't look out of the study. They'd find me soon enough if they wanted me. Nino and I stood staring at each other, both bewildered for different reasons. The footsteps halted outside the room where Akimo's body lay and someone went in. In a moment I heard the woman's voice again, a brief remark in Portuguese, harsh in its sudden businesslike tone. Remembering the coincidence of that meeting three days ago, remembering that picture of the young girl on the desk behind me, I knew at last—sinkingly, almost with a sense of anticlimax—that I'd been a bloody fool.

The footsteps rang on the stone floor, approaching the study, directed by a word from the guard who had seen me go in there. The first of the group to come through the door was Filipe. He was holding his small pistol.

"Here!" he called hoarsely. "Here he is! Traitor! Stooge!"

"Quiet," said Emmerich from behind him. The German stood watching me malevolently for a few moments, then stood aside to make way for Joana.

She was wearing slacks, a halter top and a matching headscarf, all in brilliant orange, and she looked cool and composed. She said nothing but gave me that knowing, sardonic smile. Behind her I could see Henrique and another guard slouching in the corridor.

"Judas!" Filipe yelled at me, unable to contain his excitement. "Police spy! I suspected from the start! You were in it with those two last night. Did you think we had no way of finding out?"

I turned back, shocked but still not quite comprehending, to Joana. She stood watching me, still smiling, with her hands on her hips. "You," I said. "You were the way of finding out. You came up here just to identify—"

"Akimo, yes. The policeman who questioned you—and me—after Gomes's death. We needed to be absolutely sure."

So that was why they had kept the body there. My breathing had quickened with fear and my tongue felt thick and dry, but I thought for a moment that I might still talk my way out of this. "Sure of what?" I said. "Akimo was following me. All right. That doesn't prove—"

"It proves," Emmerich snapped, "that you were lying. The gun that was found on the ground beneath him—that was the first thing that alerted us. Mauser. Police issue."

I couldn't find any words now. My only thought was that Akimo had been an idiot to the last.

"That in itself didn't prove the case against you," Emmerich said. "But then you told me last night that you had never seen Akimo before. That was a lie. And there can only have been one reason for it."

"And for the ones you told me," said Joana. "I made some discreet inquiries at the Polana after you left. I learned that there had been no call from Salisbury for you at midnight on Thursday, but that a man fitting Akimo's description had called to see you around eleven. That you weren't seen from the time you went up to your room until you reappeared in the lobby shortly after eleven yesterday morning. And that then you had two men with you who couldn't have been anything but plain-clothes *cipais*. Finally I checked with the South African trade commissioner. You didn't spend the night with him, Joe. You were under arrest, weren't you? All that time while I was trying to phone you, you were with the police. You'd been caught with the papers, and to save your neck you agreed to lead them to Barboza. Otherwise they would never have released you so soon."

"What did all that information cost you?" I asked bitterly. "A night in the hall porter's bed?"

"Shut up!" Emmerich said venomously, but Joana herself didn't rise to the taunt.

"I flew all the way up here," she said, "just to look for one second at the face of that lump of black meat in there. It was important to be certain. Sorry, Joe—it was either you or us."

"Us?" I looked at the two men in turn and then back at her. "Yes, all right, I was a fool. I should have suspected something. The way you managed to appear on the scene right after Filipe had first spoken to me—and to make it seem like a coincidence. The way you put the thought of the fishing shack into my head. And the way you stayed close to me for the next twenty-four hours, watching for giveaways, for signs of contact with the police. You got about as close as you could get, and like all the best whores you even convinced me you were enjoying it."

"Watch your tongue." That was Emmerich again.

"It's the oldest weapon, but still one of the best. Should

I have wondered whether you'd been a member of Ficamos as well?"

"From the beginning. I was in it before Gomes was. I joined for one reason, because I hated the animals who had killed my father. He was a good man, a great man, and they weren't fit to lick his boots—ignorant black brutes, spouting Marx when they could hardly read, talking about progress when they couldn't use a lavatory. I hated them, and I still hate them. I will do anything I can to pay them back."

Her vehemence was almost frightening. I said, "So you threw in your lot with Emmerich, your godfather, the man who took you into his home after your father died. That's right, isn't it? Should I have guessed that as well?"

"I took a chance that you wouldn't." She glanced at the old man and then back at me, defiantly. "I haven't forgotten how good he was to me then—a second father."

"And to him you were like the child he'd never had, no doubt, with memories to share, the old officers' mess *esprit* to keep up, and a common hatred of blacks in general and Frelimo in particular."

"We need no amateur psychologizing from you," Emmerich said. I turned to address him.

"There's one bit of logic I don't follow. You three have been in this from the start, which means you must have known in the first place where Gomes had hidden the Barboza papers. Why force me into finding them for you? You didn't even need me."

"Of course we did. Yes, we knew the documents were in the fishing shack, because Gomes told us. He phoned me in the early hours last Saturday to say he was leaving in a hurry. His background was in danger of being exposed, and the best thing he could do for all our sakes was to get out and take the money he had earned from Ficamos—from me, in effect—for providing twelve faked sets of credentials. He told me he had moved the papers temporarily to his fishing shack, and he advised me to collect them and get Barboza out of the country as soon as possible. How could we know who might not be exposed next? I'd have sent Filipe down the same day if the news of Gomes's death hadn't reached me. I didn't know now whether we dared touch the documents. They might have been discovered by the police and left as bait. We devised a plan to send someone else in for them, someone from outside who knew nothing, who could not incriminate us even if the trap should be sprung. Someone we could keep on a string for a couple of days, and watch, to make sure that the papers were quite clean. You were the perfect choice, Hickey."

I said nothing. There were no questions left.

"We had both a carrot and a stick," Emmerich said. "Joana already knew you and was sure she could use her influence on you. And then there was that file. It was one of a number that the DGS passed secretly to us, their friends in Ficamos, to save burning them and to keep them out of the hands of Frelimo."

"I see," I said dully. There was silence for several seconds as I stood facing the three of them. Then suddenly I looked at my watch.

"Twenty past one," I said. "You're too late. Barboza must be on his way to the airport by now."

"No." Emmerich smiled and shook his head at me. "After what happened last night you don't think we would leave our plans so inflexible, do you? As Joana said, we had to be absolutely sure before we could give the final signal for his departure. At present he is in a safe place in Beira, waiting for a phone call which will tell him whether to leave for the airport or not. That was the plan, surely, to arrest him at the airport? The latest check-in time for his flight is one forty-five. The drive to the airport takes only fifteen minutes, which means that he does not have to leave until one thirty. We have ten minutes in hand. A phone call to make, a taxi call to cancel: it is that simple."

Filipe had been bouncing on his heels. Now he made a nervous move towards the telephone.

"I'll call the hotel now."

"Not from here." Emmerich spoke sharply, with a sidelong glance at me. "Go out to the office."

He faced me again.

"And so you have failed, Hickey. Barboza is as safe as ever, and everything else is as before. The only thing that remains is to deal with you."

3

The little man hurried out of the room. Emmerich stood glaring at me, aware that a cat had been let out of its bag: Filipe's reference to the hotel. Gil must have been taken to the Braga. The second billet, as planned more than eighteen months ago: a risky choice now, I'd have thought, in view of the possibility that the police were still watching the place, but perhaps there'd been no alternative.

"So you would have betrayed us after all, Hickey," the German growled eventually.

"And I would have succeeded, if it wasn't for Akimo. Not that it would have helped me much. As it is, Barboza may still be safe, but he's also still stuck in Mozambique. Or shall we stop pretending now and call him Gil? Antonio Gil, ex-superintendent in the DGS, with the murders of fifty people around his neck." I looked at Joana. "Are you proud of having helped him?"

"It's not a question of pride," she said, shrugging indifferently. "Anything that harms Frelimo pleases me."

"Of course." I couldn't blame Akimo for all the mistakes. I'd made some too, and perhaps the most serious had been to treat Joana as a conveniently enjoyable body, not to wonder whether that deep bitterness of hers had ever found some forceful way of expressing itself. She had found it by clinging to people who felt and thought as she did. Now I could see why she had married Gomes: because, like Emmerich, he had shared and indulged her attitudes. When she'd discovered his impotence it must have made her twice as bitter as before.

"All that stuff you told me about Ficamos and Emmerich," I said. "That was all true. You were taking a chance telling me, weren't you?"

"You needed convincing."

"When I sent Filipe to make the first approach to you," Emmerich explained, "you did something we had not expected. You offered to buy your way out. You offered and were refused payment of twenty thousand rands as an alternative to finding the Barboza papers. . . ."

"Which made Filipe's story about the architect from Vilanculos look pretty absurd," I said. "So you decided to expand on it, right? You let Joana add just enough of the truth to give me something to chew on. Still, you stopped short of mentioning Gil's name. Even a blackmail victim might balk at helping a mass murderer."

"Enough!" Emmerich said. "There are things you do not understand."

"Quite a lot of them," I agreed. I had nothing left to lose now. "I'd like to know, for instance, exactly why you've been sheltering Gil."

He shot me a look. "What?"

"Up to now I've assumed the obvious, that you sympathized. Ficamos and the DGS, an ultra-white brotherhood of supremacist bitter-enders. But now I wonder whether it's that simple. Answer one question for me, Emmerich: How was it possible for the Flechas to be at Goronga after nightfall when they'd left here before dark to return to Beira?"

"Who said they were there at night?"

"You did, actually. You quoted Nino as saying that he'd managed to escape in the dark."

Emmerich glanced at the boy, who had sidled into a corner of the study.

"Yes, he did tell me that," the German said carelessly. "I never thought to question it. He must have got it wrong. He was confused about what had happened. And he's only an ignorant child."

"Not too confused to know night from day. Not so ignorant that you didn't have to warn him never to breathe a word to anyone about what had happened at Goronga. Maybe you should have given the same warning to the rest of your employees. I'm indebted to Henrique for some technical information: A Super Frelon helicopter can't land in the bush in darkness. Which means that if the Flechas carried out the massacre after dark they must have gone to the village on foot, *after* they'd called in here for the second time. Which in turn means they must have been guided. Even in daylight they'd needed local advice; at night they couldn't possibly have found that village without help from people who knew the country. That is, assuming the Flechas went there at all."

I was watching Emmerich's face. It reddened with anger but a sudden wariness crossed it and made him hold his temper in check.

"If there really is a discrepancy in the times," I said, "Gil could have a useful alibi. Is it him that you don't want exposed, or is it the alibi? Is it him you're protecting, or yourself?"

Emmerich spoke quietly. "Ask all the questions you like, Hickey. I do not have to answer them. For good reasons of my own I am committed to helping Gil out of the country. This way has failed; another will be found. We are back where we started—apart from the inconvenience of having you on the premises."

"You're not quite back at the start," I said. "The man who sent me here is your old friend Raoul Sousa. He already knows enough, through what I learned from Joana, to suspect that you're the one who's been harbouring Gil. Getting rid of me and Akimo will solve nothing.'

"Wrong, Hickey." His voice was grimly triumphant. A swing of the gun-turret head brought him face to face with me. "Getting rid of you will give me enough time to find an alternative way out for Gil. As long as Gil is safe, I am safe."

I remembered that exchange of letters I had read. "Safe even from Sousa?" I asked.

"Especially from Sousa."

"You're fooling yourself. You may have some kind of influence over Sousa, but that can only help you postpone what is inevitable. How much longer do you think you can play the *prazeiro*, the bush emperor, the white god?"

"Enough!" Emmerich's eyes were aflame. He looked to the doorway and signalled sharply to Henrique, who stepped into the room. He raised the muzzle of the machine carbine to point it at my stomach and jerked his head towards the door.

"Where are you taking me?" I asked. Only now was fear beginning to settle into me.

"You are no longer welcome here," Emmerich said. "When you cease to be a guest you become a trespasser. And you trespass at your own risk."

"Remember what happened to the last trespassers?" Joana said. "Sousa's gang?" There was a gleam of almost sensual pleasure in her dark eyes and I wondered for a moment, incongruously, whether she was altogether sane, whether any of these people were. Yes, I supposed I had to concede that Joana was, but she was removed from reality just as Sousa was, taking her bearings from nothing outside herself. In their own ways they were both fanatics. And her sensuousness was deceptive; like his rhetoric, it was ultimately directed inwards.

Henrique jerked the carbine to get me moving to the door. I was thinking hard and fast. I took a final look at the faces opposite me—Emmerich's expressionless, Joana's bright with a kind of gloating—and then Henrique nudged me out of the room and down the hall. The guard who'd been with him this morning, now carrying a G-3 rifle at the trail, preceded us to the front door and opened it to a blast of warm air. Emmerich followed us out.

We went down the steps to where the Mini-Moke stood. With a sort of grim solemnity Emmerich directed the guard with the rifle into the front passenger seat and myself and Henrique into the rear. Nobody spoke. The German climbed in behind the wheel, drove across the courtyard and into the factory area.

They were going to kill me. They knew it and I knew it; yet there'd been no time for panic and my thinking remained remarkably, stunningly, clear. They wouldn't do it inside the inner perimeter, I guessed, because there were too many workmen about. The canefields would be the place. A man could be killed and his body disposed of anywhere in an area of twenty-four square miles, and I knew from my trip out there this morning that even an army of searchers would be unlikely ever to find it.

A sudden memory from this morning made me glance down to the floor beneath Emmerich's seat. The handle of the long panga that he used for cutting cane protruded slightly. It was so much an accessory of the car that it had not crossed his mind to remove it. And it was less than two feet from my hand.

I looked away quickly. We were just beyond the mill and halting at a level crossing where a trainload of cane was passing. We were heading for the main gate, a couple of hundred yards further on. The body of Akimo's driver had been dumped in that cane somewhere, and Akimo himself would soon follow. Once I was out there I was as dead as they were. If I was going to act it would have to be now.

While we waited for the train to cross I calculated my move. Henrique had rested his carbine on the seat beside him, though taking care that it was out of my reach. It was essentially a close-range weapon, and although I'd seen how accurate a shot he was I reckoned it would take him a good four seconds to seize the gun, cock it, slip the safety catch and fire. Add a few more seconds for surprise, and provided I could put some cover between me and him in that time, I could be moving out of effective range. The man with the rifle was the more immediate danger. If I could disable them both, so much the better.

As the last of the railway wagons with their high bins piled with cane passed over the crossing, Emmerich eased the Moke forward. I stood up, grabbed the panga two-handed and brought it down with all the force I had on the collar-bone of the guard in front of me.

There was a crunch of bone, a gush of blood. The man gasped. Henrique made an astonished noise and tried to grab my arm. I slashed at his face with the panga but he weaved backwards and the blow missed. Then I toppled out of the moving car.

I landed on my feet, stumbled, regained my balance, dropped the panga and ran, hearing a clamour of yells and the slithering of tyres in the dust as Emmerich braked. I crossed the tiny railway line, lurched to the left and with a few strides got the last of the moving wagons between myself and them. The train was going at about fifteen miles an hour. I slowly overhauled it but knew I wouldn't be able to keep up the pace for long. At the corners of the bins there were handles for manual tipping. I leaped onto the flatbed chassis of the second wagon from the end, seizing a handle as I went, almost losing my balance as the bin swung on its pivot and stalks of cane cascaded down around me. But the driver was still unaware of what had happened. The train picked up speed. Precariously I edged my way round into the gap between the two wagons; if I wasn't inconspicuous I was at least shielded from Henrique's gunsights. It would only be a minute before the rest of the guards were alerted.

It was less than a minute before I heard the hiss of the small locomotive's pneumatic brakes and the train began trundling to a halt at the front of the mill. At almost the same moment the sirens began. Jesus, sirens! I'd forgotten the place was such a fortress. I had ridden about a quarter of a mile. I put my head round the corner and glanced in both directions. Emmerich and Henrique hadn't chased me along the track; sounding the alarm had been their first priority. Ahead, there were only groups of Africans who'd been off-loading cane onto the platform adjoining the mill. As the train slowed I slipped to the ground and made for the south-east corner of the great iron building. As long as I could reach the other end of the mill I was sure I could get across the fence and lose myself in the tall cane beyond.

But I was already too late. As I rounded the corner I saw a guard, alerted by the sirens, running across the grass towards me. He stopped when he saw me, yelled something and raised his rifle. I ducked back just in time to miss the bullet, which knocked a hole through the iron wall at head height. I ran back in the direction I had come from, towards the loading platform; there might still be a chance of reaching the back of the mill from the other side. But now, beyond the steel framework of the conveyor housings, I saw the Mini-Moke approaching. I was cut off in both directions from the only place where it was possible to cross the fence.

I stopped and looked around desperately, the howl of the sirens echoing in my head. There seemed only one other way I could go, across the open lawns to the eastern boundary, three or four hundred yards away: a hopeless prospect; I'd be a moving target for every guard on the estate. Unless I could get inside the mill and somehow through it.

On this side of the building there were no doors, just a row of three openings in the wall about twenty feet up, through which the cut cane was moved on conveyor belts to the crushers inside. There was access to only one of these openings, the one nearest me, by a steel ladder fixed to the wall. I ran to it and went up two rungs at a time, watched with passive incredulity by the black loaders.

I reached the opening and flung myself onto the steel catwalk inside just as the guard came running round the corner and let off another hasty shot. It ricocheted off a steel crossbeam with a scream. I wriggled to the right to get away from the opening and found I had come to a dead end. The catwalk led nowhere. It simply ran the width of the building to give access to the conveyors.

The noise of heavy, slow-moving machinery thundered in my ears, almost drowning the wail of sirens from outside. The whole building vibrated gently to the motion of the crushers and the electric motors that drove them. The only way of getting off the catwalk, short of jumping twenty feet and risking a broken leg, was somehow to climb down the open framework that supported the conveyor belts and rollers.

From outside, I heard Emmerich's voice indistinctly roaring instructions. I also heard the ring of feet on the ladder. I stood up and ran, footfalls echoing, to the other end of the catwalk sixty yards away. Here, in line with the last of the three milling machines, a section of railing had been removed so that maintenance men could get at the rollers and the belt that they carried from beneath the catwalk to a chute at the top of the machine. Beside the chute was a platform connected to a walkway that ran the full length of the building. Without hesitation I sat on the edge of the catwalk and dropped onto the belt.

It was made of rubber with a reinforcing of steel mesh. At the moment it was carrying no cane, presumably because the loaders had been distracted by the chase. Moving slowly upwards, I lay flat and looked back. Henrique had come through the opening at the far end of the catwalk and was running towards me, clutching the carbine. I was sure the belt would take me out of range before he got a chance to shoot. At the top, in the mouth of the chute, was a revolving steel drum with gleaming spiral blades three or four inches long that cut the cane into lengths suitable for the crushers. I'd have to be very sure of getting off the belt onto the platform before I reached that.

I was about halfway up when the whole machine shuddered to a stop. Startled, I looked back and saw that Emmerich was on the catwalk too. He was standing by a box against the wall that contained a row of switches. I realized why he'd done it when I saw Henrique jump onto the belt and come up in a crouch towards me. I scrambled to my feet and did what I could to run.

Riding on the smooth rubber had been one thing. Trying to climb it at an angle of thirty degrees, even in crepe-soled boots, was another. Within a few moments I was reduced to crawling, desperately aware that Henrique was gaining fast. He was younger, fitter, less short of breath, and he wore boots with patterned rubber soles that gave him a better grip. It took me about a minute of slithering and backsliding to reach the top. One yard short of the spiral cutters I stood up precariously, seized the rail of the platform on my right and swung myself under it. I looked back and was horrified to see Henrique only five yards behind me. He hadn't fired in case I fell back on top of him; there was now a drop of eighty feet to the concrete floor.

For two or three seconds I stood paralyzed by indecision. He'd be on the platform himself in a moment, and if I ran down the walkway he'd have a clear line of sight to me for seventy or eighty yards. The pause gave me long enough to notice a big electromagnetic switchbox bolted to the railings of the platform. It had a red button and a green one, but there was no way I could tell whether it would close the circuit that Emmerich had opened.

Henrique didn't wait till he reached the platform. Dithering there, I offered him a stationary target. He stood up on the conveyor belt and levelled the carbine at my head. I punched the green button.

The burst of shots went straight up through the roof as the belt moved beneath him, jerking him off his feet. He dropped the gun and fell on his back, arms flailing, hands clawing for a grip that would stop him sliding off the edge. It would have been better for him if he had. It took the belt only two seconds to carry him to the mouth of the chute. His right foot went under the blades first and the leg was drawn after it by the slow spiral action like a stocking into a mangle. He had time to raise his head and look at me, his face grotesque with horror and disbelief, before he began screaming. I turned and ran. Over the thudding of the mill, the gurgling scream went on for several seconds and then stopped quite suddenly. The whole machine gave a dozen spasmodic shudders as Henrique's body, offering more resistance than even the thickest cane, was hacked into six-inch lengths and fed into the crushers.

I was trembling when I reached the end of the walkway and clattered down a steel staircase to the floor. Here was the rear of the mill, the loading bay where trash was disgorged from the three machines and taken off in truckloads. The fence was forty yards away and the lorries were lining up beside it. African workmen were nudging the trash with shovels down the exit chutes into a central bin, from which it was emptied into the trucks. They stopped work to watch me, curiously but without hostility. The sound of the sirens was considerably muted in here; even if the men had heard the shots and known I was running from the guards they would probably have thought twice about challenging a white man.

I moved quickly along the queue of waiting trucks that curved away from the loading bay. When I reached the first one that was close to the fence I hopped up onto the running board. The black driver blinked at me through his open window. Suddenly there was a shout from the direction of the mill. Two guards had come round from the front of the building, one with a Doberman on a leash. Another para had seen me from further along the fence and was running towards me. I got my left foot on the side of the truck and hoisted myself up onto the roof of the cab. Belatedly the driver reached through the window and grabbed my right leg; I kicked free and jabbed a knee in his face. In a second I was standing on the roof. The barbed wire was a yard away, the top strand of it level with the roof. There was young cane on the other side, growing right up to the fence. I jumped straight into it.

The soft green growth did little to break the fall, and I landed with a bump that jarred through my body, snapping stalks at the root as I rolled on the wet soil. I got up shakily and began to wade through the cane. All sense of direction had vanished in an instant but I was guided by the confused shouting and the barking of the Doberman behind me. My only object for now was to get as far as possible from the fence before Emmerich's men began to search the canefields.

The stalks here were eight or nine feet high, giving ample cover, and the cane hadn't yet acquired a prolific growth of leaves, so it was easy enough to walk through. My main cause for anxiety was that every couple of hundred yards I would have to cross one of the driveways separating the fields. I need only be spotted once to narrow the hunt right down. No field was larger than eight or ten acres, and once it was known which one I was in it would be easy enough to surround it and beat through the cane—or even send the dogs in after me.

I went over the first gap cautiously and continued in what I hoped was a westerly direction, towards the road. Once there I intended to stop the first vehicle that came along, provided it wasn't one of Emmerich's, and go south to the hamlet of Nova Lusitania or, preferably, north to Beira. Either way I had to get to a telephone as soon as possible and report to Raoul Sousa. He wouldn't be happy with what I had to tell him—that Akimo was dead, that the Barboza plan was blown, that Gil was still at large—but he would at least have the excuse he'd been looking for for a confrontation with Emmerich, the confrontation that might have happened three months ago and had been mysteriously postponed.

As for what would happen to Gil—well, now that his escape route had been closed he could hardly be left to stay at the Braga. Probably he would be brought back to the sugar estate while Emmerich searched hurriedly for another way of getting him out.

The shouting of the guards had receded and finally ceased, and I now had less need to worry about whether they had set the dogs after me. They might be killers but they were not trackers, with no keener scent than suburban mongrels. The only sounds around me were the crashing of my own movements through the stalks and the occasional scurrying of huge rats that lived on the cane. Rats, and the snakes which in turn lived on them, were the only life that these fields supported. In the second field I allowed myself to linger for a minute under the cool spray of an irrigation jet, washing away the sweat in which heat, exertion and fear had soaked me.

I crossed two more fields, two more driveways, before encountering the first unforeseen difficulty. In the next two fields the cane had been recently cut. For a quarter of a mile ahead there was nothing but bare soil, yellow stubble and the remains of small bonfires where leaves, tailings and trash had been burnt. To cross all that open space was out of the question. Reluctantly I turned south, moving parallel to the driveway that bordered the bare field, till I came to the next gap. Here I found with dismay that the cane on the next sector was ripe, ready for cutting. The stalks stood twelve to sixteen feet tall and were so thick and dense with dry leaves that without a panga they

227

were practically impenetrable. There was no alternative but to double back and search for another way out.

Visibility was about two yards at the most, and on that flat ground there was no way of seeing any landmarks. But I guessed that I had returned to within a quarter mile of the boundary fence before I found another field of young cane that I could move through. It lay to the south. I had begun to wonder uneasily about the strategy that Emmerich might adopt in trying to find me. He knew every acre of his land and the state of the cane growth on it, which meant that he knew exactly where I could and could not go. It was not inconceivable that he'd be able to plot out the actual route I was forced to take and set an ambush on it. Less confident than I had been, I ploughed on across the field, found another that took me west and another after that which turned me to the south-east. I was zig-zagging like an erratic piece on a huge chessboard.

Luckily, when I heard the voices, I had stopped and was standing still. Otherwise my noisy progress would certainly have been heard too. Fatigue had been creeping up on me; I had taken a stalk of fairly mature cane, broken it into lengths of a foot or so, stripped off the outer husks and chewed at the sweet, fibrous core. It wasn't nourishing but it would supply instant energy. I was about to move on when the sounds drifted across to me. I stood rigid with silence. They came from the nearest driveway, fifty yards or so to my left, the voices of several men approaching from the south, with the timbre and carrying power that is distinctly African. I was reminded that I was not the only man in these fields. There were cane-cutters, drivers of trains and tractors, perhaps women employed to gather leaves and tailings, into whom I was likely to blunder at any moment. The voices came closer and I could hear now that the men were trying to argue with someone in halting Portuguese. Their speech was punctuated with clicks of annoyance.

"Our shift is off," one man kept insisting. "Our shift is off."

"Nobody is off till the *estrangeiro* is found," an authoritative European voice replied. "That's an order from Number One himself."

"It's your work, this," someone else said. "Our job is to cut cane."

"There aren't enough guards available, so we're seconding all you *macacos* to help patrol these driveways. He's forced to come this way, it's his only escape route. There'll be a bonus for the first to spot him. . . ."

The voices trailed away and I released a breath. I would have to be doubly cautious. However, I had at least learned that I was moving in the right direction; sooner or later I had to reach the southern boundary of the estate.

4

I went forward now with much greater care, parting the stalks in front of me instead of crashing through them, watching where I trod, lingering for a minute or two on the edge of each driveway to make sure no one was patrolling it. It soon became obvious that the cane-cutters who'd been pressganged into helping to search for me were showing no great enthusiasm for the job. They wandered aimlessly up and down the driveways, they sat down for rests and smoke-breaks, and above all they talked; high-toned African voices rang at regular intervals across the fields and warned me of their presence. Their negligence itself could be dangerous, though; once I almost stumbled on a man who'd fallen asleep in the middle of a driveway. There was another brief delay when I found a python lying coiled across my path devouring a cane rat. For a minute its bright black button eyes held my gaze before it unravelled its enormous mottled length and slid away.

The strain of taking extra precautions wore away at my stamina. Every so often I broke some more cane and sucked out the juice. Although there was no shortage of water from the irrigation jets, I avoided drinking any and made do with a cooling shower once in a while; water taken on the move in the heat of the day is apt to cause stomach cramps, and most of it goes to waste by way of extra sweat in any case.

For two and a half hours I kept walking, zigzagging at times to avoid open ground but heading generally south by south-west. At four thirty I suddenly broke out of the cane. I had reached the edge of the cultivated land. The sun had lost some of its heat but I had to screw up my eyes against the glare as I stepped from the shade of the green cane. The flat bush country shimmered before me; half a mile ahead would be the boundary fence, though I guessed I was now some miles west of the point where Emmerich had dropped me that morning. Once across the fence I had only to head due west to reach the Nova Lusitania road.

I wondered, not for the first time that day, whether what I had to tell Sousa would make any sense. I'd confirmed what had already been suspected: namely, that Emmerich had been sheltering Gil, a man he knew to be wanted for an atrocious crime. Emmerich was willing to kill in order to continue protecting him and to get him out of the country. But why? The obvious reason—that he was anti-Frelimo, a right-wing DGS sympathizer—seemed no longer obvious. As long as Gil was safe he would be safe, he'd said, which seemed to imply that as long as Gil remained free Emmerich was able to bring pressure of some kind to bear on the man who threatened his interests, Sousa himself. A curious triangle indeed.

My doubts about exactly what had happened at Goronga had intensified. Discrepancies about the timing of the massacre suggested that Gil might have had the makings of an alibi, though he had confirmed his guilt by choosing to go on the run. Choosing? Perhaps I was wrong there. Was it always the guilty man who ran? And was it preposterous to suggest that someone besides Gil and his Flechas might have had a hand in the killing?

I walked straight along a footpath that led towards the fence, pausing now and then to look and listen ahead of me. In a few minutes the shiny strands of barbed wire came into sight, and on this side of them the sandy track that ran parallel. I halted for a minute behind the vast bole of a baobab tree fifty yards back from the fence. There was no sign of a guard for as far as I could see in either direction. That wasn't surprising; it would take an army to mount guard effectively on a boundary this long. But something else had caught my eye. At one point, beside one of the steel uprights of the fence, the wires had been cut and the loose ends bound around a post which, in turn, was secured with a loop of wire to the upright. The whole section of fencing, twenty feet long, had been made into a crude gate. Leading where? I had part of the answer when I walked forward and crossed the track. Wheel marks, the distinctive chunky tread of the Mini-Moke's tyres, led through the gate onto the hard grass beyond the fence. There were lots of them. A kind of thin track had been worn into the ground, curving round a couple of thorn trees and vanishing into the bush.

I undid the wire loop and passed through the gate. The track went roughly in the direction I wanted, so I decided to follow it. In a minute I was deep into the bush and no longer needed to worry about being seen. My main concern was to reach the road before nightfall.

The track twisted a good deal, taking the line of least resistance among thorn bushes, acacias and baobabs. Then, like a mirage, an old fort appeared out of the bush ahead of me.

At first I saw only a high wall of rust-coloured stone blocks, broken and jagged at the top and partly camouflaged by a curtain of thorn trees that had grown up against it. Then I made out another wall at right angles to the first, this one undamaged for several dozen yards of its length, the embrasured parapets where cannon had once been positioned still intact. It was a weird sight, something from another age and another continent dropped at random in the African bush. The Portuguese had built many such *fortalezas* in the sixteenth and seventeenth centuries to protect trade routes to the interior. The trade was not worth the protection in the first place, and the routes had long since been abandoned.

I moved closer. Now I saw that the second wall formed part of a bastion, one of a pair facing north-east and south-east from either end of the first wall. As I edged round the corner to the right, keeping my distance from the building, I could also see that this end was the least ruinous part of it. The north wall had collapsed almost completely; the only part that stood higher than a couple of feet was an arched gateway at the centre. The Portuguese had often been indifferent to relics of their past in Africa, as well as careless at keeping records, so it was quite likely that the very existence of this place was forgotten—forgotten, at least, by everyone but Emmerich, for the track made by the wheels of the Mini-Moke ended here, in front of the gaping gate. It was here that he had driven this morning after dropping me with the two guards at the boundary fence.

Cautiously, suddenly aware of my heartbeats, I approached the opening in the wall. A flock of house martins broke from their nests under the ledges of the bastion and wheeled overhead, twittering excitedly. It was a reassuring sign. I paused in the gateway; through it I could see the open quadrangle which had once been a parade-ground, now overgrown with savanna grass and low bushes, and beyond it the door and window openings of the casemates beneath the ramparts, where the troops would have been quartered. Their existence in an outpost like this must have been wretched. One in three were said to have died of malaria or dysentery; the rest would be confined to the fort for months at a time in suffocating heat, unable to venture out because hostile Africans still effectively controlled the hinterland. For Antonio Gil, things seemed to have come full circle.

I spotted what had been his hiding place without difficulty, a small green tent with an awning above it, pitched in the north-west corner of the quadrangle, where there would be more shade through the day than anywhere else. Apparently he had passed some of his time digging for relics; as I went towards the tent I almost tripped over a little pyramid of rusty and misshapen cannonballs. Further on, the corroded barrels of two small artillery pieces leaned against the casemate wall. A couple of tea-chests full of stores and tools stood under a second canvas awning, together with a folding washstand and a plastic jerrycan, half empty, similar to the one I had seen in the Mini-Moke that morning.

The campsite was neatly kept, with the tent walls rolled up and a sleeping-bag spread out to air on the grass. There were no signs that the departure had been hasty, except perhaps for a shoebox that had been knocked over and its contents spilt on the ground: old buckles and buttons dug from the soil and polished to a high shine, products of the sort of patient task that a man would set himself to avoid being driven mad by boredom, things that he would discard without a thought at the moment of rescue.

Rescue? Yes, it would seem like that to him. But now that I had escaped, that second billet in Beira, the hotel, was clearly no longer a safe place for him to be. Unless there was a third alternative Emmerich would have to bring him back, either to the house or here. It could be dangerous for me to linger.

Lifting the flap of the tent, I glanced inside. There was a camp bed, a few cooking and eating utensils, a folding stool and a small table with a pile of paperback books on it. There was also, standing in one corner, a G-3 rifle.

I pushed my way into the tent, picked up the weapon, unclipped the magazine and examined it. It held a full twenty rounds of ammunition. This was one of Emmerich's arsenal, no doubt, left with Gil in case of emergency. I decided to take it. In spite of the extra weight it would be tempting fate not to, because I was still well within the reach of Emmerich and his guards. The rifle was clean and had been recently oiled. I replaced the magazine and backed to the entrance of the tent, knocking over the pile of books with the rifle butt and exposing four other items that stood behind them: a small yellow cardboard box and a row of three wide-mouthed bottles, all empty, all with identical labels. I picked one of them up. The label bore the imprint of the Merck Sharp and Dohme pharmaceutical firm and identified the contents as one hundred cortisone acetate tablets. It irritated me vaguely to realize how right Sousa had been: Gil had been dosing himself with cortisone to retain the moon-faced appearance of the Barboza photographs. Emmerich might not have a tame doctor any longer, but he must have had a tame pharmacist somewhere who'd kept him supplied.

The yellow box was empty too. It had once contained twenty-five rounds of Peters's 9-mm pistol ammunition. That meant there was another gun, and that Gil had it with him.

As I replaced the box I noticed something else, a thin bundle of folded paper that had slipped from between two of the books. I would have paid it no attention if I hadn't noticed the handwriting on one of its outer folds, a neat, crabbed scrawl dotted with smudges from a leaky ballpoint. I propped the rifle against the table, picked up the papers and unfolded them. There were four sheets of ruled foolscap, with writing on one side and widely spaced paragraphs of amateur two-finger typing on the other. Punched holes with rips running to the edges of the pages showed that they had been torn out of a binder of some kind.

I turned to the typed sides first, because they were easier to read than the handwritten ones. Each had a small inked stamp in the bottom right-hand corner with initials scribbled across it, presumably to authenticate the contents. The initials were Gil's. The pages were not numbered but followed an order prescribed by chronological paragraphing. At first the Portuguese military jargon was difficult to follow. I translated the headings and the first couple of lines as:

DIRECTORATE-GENERAL OF SECURITY
(Mozambique Delegation)
Special Group No. 55, Counter-Terror
Field Operation Report No. 14, dated 1206

Time
0600   Unit emplaned and departed air station Manga for incident report zone, map reference H9.

I sat slowly down on the camp bed, staring at the page. The significance of the term "dated 1206" had suddenly struck me. It meant the twelfth of June, the day of the Goronga incident. This was the missing operation log for Gil's Flecha unit. I read further.

> 0630 Unit arrived at incident site to find army engineers towing away damaged vehicles. Proceeded on a course of 80 degrees—

The house martins saved me. A sudden commotion came from the bastion and I stood up, startled, folding the papers and cramming them into my shirt pocket, grabbing at the rifle. As I thrust my head out through the tent flaps I heard the whine of a motor and, a second later, a faint squeak of brakes. I turned and ran for the south wall.

It was broken down to waist height at the point nearest to me, and within a few seconds I was scrambling over the pile of rubble. No car doors had banged; the vehicle must be the Mini-Moke. Emmerich. Bringing Gil back? Through the still, early evening air I could hear men's voices and the whining of a dog from the north side of the fort. I plunged into the bush beyond the wall, uncertain whether to hide or keep running. The sight of a narrow game trail twisting off to the right decided me. It was the direction I wanted. I pounded along it, determined again on only one thing—to put some ground between them and me. Once they found that the rifle was missing they would leap to the obvious conclusion.

I hadn't realized how the day's exertions had drained me. In less than a minute I was gulping for air and could feel my leg muscles quivering. Deliberately I reduced my run to a walk. After a minute I broke into a trot again but had to give it up when I'd gone a hundred yards. I was sucking in air in ragged gasps. The rifle felt made of lead and I might have been tempted to discard it if I hadn't now heard the sound that I knew I'd been secretly dreading all afternoon, the fierce yelping bark of a dog along the trail behind. Panic swelled in me. I pushed myself forward.

The barking drew closer, steadily but slowly enough to tell me the dog was still on its leash. I knew now that I'd been mad to run; once Emmerich had realized I had been at the fort he'd guessed that I could only have left in one direction—westward, towards the road. The only thing he and his men couldn't know was just how close they were to catching up on me.

The high-pitched barking grew louder. Once again I tried to run but had to stop and fight off a wave of dizziness. It could only be a few more minutes before the dog and the men closed in. Despairingly I began to realize that I would have to stand and fight.

There was no choice of tactics; it was a pure game of numbers. If there were too many of them to handle I was as good as dead already. I had only one advantage, surprise, and I had to make full use of it. I needed a clear line of sight and some cover. I strode another hundred yards through the loops and twists of the game trail and came upon a relatively straight stretch of forty yards or so. At the end of it was an acacia tree with a trunk thick enough to provide concealment. I crouched among the savanna grass at its base, slipped off the safety catch on the G-3 and cocked it. The sharp metallic click sounded very loud in the stillness of the bush, but the frenzied barking was even louder. I was pouring with sweat. My hands slipped on the metal surfaces of the rifle. I wiped them on my trousers, checked the sights and aimed down the path.

For two minutes I waited before the man came into

sight. The Doberman was hauling him along at a fast trot, one of Emmerich's guards with a G-3 slung from his shoulder. Only one? What was I to do, shoot him and alert the others? Were there others? I let him come on, to within twenty yards and then fifteen yards of where I was crouched. Suddenly the dog halted, quivering, and gave out a howl. It had got my scent.

I was on my feet and out on the path before I knew quite what I was going to do next. The G-3 was trained on the man's middle.

"Don't move or I'll blow your guts out," I said. "How many others are there?"

The guard stared at me wide-eyed. Reflexes bypass the reasoning part of the brain, and his reflexes made him let go of the dog's leash and fumble for his weapon. I made a mistake too. I shot the man first.

He flopped back on the ground, doubling over himself like a limp cushion. The dog was already coming at me, a blur of black and bronze with the leash streaming out behind, its fangs bared in an inaudible snarl. There was no chance for a second shot. Instinctively I raised the rifle across my chest and shoved it out in a protective gesture as the dog launched itself from twenty feet.

It was trained to go for the throat but it took the first hold offered; the jaws closed round the stock of the rifle as the dog's weight hit me, knocking me to the ground. The shock of the attack tore the rifle from my grasp and the dog fell on top of me, scratching and growling frenziedly as the fangs searched for my throat. I fended and punched with both fists but pain would not deter it; the instinct to kill prevailed over everything. I grabbed the muzzle with my right hand. It bit into my fingers and I let go. I could smell dust and blood and hear my breath coming in panicky gasps. I managed to get hold of the leash and drag the animal off me. I rolled into a crouch but the dog was on me again before I could reach for the rifle, knocking me down as it sprang for my throat. I parried with my left arm. The jaws took it and the fangs sank deep. Fetid breath was in my face. I got my right hand round the back of its head but this time I couldn't reach the leash or the collar. Instead I dragged backwards at its scalp. The Doberman's eyes bulged huge and red. It would not let go of my arm but momentarily it opened its jaws a fraction wider to take a better grip. I forced the arm deeper into its mouth, tearing the existing wounds as I did so, trying to get to the back where it had blunter teeth and a less certain grip. Pain was spreading like a scarlet curtain across my consciousness.

The Doberman's claws dug into my chest; it pulled backwards, worrying the arm and trying to drag it clear and get at my throat. I knew the only way to break that grip was to use the arm itself as a lever. I let go of the dog's scalp, crooked my right arm around the back of its neck and began to push upwards with my left, forcing its head back. The teeth embedded in the forearm ripped the skin in a new direction. Pain was flooding through me now, threatening to overwhelm me; if I gave in to it, my throat could be torn out in a second. I hugged the animal close to me, keeping its neck clamped down and feeling the pressure on the upper vertebrae as the head was pushed steadily backwards and up. It held on to my arm but began struggling convulsively to free itself. And then its neck broke. The lithe body stiffened, shuddered and went limp; the head lolled. I extracted my arm from the trembling jaws and stood up, sick and giddy with pain. The forearm was punctured by dozens of toothmarks and horribly lacerated; blood ran steadily down to my hand and dripped from the fingertips.

A glance back along the game trail confirmed that the guard had not been followed by others, which meant that only he and Emmerich had gone to the fort. I picked up the rifle I had dropped, walked unsteadily to the shot man and looked down at him. The bullet had taken him just below the breastbone and had blown a hole the size of a saucer through his back. He was dead. I snapped the magazine out of his rifle and put it in my pocket.

When I straightened up Emmerich was there. He stood thirty yards away at the turn of the trail, watching me with an empty face. Holding the rifle one-handed, I raised the muzzle and waved it at him. He didn't move. He was not armed.

"If I thought it would do any good I would shoot you too," I called hoarsely. "If you come after me I will."

He did not reply. I turned and walked past the carcass of the dog, then stopped and said as an afterthought, "You won't be seeing me again. But I'd expect a visit from Sousa, if I were you."

Emmerich still said nothing. Blood dripped steadily from my fingers. Dizziness washed through me again and for a few awful moments I thought I was going to spoil it all by fainting. From somewhere I gathered enough strength to stumble on along the trail.

Once I was sure Emmerich wasn't following I stopped, sat down and did what I could to stanch the bleeding from my arm. I tore open my shirt and took it off and, with difficulty, removed the T-shirt from underneath. I folded this into an absorbent bandage and wrapped it tightly round the forearm, tying it with strips of cotton torn from the shirt. If anything the pain from the bites now seemed worse, though this concerned me less than the likelihood of infection. I needed medical attention, and promptly.

By now I was too exhausted to walk for more than five

minutes at a time without resting. And even though I was grateful that the heat had gone from the sun, the approach of dusk made me anxious. I wasn't at all confident that I'd be able to find my way out of the bush in darkness, and if I was forced to spend the night out here I could be ill beyond recovery by the morning with blood poisoning or tetanus. Between rests I pushed ahead as fast as I could, moving steadily westward along a series of game trails towards the narrow rim of daylight. It struck me that Emmerich had probably brought Gil along this same route this morning, which meant he would have a fairly good idea, a better idea than I had, of just where I was likely to emerge on the Nova Lusitania road. It would take him an hour or so to get back to his house, and soon after that the guards could be out hunting for me again.

Luckily the summer solstice was only four weeks off, so it would not be dark until around seven o'clock. At six thirty I blundered out onto the deserted road. There was no point in starting to walk along it, since I intended to stop the first vehicle going in either direction. Utterly fatigued, I slumped down at the roadside, resting my back against the trunk of a fallen tree.

In the last minutes of the brief tropical twilight I examined my arm. The makeshift bandage was sodden; I threw it away. The bleeding had stopped except from a couple of the deeper bites, though, and it would probably be best to leave the wounds exposed to the air. It was too early for any signs of sepsis to be present; the whole forearm was just an ugly and fiercely aching mass of gashes, pockmarks and congealing blood.

After that I must have fallen asleep. I was startled awake by the sound of a distant motor and saw headlights approaching from the north. It was now quite dark, and when I looked blearily at the luminous hands of my watch they said twenty past seven. Half naked as I now was, I felt chilly. I groped for the rifle and used it to pull myself to my feet; my muscles had begun to stiffen. Stepping back a couple of yards to stay out of the headlight beams, I watched intently as they drew closer. Coming from that direction, this might just be one of Emmerich's vehicles, sent to look for me, but I didn't think it was moving fast or purposefully enough. It travelled at around twenty miles an hour, rattling over corrugations and jouncing on tired springs through the potholes. I braced myself. If I wanted them to stop I had to take the chance. I stepped out into the middle of the road, holding the rifle out of sight behind my right leg, and raised my wounded arm in a signal to halt.

There was a grinding of worn brake-shoes. The wheels slithered on the sandy road surface and came to a stop a few yards short of where I was standing. A diesel engine idled unevenly. I stepped round to the left, where there was an open doorway. The vehicle was an ancient bus. The driver, an African in a string vest, stared down at me through the opening. Behind him the whites of incredulous eyes stood out against a dozen black faces.

"*Onde vai?*" I asked.

The rifle was visible now and the driver glanced at it nervously. "*Nova Lusitania.*"

"*Está um médico lá?*"

"*Médico, não. Posto de socorros. Uma missão.*"

I considered. I'd be better off trying to reach Beira. On the other hand I might wait all night for a vehicle going that way, with the added risk of Emmerich's men arriving first.

"*Bom,*" I said, and went clumsily up the steps. Inside there was a tense silence, as if the passengers had all held their breath at once. They'd been shopping in Beira, by the look of it; drums of paraffin and bags of mealie-meal and oranges were stacked on the seats and in the aisle, and the bus smelt like a grocery store. The eyes followed me down the aisle to the long seat at the rear. It was empty, but for a cardboard box containing a sheep's head. I flopped down, leaning back against the hard wooden backrest and laying the rifle across my lap. The driver crashed into gear; the bus shuddered and moved off, and a minute later I was asleep again. Nobody asked me to pay my fare.

5

Nova Lusitania was a couple of dozen corrugated-iron shacks scattered round a square of hard-baked sand, and the *posto de socorros* or first-aid post was, in fact, a mission school with a tiny hospital attached to it. The building was a long bungalow that looked out across the square, and the missionary himself was standing on the porch smoking a cigarette when the bus rattled into the village at eight fifteen. I got out and walked across to him. He wore slacks and a bush shirt. He was a youthful-looking man with a mild, bespectacled face. The bus driver had told me his name.

"Padre Afonso?" I said.

"Yes."

He'd been watching me with some puzzlement. "I need your help," I said. I stepped onto the porch and raised my left arm, letting him see the wounds in the dim light that came from a lamp farther along the building. He stood still, with the cigarette poised halfway to his mouth. Then he flicked it away, took hold of my good arm and began steering me towards a screen door at the end of the porch.

"What happened?"

"I was attacked by a dog. I've lost some blood, not a dangerous amount. It's infection I'm worried about."

"How long ago was it?"

"Around five."

"In here."

The door opened into a small dispensary adjoining the hospital. Father Afonso sat me down on a chair, turned on the overhead light and examined the arm more closely. I still had the rifle with me; I propped it against the chair. Through another door I could see into a room with a row of three beds against the wall. Their occupants were invisible but there came the sound of someone stirring restlessly in sleep.

Father Afonso looked impressed by what he saw. "What kind of dog did that?"

"You know a man named Emmerich? The sugar farmer? He has vicious Dobermans."

"Ah." The priest sounded knowing. "Are you a guest of Senhor Emmerich?"

"I was. Sort of."

"Couldn't he have driven you here? Or into Beira, to hospital?"

"He had other things to do."

Charity prevented Father Afonso from pursuing the subject. I said, "Have you a telephone, Father?"

"The only one in the village."

"Please let me use it. Before we do anything else."

"Before anything else," he said, "I'm giving you as big a shot of penicillin as you can take. Some antitetanus serum too. And the wounds must be cleaned."

"If I delay—"

"If you delay this treatment you will find yourself with

septicaemia or tetanus. You have lost three hours already. Make your phone call once the arm is dressed. And then you must rest. Have you somewhere to spend the night? If not we happen, very luckily, to have a bed vacant in the hospital."

"That's good of you, Father. But I'm not sure I'll be able to stay." I wouldn't be sure of anything until I'd made that call to Sousa. A lot depended on how quickly he could act on it, and on how soon Emmerich's men were likely to catch up with me. Although I'd put a good distance between myself and them, I was pretty sure that sometime during the night they would turn up to check out the mission. On the other hand, Nova Lusitania must be a good three-hour drive from Beira; Sousa probably wouldn't be able to get a force of men mobilized and out here much before dawn. Which meant I would have to move on. It also meant that a few minutes' delay in telephoning couldn't make a lot of difference.

The priest prepared two syringes and injected me, once in the upper arm and once in the behind. Then he fetched a basin of warm water and a wad of cotton wool, cleaned the wounds with practised competence and dabbed acriflavine on the arm. He covered it with a light gauze dressing and finally brought a towel and a safety pin and improvised a sling.

"How bad is the pain?"

"Par for the course, I suppose. Bad, yes."

"I could give you pethidine, but it would knock you cold for the night."

"I'll have to settle for aspirins, then."

We went back along the porch, through the small schoolroom with its scarred desks and pictures of the Sacred Heart, to his own quarters, a book-strewn room furnished with an iron-framed bed, a wardrobe and an armchair.

Obviously it served him also as an office; there was a desk littered with papers, a portable typewriter and a crank-handle telephone.

"This isn't supposed to mix with aspirin," Father Afonso said with a grin, producing a bottle of Portuguese cognac from the wardrobe, "but I can't imagine a glass will do you any harm." I waited in slight impatience while he found a clean glass and a coffee cup and poured a stiff measure for me and a smaller one for himself. "What number do you want?" he asked, picking up the telephone handset.

"Beira. The Governor's residence. I want to speak to him personally."

I sipped brandy while the priest cranked the handle. "Do you think he'll come to the phone?"

"When he's told my name, yes."

Father Afonso gave me a puzzled look. "That's odd. It sounds dead."

A chill went through me. "Has that happened before?"

"Never." He cranked again and put the receiver to his ear. "There's not even any static."

"Where is your exchange?"

"At Lamego, about eighty kilometres to the north."

I banged my glass down angrily on the desk. "God damn it, I knew I shouldn't have waited! The cable must run past Emmerich's place. And he's cut it, I know he has!"

The priest watched me without expression. "Why would he do that?"

"Because he wants me killed, that's why. Because I've got information that could hang him and he wants to stop me getting out with it. Thanks to you, he's probably going to succeed!"

I regretted this outburst immediately. It wasn't the priest's fault; Emmerich had probably cut the telephone cable as soon as I'd escaped, just as a precaution.

"Look, I'm sorry, Father," I said. "You may find this hard to believe, but I escaped from Emmerich's place because he was going to kill me. It's vital for him to stop me from reaching help."

"I'd been wondering about the rifle," Father Afonso said mildly. "It hasn't left your side since you arrived. Well, help is here."

"Not the kind that'll do me much good, unfortunately. Emmerich's men will come here looking for me. If they find me they'll take me away."

"They can't remove you from a hospital against your will."

"Don't you believe it. Do you have transport here?"

"The mission jeep. But the only way back to Beira is the way you came in."

"Past Emmerich's place—and he'll have the road blocked. What about to the south?"

"The road travels fifty kilometres to Sofàla and ends there. And Sofàla's phones are on the same cable as mine." The priest hesitated. "There is an Indian trader down there with a short-wave transmitter. He uses it for ordering stores from Beira, but he has occasionally put an emergency call through on the police frequency. Would that be any use to you?"

"Yes." I downed the rest of the brandy. There was no way of guessing how much time I had now. "Will you lend me the jeep, Father?"

He was shaking his head. "You're in no condition to drive. I have been watching you; you are suffering from shock and you're much weaker and more exhausted than you realize. You might well collapse over the wheel. Give me your message. I will have it sent."

"You must understand. If they come here and find me—"

"If they find you and this vital message has already gone

247

then their purpose is defeated, surely? There would be no point in their abducting you. Besides, it is of the utmost importance that you should rest."

Maybe he was right, I thought suddenly. I had to stop running sometime. There was no reason why the priest should not know the whole story, and in fact the more people who knew it the better. It would shift the focus of Emmerich's attention away from me; it would also make me awkward to eliminate.

"All right," I said. "Drive to Sofala. Get through on the radio to the police in Beira and get them to connect you somehow, anyhow, to the District Governor. He's a man named Raoul Sousa. He'll speak to you personally if you tell him you have a message from Hickey. H-I-C-K-E-Y. Write down what I tell you; it's important that there should be no confusion."

Father Afonso found a pencil and a blank sheet of paper on the desk and I dictated the message as a series of bald facts. The Barboza plan was blown. Emmerich had killed Akimo. Gil had been hiding on Emmerich's property; he had been moved to the Hotel Braga this morning but was possibly back with Emmerich now. I spelt out all the names. At the end the priest looked at me with a frown.

"Excuse my asking, but this person Gil . . ."

"The same one, yes."

"That's incredible! I thought he had left the country, vanished."

"I'll tell you the story later, Father. Please go now."

"Yes. It's just that—well, I gather you must be part of some attempt to capture him, and I am glad of the opportunity to help you. Forgiveness is at the heart of Christianity, Senhor Hickey, and I have tried hard to forgive this man Gil. I have not yet succeeded. I saw the results of what he did, you see, at Goronga."

"Of course." Suddenly I recognized the name: Father

Afonso Rodrigues, the priest who had given evidence at the United Nations inquiry. "You were the first European on the scene, the man who first exposed the massacre."

"I am leaving now. I shall be away about two hours. The sister will show you the bed in the ward."

A minute later he left. I stood on the porch watching the tail-lights of the jeep recede down the road to the south. I was relieved that the message was on its way, but apprehensive of what might yet happen tonight. What if the Indian trader's radio had shorted out? What if he couldn't raise Sousa? I could have insisted on accompanying the priest to Sofala, I supposed, but if things had gone wrong on arrival there'd have been nothing I could do to change them. And it would only have delayed the confrontation with Emmerich, not prevented it. Meanwhile I must sleep, gather strength.

An African nun appeared and led me through the dispensary into the little hospital ward. It was no bigger than the schoolroom, with just enough space for two rows each of three beds. A blue nightlight shone at this end of the room. The bed beside it was empty. The other two in the same row and the two opposite them contained African men, apparently asleep. Their heads were gaunt black silhouettes against the pillows. In the far corner was a cot with a small child curled up in it.

"Malnutrition," said the nun softly, following my gaze. "We don't have the luxury of separate wards for children. Or women. She is fortunate enough to have come here in time; many die in their villages without medical help. Even a revolution cannot create hospitals and doctors overnight."

"And the others?" I said, indicating the men.

"Blackwater fever. A complication of malaria. We can only admit those with complications."

She left, promising to return with some soup. She had

given me a clean hospital nightgown of light cotton and I changed into it, removing my sling before coaxing the injured arm into the sleeve. The pain had eased from its earlier agony to a throb that was still distinctly uncomfortable. I found a small bathroom beside the dispensary and splashed water on my face, glancing at the reflection in the small mirror above the basin. I'd been through a hell of a day, and it showed. The ruddiness of fresh sunburn only helped to emphasize the pallor beneath, and there were deep hollows round my eyes. I returned to the ward. I propped the G-3 up against the wall beside my bed, then remembered something I had not yet had time to do. From the pocket of the torn and sweat-stained shirt I had taken off I removed the four sheets of paper I had found in Gil's tent. Climbing into bed, I began with some difficulty to study them by the dim blue glow of the nightlight.

This time I tackled the handwriting on the back of the operation log as well as the official typewritten entries on the front. It was quickly apparent that they were meant to be read together. The typing had been done by some DGS clerk, probably to Gil's dictation, within hours of the unit's return from Goronga. The writing must have come later, perhaps after the pages had been torn out of their binder; they enlarged on the rather terse typewritten paragraphs, expanding in an informal but quite detailed way on the official accounts of events of last June the twelfth.

Once my eye became accustomed to the crabbed handwriting it wasn't all that hard to decipher. In a few minutes I was able to match up the typed and the written entries and read them right through:

0600: Unit emplaned and departed air station Manga for incident report zone, map reference H9.

0630: Unit arrived at incident site to find army engineers towing away damaged vehicles. Proceeded on a course of 80 degrees to Açúcar Emmerich estate to request guidance.

Gil's note: Maps bloody inadequate as usual. Half the villages we could see plainly from the air weren't shown. Heinrich Emmerich most helpful; knows the country like his own back garden. We got all the villages in 20 km square pinpointed and set off to visit them. Emmerich was sending his own security guards out on a march to the east; can't say I would trust that rabble myself—a crew of thugs, deserters and rapists—but they're his problem.

0745: Unit visited first suspect village in the target zone, deplaning in a clearing 200 m north. Villagers questioned.

Gil's note: Garanga, Goringa, or some such, they called it. Macacos too frightened to talk—the old story. I gave them the usual treatment: Did they want their huts burned down, themselves moved out? Eventually I took the old headman aside and got what I could out of him. Warned him he'd better be telling the truth, or we'd be back. We'd wasted far too much time.

0915: Unit proceeded to Usa and conducted further questioning.

Gil's note: More co-operation here—it seemed my reputation was known! Armed with some good stuff now, we carried on towards a placed called Chiculezi.

The nun brought me a bowl of potato soup and a bread roll on a tray. It seemed she would be on duty all night, so I asked her to give me immediate warning if any vehicles came into the village from the north. She glanced at the rifle beside the bed, nodded and left; I guessed Father Afonso had given her a quick briefing.

I hadn't much appetite. I ate half the soup and then put

the tray aside. Exhaustion was creeping up on me again, but I wanted to stay awake long enough to finish reading the log.

The morning had worn on in much the same way, with Gil and his men hopping from one village to the next on the trail of the guerrillas. They expected co-operation from the people they questioned, and when it wasn't offered they bullied and intimidated; Gil made no secret of the fact. They seemed to have travelled in a loop, for they were again a few kilometres south of Goronga in mid-afternoon when they were suddenly attacked.

1515: Aircraft came under light machine-gun fire on starboard quarter. Unit landed and deplaned in attack formation.

Gil's note: Contact at last! We heard the bullets ricochet off the rotor blades above us and I saw that the pilot had some trouble putting the chopper down. The terrorists kept blasting away at us from beyond a dry riverbed. We returned fire. After a minute there was no further response and I guessed they were pulling out. We knew by now that we outnumbered them. I sent sections 1 and 3 forward to cover their flanks and took 2 back to the Frelon, intending to carry them over the enemy's head and cut off his retreat to the north. Now, disaster! The pilot told me the gunfire had damaged the linkage system on one of his rotors. He couldn't get enough lift for takeoff. He had already signalled for a replacement chopper and mechanics, but it would take them forty minutes to reach us. We couldn't leave the Frelon unguarded in case the enemy doubled back. How I ranted and swore! We had had the bastards in our grasp. Now I could feel them slipping between our fingers.

And so they had. The two sections that had been sent forward soon lost contact with Raoul Sousa's guerrillas, who were lightly equipped and faster on the move. The second helicopter arrived just after four o'clock. The log was oddly bare of official entries for the next hour and a half but there were a couple of written notes by Gil, reflecting his frustration and anger at what had happened. He recorded that the new Frelon had picked up the two sections which had been sent forward, but gave no account of what the Flecha troop had done from then until it became too dark to continue searching. He mentioned his intention to return and continue the hunt the next day, adding cynically that by then the quarry could be a hundred kilometres away.

The final entries were in the brusque language of the official report:

1750:   Unit called at Emmerich estate.
1835:   Unit returned to base.

On the face of it, it seemed clear enough what the day's events had led up to. Gil was obviously not a man who took setbacks easily. Infuriated by his failure to kill or capture the guerrillas, sometime after four o'clock he had taken his men back to Goronga. It wasn't clear whether they'd intended punishing the headman and his people specifically for giving wrong information, or whether they were singling out Goronga as an example to other Africans in the area, as a grim reminder that the Flechas were not to be trifled with. For whatever reason, the massacre had happened. But there remained that discrepancy in the timing of it. The entries in the log bore out what Henrique had told me, that the Flechas had left Emmerich's place before nightfall, around six o'clock, while Nino claimed to have escaped from the killers in the dark. The log wasn't infallible, of course; Henrique and Gil might have been lying as easily as Nino. But certainly someone was lying.

Neither the official log nor his own notes actually incriminated Gil, but I could see now why he had stolen the sheets from their binder. They mentioned Emmerich's name, and once Gil had gone underground he would want no hint to emerge that the two of them were even acquainted. However, this didn't explain why he had kept the papers rather than destroy them, or why he had expanded on the log entries with details from his own memory. Could he, at the time, have had a reason to want an exact record of certain times and locations, a reason which no longer existed, so that the papers had been left behind, forgotten like the rusty cannonballs? Mulling over this question, I fell asleep.

6

It seemed only a few minutes before the nun was shaking me gently but insistently awake. When I looked at my watch, however, I saw it was a quarter to eleven.

"There are men," she said. "Across the square."

A combination of aspirin and exhausted sleep had made me extremely groggy. I swung myself out of bed, shaking my head in an effort to clear it, and groped for the rifle. My vision was blurred and unfocused. I got hold of the G-3 and made my way unsteadily to the door. The nun stayed behind, looking apprehensively round at her sleeping patients. I regretted having slept at all, though I supposed I could not have stayed awake anyway. I could hear men's voices outside now, one that spoke in clear, measured tones, another booming through an amplifier across the square. Emmerich's voice.

I walked through the dispensary and out by the screen door onto the porch, feeling the nightgown billow round me in a cool breeze. The door slammed behind me. A pair of powerful lights came on, illuminating and dazzling me, distorting my vision even more. They were the headlights of a Land Rover. I could just make out its silhouette, and the shapes of two or three men deployed on either side of it, facing me from the opposite side of the square.

"Hickey?" one of them called.

"Yes."

"You're to come with us."

"Who says so?"

"He does."

The amplified voice was ringing out again, slurred and unintelligible through the short-wave static. Emmerich wasn't present; he was at the transmitter in his study, drunk. I stepped forward, raised the rifle muzzle, and rested it on the wooden veranda railing to point at the vehicle.

"Tell him I like it here," I said. "I don't care much for his hospitality."

"Don't be funny."

"Tell him I'm staying here, but that Sousa is on his way. To arrest him for killing a policeman and harbouring a murderer."

"Sousa!" There were a couple of incredulous sniggers. "You know what happened the last time he called on us? We chased him halfway across the country. What are you going to do, Hickey, come with us or fight? There are three guns lined up on you."

I could see a little better now. I had made out a dozen or so African villagers, sleepy and bewildered, drifting from the tin shacks around the square to stare at the scene.

There was a cold core of fear inside me but I knew I had to keep sounding confident.

"You'd better think before you start any shooting. There are witnesses."

"A crowd of bare-arsed *macacos*? What do they matter?"

"They happen to be running the country nowadays. You're not going to learn until it's too late, are you, you and Emmerich and the rest of the stranded colonial flotsam who haven't managed to adapt? The tide has gone out for you—and for good."

Someone cocked a rifle with a snap. I spoke again into the blinding glare of the lights.

"Get back to Emmerich on that short-wave set. Tell him this. You've arrived too late. A radio message has gone to Sousa. He knows everything. So does the priest from this mission and the Indian trader at Sofala. Killing me will solve nothing. Are you going to kill the priest and the trader as well? And Sousa?"

In the short silence that followed I heard the sound of a car approaching from the south. Father Afonso. Jesus! He couldn't have picked a worse moment to return. What if Emmerich's men called my bluff? What if the priest hadn't got through to Beira? Would he be willing, or even able, to lie to them?

"We know nothing of that," the para called. "Our orders are to take you back before you do any damage."

"The damage is done. Just repeat what I said to Emmerich."

"You know what he'll say. He'll want proof."

I took a deep breath and pointed. "Here it comes."

Heads turned to face the south. We waited for what seemed a very long minute before the jeep swept into the square and pulled up in front of the mission. Father Afonso doused the lights and switched off the engine. He sat for a couple of seconds summing up the situation before climbing out and walking into the glare of the headlights to face Emmerich's men. Standing in the middle of the square he looked soft-featured and suddenly vulnerable.

"This man is a patient in my hospital," he said. "What do you want with him?"

"We're persuading him that he's well enough to be discharged, padre. Senhor Emmerich wants to talk to him."

"He will go nowhere against his wishes."

"You'd do well to keep out of the argument. This is—"

"Tell them where you've just been, Father," I interrupted. My stomach felt tight.

"Sofala. The Indian trader's."

"And tell them exactly what you did there."

For an awful moment he hesitated and glanced round at me, and I knew that he really was incapable of lying. Then he faced the guards again.

"I have spoken by radio to Governor Sousa. I have repeated to him what Senhor Hickey told me—that Senhor Emmerich has been protecting Antonio Gil, the man responsible for the killings at Goronga last year. That he is also responsible for the death of a man named Akimo."

Relief surged in me. I said, "What was Sousa's reply?"

"He will personally arrest Emmerich tomorrow. Any attempt to resist will be met with force."

"Words," the guard replied, though his tone was now much less confident. "That is all just words."

"You disbelieve a priest?" I demanded. "Does Emmerich disbelieve? Ask him."

There was a buzz of excited conversation, not from the paratroopers but among the Africans grouped around them. Father Afonso and I went on facing the headlights. The silhouette that was nearest the passenger door of the Land Rover made a grab for the transmitter microphone, and a moment later the incoherent voice echoed across the square again. There were several exchanges in Portuguese, none of which I could follow. Then my own name came booming at me over the static.

"Hickey? Listening? I hope so. Very well. A game doesn't give you the set. I still have men who are loyal to me, who'll be a match for all the *macacos* Sousa can send against me. If it comes to a fight, then I fight. You can tell Sousa that." Emmerich paused. "You can tell him something else, too. We had an agreement, he and I, and he has broken it. The truce is over. I can still destroy him."

He stopped there. I opened my mouth to reply and realized I would not be heard. The men made a concerted move to the vehicle. There was a sound of boots scraping on the metal deck, and then doors slammed and the lights flickered as the ignition key was turned. The engine came to life with a roar and the Land Rover swung into a violent U-turn that sent the villagers scattering; it raced away up the road to the north, leaving the disembodied voice echoing in my brain.

Destroy? What did he mean?

Father Afonso came up the steps on to the porch, fumbling in the pocket of his bush shirt. He took out his cigarettes and I noticed with surprise that his hands were shaking.

"Not used to scenes like that," he said with an embarrassed grin. "Strange words he used there."

"Yes."

"I wouldn't have thought he was in any position to threaten a man like Sousa. He must know his days are numbered—but then some of these old *colonos* are very stubborn. Well, I expect you could do with another brandy. I certainly could."

He lit his cigarette and then led me through the schoolroom again and down the short passage to his quarters.

When I had sat down and he had poured the drinks he said, "You were right. The Governor agreed to speak to me as soon as I mentioned your name. As it happened he remembered mine as well, from the UN inquiry."

"You told him everything?"

"He wanted to know much more, of course. I could only repeat the facts you had given. He said he would act upon them at once. He also said he would send someone to collect you early in the morning."

I drank some brandy. "Tell me about Goronga, Father. I mean your own experience of it."

"I told everything I knew to the UN." His mild dark eyes searched my face and he blew out some smoke. "Have you read the report? It's all there."

"I read the report. I wasn't too impressed with it." I knew that Father Afonso was a good man who would have told the truth as he had seen it; what I wanted to know was how he had seen it. "I'm just interested in your personal impressions. How did you first hear about the massacre, for instance? What form did the information take?"

"A woman came to see me on the morning after it had happened. That was Thursday, the thirteenth of June. She was from a neighbouring village named Usa. She had gone to Goronga at sunrise to visit her cousin. She saw the bodies and came straight here—rather as you did, by begging a lift on the bus. I don't know why she chose to report it to me. Perhaps she thought I was the only European in the vicinity who would listen and believe."

"What exactly did she tell you?"

"That the Flechas had been to Goronga, burned it down and killed most of the inhabitants. Perhaps even all of them."

"She didn't see it happen, and so she was assuming. You took that assumption for a fact?"

"Why, yes, I suppose so." Father Afonso stubbed out his

cigarette, removed his glasses and began to clean them with a front flap of his bush shirt. Without them his face had a fragile myopic look. "At least, I never found any reason to challenge the assumption. Do you think I should have?"

"No," I admitted. "I'm puzzled by some discrepancies in the evidence, that's all."

"I'd heard that the Flechas had been out hunting guerrillas the day before, and I knew something of their methods. It was the talk of every village. They'd even visited Usa, where this woman lived, and roughed up a couple of the young men."

"What did you do?"

"I took her and a couple of our workmen in the jeep. I thought it was as well to have some witnesses. We drove north until we were as close as we could get by road to the village, and then walked through the bush. It took more than two hours. I need hardly describe what we found. Vultures and jackals had been at some of the bodies. I left the men there to keep the scavengers away and came straight back here. I telephoned the Governor in Beira and spoke to him personally. It was a Portuguese governor then, of course. A few months earlier such a call would have achieved nothing. The incident would have been hushed up; I might have been arrested to keep me silent. But senior officials were in a peculiarly sensitive position at that time. There had been a coup at home, and they were anxious to show their loyalty to the new left-wing regime. They were also committed to ending the war, and yet they were still fighting it. The Governor realized that more harm could come to him from suppressing such an incident than from exposing it."

"So the Portuguese authorities themselves never questioned that their own men had been responsible?"

"Why should they have? They knew the methods of the Flechas too. Counter-terror was based quite frankly on intimidation and reprisals. There'd been other incidents—nothing on this scale, but occasions when huts had been burnt, cattle slaughtered. Sometimes Frelimo supporters would be taken away and simply vanish."

"Did you go back to Goronga?"

"Immediately I had made the phone call. By the time I got there a detachment of police had arrived in a helicopter and recruited help from the nearest village. The most urgent task was to bury the bodies."

"So the question of autopsies never arose?"

The priest smiled and shook his head. "Out in the bush in this climate, Senhor Hickey, such luxuries can rarely be afforded. The bodies were twenty hours old before we could bury even the first of them. The stench was appalling. Besides, there could be no disputing the cause of death; bullet wounds were clearly visible on all of them."

I nodded slowly. You couldn't blame Father Afonso for his ingenuousness any more than you could blame the police for wanting an unpleasant job over as quickly as possible, but here was further confirmation of the sloppiness of the investigation. I said, "Where do you get that figure of twenty hours?"

"Perhaps it was eighteen, I don't know. No, I remember now, it was certainly twenty. It was just after four that afternoon when we buried the first body, and the killings had taken place just before eight the previous evening."

"Are you guessing, Father?"

"Not this time. Wait, I'll show you."

He put down his drink, turned round and opened the bottom drawer of his desk. He brought out a small plastic bag, crossed to the bed and shook the contents out on it. There were a couple of dozen trinkets of various kinds: cheap jewellery in bronze and copper, semi-precious stones, a wristwatch, wooden beads on a leather thong, a fountain pen.

"I collected these," Father Afonso said, "in case relatives turned up to claim them. Very few ever did. Some things I removed from bodies, others were lying about on the ground. This"—he picked the wristwatch off the pile—"apparently broke when the man wearing it fell and jarred his arm against a stone. So assuming it was correctly set, it shows the exact time of the shooting."

I took the watch. It was a cheap make designed to look expensive, with a chunky steel case and a black face marked with mostly useless sets of figures in luminous green: made in Japan and probably fitted with a cheap Russian movement, the pride of a man who had probably saved for a year to buy it. The glass was broken but the case was intact. The hands were stopped at seven minutes to eight.

I held it up to my ear and shook it. It claimed on its backplate to be shockproof, among many other things, but it sounded as though the mainspring was broken.

"Did you mention this at the inquiry?" I asked.

"No." Father Afonso looked surprised. "It never occurred to me. I mean the question of time never came up, and I saw no reason to raise it. It could not have made any difference, could it, whether the killings had happened at seven or eight or nine o'clock? They had happened, that was what really mattered."

"It might have made a lot of difference," I said, impatient with him again.

"I don't understand how."

"I used to be a policeman, Father. I have a tidy mind that likes to sort things into sequences, time sequences most of all—and I've got a time sequence here that doesn't make sense. What would you say if I told you that the Flechas' official operation log showed they were back in their barracks at six thirty-five that evening? That's an hour and a quarter before the time shown on that watch."

"I don't know," the priest said, nonplussed. "Such records can be falsified, of course."

"Of course. And so can evidence. In this case it probably didn't need to be falsified because the committee never looked beyond what seemed obvious. They never found out, for instance, that on the twelfth of June there were not one but two groups of men out hunting for that guerrilla band, calling on villages, behaving in much the same way towards the people they questioned."

"Two? The Flechas and who else?"

"You saw some of them tonight."

"Emmerich's men?" Father Afonso's jaw had dropped. "You don't think they . . . ?"

"I don't know," I said. "I can only tell you this: They're a tough, mean bunch, just as capable as the Flechas of doing what was done at Goronga. They were out looking for the Frelimo band that day, and they'd been out the day before. I heard it from one of them. He was careful to say they went nowhere near Goronga. And he claimed they were back on the estate by nightfall."

"They could have gone to Goronga after that."

"Easily. They know the country round here; they'd have found their way in the dark. Emmerich has a secret. There was a survivor of the massacre, a boy called Nino who was shot in the leg but managed to escape. Emmerich has him working as a houseboy. He wouldn't let him near the UN committee, and now perhaps I can see why. Nino might have been able to give some pretty damning evidence. So might Gil, for that matter."

A pair of vertical furrows had appeared at the centre of Father Afonso's brow. "You don't seriously suggest that Gil might be *innocent*, do you? A man with a record of brutality—"

"I don't know enough to suggest anything, Father. What

I do know is that a refuge can also be a prison, even a refuge out in the bush. I've wondered all along why Gil stayed on for eighteen months in Mozambique when he could have left—in theory, anyway—at any time he chose. In practice he couldn't leave without Emmerich's help; he was trapped out there just as thoroughly as he would have been in a cell, because Emmerich chose to keep him there."

"But why?"

"For one of two reasons, maybe both. Gil knew something about the massacre at Goronga that Emmerich did not want revealed. He was also useful to Emmerich in some other way that I haven't fathomed out, but it's connected with trying to stop Frelimo's taking over his property, and perhaps with that odd threat you heard, to destroy Sousa. He intended to keep Gil on a string until things in that department were settled, but suddenly last week he found himself in danger of exposure." I told Father Afonso about Gomes's death and the discovery of the thirty thousand dollars. "Emmerich realized that the money might be traced back to him and lead to Gil's capture. He decided the Barboza papers would have to be used after all. Gil alive and free in Brazil was more valuable than Gil stuck in a Frelimo prison."

"You say it's possible that Gil had an alibi for the night of the massacre," the priest said. "If so, I don't see why he went into hiding."

"You've supplied part of the reason yourself, Father. When the woman who discovered the massacre told you the Flechas had done it, you never questioned the assumption. Nor did anyone else, least of all the UN committee. The DGS were discredited, and all the circumstantial evidence pointed straight at Gil. Besides, as you say, he had a brutal record. Nobody would have been in the mood to listen to his story. That's *poder de opinião* for you," I said, and recalled another quote from Joana. "Facts don't matter so much as the disposition to believe. Guilt isn't the only thing that makes people run, Father. Sometimes fear is enough."

I finished my brandy and stood up. The priest accompanied me to the hospital ward. "The truth should come out once Emmerich is captured," he said.

"If they take him alive."

"Do you really think he'll fight?"

"Yes."

I had carried the rifle from the priest's room. Now that the danger was past I decided to unload it. When Father Afonso had gone I sat on the edge of my bed, unshipped the magazine and pumped out the round in the breech. I stood the G-3 against the wall and then found myself staring at the cartridge in my palm. What memory was it trying to prompt out of my subconscious, what comparison was it inviting me to make?

I remembered. I would have done it earlier if fear and exhaustion hadn't driven the intention from my mind. I grabbed my soiled clothes from where they hung over the footrail of the bed, dug into the trouser pockets and found the two discoloured cartridge cases that I'd unearthed that morning from the vegetable garden at Goronga. With the live round between the thumb and forefinger of my right hand, I took the spent cartridges in my left and held the three shells up side by side, comparing their silhouettes and then turning them round to examine length, diameter, circumference. Even by the dim glow of the night-light the comparison was easily made.

It was incredible but undeniable. Without expecting it I'd found another of those loops that loosened a whole tangle. I'd had misgivings before about what had happened at Goronga, but this was much more; this was bewilderment giving way to disbelief and then to a kind of terror. Was it conceivable that a lie, a simple but monstrous deception, had endured since the night of the massacre to this very moment, a lie that I had been helping to enshrine as the truth? I wanted to know, and yet I was afraid of knowing.

PART SIX
Sunday, November 23

1

Sousa sent for me at six in the morning.

The nun woke me again to whisper anxiously that two soldiers had arrived and were asking for me. I got up, feeling dreadfully stiff and shaky, looked out through the dispensary door and saw them standing in the dawn half-light at the end of the porch, a pair of slouched figures in shabby camouflage and forage caps, brown-paper cigarettes in their mouths and Kalashnikovs slung from their shoulders. They didn't look in any great hurry to leave, so I went back into the ward and let the nun untie my bandage and wash and re-dress the bites, which she told me were healing satisfactorily. The pain had receded to a dull ache. She gave me another injection and fetched from the dispensary a small box of penicillin tablets that I was to take with me. I decided to leave the sling off. When I was dressed and washed she brought coffee and a buttered roll, which I wolfed down hungrily before going outside.

I took the rifle and the two magazines. Father Afonso

had come out on to the porch, wearing a surplice in preparation for mass, to say good-bye. I thanked him warmly for his help. The Frelimo men ambled forward and one of them jerked his head at the jeep.

"*Para lá, camarada.*"

I followed him down the steps. He hopped into the driver's seat, I climbed in beside him, and the other man squatted on the narrow deck behind us. Without another word we set off.

The quick tropical dawn had turned the eastern sky into a band of gold mottled with dark cloud. It looked as though the weather was at last preparing to break. The road wound unevenly through the bush ahead, a thin ribbon of pale sand reaching northwards, and the jeep bounced and shuddered as the black man pushed it relentlessly through potholes and corrugations and over precarious little bridges. Nobody spoke. The man on the rear deck clung to a safety bar with one hand and used the other deftly to roll and light a succession of cigarettes.

In forty minutes or so we were approaching Emmerich's property. The canefields came into view on the right, a still green sea in the early sunlight, and after another three miles we reached the sign that pointed to the factory area and the house. Here a group of vehicles was drawn up, another jeep and four Berliet troop-carriers, battered old trucks abandoned by the Portuguese and patched up by Frelimo. They were packed with armed men. Four or five others stood by the jeep, among them Raoul Sousa.

He was dressed in camouflage gear and wore a revolver in a leather holster on his hip. The outfit looked tailored, like the cotton drill, but suited him, and there was a spring of nervous self-assurance in his stride as he approached me. But he did not look pleased. I stepped clumsily out of the jeep.

"The bird is flushed," he said, "but not yet captured. Your information was wrong."

"What information?"

"About the Hotel Braga. He was never there."

"Are you certain?"

"I have had the woman, Filipe's wife, in for questioning. She is telling the truth. She was kept in ignorance of everything. She knows nothing about Gil and he has not been near the hotel. Besides, we kept the place under surveillance after you left it. He could not possibly have got in without being seen."

Puzzled, I said, "I'm certain the hotel was mentioned. Filipe had to phone Gil there, to warn him not to go to the airport. . . . It slipped out; I wasn't meant to hear. What about Filipe, has he been seen?"

"Not since he left with you on Friday night. But yesterday evening he telephoned his wife and asked to speak to the South African, Slater. Soon afterwards Slater walked out of the hotel. He has not been back either, though he left his belongings in the room."

"Jesus," I muttered. "Did you ever get round to checking his credentials?"

"He is exactly who he claims to be, an engineer contracted for a consulting job at Cabora Bassa. Mysterious." Sousa shrugged. "But Filipe and Slater can wait. What matters is to get Gil and Emmerich. I expect to find them both here."

"I wouldn't be so sure." Until now I had shared this belief, but the suggestion of Slater's involvement gave the picture a new perspective. Perhaps Gil's protectors had resources that we hadn't guessed at: yet another hiding place, another route out of the country. But Sousa sounded confident.

"Where else could he be? There would be no point in

leaving the property unless he could also leave the country. We are taking every precaution, of course; there are roadblocks on all roads out of Beira, we are screening passengers on all flights out and we have extra men on the docks and at the border crossings into Rhodesia; that is the only neighbouring country where he would have any hope of refuge. But he knows the Barboza papers are useless, and he has no others. He must surely be here."

I glanced round at the men he had brought with him. They numbered about eighty, the size of three infantry platoons, and were dressed in an assortment of camouflage outfits and cast-off Portuguese fatigues. Few had boots, most were wearing tennis shoes and a couple were barefoot. The Russian rifles were the only standard equipment.

"Do you think you're strong enough to do the job?" I asked. "Emmerich's got forty rifles and six machine-guns in there, plus a tough bunch of mercenaries."

"These men may not look much," Sousa said, gesturing at the trucks, "but they are fine soldiers. Some of them fought the Portuguese for seven or eight years. They dispelled the myth that black men have no stomach for battle. I do not expect serious resistance."

His arrogance irritated me. "It was serious enough the last time you attacked them," I said. "In June last year. Remember?"

Sousa's look was swift but calculating. "Emmerich must have been boasting to you. It was nothing to be ashamed of. We attacked, we were fought off, we withdrew. Guerrillas do not engage superior forces. This time things are different. We carry the lawful authority of the country with us; the paratroopers may sneer at that authority, but they know that in the long run they cannot win. They lack the motivation to fight."

"Emmerich will fight."

"Then he will be killed," the black man said flatly.

"Making it easier for you to take over his property."

"You've been listening to his talk. That is dangerous."

"Spying on his correspondence, actually. You gave him seven days to hand over the estate or have it taken by force. That was three months ago. What happened? Did you suddenly go soft on capitalists? Or did he somehow persuade you, that day that you met, to change your mind?"

He watched me blankly. "There were special circumstances," he said. "They have nothing to do with you."

"They must have been special," I said. "He claims to be able to destroy you."

"He is a blusterer. He has always overestimated himself."

Sousa turned away, glancing at his wristwatch, and spoke to the men lounging by the jeep. One of them climbed behind the wheel; the others walked to the cabs of the trucks, got in and started the engines.

"You will ride with me,' Sousa said, facing me again. "In the event of trouble you will stay at the rear, with the vehicles. I do not want the responsibility of having a foreigner killed or injured."

"A slightly comical notion, in view of what's happened to me over the past two days," I said. He didn't seem to see anything funny in it. "There'll be trouble, all right," I added, "and I don't intend to be anywhere near it."

We set off in convoy. I sat in the leading jeep with Sousa and his driver, followed by the four truck-loads of soldiers; the jeep that had fetched me from the mission brought up the rear.

The drive between the canefields to the mesh gates took only a few minutes, and as we approached them, slowing to a crawl, it became obvious that we were expected. Six of the guards were drawn up in a line behind the gates, their rifles held at the trail. Another stood behind them with a Doberman on a leash. The factory area was silent and empty; nobody worked on a Sunday, and the workmen must have been told to keep to their compound. Beyond where the guards stood, others were occupying sandbagged positions at a corner of the office building and outside the mill. They had spent the night preparing for a siege.

Sousa told the driver to stop when we were twenty yards short of the gates. He hopped lithely off the rear deck of the jeep. The trucks squealed to a stop behind us while Sousa walked alone up to the guards.

It took some courage to do it. They knew who he was and did not trouble to hide their hatred. One of them spat on the ground. A couple raised their weapons fractionally. The dog snarled, straining at its leash. From where I sat I could hear everything that was said.

"Do I need to identify myself?" Sousa asked.

"No, *macaco*."

"You will open the gates and let me in. I have business with Emmerich."

"No one comes in today."

The man who spoke was short and paunchy, with holes through the epaulets of his faded green shirt where an officer's shoulderboards had been pinned. He scowled at Sousa defiantly through the mesh.

"I will not argue with you," the African said. "We are here to arrest Emmerich and a man he has been protecting. We will get in by force if necessary."

"Like the last time?" said one of the paras.

They all laughed, rather too loudly, with the momentary release of nervous tension. In the pause that followed the dog growled and whined. Sousa said nothing but swung round and snapped his fingers at someone behind me. There was an expression on his face that I hadn't seen before, a look of violent anger held precariously in check. It lasted only a moment. From behind me came the sounds of Frelimo soldiers scrambling down from one of the trucks, and in a few moments they had filed past me, twenty of them, to form a wide semi-circle behind Sousa. For nearly half a minute the two sides stood confronting each other, the motley Africans and the outnumbered whites, all nervously clutching their weapons. The paratroopers now seemed less sure of themselves, and I wondered if Sousa had been right. Would they back down because they hadn't enough reason to fight?

"We shall come in now," the black man said calmly to the ex-officer. "Notify your colleagues in the other positions. Tell them that as long as they lay their weapons on the ground and raise their hands none of them will be harmed. Tell them that, and then open the gates."

"And if I don't?" said the guard, summoning up some bravado. "You think this crowd of ragbags could fight their way in?"

"I know they could. So do you. It may be hard for you to accept because you cling to your belief in your superiority, especially at fighting. I advise you not to put it to the test. You must learn. The day of white supremacy in this country is over. You work for a man who encourages you to think otherwise, to believe that nothing need change as long as he is here, running this estate like a feudal manor. Today the change is coming. I would like to make it easy for you. Even if you managed to fight us off we would be back tomorrow, in greater strength. Is it worth dying for, just to delay what cannot be stopped?"

The guards stared in unison at Sousa. There was nothing left for either side to say. The tension was at breaking point, and no one could have anticipated how it would break.

The Doberman had been pulling on its leash in a frenzy

of frustration. Suddenly the collar parted and it streaked through the line of men to hurl itself at the gate in front of Sousa, snarling and dancing on its hind legs as it tried to get at him through the wire. With a swift, certain movement he pulled out his revolver, thrust its muzzle through the mesh and between the dog's jaws, and fired. Its lower jaw blew off, blood spurted from its gullet and it fell writhing to the ground. The dog's handler and two or three other guards lifted their rifles and in the same moment stopped, forming a frozen tableau as they stared into the muzzles of twenty Kalashnikovs pointing at them through the fence.

"A dog is not worth dying for either," Sousa said, and shoved his gun deliberately back into its holster.

The ex-officer glanced round at the other guards, seeking confirmation of what now seemed inevitable.

"Wait," he said to Sousa, and turned and went into the gatehouse. For a minute we all listened to his voice and to the crackling replies on the walkie-talkie. No one paid any attention to the dying dog, which lay whimpering and trying to snap convulsively with its missing jaw. Then the man came out with a bunch of keys, walked to the gates and undid the padlocks that secured them.

"Emmerich won't surrender," he said shortly. "He told me to say so."

"Is he up at the house?"

"Yes."

"Who is with him?"

"The woman. And the houseboy.'

"And Gil?"

"I wouldn't know." The guard licked his lips nervously. "I know nobody of that name."

Sousa gave him a curt nod. "Lay down your weapons," he called to the other white men.

They obeyed. The gates swung open. A party of men was detailed to collect the guards' rifles and we drove through, followed by the trucks, past the refinery and the mill, the loading platform and the conveyor on which Henrique had been killed. The whole place was still and weirdly silent. At the sandbagged strongpoints they had set up the guards stood with their hands in the air, and at every one we passed Frelimo men would drop off the trucks to take their weapons from them. I was still amazed at the ease with which Emmerich's defence had been made to crumble. Sousa had been right again.

A few off-duty workmen had begun emerging from the compound. They watched in neutral silence as we drove by and turned up the slope towards the house. When we were thirty yards short of the fence and the row of casuarinas that divided the factory area from the private grounds, we heard the first burst of machine-gun fire.

The driver hit the brake hard. I dived out of the jeep and rolled on my injured arm, sending the pain lancing through it and realizing as I crawled for cover behind the front wheel that the move had been unnecessary. The bullets had pocked the lawn forty yards or more in front of us. Sousa had leapt out of the jeep on the other side and was signalling wildly to the rear. The black soldiers, jumping from the trucks, were scattering and scrambling for cover. Whether or not the machine-gunner had aimed short, as a warning, his four or five shots had signalled his intention to defend the house.

Responding to Sousa's shouted orders, some of the Frelimo men went forward in a crouching run to form an L along two sides of the low split-pole fence. Through the gap in the fencing where the road entered the private grounds I could just see the rear of Emmerich's house, perhaps a hundred and fifty yards away. The back doorway was sandbagged and the steel shutters that he had used during the war were in place.

It took a minute or so to get all the men into position, and then Sousa himself got to his feet and ran forward. He'd forgotten about me, and about his instruction to me to stay back. I went after him. The machine-gun barked abruptly once more as we reached the fence and dived to the ground in front of it. The bullets threw up half a dozen spurts of sand, well inside the garden. Suddenly I remembered Emmerich's short-sightedness; that was him on the gun, for sure. With his private army around him he had seemed such a formidable enemy until now that the idea of his blasting harmlessly away at us was faintly ludicrous.

I crouched at the edge of the gap and watched two soldiers across from me setting up a light machine-gun on a tripod. Sousa squatted a few yards to my left, peering through a crack between the wooden posts, waiting for the next burst of fire so that the position of the gun could be pinpointed. Behind us some workmen and a group of the disarmed guards had drifted up the slope to watch the action.

"I've got a feeling Gil isn't there," I called to Sousa.

"Why?"

"There's only one gun and I bet Emmerich is on it. He's got bad sight; that's why the shots are falling short. Gil would be shooting too, if he was in there. So would Filipe. All you're up against is one short-sighted old man and a woman. And Nino, of course."

"Nino?"

"The houseboy." I weighed my next remark carefully. "He survived Goronga. It would be a pity for him to die now."

"He *what*?"

276

"Survived the massacre. He escaped just before the shooting started. He was wounded in the leg. He managed to reach the canefields and Emmerich took him in."

Sousa wriggled towards me along the grass in front of the fence. The look on his face was very like the one I had seen when he'd first talked about Goronga, as though emotion were swelling inside him and threatening to burst violently forth.

"You mean the man who harboured Gil also gave protection to this Nino?"

"Seems odd, but yes. Nino is devoted to him. He knows no other home."

The black man stared abstractedly at me for a few seconds. Then we both flattened ourselves as the machine-gun jabbered once more. The paratroopers behind us scattered but again the shooting was wild, too high this time, smacking into the trunks and branches of the casuarinas above. And this time we had seen where it had come from. There was a dark opening about halfway up the steeply sloped roof of the bungalow, perhaps a skylight in the loft, and little puffs of white smoke had been visible against the darkness of the recess behind it.

"Enough!" Sousa said grimly. "We go in and take him."

There was suddenly a wildness in the black man's manner. He yelled something to the machine-gun crew across the gap, then snapped out instructions to the line of men crouching below the fence on the left. I caught the word *granadas*.

"Just a minute," I said, grabbing his arm as he was about to move away. "To go in there with grenades is madness! You'll kill them all!"

"He chooses to fight, not I. And they choose to remain with him."

"You don't need to kill them. He's an old man who

can't even shoot straight. Gil isn't in there, I know he isn't. And Emmerich is the only one who can tell you where to find him. You have to take him alive!"

Sousa's eyes glinted feverishly. "Don't tell me what to do, Hickey. I've done this kind of thing before."

"And failed, I seem to remember. Emmerich can't cover the approaches to the house on more than two sides, and even that's stretching his resources. You can send your raiding party up through the malala grove to break into the house on the other side, where he's unprotected—"

"What are you doing here?" he demanded savagely. "I told you to stay with the vehicles. Go back there!"

"And risk getting shot? Even with a stray bullet? No. You can't fool me, Sousa, I've done this sort of thing too. If you could get just one man into that house he could disarm Emmerich. I could do it myself. I will, if you'll let me. You don't need to kill him. Or is that what you really want to do?"

The black man said nothing. He seemed suddenly to become aware of my grip on his arm and broke it with a violent jerk and crawled away to the left, where a dozen or so of the Frelimo soldiers had moved down the line to squat in a circle—an assault party. A couple of them had unslung their rifles to allow freer movement and were clipping pineapple-shaped Mills grenades to their belts. I knew now that the handling of all this was quite wrong. By staging a frontal assault Sousa was provoking a crisis that could only end in one way, his way. But why? That feeling I'd had last night, of wanting to know but fearing the knowledge, was strong again.

Behind us the Portuguese guards were talking calmly as they waited to see what would happen to the man they had deserted. Then the Frelimo machine-gun opened up from the gap in the fence. Bits of tile were shot away from the roof as bullets poured into and around the skylight opening. At almost the same moment the assault party, crouching now in a line to Sousa's left, scaled the three-foot fence and began to move in a zigzagging run across the garden.

The Frelimo gun was a belt-fed MAG, presumably captured from the Portuguese, and its fire was continuous and devastatingly accurate. Emmerich was only able to lift his head for long enough to return two or three shots at a time, and then they went wild. For me the whole thing had suddenly become ugly, pointless and absurd: eighty soldiers besieging a stubborn, short-sighted old man. Yet it wasn't that pointless. I had little enough sympathy for Emmerich and Joana, but at that moment I had even less for Sousa. I scrambled to my feet, leaped over the fence, and went after the soldiers.

Over the noise of the MAG I heard Sousa's scream from behind me.

"Hickey! Stop!"

I ran straight on. There was plenty of room for concealment among the dense tropical shrubs and trees that dotted the lawns, but I took a gamble on Emmerich's erratic shooting and went unswervingly for the house. Ahead of me the black soldiers, darting from one patch of cover to the next, were closing on it rapidly. From behind I heard Sousa shouting again and glanced round to see him loping after me, his revolver in his hand. What the hell was I doing? I didn't even know. Infected by the insanity of the business, I was conscious only of some need to stop the senseless killing.

I had overtaken most of the soldiers by now. The cover nearest the bungalow was a row of hibiscus twenty yards from the rear door, and as I reached it one of the black men broke away a few yards ahead of me and raced for the house. He stumbled and skidded the last few yards. I went after him. The Frelimo gunner stopped firing; in the short silence that followed, what happened probably looked from a distance like some lunatic ballet.

The soldier threw himself at the wall directly under the skylight and stood with his back pressed to it, below the maximum declination of Emmerich's gun and hidden from his sight beneath the roof eaves. He unclipped a hand-grenade from his belt and ripped out the pin that would spring the detonating lever as soon as he released his grip on it. I ran at him. He stepped away from the wall, turned and dropped his right shoulder to bowl the grenade. I dived forward and seized his fist in both hands.

Off balance, he toppled to the ground and I fell with him, my hands locked around his thin brown fingers. All our concentration was fixed on the bomb that we clutched between us, knowing that once the lever was let go we had about four seconds to live. The black man's face was distorted by fear as we writhed on the grass in a desperate game of arm-wrestling. But he still had one hand free. He groped at his belt, pulled out the short bayonet from its scabbard and slashed at my hands. Involuntarily I released my grip. The soldier hacked open the knuckles of his own right hand and let go of the grenade.

The lever sprang off. We both watched in horror as the bomb rolled for three yards across the lawn, smoke pouring from its baseplate as the fuse inside it burned. Then another lean brown hand reached down to grab it; in one fluid movement Sousa picked up the grenade and flung it into the skylight.

In the breathless second that followed there was a movement at the back door of the house. It opened and slammed shut and a figure came round the edge of the heap of sandbags. I caught a flash of familiar orange. Sousa dived for the revolver that he'd dropped on the ground. Then the blast knocked all of us over.

The grenade exploded with a muffled *crump* and a flash, blowing out the side of the roof. Tiles and bits of the shattered skylight frame were flung high in the air, and from the swirling smoke in the loft Emmerich's body rose several feet like a grotesque and ungainly bird, described a short arc, and landed with a doughy thud on the lawn.

I stood up, my gaze riveted on the shapeless form, aware of Joana, a few yards away, getting shakily to her feet and staring too. The soldier who'd slashed his hand open sat looking at it numbly. Other men were forcing open the rear door of the house; there was no sound or sign of movement from within it. And Sousa was facing me, smothered in dust from the explosion and red-eyed with anger.

"I could have shot you while you were running, Hickey. I probably should have. Are you mad?"

"Possibly. Mad enough to wonder whether you were planning to kill Emmerich all along. And mad enough to try to stop you."

"You must . . ."

His attention went to Joana, who was being pulled towards us by two men, each of them gripping a wrist as if they were afraid she would scratch. Somebody else was laying sheets of newspaper over Emmerich's body. Whatever he had been, this was a messy, undignified end. And unnecessary. Neither bad tactics nor the possibility of Gil's being in the house was enough to explain it; nor was plain hostility. I remembered the exchange of letters and the old man's threat, in drunken, amplified clarity over the radio last night, to destroy Sousa. Had Sousa forestalled destruction by killing Emmerich?

Joana and the men who were holding her stopped in front of Sousa. She had torn her orange slacks and grazed an arm in the fall, and she was trembling with shock. Her face was empty as she looked at me, but there was a flicker of venom in the dark eyes as they settled on Sousa.

"So you've got what you wanted," she said bitterly.

"I want nothing for myself. Is Gil in there?"

"Of course not."

"Where, then?"

"If I knew do you think I would tell?"

The revolver was in his hand and he made a move as if to jab her with it, but she held him with her look.

"Do what you like, *macaco*, you will learn nothing from me. I know nothing. But I can tell you this much: Gil will soon be safe and I will be glad to have helped him. Only Emmerich knew the details—where he was, where he planned to go. He also knew that you would kill him, that the information would die with him. At the last minute he told me to leave the house; there was no point in all of us being killed. He was twice the man you will ever be."

"You will be questioned," the black man said, his manner now calmer and rather remote. "If you are hiding anything it will go badly for you."

I thought she might spit at him; it was the kind of gesture she would make. But her gaze met mine for a moment as one of the Frelimo soldiers jerked at her wrist.

"You. Have you no pride—a white man siding with this filth?"

"I didn't side with anyone, Joana," I said. "I'm doing what you and Emmerich were doing—trying to survive. And I'm better at it than you were."

When she'd been led away I said to Sousa, "What'll happen to her?"

"If she is telling the truth, nothing. Probably we will put her on a plane to Portugal."

That in itself would seem like a kind of sentence. I suspected she had only stayed on in Mozambique to indulge her bitter wish for revenge.

Sousa went to the back door of the house, which was now open. I followed. A few men were inside, some of them picking through the wreckage in the kitchen and another of the back rooms. Part of the rear wall had been blown away and a section of ceiling had collapsed under the weight of sandbags with which Emmerich had fortified his position in the loft. The bags lay split and disembowelled on the floor. As we passed from the kitchen into the corridor that ran the length of the house, there came an urgent shout from the left. Sousa and I exchanged an incredulous look. I recognized the direction: the livingroom. We both ran towards it, the black man with his revolver in his hand.

In the doorway we stopped. A Frelimo soldier stood in the centre of the big room, pointing his Kalashnikov vaguely at a figure in white drill who stood behind a blackwood chair in the far corner, his arms around the backrest as if it offered some sort of protection, a breadknife clutched incongruously in one hand. It was Nino. His gaze went to us in confusion as we filled the doorway; we had blocked what he must have imagined was his only exit. But he could have nothing to answer for, no need to escape.

"The houseboy?" said Sousa softly beside me.

"Yes."

The soldier took a step towards Nino, who made an uncertain gesture of self-defence with the knife. The man shrugged and stayed where he was; Nino didn't matter. I drew Sousa into the room and off to one side of it, leaving the door open and clear; it was the kind of thing you do to a trapped animal, trying to show you mean no harm and encouraging it towards the escape route. And Nino understood. He hesitated, then edged around the chair and came hobbling towards the door. I wanted to speak to him, reassure him that he had nothing to fear.

He paused when he was a couple of yards from the doorway and the same distance from us. His face was soaked in sweat and his eyes rolled in terror. I held up my hand, trying to discourage him from running.

"Wait," I said. "There's no need to be afraid, Nino."

Perhaps he understood, perhaps not. For the second time in his life he was living in a nightmare that was beyond his comprehension. His manic stare went from my face to Raoul Sousa's, and the quality of his expression changed, sharpening fractionally as though an ill-defined fear was brought suddenly into focus. Then he moved. He made a clumsy slash at me with the breadknife and ran for the door. Dodging the blow, I reached out to grab his arm. At that moment Sousa shot him.

With the same decisive swiftness I'd seen when he had killed the dog, he thrust his revolver out at arm's length and fired. I couldn't have stopped him. Nino was blown out of his tennis shoes. He did a floppy somersault and then lay still on his side, his brain scattered in damp grey globules across the polished stone floor.

I turned speechlessly to Sousa. He was returning the gun to its holster, his manner calm but his face wearing that look which told me the inner volcano had been close to erupting once more. I stepped over to Nino, then realized the action was futile. The bullet had gone into his right ear and blown away the left side of his head.

A sick anger flooded through me. "Why?" I demanded, turning to face Sousa. "Why the fuck did you do that?"

"He'd have stabbed you. He was dangerous."

"Like shit! It was chicken slaughter."

The room stank of exploded cordite. Sousa said nothing but gave me a long, searching look. Did he wonder whether I had guessed the answer to my own question? A lot of things were suddenly making sense: another tangle, another loop, this time surely the final one? I knew what that look in Nino's eyes had meant before he'd tried to run. I knew, and I was afraid.

Sousa shrugged, deciding that it couldn't matter what I was thinking. "He was a madman," he said.

"He was fifteen," I replied numbly.

2

Joana had not been lying. There was no trace of Gil in the house, or of Filipe, no suggestion that they had returned to Emmerich's place even briefly in the time since my escape. I gave Sousa directions to the fort on the south side of the estate; he sent a party of men to check it out, but I knew they would find no one there either. Emmerich's visit there yesterday had not been to return Gil to his hideout but to remove the evidence of his stay —which left only Beira. Somewhere in the city the two fugitives must be holed up in the hiding place which I had mistakenly understood to be the Hotel Braga. I still didn't know how I could have misinterpreted that reference to the hotel.

However, in spite of Joana's confident assertion that Gil would soon be safe, almost certainly he and Filipe were trapped. Roadblocks had been set up all round Beira, and security at the airport and the docks was tight. No refuge in a town could be as safe as the one Gil had had in the bush; sooner or later desperation must drive him into an escape attempt, and this seemed to be what Sousa was counting on. Brazil was out of the question now, but there was still Rhodesia, a bastion of white supremacy which had given sanctuary to other wanted DGS men. If he could reach the border he could be reasonably sure of the same treatment. But the border was two hundred miles from Beira, and to Gil that must have seemed a very long way.

Where did Slater come into the picture? That was the one question no one was even trying to answer. After taking Filipe's phone call the previous evening he had simply walked out of the hotel and vanished.

Livid clouds were massing on the eastern horizon when I rode back to Beira with Sousa. To my surprise he announced suddenly that he was sending me back to Johannesburg that afternoon.

"You have played your part. Gil is flushed; there is nothing to do now but wait. The plan to plant the Barboza papers failed, but not through your fault. You have proved your dependability. And earned this."

From a big plastic bag that was stuffed under his seat he produced the DGS file, scorched along one edge. The Frelimo men had blown the safe in Emmerich's study with a charge of gelignite, and I'd seen Sousa removing the money and documents from it.

"Keep it or destroy it," he said. "I suggest the latter. There is a flight to Lourenço Marques at four o'clock connecting with one to Johannesburg at five thirty. You have a return ticket, of course; if you encounter any trouble making reservations, let me know. Until you leave you may as well return to the Braga and rest."

He was uncommonly affable. He was also eager to have me gone, and I was so pleased at the prospect of departure I tried not to think about the reason. It was all over, I told myself. My passport was safe, my skin was mostly whole, and in a few hours' time my life would begin returning to something like normal. That was all I should care about. I spent the next half hour of the journey shredding the file into thousands of tiny pieces and scattering them in the dusty wake of the jeep.

It was odd to find Senhora Pereira still running the hotel as if nothing had happened, perhaps gaining some comfort—or distraction, anyway—from the daily round of berating the cook and prattling with her guests. But her eyes were hollow and there were signs of strain in her manner.

"A foolish man," she muttered to me as I filled in a new registration form. "Most foolish. Relying upon his gambler's judgment, always expecting the big win that could cover the small losses. Why he could not talk to me about his problems I do not understand. What sort of future has he left me with? To be the wife of a fugitive from the law—or of a prisoner in a black man's jail."

She had been closely questioned by the police and by Sousa himself, and they were satisfied that she had known nothing of her husband's involvement in the Barboza affair. And certainly he would have made just as sure that she had no idea of his present whereabouts, although a couple of Frelimo soldiers had been stationed round the hotel against the unlikely possibility that he might try to sneak back.

Senhora Pereira led me to my old room. When she had left the first thing I did was pick up the phone and ask for the local office of DETA. The pleasant-voiced girl who answered was able within a minute to give me reservations on the four o'clock flight to Lourenço Marques and the connection from there to Johannesburg. She advised me to be at the airport by three fifteen to have the return portions of my ticket filled in and to clear security.

It was only eleven in the morning, but I felt as though

a whole and very tiring day was behind me. I'd salvaged my overnight bag from Emmerich's place, so I did at least have a change of clothes. I shaved and bathed, keeping my bandaged arm gingerly clear of the water, then phoned Senhora Pereira and asked for someone to call me at two thirty. I drew the curtains, turned on the air-conditioning, lay down, and was asleep within a couple of minutes.

Filipe's wife woke me herself, rapping hard on the door and muttering when I went to open it about the porterwaiter having disappeared again. Then she said, "That friend of yours. What am I to do with his belongings?"

She still seemed to think there was some connection between Slater and me. I said, "I've no idea. He still hasn't come back?"

"Nor paid me a single centavo, for all his talk about how rich and important he was. He told me he was to fly north at twelve o'clock today, but there are his things, still in the room. Does no one tell the truth any more? Shall I leave them, take them out, or what?"

"It's really a matter for the police," I said. I hadn't given a second thought to Slater's disappearance, but now I was struck by an idea. "They searched his room, presumably. Did they remove anything?"

"Nothing."

"Do you mind if I look around it?"

Her dumpy figure preceded me down the corridor into the far wing of the hotel. She unlocked Slater's door with one of a bunch of keys pulled from her overall pocket. The bed had been made and the room tidied. I opened the old-fashioned wardrobe: A pinstriped suit and a laundered safari jacket hung on the rail; the underwear and socks and the shirts made in Hong Kong were stacked on the shelves. There was nothing in the drawers of the bedside table and nothing on top of it but the telephone and a small blank jotting pad. On the luggage stand, beside his empty grip, stood a briefcase, which I opened, glancing through the papers it contained: three or four reports by engineers on the Cabora Bassa site about the problem with the water turbines that he'd been commissioned to solve, along with a copy of his contract and a few pages of scribbled technical notes. If Slater's role as an engineer was a cover it was certainly a well-researched one. Yet there was a puzzle; the identity papers he'd shown me so readily weren't here, the papers that would admit him to the Cabora Bassa site. Since the police apparently had not taken them from the room, Slater must have carried them with him when he'd walked out of the hotel. Natural enough, I supposed; it meant nothing.

I had wondered idly whether we'd all got the wrong idea about Slater, whether he'd really gone to Cabora Bassa after all. He might have spent the night with some black prostitute, overslept, and rushed to catch the midday flight. But no. The briefcase full of technical reports was surely just as important to him as those identity papers. And there was the matter of that phone call from Filipe, a few minutes after which he had left the hotel.

So Slater had vanished, as thoroughly and untraceably as Filipe and Gil, at least for now. I looked at Senhora Pereira and shrugged. "Sorry. I'd thought I might find some clue as to where he'd gone."

"What am I to do, senhor?"

"I'm afraid I just don't know." I glanced at my watch. It was twenty to three. "Can your switchboard find me a taxi?"

"Of course."

I went to the phone and picked up the receiver. While I waited for the operator to answer I found myself gazing vacantly at the jotting pad on the bedside table. It was blank, yes, but the paper was thin and with the afternoon light reaching it from this particular angle—at a slant from the shaded rear window of the room—I could see on the top sheet an impression of handwriting, a tracing of something that had been written on the sheet above, now torn away. And from the notes I had glanced through after removing them from the briefcase I recognized Slater's scrawl.

The operator came on and I asked him to order me a taxi to the airport. Then I looked more closely at the tracing on the pad. It wasn't difficult to read. It was the kind of cryptic note in which a man records the essentials of a telephone conversation: *Grande, Ponte Gea, 600 esc.* It was easy to see how inexperienced policemen might have overlooked such an item when they'd searched the room. Unless they *had* seen it and had found it meaningless.

"Ponte Gea," I said. "Isn't that somewhere in Beira?"

"The most fashionable district in the city, senhor. At least it was, before independence."

"Far from here?"

"Just a few minutes."

"Grande. Who could that be?"

"Not who, what." She looked surprised at my ignorance. "The Hotel Grande, senhor, the best hotel Beira has ever had. Sadly it was too good for Beira, too expensive to attract enough guests and too costly to run. It was closed twelve years ago—a temporary measure, they said, but it never reopened. For that, I must admit, we cannot blame Frelimo."

The note made no kind of sense. If Slater had been thinking of changing hotels, why pick on one that existed only in name? Maybe he hadn't known it was closed—but even so, where had he dreamt up the figure of six hundred escudos? Unless the money and the hotel were not connected. He could have arranged to meet someone outside the place. But the money—what would Slater have been likely to spend six hundred escudos on if not a hotel room? A girl? Yes, one of the black girls for whom he seemed to have such an appetite. Had someone fixed up for him to meet a whore outside the Hotel Grande? I wondered why I was bothering to ask these questions; Slater was no concern of mine. Then I remembered, again, the phone call he had taken from Filipe. And at the same moment I recalled the scene in Emmerich's house when Filipe had let slip the word "hotel" in a reference to Gil's hiding place.

Conditioning plays tricks on the mind. It had never occurred to me that he might have been talking about any hotel other than his own, the Braga. I turned to Senhora Pereira.

"Did Filipe ever have any connection with the Grande?"

"But of course, senhor. He was assistant manager at the time it closed. It was only because he lost that job that we bought this place."

I remembered now; she had referred to another and better hotel, without naming it, the first time we'd met.

"And it's empty, deserted?"

"I believe some of the cleaners were kept on, as a small maintenance staff. The place is still furnished and equipped, you see. Once in a while there is talk of reopening it, but it remains just talk. What are you—?"

"It was nothing, just a thought." I didn't want to alarm her, though I could feel something tautening inside myself like a steel spring. The Hotel Grande: Could that be the second billet, Gil's present hiding place? Could Filipe have phoned Slater from there the evening before? I shouldn't be asking myself questions any longer, I thought. I had a plane to catch in an hour's time and I was leaving

Gil and Filipe and their problems behind. I left Slater's room and returned to my own, threw my clothes into my bag and went out to the lobby.

Senhora Pereira refused payment for the room. "It is the least I can do. My husband has caused you so much inconvenience."

"To put it mildly. But thank you."

The cab had arrived a few minutes early and was waiting at the front entrance, an Indian in a cheesecloth shirt at the wheel. With the fact of departure now upon me I felt oddly reluctant to go. I knew, in spite of all my attempts to ignore the fact, that I was leaving unfinished business, unanswered questions, behind me. Hell, I told myself, it wasn't my business to finish and the questions weren't for me to answer. I must get moving and not look back, keep telling myself I was lucky to be alive. But somehow there was more than just self-preservation involved. It would be so easy to follow up that shred of information I had just acquired; I felt that if I went without doing so I would be leaving some small part of my integrity behind.

"Airport?" the Indian asked.

"Yes." I hesitated, then said, "I've got a little time to spare. Stop at the Hotel Grande on the way."

"It's not—"

"I know. Take me there all the same."

Ponte Gea was, as Filipe's wife had said, just a couple of minutes away, a district of cool suburban villas struggling to keep up appearances after the Portuguese exodus. Many of the houses were shuttered, many of the gardens overgrown. The Grande was a big hotel, a three-storeyed building rambling over a couple of acres of lawns and shrubberies which had been reasonably well kept. The building itself, though, had suffered from the kind of neglect that tropical conditions quickly aggravate. The balcony railings were rusted, the colourless plaster was flaking and large areas of the walls were stained black by rushing rainwater. The general effect as I walked up the sweeping driveway was one of mournful decay, though a look through the glass front doors showed the interior to be in remarkably good repair. The lobby floor was polished, the furnishings were still in place and a notice above the reception desk said in Portuguese and English that accounts should be settled weekly. The careless optimism was very Portuguese; it was as if they were expecting guests at any moment. Like Beira itself, the Hotel Grande seemed to be living in hope of better days which were never likely to arrive.

I gave one of the glass doors a push. To my surprise it swung open, and I stepped into the lobby. Something in me found the possible proximity of Antonio Gil less frightening than tantalizing. I couldn't have explained. The most wanted man in the country, dangerous and certainly armed, might just be in this building; what was I doing entering it on my own? I didn't know. If the door hadn't opened I would probably have gone back to the taxi and ridden to the airport.

As it was, I moved quietly across the lobby—vast, dark, cool and deserted. At one end wrought-iron partitions divided it from a huge lounge; at the other a wide marble staircase led up to the first floor. Undoubtedly the cleaners were about somewhere or the doors would not have been left unlocked, but on a Sunday afternoon their activity was bound to be at a low point. Was it conceivable that a stranger could have spent the past twenty-four hours in the building without their noticing? Hardly. The former assistant manager would have found a way round that, by bribing them to keep quiet or, more likely, by pretending to an authority he no longer had. Uneducated

Africans still, out of habit, tended not to question the orders of a white man. All the same, the hotel would have to be considered a very temporary refuge.

I had only a few minutes. Where did I start? Up the stairs seemed as good a direction as any. On the first floor I found myself at the junction of two long passages at right angles to one another, each of them a dim hundred-yard corridor reaching away to where a high dirt-stained window at the end admitted a rectangle of light. It was even quieter here than in the lobby; my feet sank into the thick pile of the carpet as I moved cautiously to the nearest door and tested the handle. Locked. What else should I have expected? There were about fifteen doors on either side of each corridor, with nothing to indicate from the outside that any of the rooms might be occupied. The only thing that could possibly help would be noise; nobody in this intense silence could move about normally without being heard.

At a measured pace I went to the end of the corridor on my right, turned, retraced my steps and covered the passage on the left in the same way. Nothing disturbed the hermetic stillness. I climbed to the second floor and repeated the procedure, listening as I padded down the corridors for any sound that might escape from the rooms. Gradually I began to think I was wasting my time. The tracing of the note on Slater's pad had been the flimsiest of clues, after all. I glanced at my watch; it was just on three o'clock. Time I left and caught that plane. I was near a west-facing window at the end of one of the corridors; I looked out through one of the dirty panes to make sure the taxi-driver had parked his cab where I'd told him to, further down the street. It was there; he was reading a newspaper. I turned away and heard a sound so unexpected that it froze me. It was the gurgle of running water, very close but very faint.

It took a few seconds to work out where the noise was coming from: behind the door immediately on my left as I faced down the corridor. The number on the door was 246. For almost a minute I stood utterly still, listening, hardly daring to breathe. Then I relaxed. There was no other sound, just the thin, steady trickle of water down a pipe or into a plughole. A tap in need of a new washer, nothing more. Yet even in telling myself this I opened another area of doubt. Was it a leaky tap or one left accidentally open? I listened for a while longer to be certain there was no movement from inside, then cautiously tried the door of room 246. It was locked.

I'd pushed my luck a long way already, and the urge to stop now was strong. But curiosity had grown even stronger. I went to the window in the end of the passage, forced it open on rusted hinges, and, leaning out, saw the balcony of room 246 on the right, the crumbling plaster of its nearest edge barely three feet from the windowsill. It would take only another minute to get across there, look through the glass doors into the room and satisfy myself finally that the trail I'd been following was a false one.

First pushing the window as wide as it would go, I hoisted myself onto the sill, stood up and took a firm grip on the right-hand edge of the window frame. I probed out with my left foot until I felt it touch and then settle on the balcony rail. Now came the tricky part, transferring my weight from right foot to left and stepping across the gap quickly and smoothly enough to drop onto the balcony floor. The alternative, if I lost my balance, was a thirty-foot fall. Hugging the wall, with my legs straddling the gap, not daring to look down, I steadied myself. Then I sprang. Both feet were on the rail. For a second I teetered back before flinging myself forward and down to land jarringly on my hands and knees on the balcony floor. Pain shot through my injured left arm.

I stood up, realizing as I did so that because of the narrowness of the window-ledge I wouldn't be able to go back the way I had come. The realization was a little late; and it was driven from my mind in a moment as I pressed my face to one of the pair of glass doors and looked inside.

I should have been prepared for what I saw. Why else, after all, had I followed the lead that had brought me here? But the actuality came as a shock: the fact, immediately recognizable, that for the second time in twenty-four hours I had discovered a hideout of Gil's, and that once again Gil was no longer in it.

The rim-lock on the balcony doors was engaged, but there was a key on the inside. I hadn't time to be delicate. I stepped back, raised my right foot and used the heel of my shoe to kick out the middle pane of one door. It made less noise than I'd expected. I reached through the hole, turned the key, and was inside in a moment.

There was no need to examine anything in detail. The rumpled twin beds, an overflowing ashtray, the soiled paper plates and a half-empty bottle of Haig on the dressing-table told their own story. So did the small tin trunk which seemed to have been dragged from beneath one of the beds and left with its lid open to display cartons of cigarettes, another bottle of Scotch, chocolate bars, tins of ham and packets of cream crackers; and the bedside telephone, from which a dialling tone burred when I picked up the receiver, meaning it was plugged through the switchboard to an outside line. The former assistant manager of the Grande, no doubt with the help of his old skeleton keys and some influence over the African maintenance men, had had this second billet well prepared. Since the hotel was being kept in usable condition the room would have electric current, water, and a toilet in working order. A supply of dry rations would make any fugitive self-sufficient, and a telephone link with the people helping him from outside would make him feel secure.

As if I needed any more persuading, I spotted another cortisone acetate jar in the wastebin. Gil had been brought here from his hideout in the bush yesterday morning to await a call that would tell him one of two things: either that I wasn't double-crossing him, that the Barboza papers were safe to use, and that he could leave for the airport—or that the plan must be aborted. The call had been negative and he had stayed on here. Later he had been joined by Filipe, also a fugitive by then, and presumably they had spent the night here. But where were they now? Where could they possibly have gone with any hope of finding safety?

A sudden alarming notion occurred to me, that they were out temporarily and might be back at any moment. But a quick check of the wardrobe disclosed no clothing, baggage or personal effects of any kind. Gil, at least, must have carried some baggage with him from the start, since on the intercontinental flight he'd planned to take it would have invited unwelcome curiosity if he'd gone empty-handed. So whatever he had brought with him to room 246 he had taken away again. But where?

The insistent trickling of water penetrated my consciousness once more, reminding me of how my attention had first been drawn to this room. The louvered wooden door to the bathroom was closed. I stepped over and opened it. The first thing I noticed was the blood, congealed into a sticky mess on the stone floor and caked in thick rust-brown blotches where it had soaked into the bath-mat. Then I saw what was causing the slow leakage I had heard. The bath was full; the cold tap was running weakly and the surplus was gurgling off through the overflow outlet. In a bath full of water which blood and a corroded tank had combined to turn to the colour of strong tea, Aubrey Slater floated face down. His hair was splayed out and moved with the slight motion of the water like thin seaweed just below the surface, and the ugly gash behind his right ear was white and water-sodden.

For a second or two nausea threatened to bubble up but I managed to suppress it. Police work had given me a strong enough stomach to do what I knew I must. I took Slater by the shoulders and rolled him onto his back. Water slopped over the rim of the bath onto my shoes. The body had already started to swell. Avoiding as best I could the sight of the bloated, staring face with water welling from the open mouth, I went with some difficulty through his pockets. I found a silk handkerchief, a gold Parker pen and a billfold full of sodden hundred-escudo notes; this also contained the smudged original of the tracing I had read on his jotting pad: *Grande, Ponte Gea, 600 esc.* There were no credit cards, no travellers' cheques, though it was inconceivable that a man like Slater would be without such things. Above all there were no identity papers. Those documents that he'd needed for his trip to Cabora Bassa, that he'd complained in his loud voice to me and everybody else about, were missing. They were not in his hotel room and they hadn't been removed by the police.

I left the bathroom gratefully, went to the dressing table and took a mouthful of Gil's Scotch. Funny, I thought, how when you start behaving like a criminal you become suspicious of everyone. Slater had been just Slater, an engineer with a weakness for black prostitutes and too loud a mouth. Filipe had known enough about him by last night to be able to lure him here—perhaps with the promise of a special girl, private surroundings—where he'd been hit over the head and drowned.

I was ready to back a hunch. It was ten past three. I was

probably going to miss that plane anyway. I went to the table between the two beds and found a Mozambique phone directory in the drawer. The girl who took my call in the DETA office was the one I'd spoken to earlier. I asked her what flights had left for Tete today.

"None, so far. There is only one on a Sunday, at four thirty."

"Is that all? A friend of mine is on his way to Cabora Bassa. I could have sworn he said he was leaving at midday."

"Not with us, sir." She paused. "You aren't confusing us with the Zamco shuttle?"

"The what?"

"Zamco, the company that manages Cabora Bassa in conjunction with the Portuguese government, has a private flight every day from here to Songo and back. That's the airport on the dam site itself. It's the most direct way there, but it's strictly for people on company business, of course."

"Of course."

I thanked her, put down the receiver and looked up the number of Zamco's office in Beira. Luckily a home number was given for their representative, one Senhor Carvalho.

Sunday afternoon isn't the best time to approach anyone on business. I woke Carvalho from his siesta. He confirmed grumpily that the shuttle for Songo had left today at twelve o'clock, as usual. It was part of his job to organize it; there was a constant stream of people to and from Cabora Bassa—visiting engineers, men and their families going on leave—and the company found it easier to run their own 32-seater Fokker Friendship back and forth than to use the DETA connection through Tete. He listened with some impatience to my explanation that I was trying to find out whether a friend of mine had been on the flight. The passenger list was now locked away in his office, he said, clearly implying that he hoped I didn't expect him to travel in to the office and look it up. What he could tell me was that the plane had been full.

"Meaning everyone who had a booking was on board?"

"Correct."

"And there was no trouble with security?"

"Of course not. Why do you ask?"

"It's just that—well, my friend wasn't sure that his papers were completely in order. The police these days. . . ."

"Ah, but we have our own security, senhor. Most of it is put into effect long before anyone is permitted to make a booking on the plane. Nobody who is issued with an identity card by Zamco could possibly be a security risk, whatever the black police might wish to think. Besides, they cannot interfere. Our plane does not depart from the main terminal but from our own small hangar on the other side of the airport."

"You mean your passengers aren't subject to routine security checks?"

"Certainly not, senhor. We are jealous of our independence. As long as your friend had a seat reserved and could produce his ID card you may be sure that there would have been no difficulty."

"That's good," I said. Glad to get rid of me, Carvalho hung up and I sat staring numbly at my reflection in the dressing-table mirror. It had seemed hardly credible that even with a new set of false papers—inadequate papers, but better than none—Gil should put in an appearance at an airport where Frelimo's security men were on the lookout for him. This made a lot more sense. Under the Portuguese he himself had been in charge of security at Cabora Bassa; he would know the system inside out and be able to exploit any of its remaining weaknesses. In this case there were two weaknesses: the absence of a photograph on Slater's identity card, and the failure of the police to double-check people who'd already been cleared by Zamco's own screening process. The two nets didn't quite overlap, and a particularly wily fish had managed to slip between them.

Slater had been murdered for his identity papers. He'd just been unlucky enough to be around with something that someone else wanted badly, and once the Barboza plan had failed, Slater's fate was sealed. It was a desperate gamble that Gil was taking, but so far it seemed to have paid off. Tete was around two hundred and fifty miles north-west of Beira, and Songo was another seventy or eighty up the Zambezi from there—a couple of hours' flight in all for a piston-engined plane, and a long way from where Gil was thought to be. At this moment he was somewhere in the vicinity of the Cabora Bassa dam, masquerading as Slater. But it was a deception he could not hope to sustain for long. He was still in Mozambique, still wanted. And if he had travelled alone, where was Filipe?

The questions could wait. The important problem was what I was going to do about the things I had learnt. I could do nothing, which seemed much the wisest course. I could tell Sousa, which would mean that Gil was as good as dead. Or I could try to find Gil on my own.

This idea startled me. Why should I get involved? Because, I realized, it was more than a question of unfinished business now. Whatever else I told myself, I knew I had become obsessed with the subject of Goronga. I had a pretty good idea what had happened there; what I needed was to hear it confirmed. If there was a chance of finding out for certain I had to take it, even if it meant confronting Gil himself. He was the last survivor of what had passed on that night nearly eighteen months ago; once he disappeared or was destroyed there would be no one else to ask.

It seems odd, looking at it now, but at the moment I

was strongly aware of a feeling, uncomplicated by any personal motive, of loyalty to the truth. Self-preservation had receded into the background. I was willing to risk a lot for the sake of talking to Gil. And the only way of talking to him was to find him before Sousa did.

Once more I picked up the phone. When I had finished my third conversation of the day with the girl in the DETA office I went to the door, unlatched it and put my head cautiously out into the corridor, looking and listening. There was still no sound but the trickling of water from the bath behind me, still no sign of the hotel maintenance men. I reckoned Slater was safe from discovery until tomorrow morning at the earliest.

When I left the hotel and walked down the street to the taxi I found the outdoor light dramatically subdued. The banks of dark cloud that had been building all day from the seaward side had moved far enough inland to obscure the westering sun. It was as hot as ever, but with a heavy, expectant stillness in the air. Sometime soon those vast purple layers would topple over on us to release the fury of the delayed summer rains.

The Indian driver folded away his newspaper and yawned. "The airport now?"

"Yes," I said.

3

I got there in time to see the departure of the Lourenço Marques plane that I was meant to be on. Luckily, and perhaps understandably, Raoul Sousa had assumed I would be glad to leave and had not sent anyone to make sure I did. I went to have my ticket altered and to check in for the flight to Tete with a connection to Songo, the airport adjacent to Cabora Bassa, at five forty-five. At the counter I met with some officiousness from the ticket clerk.

"Not my business, senhor, but have you a visitor's permit for the dam?"

"No."

"They won't let you beyond the airport without one."

"I'll depend on talking my way through."

"You are wasting your time, senhor. The Portuguese government still controls Cabora Bassa, and Zamco is responsible for security. They do not welcome casual visitors; if you arrive without the right documentation you will be put back on the plane."

"Let me worry about that. Just give me the ticket."

The truth was that I hadn't the faintest idea how I would deal with the authorities at Songo. The important thing was to get there. The flight up-river from Tete was the last one of the day, and if I was to hang about here trying to get a permit I would be certain to miss it.

Beira airport was stiff with security men. On the way into the departure lounge my grip was opened and I was body-searched. And in addition to the usual passport check that was made even on internal flights, a black PSP man studied my ticket, compared my face several times with the passport photograph and asked me questions. I said I was on my way to see a friend working on the Cabora Bassa site. With a reluctant air the policeman banged a rubber stamp down on my departure form.

The Boeing was half full. There were a few whites, some Indian families—those hardy survivors who weathered political upheavals in Africa by lying low—and the inevitable Frelimo soldiers, who had checked in their Kalashnikovs as baggage to be stowed in the hold.

We rose steeply into the dark clouds above the Pungwe

estuary and I wondered again about my motive for setting off on this journey. The truth? It sounded corny, but I had rediscovered a respect for the truth. Emmerich and Nino, two people who had known what had happened at Goronga, had not died entirely by accident. Only one man was left who might tell me. Gil was a desperate man who would kill without compunction—the way he had dealt with Slater was proof of that—but I didn't want to see him shot down like a dog and taking that knowledge with him. Which meant staying a jump ahead of Sousa.

When the drinks trolley came round I ordered a double Scotch and used it to chase down a penicillin tablet. My arm was still uncomfortable. Soon after that I fell into a doze, waking up when the warning came to fasten seat-belts for the descent to Tete. The town came into view only after we had bumped through the cloud cover at a few hundred feet, a sprawl of low buildings straddling the wide, greasy-green Zambezi and surrounded by scorched bush. The airport was on the north side of the river; as we touched down the rain that had been threatening all day finally came sheeting onto the runway.

The passengers scuttled for the terminal, a shed open on two sides and fenced off from the apron. It was only forty yards from where the plane was parked, but we got thoroughly soaked all the same. I forced my way through the crowd sheltering from the storm to the DETA desk, where a harassed girl had to shout to make herself heard over the hammering of rain on the iron roof. After checking in for the Songo flight I crossed to the open bar counter, squeezed in among a row of Frelimo soldiers with their wet uniforms gently giving off steam, and fortified myself with another Scotch. I was getting nervous. Very nervous.

Fifteen minutes later an announcement in Portuguese went racketing incomprehensibly off the walls of the shed and I gathered that the plane for Songo, Magoe and Zumbo was ready to take off. It was an eight-seat Cessna Businessliner parked close to the terminal. I ran out to it through the downpour.

This time the plane was full. Four of the passengers were South African and German engineers returning to their jobs at Cabora Bassa, who for one reason or another hadn't been able to take the company shuttle. Of the other three besides myself, two were missionaries and the other a Portuguese storekeeper, all bound for bush stations higher up the river. The pilot swung the plane onto the end of the runway, built up the revs and let it surge forward, tyres hissing on the wet tarmac. We made a wobbly takeoff and a couple of minutes later were bucketing about in successive layers of tropical turbulence.

Cabora Bassa came into view after twenty minutes, the rocky gorge where the Zambezi in its natural state had narrowed from a width of half a mile to rush between towering granite cliffs in a millrace two hundred feet wide. The dam had been built halfway along the gorge; through the rain and mist it looked like a great pale wedge of putty shoved in to block a crevice in the earth's crust, with the green lake that had formed behind it stretching to the horizon. The surrounding bush was grey and utterly desolate. Did Gil expect to find refuge out there, or did he have some other plan? Either way, he was out on his own and pretty near the end of his resources. So was I, for that matter.

The Cessna banked to give us a glimpse of Songo, perched on the plateau south of the dam and slightly down-river from it, identical prefab bungalows spaced out against the striking artificial greenness of irrigated lawns. A company town, and still an enclave of white exclusiveness because of the importance of the dam and the fact that Frelimo couldn't do without the skills of the white foreign technicians and engineers. I still had no clear idea of how I would deal with the company officials.

Rain was pelting down as we landed and taxied in to the tiny airport building. It was the kind of bush airfield I'd been to a hundred times before, except for the security. Armed guards in glistening oilskins were out on the apron, and to get into the building we had to pass through a little glassed-in vestibule. Those who were flying up-river were given transit cards and sent through to wait in the main hall. The rest of us had to line up and show our papers to a Zamco security officer and a Portuguese official who sat next to him behind a table. I was the last in the queue of five who had left the plane.

"Company ID card?" said the security man.

"I'm not with the company," I said.

"Visitor's permit?"

"I haven't got one." It seemed best to tell as much of the truth as possible. "Look, I came up in a hurry to find someone—a man I believe flew in on the shuttle today. There wasn't time to apply for a permit. I have to see him urgently."

The security officer looked unimpressed. He was a young white South African, one of the kind that you find working in every odd corner of the continent that will let them in. A card pinned to his khaki uniform shirt identified him as N. J. Lowden.

"Nobody gets in here without prior approval," he said.

"I know that. I'm asking you to bend the rules slightly, just this once. All I want to do is talk to him, on a private business matter. It's important."

"Who is he, anyway?"

"The name is Slater. He's an engineer, up here for a few days on a consultancy contract. At least I think he's here. Perhaps you met him when the shuttle came in?"

"I wasn't on duty then." Lowden frowned at me. "You came all this way without being sure he was here? Why didn't you phone? The company guest-house is on the phone; he's sure to be staying there."

"There wasn't time. Besides, I had to see him personally."

"I don't know whether to believe that, but it can't make much difference anyway." Lowden's tone was friendly enough, but if anything firmer than before. "We just can't have people arriving out of the blue like this, you see. If you'd phoned us first, explained the circumstances—"

"I couldn't, I tell you." But I'd begun to realize I was up against a brick wall of intransigence. This, paradoxically, was part of the security barrier that Gil himself had erected around Cabora Bassa. I was going to have to take a gamble. I said, "Let me talk to Slater on the phone."

He considered for a few seconds. "Tell you what. I'll call the guest-house myself, see if he's there, ask him if he wants to talk to you. If he does you can have two minutes on the phone, and then I'm putting you back on that plane. If he doesn't—well, the same thing will happen."

"That plane? It's flying up-river."

"Right. I'm afraid we have no facilities to cater for uninvited guests. What's the name, anyway?"

"Hickey," I said resignedly, and spelt it for him. I couldn't explain that Slater wasn't really Slater and that the last thing in the world he was going to do was speak to me at someone else's suggestion. I'd been counting on taking him by surprise for myself, convincing him that I was here on my own and not on someone else's behalf—particularly Sousa's. As it was, the moment that he learned I was looking for him he would run. Assuming he had somewhere to run to.

Lowden, leaving his Portuguese colleague to keep an eye on me, opened the door from the vestibule into the pillared hall and crossed to an office in the far corner. I sat down on one of a pair of hard chairs facing the table, watching the rainwater run in a solid wall down the outside of the sheet glass and confronting my failure. Assuming Gil was here, staying at the guest-house and pretending to be Slater, he would probably have no choice but to take the security man's call. Again he would be flushed but not captured, scared off probably for the last time. And the questions I wanted to ask him would go finally unanswered.

The small plane still waited on the apron. Through the curtains of rainwater that separated the glass of the vestibule from the windows of the main building I could dimly see a dozen or so figures in the main hall: airline officials, passengers for up-river waiting for the signal to board, and perhaps friends seeing them off. Up-river: Magoe and Zumbo, twenty and forty minutes' flying time respectively, godforsaken little trading posts and mission stations, at one of which I would have to spend the night, perhaps a couple of nights, before I could return to the relative civilization of Beira. And just how would I explain this escapade to Sousa?

A couple of minutes went by before Lowden returned, wearing a puzzled look.

"Your friend arrived here this afternoon, that's for sure. He had a room reserved in the guest-house but he never checked in. Why was that, do you think?"

"I've no idea," I said, but my mind was set racing. Could it be that Gil hadn't intended to spend much time here, that he was using Cabora Bassa as a stepping-stone to somewhere else? If the Slater identity could get him in through the security screen, presumably it could get him out. But where was there to go from Songo?

Lowden shrugged. "He's probably met someone and

gone boozing at the club. There's eff-all else to do here on Sundays. And now I'm afraid you must leave."

I stood up. I was becoming reconciled to the fact.

"They've got a spare seat as far as Magoe. I've arranged for you to have it. There'll be an extra fare for you to pay, of course. If DETA would listen to us and not let people without clearance on board for here in the first place. . . . Anyway." He shrugged. "There's a few minutes' delay in departure, but we may as well stroll out and wait."

I picked up my grip and followed him from the vestibule, across the hall to where the other passengers stood waiting by the glass doors that led out to the apron. I stopped, made a half-turn to say something to Lowden, and found myself standing beside Gil.

It was that simple. There he was, two feet away from me, a big, heavily built man in a biscuit-coloured suit, clutching a cardboard suitcase and waiting a little apart from the others to be allowed to board the plane. The plane I was going on. He didn't look nervous, but he glanced quickly round as he became aware of me. Something shrivelled inside me in the moment before I realized that he couldn't have recognized me. He would know my name, nothing more. But there could be no question about who he was: the hawklike features blurred at the edges and the pale, heavy face bloated by cortisone were unmistakable, and the widow's peak, the moustache and the rimless glasses that had been in the Barboza photographs were all there. I wasn't sure whether I'd been staring.

"Are you for Zumbo?" he demanded suddenly. His stare was fierce, even through the tinted contact lenses.

"Magoe," I said, almost choking on the word. But Gil seemed not really to have listened. He addressed Lowden beyond my shoulder, in English.

"This plane should have left by now. Why the delay?"

"Charter coming in from Beira. Unscheduled."

For a couple of minutes we all stood staring across the airfield. In the foreground the pilot, under an umbrella, kept an eye on the African loader who was fitting baggage into the forward hold of the Cessna. Once he looked at his watch and gestured to someone in the control tower. Dusk was closing in, and he'd prefer not to have to land at those up-river strips by the light of gas lamps. By now I had recovered enough from the astonishment of meeting Gil face to face to make a calculation. Zumbo was the last Mozambican village on the Zambezi; it stood just a couple of miles east of the point at which the boundaries of both Rhodesia and Zambia met up with Mozambique territory. That would be where Gil was heading—Rhodesia, the best haven after Brazil for those DGS men who had escaped the roundup eighteen months ago. Right after his arrival on the company shuttle this afternoon he must have booked himself on the onward flight, knowing this was the one airport in Mozambique where Frelimo would not be around to see his departure, knowing, too, that his arrival at a desolate up-river airstrip would almost certainly go unnoticed by anyone who mattered. With luck he'd be able to walk those few miles through the bush tonight and reach safety by morning.

What should I do? Stop him? Carry on pretending that I didn't recognize him? I was at a loss to know. All I could be sure of was that the urge to talk to him was still there, overriding every other consideration. Standing there with Lowden and the missionaries and the storekeeper I could do nothing. On board the plane, confined within a space from which he couldn't escape, I could safely identify myself and ask the questions that had acquired such a terrible, irrational importance.

We watched the incoming aircraft appear against the fading light to the south and belly down on the wet runway, arcs of water scything up behind its wheels. It was another light plane, a twin-engined Piper with the markings of some Beira charter company: one of the Zamco executives, at a guess, arriving in style. It slowed at the end of the runway and turned onto the apron to park beside the Cessna. Our pilot was making signs at the control tower again but apparently he had still not been cleared for takeoff. Gil shifted his weight impatiently from foot to foot.

"Again delay," he muttered to Lowden. "Why?"

"This bigwig is landing on us by surprise. The tower was told to hold your flight till he got here."

"Why?" I asked uneasily.

"I don't get told that sort of thing, Mr. Hickey. You'll be on your way in a minute or two, don't worry."

It was the first time he had addressed me by name. I sensed the sudden sharp turn of Gil's head. As I swung round to face him I saw behind the glasses and the dark contact lenses the burgeoning light of recognition in his eyes.

"Hickey," he said softly. "Your name is Hickey, is that right?"

"Yes." There was no point in trying to pretend. "Yes, I'm the one. Don't panic. I want to talk to you, that's all."

"Who sent you?" he demanded. His eyes blazed at mine and his voice was a fierce whisper. "Who?"

"Nobody," I said quietly. "Believe me, Gil, I just want to talk. Let's get on that plane and—"

"No!"

Whether it was the use of his name or the thought of being trapped in the plane that alarmed him I didn't know. He dropped the cardboard case and began backing away from me, groping with his right hand under his crumpled jacket, elbowing aside the two missionaries who stood behind him.

"What the hell's got into him?" Lowden said blankly.

Heads were turning; the hum of conversation died down in the awareness that someone was making a scene. The rain drummed against the windows.

"Where are the rest?" Gil demanded, his voice now ringing round the hall. "You can't have come alone. Where are they?"

He tugged the gun out of his waistband, an Astra automatic which he waved at me as he continued backing away towards the rear doors of the building.

"Hey!" Lowden stepped forward. His tone was still incredulous. "Are you crazy, man? Put that gun down!"

Gil had reached the end wall, a few yards from the doors that led out into the forecourt, and stopped and stood with his back to it. He swung the pistol away from me to point it at the advancing security man.

"Did you hear me? Put it down."

"Stop there," Gil said.

"Better do as he says," I called urgently.

"One step closer," Gil said, "and you're dead."

There was enough menace in his voice to make Lowden see the sense of obeying. He was unarmed. He stopped walking and stood facing Gil, a gap of ten yards between them.

"Look, I don't knew what you think you're doing, but you won't get away with—"

"Quiet," Gil snapped. His eyes darted round the room and settled on the South African again. "You have a Land Rover parked outside. I've been waiting here for the past hour; I saw you arrive in it. Slide the keys across the floor to me. And don't try to do anything stupid."

Lowden hesitated for only a second. There were armed guards around the building, but the nearest of them was out on the apron in the rain, unaware of what was happening inside. He dug into his trouser pocket and brought out a leather keyholder, bent down and sent it slithering across the polished floor to stop at Gil's feet. The rest of us watched in silence. Without letting the gun waver from Lowden, Gil bobbed down swiftly and scooped up the keys with his free hand.

"Go back to where you were," he ordered. "Hickey, you come here."

Belatedly realizing there was some connection between us, Lowden glanced at me and said, "You know him? This isn't . . . ?"

"Slater, yes. Only he isn't really Slater. His name is Gil and he's wanted for the massacre at—"

"Shut your mouth!" Gil said savagely. "And come here!"

Lowden stepped back and numbly I walked forward to stand where he had been, a few yards in front of Gil.

"Closer," he said.

I kept walking until I was six feet from him and he jerked the pistol a fraction to signal me to stop. It pointed at the middle of my chest. Gil's eyes glittered as he watched me—the eyes of a survivor, fierce, alert and intelligent. No one in the hall stirred, but a movement from beyond the doors that led out to the apron told me that the passengers had alighted from the newly landed plane and were running towards the building. Gil saw it too, and then the eyes were back on my face, the gaze boring into mine.

"Quickly. Where is Sousa? How do they plan to take me?"

"There is no plan. I came here on my own."

"You dare lie to me?" His arm suddenly shot out and the wide muzzle of the pistol was pointing between my eyes. "You have done more than anyone to ruin things for me, Hickey. It will not just be easy for me to kill you, it will be a pleasure. Now tell me. What are the arrangements?"

"I tell you there aren't any. I'm here alone. Sousa doesn't know. I came . . . to talk to you."

It sounded lame as I said it. "Talk?" Gil demanded. "What is there to talk about?"

"About Goronga. I've learnt some things. About the real reason why you're running."

"Tell me the arrangements. I won't ask again."

He hadn't listened; he wanted to hear only one thing. Staring into the gun muzzle, I felt the blood surging in my head. The more I denied the existence of a plan to trap him the angrier he would get.

"You've got to believe—" I begun, and then saw his eyes flash to the doorway facing the apron. I looked too. Raoul Sousa was coming through the door.

4

He saw us at the same moment we saw him, and for a fraction of a second everyone was too paralyzed with astonishment to do anything. Two or three Frelimo soldiers were crowding through behind him, their camouflage outfits soaked with rain.

Sousa's eyes were wide and white in the thin face. He grabbed for the revolver on his hip. Gil made a guttural sound, swung his pistol away from my head and fired twice at the doorway. I didn't see whether he hit or missed; I was already diving for cover behind the nearest pillar. The sound of the shots was shattering, twin explosions merging into one with the echoes overlaid by footfalls, breaking glass and hysterical screams as the people in the hall scattered and the men in the doorway fell back. Then Gil turned and ran. He reached the exit in a couple of strides and was out of sight a second later.

I scrambled to my feet, ears ringing with the reasonance of the shots. Glancing round the pillar, I saw that one of the Frelimo men had been hit and had fallen back through the glass door. It wasn't Sousa; he had freed himself from the tangle of bodies and was sprinting towards me. Then Lowden seized me by the shirt collar and swung me sharply round to face him.

"Is that really Gil? And did you know all along?"

"Yes."

"You stay with me. You've got some explaining to do."

He let me go and we ran to the exit door together. We got out in time to see the open Land Rover, twenty yards away, pull off and accelerate in a lather of pale mud down the unsurfaced road to our right.

"He's heading for the dam," Lowden said. "We'll get after him."

He turned to go back into the building and collided with Raoul Sousa. He tried to shove the black man aside but Sousa reached out a bony hand and grabbed his arm.

"Where are you going?"

"To find transport. Get out of—"

"Wait. I am here to take him."

"It's nothing to do with you."

"It's everything. Do you know who I am?" Sousa's eyes were wild again and his nostrils were distended.

"They told me you were coming," Lowden said. "But this is our problem. We'll handle it our way."

"No. He is a wanted murderer and he has just killed one of my men. Where does that road lead?"

"To the dam."

"And what's beyond that?"

"Just bush. What the hell else is there here?"

"Get your transport—and more men. I have two left; we will come with you."

Lowden gave the black man a hostile stare but then

turned and ran back into the terminal. Even on Zamco's property, the authority of Frelimo had to be respected in a matter like this. Sousa turned to me.

"What the devil are you doing here?"

"I followed a hunch. I might ask you the same question."

"Filipe Pereira was arrested three hours ago," he said. "He had walked twenty miles from Beira along the railway line towards the Rhodesian border. He talked, and quickly. He is anxious to save his own skin. Gil was planning to take that flight north and get into Rhodesia through the bush. I had the takeoff delayed until I could get here."

"You didn't need to come. They could have arrested Gil and held him for you."

"I wanted to see the business through to its conclusion. How long have you known he was here?"

I had no chance to reply. From a gate some way to the left of the terminal a red airport fire-tender roared onto the road, Lowden at the wheel, half a dozen Zamco security guards and the two Frelimo soldiers clinging to the rails along either side of the water tank. It slithered to a halt beside us and Lowden gesticulated from the window.

"If you've hidden anything from me, Hickey—" Sousa glanced at the vehicle. "Stay close to me," he said, and ran for the door at the far side of the cab.

I jumped onto the running board of the fire-tender, gripping a vacant bit of rail between two of the guards just as it began to move. The wheels spun and slithered in the mud as Lowden stood on the accelerator; then we were racing down the road between the suburban bungalows and the green gardens hacked out of the bush. Gil in his stolen Land Rover had perhaps two minutes' start on us, and I could see the fresh gouges of the tyres in the mud along the road ahead as I clung to the rail. The rain was as heavy as ever; I was soaked within a minute. The guards and the Frelimo men crouched on the running boards, shielding themselves and their rifles as well as they could against the downpour.

The township gave way to bush as we drove on towards the edge of the escarpment that dropped suddenly into the Cabora Bassa gorge. When we reached the crest and began to descend by a series of giddy hairpin bends towards the dam we could see the Land Rover, a long way below, sliding on the muddy road surface as Gil took the corners at a reckless speed. In the heavy fire-tender Lowden had to be more cautious. One bend taken too wide would have sent us rolling a thousand feet down the slope into the dull green lake.

Huddling between the high granite cliffs, the dam when viewed from above looked small; it was only as we drew closer that I began to get any real idea of its size—a towering mass of concrete five hundred feet high holding all the strength of the Zambezi behind its curved wall. Below ground, water inlets were feeding the turbines of the enormous power station that had been dug out of the rock and now pumped electricity halfway across Africa. Beyond the wall, where the trapped water of the river was released again, it surged at a dizzying speed on to rapids that stretched down the gorge for as far as I could see. The precincts of the dam were vast, and Gil knew every square yard of them. It could not be by chance that he'd driven this way, but because it offered him the best hope of escape. Darkness was falling; within half an hour, assuming he could get clear of the dam-site, he'd be able to hide in the bush and know that he was safe till morning. There was no refuge for him out there but there was temporary security, and he was a resourceful man.

The Land Rover was out of sight now, somewhere on the shoulder of flat ground around the southern end of the dam wall. What would he do, run across the top of the wall? Hardly. It was too exposed and at the other end there was nothing but the bare cliff face.

The fire-tender continued its roller-coaster progress down the slope, with the dam looming larger in front of us as we descended. Rain was still bucketing down, but I was too wet for it to make any difference. At the foot of the cliff the road straightened out and ran parallel to the lakeshore for a couple of hundred yards before it reached a paved car-park adjoining the south end of the wall. Twenty or thirty vehicles were lined up here, cars and trucks belonging to men working in the power station down below. Among them was Lowden's Land Rover.

The tender slithered to a stop beside it. Sousa and Lowden scrambled out of the cab and I hopped off the running board with the guards.

"He could have gone one of two ways from here," the security man was telling Sousa. He pointed ahead to where the road narrowed to enter a tunnel in the rock on the right shoulder of the dam. "In there, down to the underground turbine rooms, or that way"—he was pointing now to the top of the dam wall, more specifically to a concrete shelter at this end of it, with an open doorway through which the top of a flight of stairs could be seen—"down into the inspection galleries. You'd have a job winkling him out of there."

"You mean inside the dam wall itself?" Sousa asked.

"There are ten galleries running through the wall horizontally at intervals of around fifty feet. The engineers use them to make daily checks for stress, seepage. . . ."

"And that stairway connects them? Where does it come out?"

"In the base of the wall on the north side."

"That's where he'll have gone," Sousa said decisively.

"On this side of the river he'd be trapped. Across there his chances are far better."

He snapped his fingers and ran for the staircase, the Frelimo soldiers and the Zamco guards falling into line behind him. Lowden and I brought up the rear.

The stairway was narrow, steep, dank and badly lit by overhead lamps enclosed in mesh, an interminable-seeming slope running down the inside face of the east side of the wall. At regular intervals it switched a few degrees to the right to follow the curve of the wall, so that there was no way of seeing more than forty feet ahead at a time. At the same intervals there were landings from which the horizontal inspection galleries ran off to the left. Here in the bowels of the dam there was constant vibration as thousands of tons of water poured through the inlets to drive the vast turbines. There was also a feeling of claustrophobia, brought on by the closeness of the raw concrete walls that boxed us in. The ventilation was bad. I found myself short of breath, falling behind the white guards and black soldiers who were racing in single file after Sousa. Running downhill can be as exhausting as running up. I was beginning to feel the effects of my deep-rooted exhaustion, and I was not entirely convinced that we were going the right way in any case. Gil was too cunning to do the obvious, I thought, to expose himself on the dry riverbed at the foot of the dam knowing his pursuers were only a couple of minutes behind.

We were about halfway down the staircase and the rest of the men were half a flight ahead of me when I felt a sudden dizziness that forced me to stop and lean back hard against the wall. To fall here could mean going in a long tumble down the stairs. I pressed my back to the wall for a minute and sucked in air, feeling the clammy sweat on my face, hearing the receding footfalls of the men echoing down the stairway. And then I heard other feet, closer, higher up the steps.

They were climbing, steady but fast. Someone had come out of one of the inspection galleries and was going back up to the head of the stairs. Someone? It could only be one man. I glanced down the stairway; Sousa and Lowden were out of sight and hearing, probably a hundred feet below me by now. I turned and went scrambling up behind the receding footsteps, knowing that my instinct about Gil had been right. He had double-guessed Sousa, and he knew the layout better than any of us. He'd stopped and hidden along the third or fourth gallery down, waited until we passed and was now heading back to where he'd come from. If he intended crossing the river he knew of some better way than this.

A minute ago I had felt immobilized by exhaustion, but now a new surge of energy sent me slogging up the stairs. Gil must have heard the ring of my footsteps as I heard his, and he increased his speed. We couldn't see each other because of the regular changes of direction in the staircase, but we paced ourselves by our footfalls. And I was gaining slightly. He was overweight, out of shape, bloated by the cortisone; in spite of my tiredness I had more reserves of strength than he did. Nevertheless, he reached the head of the stairs a full minute ahead of me, and when I broke out into startlingly fresh air and blinding rain he was nowhere in sight. But the Land Rover was still in the car-park, which meant he could only have gone one way: into the tunnel that led to the underground plant.

I took a few seconds, as I struggled to get my breath back, to glance over the balustrade of the dam wall. Far below, the guards and the Frelimo men came spilling out of the opening in the wall where the long staircase ended. In the gathering dusk they were faint, minute figures against the pale sand of the riverbed. From there, the only way up the cliff on the north side of the river was by a tortuous footpath. If Gil had taken it he would have been left exposed to view and to gunfire from below; the fact that he wasn't visible meant that at this moment Sousa was realizing he had come the wrong way. And he would double back. I had only a few minutes in hand.

I ran to the mouth of the tunnel. The lighting was better here than on the stairway, designed for constant use, and I saw him at once: a hundred yards ahead, walking fast, with the pale suit flapping about him. I went after him, my footfalls ringing against the rock walls. He heard me, glanced round once, and began to run.

When he'd gone another twenty yards the tunnel took a turn and I lost sight of him. As I approached the bend I became aware that the constant low hum of machinery had increased in volume, and when I rounded the corner noise and harsh light burst in on my consciousness. The turbine room opened up in front of me, a vast cavern cut out of the belly of the mountain, its granite walls shored up with concrete. The whole place vibrated gently to the thunderous drumming of the five great turbines and the generators which they drove. The tunnel had brought me out on a landing about twenty feet above the floor, with steps leading down to it. I could see Gil sprinting across the open space on the right of the generators towards a sliding steel door halfway along the chamber—about a hundred yards away. I bounded down the steps and followed him. A couple of technicians in white overalls stood watching us bemusedly.

Gil reached the door and slid it open. He glanced back at me once before disappearing through it. I should have been warned. I ran on, noticing one of the technicians heading for a telephone on a console beside the nearest turbine. I reached the door in twenty seconds, ran through it and almost went headlong over the rail of a narrow steel catwalk into the black water that swirled in a huge concrete tank a hundred feet below. I staggered against the railings, making an involuntary half-turn and so catching sight just in time of the movement close behind me, the raised arm with the heavy pistol gripped flat in the palm. I shot out my forearm, parrying the blow before it had gathered half its strength, and the Astra fell out of Gil's hand, slid over the edge of the walkway and fell into the water far below. I hit him in the mouth; he staggered back against the chest-high railings and groped with his left hand for something under the right flap of his jacket. Another weapon. I moved in close, seizing the hand and pinning it against his hip, feeling the outline of a hunting knife still in its sheath under his waistband.

He tried to knee me in the groin. With my left hand I grabbed his leg behind the knee and jerked upwards. He fell on his back and I dropped on top of him.

He fought to raise his back from the floor. I pushed down his shoulders and sat straddling his middle. He grunted and heaved with the effort of trying to roll me off him, but my weight was too much for him. My thigh was across his waist, so when he tried to claw for the knife again he couldn't get at it. The glasses had fallen off and his face was vicious with desperation. He reached up to gouge at my eyes. I fought his hands away and got his arms pinned down on the steel floor. The railings were only a foot away; beyond them was the hundred-foot drop into the surge chamber, where water from the turbines thundered through another huge, harshly lit cavern before rushing into the tailrace that took it back into the river.

"Listen to me!" I yelled over the noise. "You haven't got much time!"

He went on bucking and struggling, staring wildly up into my face.

"Listen, God damn you! I meant what I said at the airport. I didn't come to trap you, I didn't lead Sousa here. He found out where you were because Filipe was caught and he talked. No, listen! I came to find you because I want to know about Goronga. Because I think I know what really happened there—and because you're the only man left who can tell me whether I'm right. Tell, me Gil. It'll make no difference to what happens to you. If they get you they're going to kill you."

He stopped trying to fight and lay panting under my weight, the fat face clammy with sweat. Then he spoke hoarsely through the roaring of the water below.

"Yes, they'll kill me. They'll make sure of that."

"Tell me about Goronga."

"What the hell is it to you?"

"Nothing. I have to know, that's all."

"Then they will have to kill you too."

"Not necessarily."

Gil said nothing for a few seconds more until I prompted him.

"Were you there, or weren't you?"

He closed his eyes and shook his head wearily, as if he had answered the same question many times before and grown bored with it.

"Say it," I insisted.

"I wasn't there."

"Then who was? Emmerich? His men?"

"Not them either."

"So what happened?"

"How do I know? I was back at the barracks. The first I knew of it was the next evening. Of course, nobody was going to believe that."

"You fled, went underground. Why?"

"What would you have done?"

I understood and nodded. "The evidence pointed at you. You'd have been arrested anyway, as part of the roundup of DGS men, and you didn't have a hope in hell of getting a fair trial. Not that you were an unblemished lamb, exactly; Slater, yesterday, wasn't the first man you've killed in cold blood, was he? I think you were quite capable of killing fifty people at Goronga, that in the right circumstances you would have killed them. It just so happens that you didn't, though for all the difference it made you might as well have. Your disappearance confirmed your guilt, and nobody ever bothered to look any further."

Gil sighed heavily. "It's a matter of what people want to believe."

"Poder de opinião," I said. "You knew the truth. So did your men in the Flecha troop. And Emmerich, the man you'd arranged to go to if and when you needed protection. But none of that was going to help. Nor was the log you stole or the notes you made on it. The best you could hope for was to get out of the country. Instead of helping you do that, Emmerich prevented you. He kept you living out in that tent in the bush for eighteen months, refusing to let you have the Barboza papers, using you as a pawn in his struggle to retain control of his property. More than a pawn, in fact. You and the boy Nino between you provided him with a hold over Sousa. You knew the truth of what had happened at Goronga, and Nino had seen the killers himself. Why produce him at the UN inquiry when he was much more valuable under Emmerich's own roof, living with that knowledge? And why send you away to Brazil, where you might disappear forever?"

"You say I was capable of doing what was done at Goronga," Gil said neutrally. "Perhaps that is so. The fact is that I had no reason to destroy the village. They helped me. They were doubtful at first, they took some persuading of the gentler kind—but in the end the headman agreed to give me information. He told me which direction Sousa's band had taken. They did not like Frelimo any more than I did. They would have helped them only under threat of reprisals."

"A fact that was twisted afterwards. They were made out to be pro-Frelimo people who'd been punished for deceiving you."

I released his arms and stood up. He lay there and looked at me blankly.

"What now?"

"I don't really know."

I glanced along the catwalk in both directions. It formed one side of a gallery that ran all round the surge chamber, high above the dark maelstrom below. There was no way out except through the door by which we'd entered. I said, "You weren't planning to escape this way?"

"No. I saw you were the only one following."

"So you brought me in here to kill me. Then what?"

He sat up and shrugged resignedly. "At the end of the turbine room there's another tunnel. It follows the tailrace down to the riverbank. From there is a way across beneath the dam wall and up the north side of the gorge. It would have been dark by the time I got there."

"It's just about dark now."

He watched me uncertainly.

"You'd better go," I said.

Gil scrambled to his feet, incredulous, hopeful, but still wary.

"Why?" he asked. "What's in it for you?"

"Nothing that I can think of. I don't know any good reason for letting you live. I don't want to do Sousa's work for him, that's all. He'll be here soon. Go."

He stepped towards the door and then turned. "I'll remember this, Hickey."

"I'd rather you didn't. You could still get caught. One final thing: If you didn't do it, who did?"

The look he gave me was calm and serious. "I think you know the answer to that. Otherwise you would not have come so far to ask."

He swung round and I watched him walk to the door. We had both been deceived, cheated, used, by one side or the other in the Barboza affair, and it was only by luck that I hadn't had to pay as high a price as Gil. He'd still need luck, lots of it, if he hoped to get away.

His frame filled the doorway and he stood for a second looking out into the turbine room. Then he gave a peculiar grunt. An instant later there was a bang that echoed at length off the high walls, like the sound of tearing paper. Gil came lurching back on to the catwalk with both hands clutched to his left side. There was a bewildered look on his face. He tottered past me, bumped into the railings and spun against them, stopping several yards down the walkway. Blood was already welling from the wound in his flank and running over his splayed fingers.

I turned to the door. The first man through it was the one who had fired the shot, one of the two Frelimo soldiers. He saw Gil slumped against the rail, stopped beside me and raised his Kalashnikov deliberately to his shoulder. I grabbed its stock, two-handed, twisted it aside and shoved the man back into the doorway. Sousa and Lowden and the Zamco guards were crowding through now. I planted myself in the centre of the narrow catwalk, arms outstretched, interposing myself between them and Gil. Lowden stopped in front of me; Sousa thrust his way forward, his revolver drawn.

"Out of the way!"

"Don't shoot! I've already disarmed him."

Sousa tried to force his way past me but I grabbed the front of his camouflage jacket and shoved him back. The revolver swung to point at me.

"You're looking for trouble again, Hickey."

"You don't have to kill him. But then that's why you came here, isn't it? To make sure he died."

I glanced over my shoulder at the Portuguese. He stood three or four yards behind me, gasping for breath, with one hand clinging to the railings and the other still pressed tightly to his side. He watched us dully, frowning as if he couldn't quite make out what was going on.

Sousa's eyes were very bright and his face was contorted with that old inner turbulence. "For the last time, Hickey, get out of my way. Otherwise I shoot."

"In front of them?" I jerked my head at Lowden and the white guards crowded behind him. The technicians from the turbine room had come through as well. "You'll need a better excuse, Sousa. Those are independent witnesses, not your faithful soldiery. You intended getting rid of Gil for the same reason you got rid of Emmerich. And Nino. Because they were embarrassments to you. Just as Gil is. There's nothing I can do to keep him out of your hands, but it's damned certain you're not going to let him live—even if he does survive that bullet wound. Gil is your last embarrassment, isn't he? That's why I have to speak now."

I was taking a hell of a chance, in spite of the witnesses. The gun was still trained on me and I saw that the hand which held it was trembling slightly. The guards and the Frelimo men hovered restlessly behind Sousa, not knowing quite what was happening. The rush of water from beneath us filled the few seconds' pause before I spoke again.

"Over the last few days I've been picking up bits of information from here and there, and I've built up in my own mind a sort of case for the prosecution. It's not a case that's likely ever to reach court, but if it did I'd be reasonably confident that it would succeed. It's a case against you, Sousa. And it concerns the massacre at Goronga."

His face was a scarred mask.

"I won't go into all the details," I said. "The case rests on three facts. Fact one: the killing could not have been done by the Flechas. I've established beyond any doubt that the incident took place shortly before eight o'clock at night. By that time Gil and his unit had been back at their base for nearly an hour and a half.

"Fact two: although it's generally supposed that Goronga was destroyed for supporting your guerrilla band, it was not a pro-Frelimo village. Not only that, Sousa; when Gil and his men landed and questioned the headman he gave them the information they wanted. He actually told them which direction you had taken and where he thought you were heading. It was that information Gil was acting on when he got so close to you later that day. If it wasn't for an unlucky accident that grounded their helicopter, the Flechas would have killed or captured most of you. Gil believed that, and I think you did too.

"Fact three: and here we actually have an exhibit." I fished in my trouser pocket and brought out one of the two cartridge cases I had found. I held it up high for everyone to see. "This and a whole lot more spent shells, all identical, were buried in the vegetable garden of the village."

Gil made a gasping noise behind me and I glanced swiftly round. Staring glassily, almost paralyzed by pain and shock, he had managed to lurch a little closer to us along the rail. But as I watched he slid slowly to the steel floor and lay on his side, clutching his wound with both hands.

Everyone else was listening to me with rapt attention, Lowden with a frown creasing his forehead, Sousa with sweat gleaming in the grooves of his facial scars. Involuntarily he had lowered the revolver and it hung at his side. I took a step forward, reached out to the Frelimo man who had shot Gil and pulled the rifle out of his grasp. I worked the bolt and pumped a round of ammunition out of the breech. Then I handed back the weapon and held up the gleaming live bullet and the corroded shell-case side by side.

"The cases are identical. They take a high-velocity seven-point-six-two-millimetre bullet. The G-Three rifle that was standard equipment for the Portuguese is exactly the same calibre, but the NATO cartridge case is a different shape, longer and more slender. The two types are made for different breeches and are not interchangeable. The bullets that were fired at Goronga came from Russian Kalashnikov rifles—as used by Frelimo."

Sousa was trembling all over now.

"There was one other thing—not a fact, an intangible, but it was what finally convinced me. This morning, at Emmerich's house, when Nino saw you, the look on his face told me as much as if he'd said it. He recognized you, Sousa. And he had reason to fear you. That's why he ran, and that's why you shot him."

Again the cavern was filled with the roar of water from below. Through it, I could hear Gil's harsh breathing behind me.

"It wasn't Gil and his Flechas who destroyed Goronga. It was you, Sousa, and your guerrillas, all now safely scattered about in their home villages. The inhabitants of Goronga were killed not because they had deceived Gil but because they'd betrayed *you*. They had to learn, didn't they? They and everyone else had to be shown that only one loyalty was possible—loyalty to Frelimo.

"Perhaps you went further than you'd intended. Or perhaps you took fright afterwards. At any rate, you gathered together the only evidence there was on the site, all the spent cartridges, and buried them before you left.

"You'd planned to make an example of Goronga, but the plan misfired in a way you couldn't have imagined. The crime was blamed on the Portuguese.

"It's understandable, in retrospect. There didn't seem any reason why African nationalists should kill their own people—and there was no suggestion that your band was even in the vicinity at the time. The Flechas were Africans themselves. One group of black soldiers in camouflage gear looks pretty much like another, and your men would have been speaking Portuguese. Perhaps some of the villagers themselves didn't know who was killing them—or why.

"You must have been amazed, Sousa. And by then you must have seen some of the reaction to the incident and thought that the best thing to do was join in the chorus. Did you also have regrets?"

He didn't reply. Perhaps he couldn't. His face poured sweat, his eyes were wide and maniacal, and although I knew that he could still kill me I was sure he wouldn't try. There was a strange impotence about him.

"Dead people don't learn," I said. "I suppose you managed to forget that, if you'd ever been aware of it. You thought it was all forgotten, until three months ago when you made your first move to nationalize Emmerich's property. He'd been expecting it, and he had his weapon ready: blackmail. He went to see you in Beira and warned you that he knew the truth of what had happened at Goronga. He threatened to use Gil to expose you unless you left his property alone.

"You sat and worried for three months. And then, by chance, the Barboza papers turned up—in my hotel room. You realized then that Gil was still in the country and that there was a chance of destroying him and making yourself safe once and for all. You sent me to lure Gil into the open, knowing that once you'd got him you could eliminate Emmerich as well. And it worked, even if it was messier than you'd intended. It turned out that Emmerich had another small card up his sleeve: the boy Nino. You got rid of him too, in very unpleasant circumstances. And Gil went on the run and you had to chase him up here. But it worked. There he is—he's yours.

"That's my case, Sousa. The proof is all there if anyone wants to find it. Nobody will, though. To do that would mean more than just opening an old wound. It would shatter an illusion, destroy the value of Goronga as a symbol. I just thought you might as well realize that there's still someone around who knows the truth."

At one point the terror on his face had seemed to threaten a breakdown. Now it was edged with relief; the knowledge that there was no proof was sinking in, an awareness that in spite of all the talk nothing had changed. Even the fact that a dozen men had been listening would do no more than create rumours. Yet he couldn't meet their gaze, now, or mine. He turned to grip the rail and stare intently out across the surge chamber.

I stepped aside from where I had stood in the centre of the catwalk. "Better move him before he bleeds to death," I said to Lowden, indicating Gil.

It seemed that the South African had already notified the company hospital. There was a stretcher waiting in the turbine room; to get Gil onto it he would have to be man-handled off the catwalk. Lowden and another guard came forward. They heaved the wounded man on to his back and then propped him up in a sitting position. He was still conscious; the movement made him snarl with pain. His face was grey and his bulging eyes seemed fixed on one thing—the figure of Sousa.

Kneeling beside him, the men tried to get his arms around their shoulders, but he grimaced and shook his head and kept his hands under his blood-soaked jacket, seeming to lessen the pain by clutching his wounded flank as tightly as he could. Instead, they gripped him under the armpits and dragged him clumsily to his feet. Supporting most of his weight between them they propelled him on buckling knees towards the door. The rest of the guards fell back.

Sousa still gazed out at nothing. He had to step aside as the wounded man was taken past him. He turned towards me and his dark eyes met mine briefly, blankly.

"It didn't seem right," I said, "that you should sleep too peacefully."

I don't know whether he heard, and I never got the chance to find out. Gil made his move with the speed of a striking snake.

I was standing a couple of yards behind him as he was guided towards the door, and at first I though he had stumbled. Suddenly he'd knocked Lowden aside and was lurching towards Sousa. Then I realized that the movement was swift and deliberate, that he wasn't as helpless as we'd thought, that he'd thrown every ounce of his remaining strength into the lunge. And that one of the hands that came from beneath his jacket was holding the hunting knife, unsheathed. I'd forgotten all about it. The eight-inch blade gleamed with blood from his own wound in the fraction of a second it took to thrust it outwards and up. Nobody had time to stop him, not even Sousa himself, who was still holding his revolver.

The thrust was powerful enough to lift the black man

off his feet. Gil drove the knife in up to its hilt just below the navel and ripped upwards, stopping only when it reached the breastbone and then raising Sousa's thin frame on the end of it like a speared fish. Blood gushed out of him. He rose a couple of feet into the air and when Gil let go he fell back with his shoulders against the railing, staring incredulously down at the hilt of the knife still sticking out of his chest, and at a length of pink intestine that began to slide out of the awful wound.

Recovering from our shock, we all rushed at Gil. Lowden got to him first, grabbing the collar of his jacket from behind. But now Gil had taken Sousa under the armpits and was shoving him upwards and back across the chest-high railings, seized by some terrible need not just to kill but to destroy utterly.

As he felt himself pushed over the railings Sousa grabbed Gil around the neck, survival instincts working even as his guts were spilling out, and for a second they teetered in grotesque imbalance, smothered in blood and hugging each other like lovers. The thin fabric of Gil's jacket ripped off in Lowden's hand as he began to fall. I got hold of a foot but the shoe came off in my hand. Sousa was right across the rail now, and dragging Gil with him.

They fell abruptly over the edge, clutched in their terrible embrace, and they were still clinging to each other when they hit the black water at the bottom of the surge chamber a hundred feet below. The splash was obliterated at once by the racing current.

They went under for eight or ten seconds. When they came to the surface they had separated, two tiny figures flailing involuntarily against the enormous force that sucked them towards the mouth of the tailrace. They were visible for only a few moments more before they were dragged down to be shot through the tunnel into the river and broken on the rapids of Cabora Bassa. Gil went under first, the pale suit flapping about him like the fins of an ungainly fish. Sousa followed, rolling once on his back to show a gaping mouth and the whites of eyes that stared enormously up at us from the thin black face. Whether they stared in terror or in death it was impossible to say.

J. BARNICOAT
CASH SALES DEPT
P.O. BOX 11
FALMOUTH
CORNWALL TR10 9EN

Please send me the following titles

Quantity	SBN	Title	Amount
————			————
————			————
————			————
————			————
————			————
			————
		TOTAL	————

Please enclose a cheque or postal order made out to **FUTURA
PUBLICATIONS LIMITED** for the amount due, including 10p
per book to allow for postage and packing. Orders will take
about three weeks to reach you and we cannot accept responsibility for orders containing cash.

PLEASE PRINT CLEARLY

NAME..

ADDRESS...

....